KATHLEEN V. DOUGLAS
27 Double Eagle Dr.
Marshfield, MA 02050

The Dark Queen

The Dark Queen

A Novel

SUSAN CARROLL

BALLANTINE BOOKS • NEW YORK

Copyright © 2005 by Susan Coppula
Excerpt from *The Courtesan* by Susan Carroll
copyright © 2005 by Susan Coppula

Published in the United States by Ballantine Books, an imprint of The Random
House Publishing Group, a division of Random House, Inc., New York.

Ballantine and colophon are registered trademarks of Random House, Inc.

ISBN 0-7394-5245-2

Printed in the United States of America

Text design by Susan Turner

To Kay Krewer and Armin Weng,
True friends for all time, whether it be
the nineteenth century or this one.

And to the memory of Fred Zimmer,
Gentle farmer and philanthropist.

Acknowledgments

THIS NOVEL HAS PROVED A LONG JOURNEY FOR ME, MORE DIFFICULT than most. I could never have arrived at the end without the unfailing support and enthusiasm of my agent, Andrea Cirillo, and the staff at Jane Rotrosen. Nor could I have brought this work to a satisfactory conclusion without the patience of my publishers at Random House and the talented and insightful editing of Shauna Summers and Charlotte Herscher.

I also have many friends to thank for making my long hours at the computer more bearable: Carol Boomershine for her constant encouragement, my dear friend Kim Cates, her husband Dave and daughter Kate, for always being there for me, my own personal cheering squad, the ladies of Monday night, Stephanie Wilson, Sheila Burns, Gina Hinrichs, Amy Lillus, and Trudy Watson. My daughter Serena for never losing faith in her mom.

And lastly but not least a very special thanks to the three ladies who inspired me to write this tale of the Cheney sisters . . . my own siblings, Dorothy, Jean, and Janet. It was from them that I learned of the special love and unshakeable bonds of sisters.

Author's Note

THE DARK QUEEN DEPICTED IN THIS BOOK IS BASED ON AN AL-chemical mix of myth and fact. Throughout Catherine de Medici's reign, rumors of her use of black magic abounded. Many believed her to have been a witch and a notorious poisoner, although there is no evidence to back up these claims. It is known that she did employ a band of beautiful women she called her Flying Squadron to seduce her enemies at court. And she was undoubtedly mistress of the arts of political intrigue.

Combining a little fact with fiction, relying mostly on legend, embellished by the powers of imagination, I created this tale of the Dark Queen. By no means do I claim to be putting before you an accurate portrayal of the complex woman who was Catherine de Medici or of the events that led to that murky night in August 1572. Centuries later, historians still argue over who was to blame for the tragedy of St. Bartholomew's Eve and debate the elusive character of that "Italian woman," as her subjects called her. For more information about French politics and history, I respectfully refer you to the domain of scholars and historians.

My realm is one of fantasy, romance, and adventure in the country of long ago and the land of might have been . . .

The Legend . . .

Long ago there lived a group of women known as the Daughters of the Earth. These women were revered for their wisdom and knowledge, skilled in all the arts of healing and white magic. They lived in a more innocent and peaceful time, when men and women were deemed equal and shared in the governing of their kingdoms.

But as time passed, the balance of power shifted, men coming to dominate with their warlike ways. Women were slowly denied more of their rights to govern and to learn.

Most of the Daughters of the Earth sorrowfully accepted these changes and gave up their power. Some became embittered and took their vengeance by learning to employ the darker arts. But a brave few persevered, struggling to keep the ancient knowledge alive. They passed on the secrets of the white magic from mother to daughter for generations. It was an increasingly dangerous proposition, for the Daughters of the Earth were no longer revered as wise women.

They had come to be known by a far more sinister term . . . witches.

Prologue

THE BRIDE WAS LATE.

The crowd gathered outside the cathedral grew hot and restless. Murmurs, low at first, then steadily louder, rippled through the throng of townspeople lingering to gawk. Ariane Cheney was not coming. No one was particularly surprised.

She was known as the Lady of Faire Isle, and all the women who inhabited that island had a reputation for being contrary and strange. None more so than Mistress Cheney, and the lady had made no secret of her reluctance for this marriage. The comte was rumored to have all but wooed her at the point of his sword.

As the sun rose higher in the sky, the bishop drew farther back into the shelter of the cathedral portico. Straining beneath his heavy miter, His Eminence showed signs of impatience, his clerics wilting in their flowing vestments. The wedding guests exchanged disgruntled glances, shifting wearily from foot to foot.

The bridegroom appeared unperturbed. Mounted upon a

richly caparisoned stallion, Justice Deauville regarded the street leading toward the cathedral with unwavering arrogance.

The Comte de Renard was a man cut on a grand scale, a veritable giant, well over six feet of solid muscle and long limbs. The broad span of his chest strained beneath a satin doublet studded with sapphires. Uneven lengths of golden-brown hair fell past his shoulder, giving the impression of a man too impatient to sit still for his barber. Although clean-shaven, his face was rough-hewn, with a square jaw and a nose that appeared as if it had been broken at some point in his past.

Exactly what that past was no one seemed able to say. Many in Brittany scarcely remembered that the late Comte de Renard still possessed an heir until Justice Deauville had turned up a few months ago to claim his inheritance. Despite his elegant attire, he looked more like a man one would fear to encounter alone in a darkened alley than an aristocrat.

Even though weariness spread through the guests and attendants, no one dared suggest to the comte the possibility that his bride was not coming, not even the bishop. As the morning waned, only one rider ventured to nudge his horse out of the line of gold-and-black-clad retainers, an old man with a shock of white hair and a lifetime of adventures mapped across his craggy face.

Toussaint Debec had faced down Turks in the Middle East, Venetian pirates in the Mediterranean, even the monks of the dreaded Inquisition. He had one other advantage over everyone else. He had known Justice Deauville since he was a boy.

The old man brought his mount calmly alongside the comte and remarked, "Well, lad, it doesn't appear to me as though you are going to be married this day."

"She will come." Renard's gaze remained upon the empty street.

"I warned you that you were being too high-handed with Mistress Cheney. She is not like other women. She—"

"I know exactly who the Lady of Faire Isle is," Renard interrupted.

"Then you should have known you could not just issue commands to her."

"I am the Comte de Renard now. I can command anyone."

"Not this lady!"

"She *will* come," Renard stubbornly repeated.

"Why? Simply because you ordered her to?"

"No." An odd smile played about Renard's lips. "Because she won't be able to help herself. I am her destiny."

"Oh, Lord!" Toussaint muttered, rolling his eyes. But just then a shout rose up from the crowd.

Some half dozen of the comte's own retainers came into view, escorting a gilt-trimmed coach pulled by a team of snow-white horses, plumes fastened to their manes. The townsfolk surged into the street to gape.

As the coach drew to a halt in the square, Renard shot Toussaint a look of pure triumph. Renard dismounted, tossed his reins to one of his squires, and strode toward the coach. Brushing the footman aside, he yanked open the carriage door.

Heavy curtains had been drawn across the windows, leaving the interior dark after the glitter of sunlight. Squinting, Renard could just make out the willowy form of his bride seated in the corner, the billows of her satin gown spread out around her, a heavy veil concealing her face.

"My lady, I was just starting to fear that I would have to—" Renard's eyes adjusted to the darkness.

There was something very wrong in the way his lady slumped against the cushions, a fear that was confirmed when he took hold of her gloved hand.

"What the devil!" Renard hauled his bride from the carriage none too gently. Her veil caught on the coach door, tearing free along with a long brown wig, leaving exposed a round head of cloth stuffed with straw, as was the rest of the satin-clad body Renard clutched in his hands.

He stared in astonishment at the muslin head painted with gray eyes and a mocking vermilion smile. A hush fell over the crowd, and then Renard heard the first titter of laughter.

For a moment, time fell away from him and he was not the all-powerful Comte de Renard, but only Justice Deauville, an ungainly boy picking himself up from the dirt of the tournament field while the crowd snorted with derision.

The sharpness of the memory surprised him, as did its ability to hurt. But he was quick to shrug it off. There were many years between him and that raw, awkward boy, a lifetime of experience that had given him, among other things, the ability to laugh at himself.

His jaw relaxed. Renard flung back his head and roared. After a flicker of uncertainty, the crowd joined in, the entire square ringing with laughter. As Renard finally subsided, he found Toussaint at his side, grinning up at him.

"Now, lad, perhaps you are finally willing to admit you made a mistake trying to force that woman to marry you."

"I made only one mistake, old man," Renard retorted, "and that was in not going to fetch Mistress Cheney myself."

Renard thrust the straw bride at the dismayed Toussaint. The comte wheeled about and remounted his horse. He then galloped away, leaving the entire square gaping after him.

Putting the spurs to his mount, Renard tore through the streets, and out the city gates, following the road that led down from the town. Only when he reached the rocky stretch of beach did he rein to a halt.

Off the coast, the Faire Isle could be seen, its outline growing dimmer by the moment, disappearing in the haze. The place was not, properly speaking, an island, but connected to the mainland by a rocky isthmus of land just wide enough to support a road.

Renard urged his horse toward that narrow channel, but the skittish stallion balked, all but rearing back on its haunches when Renard tried to force it forward.

The horse was showing better sense than he. The road leading to the Faire Isle was treacherous on a fair day, but in fog or storm, the passage could be lethal. The sea had claimed more than one rider foolish enough to attempt it.

As the mist thickened, Renard reined in his mount and watched the island disappear as though it had been veiled by a sorcerer's magic. Or perhaps, more aptly, a sorceress.

Renard expelled a frustrated sigh. Toussaint had been right. The comte would not be married this day. The old man was also right that Renard's blunt approach had not worked with Ariane Cheney.

But he had learned long ago that the meek did not inherit the earth. Being patient and gentle meant being ridden over roughshod and having the woman one loved married to someone else.

The fog blurred before his eyes and he was hurled back across the years. Once more he stood shivering and bleeding on Martine's doorstep while she gazed up at him with dismayed blue eyes before slamming the door in his face.

Renard shook the memory off. So long ago, and what did it even matter now? Except that his experience with Martine had taught him a hard lesson.

When a man wanted something, he had better be ruthless when going after it, whether it was a parcel of land, a horse, or a woman. Of course, he was obliged to admit that the Lady of Faire Isle was no ordinary woman.

With a recalcitrant bride like Ariane, a man might be obliged to resort to more devious methods. Especially a man determined to marry a witch.

Chapter One

THE CHAMBER LAY HIDDEN BENEATH THE OLD PART OF THE house, far from prying eyes. During Roman times, when a fortress had stood on the island, the room had been part of a catacomb of prisons, a dark place where frightened souls had been imprisoned awaiting torture and death. But that had been centuries ago.

The chains and manacles were long gone, the stone walls now lined with jars of herbs, dust-covered bottles, and books preserving knowledge forgotten by the rest of the world. The grim place had been completely transformed by feminine hands into a repository of ancient learning and a keeper of secrets. There was enough evidence stacked upon these shelves to get a woman condemned for witchcraft seven times over.

No one could have looked less like a witch than the young woman stirring the hearth's bubbling cauldron. Ariane Cheney was tall and thin, her slender form clad in a russet-brown gown protected by the apron knotted round her waist.

The orange-red light of the torches imbedded in the walls flickered over her grave features; her thick chestnut hair was demurely bundled beneath a kerchief. Ariane had an unusually solemn face for a woman barely one and twenty, her pensive gray eyes seldom given to laughter, her lips rarely transformed by a smile.

She had little to smile about these days since her mother's death. With her father still missing, that left only Ariane to protect and care for her two younger sisters. Speculation grew daily that the Chevalier Louis Cheney's grand voyage of exploration had come to disaster, that the Chevalier was either lost at sea or killed by natives on some hostile foreign shore.

Ariane gave the contents of the cauldron one final stir, then carefully ladled some of the clear liquid into a thick clay flagon. She carried it over to the long wooden worktable. The powder she had ground rested in the bottom of the iron mortar, a concoction partly gleaned from her books, partly from her own ingenuity.

Setting the flagon down, Ariane scooped out a spoonful of the powder. She hardly knew how much to use. It was a matter of guesswork. Ariane closed her eyes and sent up a silent prayer.

"Oh, please, please let this work." Opening her eyes, she carefully ladled the powder into the flagon. She watched anxiously, preparing to give the potion a stir, but she never got the chance.

The reaction was immediate and violent. The liquid began to smoke and hiss, bubble and foam. As the potion roiled over the sides of the flagon, Ariane emitted a cry of dismay. She grabbed for a cloth to check the mess, but the spitting flagon forced her to retreat.

She backed away, flinging up one arm just in time as the vessel shattered, spraying the chamber with flecks of red foam and broken pottery. An acrid haze hung over the room, a sharp stench that caused Ariane to choke and her eyes to sting with tears. She flapped her cloth to clear the air and then mopped her eyes to survey the damage.

She was not hurt, but her potion had left a scorch mark on the table and burned tiny holes in her apron. Ariane had failed.

If only Maman was here to help me, Ariane thought, the familiar ache of loss tugging at her heart. It was a wish she made a dozen times every day.

Evangeline Cheney had been a true descendant of the Daughters of the Earth, as learned in the old ways as any woman who had ever lived. She had been known as a leader among wise women, the Lady of Faire Isle, a title that had passed to Ariane, but she had never felt equal to slipping into her mother's shoes.

It had been over two years since Ariane had watched the life ebb away from the once-indomitable Evangeline. Still, not a day went by that she did not miss her mother's gentle strength, the wisdom of her counsel.

Oh, Maman, Ariane thought, *to be able to hear your voice again.* She wondered, would it really be so dreadful, to summon her mother's spirit, just this once? She knew well what her mother's answer to that question would have been. Evangeline Cheney had taught her three daughters many marvelous things, but she had solemnly adjured them against any meddling with dark magic.

Ariane forced her attention back to the mess she had made of her workshop. She had most of the broken pottery picked up when she realized that someone was shifting the trap door that concealed the way down to the hidden chamber.

"Ariane?"

Gabrielle's voice floated down to her from the regions above. Ariane had just enough time to dump the shards of pottery into the ash bin before her sister came down the twisting stone stair with all the air of a grand duchess about to make her curtsy at the royal court.

The girl had been cutting and refitting one of her old gowns again in an effort to appear more fashionable. What had once been a sweet and simple frock had been dyed carnelian and trimmed in a rich pattern of gold embroidery. The full skirts flared out over a farthingale and opened in the front to reveal a cream-colored underskirt frothing with lace. But it was the bodice Ariane eyed with misgiving, cut too low and displaying far too much of Gabrielle's generous bosom.

As she descended the stairs, Gabrielle lifted her skirts, managing to keep the gown clear of any stray dust with one elegant twitch of her hand. Her hair was of fairest gold, her face noted for its alabaster complexion, full red lips, and jewel-blue eyes.

She was so perfectly lovely that it often made Ariane's heart ache to look at her. Perhaps because she missed the days when Gabrielle had not been quite so concerned about her appearance, when her little sister had torn about Faire Isle barefoot, her curls in a flyaway tangle, a smudge of paint on her cheek, as she had demanded a fresh canvas to work upon. Her hands had been callused, her nails broken from her latest effort at sculpting.

Now Gabrielle's hands were soft, her nails perfectly manicured. It was her eyes that seemed in danger of turning hard and brittle.

"Ah, there you are. I have been looking for you everywhere," she complained. Gabrielle rarely visited the hidden workshop, and Ariane was disturbed to realize that she had not made any effort to close the concealing door above them.

"Gabrielle, I do trust that you remember this is supposed to be a *secret* room."

"It is not as if all our servants don't know that the room is here and that we are witches."

When Ariane frowned at her, Gabrielle rolled her eyes and amended, "Oh, pardon me, I forgot. *Witches* is a bad word. I should have said *wise women*."

"And what about any chance visitor?" Ariane demanded.

"There is no one here. Not unless you count your noble suitor."

"What! Renard is here?" Ever since Ariane had awakened that morning to discover the mist burned off the island, she had feared his return.

"Just teasing," Gabrielle grinned.

Ariane recovered her breath. "Blast you, Gabrielle. It is nothing to jest about. You know I have been dreading the comte's return."

"Ah, well, if you will persist in rescuing these stray men—"

"He was lost in the woods. All I did was point him to the right path," Ariane retorted. The first time she had met Renard was on the mainland and he hadn't seemed frightening or intimidating, only a man who had lost his way in the woods. The Deauville forest covered many acres and could be a treacherous place, full of wild boar and the occasional wolf. Ariane had simply led him back to safety.

She had fully expected that to be the end of the matter, never dreaming that the next time she saw Renard, he would coolly inform her that he had selected her to be his comtesse and he was arranging their wedding. Ariane had puzzled over Renard's actions so much, it threatened to bring a permanent crease between her eyes.

Gabrielle noticed the familiar frown gathering on Ariane's brow. "Oh, do stop worrying, Ariane. After the wedding gift we sent Monsieur le Comte—"

"The gift *you* sent," Ariane corrected. "You should not have done it, Gabrielle. I don't think it was wise to insult the comte."

"Pooh! Insults are the only way to be rid of a man as overbearing as Renard. I doubt he'll trouble you again."

Gabrielle's prank of the straw bride might have temporarily forestalled the comte, but Ariane feared that Renard, like the Deauvilles before him, was not a man to be easily defied.

Ariane turned to clean up the rest of the potion spattered

across the table. As it cooled, it turned darker, assuming the appearance of spilled blood.

Gabrielle sashayed around Ariane, glancing down at the mess and wrinkling her nose. "What in the name of all the saints have you been doing down here?"

"Nothing of any success. I was trying to develop a potion to add to the soil and hopefully double our grain crop this year."

"I thought Maman said we should never attempt to perform black magic."

"This is *science.*" Ariane lifted the sopping rag and tossed it into the dustbin. Gabrielle peered at the scorch mark on the table.

"It looks to me like the kind of science that destroys crops instead of growing them."

"I don't seem able to get the formula right, but I have to do something to generate more funds."

Funds that were badly needed to pay off the debts their father had left and insure that her sisters had dowries if Papa did not return. But that was not something that ever concerned Gabrielle.

She shrugged. "Why don't you try turning lead into gold instead of attempting to burn the house down?"

Ariane glared. Repenting of her teasing, Gabrielle sidled closer to wrap her arm around Ariane's shoulders and give her a light hug.

"Your fretting is going to give you permanent wrinkles. I have told you before, a woman's fortune is in her face. You would be better off trying to develop some new skin creams. I could certainly use a new perfume."

"Another perfume is the last thing you need, Gabrielle. I remember a time when you were far more interested in concocting new shades of color for your palette."

"Childish stuff, my dear sister. Dabbling with paints certainly won't ever do anything to make a *woman* rich and famous.

No one is ever going to commission me to paint their portrait or design frescoes for their palace. There is only one way a woman can succeed in this world."

Gabrielle tossed her head, smoothing one hand down her generous curves. "A girl has to learn how to best employ her other talents. How do you like my new gown? I just finished it this morning."

"It is far too opulent for this island."

"I have no intention of remaining buried on this island the rest of my life."

Ariane hated it when Gabrielle talked in such cynical fashion, even though she knew the cause of it, the deep hurt that lay behind Gabrielle's bitterness. But any attempt to draw Gabrielle out would only lead to another of their quarrels and Ariane didn't have the heart for that at the moment.

If she emptied the cauldron and started all over, she might have another chance at brewing the formula before supper. But she would accomplish nothing with Gabrielle hovering at her elbow.

"You said you were looking for me," Ariane reminded her sister. "Was there something particular you wanted?"

"I just thought I should tell you what Miri has done now."

"Oh, Gabrielle, please!" Ariane's younger sisters had once been inseparable, but of late, Gabrielle and Miribelle's constant bickering was enough to drive her to distraction. With all her other worries, she was in no humor to mediate another quarrel.

"Aren't you getting a little too old to come tale-bearing to me about Miri?" Ariane asked.

Gabrielle flushed, her sophistication deserting her, her lower lip jutting into a childish pout. "Very well. I only thought you would want to know, but never mind."

Pivoting on her heel, she flounced back to the stairs with the dignity of an offended princess. Carefully gathering up her skirts, she marched upward, all the while proclaiming, "I simply believed you would want to be told if Miri stood in danger of being arrested, even hung—but oh, well, forget I said a word."

Ariane suppressed a groan. Gabrielle had a penchant for melodrama, but it was not nearly as great as twelve-year-old Miribelle's flair for landing herself in trouble.

Ariane hastened to the foot of the stairs and peered up anxiously. "All right. Perhaps you had better tell me. She hasn't been trying to set Madame Pomfrey's doves free again, has she?"

Gabrielle had already scrambled through the trap door, but she glanced back down. "Even worse. She has freed someone's horse."

"Oh, Lord, not again."

Ariane paused long enough to extinguish the torches and make all secure before following Gabrielle up the stairs.

ψ ψ ψ

ARIANE BLINKED AS SHE EMERGED INTO THE BRIGHT SUNLIGHT OF the courtyard. The man-made pond sparkled, the reflection of the ivy-covered stone manor behind her shimmering in the blue waters. A fine solid building with a single square tower, Belle Haven was nowhere near as large and grand as the château on her father's estate in Brittany or his elegant town house in the heart of Paris. But Maman had far preferred the snug dwelling on the Faire Isle, something that had always mystified Papa.

Papa had wanted to pull down Belle Haven and erect instead a fairy-tale castle of whimsical proportions, soaring turrets, and costly glistening windows, but Maman had managed to gently discourage him.

What Louis Cheney had never realized was that all his wife had ever wanted was his love, his constancy, and his presence by her side . . . especially when she had lain dying.

Ariane hastened past the herb garden, chasing away a straying hen as she did so. Most of the outbuildings—the chicken house, the granary, and the milking shed—were like the main house, simple and unpretentious. Only the stables had been reconstructed on a grander scale to house Papa's horses. But the horses were gone now, sold off to help finance the building of Papa's ships, leaving the stables largely empty, at least of horses.

As Ariane slipped through the stable's broad double doors, she was assailed by the scent of sweet hay and horse sweat, mingled with other animal odors. The first stall played host to a litter of abandoned bunnies Miri had tucked cozily into a wooden crate. A sparrow whose wing she hoped to mend chirped in a cage above the door.

Farther down the row, Miri's pony champed its hay, oblivious to the shrill whinnies emanating from the last stall. Ariane headed toward the spot where Miri had housed her latest acquisition.

Dear lord! This new guest to the stables hardly fit into Miri's usual category of injured strays. A sleek thoroughbred with a glossy coat of dapple-gray pranced restively. Ariane's youngest sister was in the stall, comforting the creature.

Clad in a tunic and rough wool breeches, Miri could easily have been mistaken for a peasant lad, but for the straight lengths of white-blond hair that shimmered down to her waist. She barely came up to the horse's shoulder and as the stallion attempted to wheel away from Miri, Ariane feared seeing her petite sister trampled. But of course Miri was quite adept at handling horses.

Miri moved in carefully, crooning words of endearment in an enchanting, silvery voice. The horse pricked up its ears, twitched a little, and then stilled. Miri held out her delicate hands as though begging leave to touch. Continuing her low song, she melted closer, patting the stallion's neck. The horse nuzzled against Miri's brow, its soft breath stirring the moon-gold tendrils of her hair.

Ariane watched, spellbound. Miri, unaware of her presence, continued to stroke the horse, lost as usual in her own little world.

Ariane blamed herself. She had all but allowed Miri to run wild after their mother's death when the child had grown so pale and withdrawn. Miri's only solace was tearing about the island on her pony and rescuing injured animals.

But Miri had clearly gone too far this time. This exquisite gray had not come from the Faire Isle. The island was only thirty miles wide and most of the mounts owned by local people were sturdy ponies like Miri's. The stallion's owner had to be a mainlander, not some outraged peddler from town that Ariane could easily placate with a few coins.

The situation was not improved when Gabrielle swept into the stables in a rustle of silk. Ariane frowned, wishing her other sister elsewhere. Miri could be hard enough to deal with, in many ways as recalcitrant and skittish as that stallion. Gabrielle's mischievous presence could only aggravate the situation.

"Miri?" Ariane called softly, so as not to alarm the stallion.

Miri snapped out of whatever strange communion she shared with the horse. She turned to face Ariane, her eyes shining. Fringed with pale gold lashes, they were an unusual shade of silvery blue, almost opaque and as changeable as mist.

"Oh, Ariane, I was out looking for unicorns and look what I found instead. His name is Hercules. He is a little nervous about being in the stable, but I have promised him that later he can roam free in our paddock."

"You *found* this horse, my dear?"

"Aye, isn't he a beauty? Almost as good as finding a unicorn."

"A unicorn wearing a bridle?" Gabrielle piped up from behind Ariane.

Miri scowled at her. "Unicorns don't wear bridles, Gabby."

"That horse certainly had one when you rode him home.

A saddle and a blanket, too, although I don't see them now."
Gabrielle picked up a pitchfork and prodded at a pile of hay. "I
daresay Miri has hidden it all away somewhere."

"I didn't! I haven't hidden anything," Miri said. But when
Ariane tried to hold her gaze, Miri avoided her eyes.

"Miri?" Ariane prodded.

Her little sister turned back abruptly to petting the horse,
but a telltale flush stole across Miri's tanned cheeks.

"Miribelle!"

Miri's lips firmed in a stubborn line. She emerged from the
stall, her chin raised in defiance. "All right. I didn't find him. I—
I *liberated* him."

"Oh, Miri," Ariane sighed and Gabrielle laughed.

Miri flashed them both an indignant look. "It is true. A great
ogre had enslaved this poor creature. Hercules wanted to escape
that bully and come away with me."

"And how do you know that?" Ariane asked.

"He told me so."

"Oh, Lord," Gabrielle teased. "Not another talking horse.
And what language does this one speak?"

"He speaks *horse*," Miri snapped.

Ariane addressed Miri in the most patient tone she could
muster. "Dearest, how many times must I warn you? You must
not go about declaring that you can talk to horses."

"But I can," Miri insisted with a look of hurt bewilderment.

"Aye, my love, but that is exactly the sort of thing that makes
people nervous. If anyone from the mainland should hear you, it
might get you charged with witchcraft."

"Or clapped up in a lunatic asylum." Gabrielle ventured
closer for a better look. "I must admit this horse is better than
that old nag you 'liberated' from that peddler. If you are going to
be hung for horse theft, it might as well be for a thoroughbred."

"No one is going to be hung," Ariane said when Miri's eyes

rounded in alarm. "But that horse must be returned to its owner at once."

"Oh, Ariane, no!" Miri positioned herself squarely in front of the stall. "I gave Hercules my word of honor that he'd never have to go back to that terrible man. Why, do you know what that horrid person was planning to do to poor Hercules?"

Miri whispered as though trying to spare the horse's sensibilities. "That ogre threatened to—to *unman* him."

Gabrielle erupted into uncontrollable laughter that only added to Miri's indignation.

"I assure you Hercules does not find the prospect of being gelded so amusing," she said fiercely.

Gabrielle only contained her mirth when Ariane administered a surreptitious warning pinch to her arm.

Ariane said, "Miribelle, please try to be sensible. That stallion is obviously a valuable animal. You can't spirit it away simply because you don't approve of its master."

"The ogre is not Hercules's master. Hercules is a creature of the earth, the same as you and me. He ought to be free to choose where he wants to be."

"I do hope the man you liberated him from shares your charming notions about the rights of horses," Gabrielle said.

"I don't care what he thinks, horrid beast. He may go to the devil."

"Who was he, Miri?" Ariane demanded.

"I don't know."

"Miri—"

"Truly, Ariane, I don't. Except for Papa, all men look alike. This was just some great ruffian riding along the road from the harbor. Already struggling to escape, when Hercules scented me, he called out for help. I whistled to him and he managed to brush off that huge brute and gallop toward me. I leaped up on his back and we were away like the wind."

Ariane was aghast. "Miri, you not only took this man's horse, but you left him injured on the road?"

"The oaf wasn't hurt. He jumped up almost immediately. He tried to run after us. He was shouting and cursing."

"I can well imagine he might," Gabrielle said dryly.

Ariane pressed her hand to her brow. If the man was able to describe Miri, she would be readily identifiable.

Here on the island, the fact that she was Evangeline Cheney's daughter would afford Miri protection, but even to be hauled off to answer charges would be a devastating ordeal for the shy, withdrawn girl. And there was always the great danger of what her naïve sister might be induced to say in her own defense.

"The horse begged me to rescue him. How was I able to ride him? Why, I simply charmed him with my song."

Most of the people of Faire Isle would understand, but Ariane could just imagine how such an explanation would fall upon a stranger's ears. What began as a trial for horse theft could be twisted into a suspicion of bewitchment. The best way of averting any such disaster would be to return the horse to town and find the owner before the matter took an uglier turn.

"Miri, what did you do with the saddle and bridle you removed from Hercules?" Ariane asked.

Miri didn't answer. She folded her arms and ducked her head, her stubborn face disappearing behind her shimmering lengths of hair.

While Gabrielle searched the tack room, Ariane clasped Miri by the shoulders in desperation, her patience starting to slip. She was as close as she had ever been to giving her little sister a brisk shake when she was interrupted by a discreet cough.

Fourche, their groom, emerged from one of the unused stalls at the end of the stable. The old man had been hiding in there, listening. He approached Ariane, looking sheepish, flushed to the bristly ends of his short gray hair. As well he might. Ariane had given him strict instructions to come to her at once if Miri ever turned up at the stables with another "liberated" horse. But Miri had the old man as enchanted as any of her animals.

Fourche swallowed hard. "Begging your pardon, milady, but here is what you are looking for."

"Fourche! No!" Miri said, her eyes reproachful and pleading.

The groom cast her an anguished glance before handing over the bridle to Ariane. "There is some sort of emblem on the headpiece that will likely help identify the owner."

Ignoring Miri's chagrined cry and attempt to snatch the bridle, Ariane studied the leather workmanship. It was of fine quality and just as Fourche had indicated, there was a silver engraving on the headpiece, a bold and arrogant letter "R" entwined with the symbol of some small animal. A fox.

Ariane's heart missed a beat. The emblem was not unfamiliar to her. She had seen it before, emblazoned on a signet ring adorning a large, powerful hand.

"What is it, Ariane?" Gabrielle asked. "You look as white as your apron. What did you find?"

Numbly, Ariane held the bridle out for her inspection. "Renard . . . it was Renard's horse Miri took."

"*Merde!*" Gabrielle gasped.

Ariane forgave her sister the vulgarity. She almost felt like swearing herself. Old Fourche's jaw dropped open. Only Miri appeared undismayed.

"Who is Renard?" she asked.

"I swear, Miri! You truly do live on a different world from the rest of us." Gabrielle rounded on her. "The Comte de Renard is Ariane's suitor."

Miribelle's eyes widened. "Ariane has a suitor?"

Gabrielle flung up her hands in exasperation. "Where were you last week when Renard sent that magnificent coach to fetch Ariane to their wedding? The entire island was abuzz about it, thinking the king himself was descending upon us."

Miri clutched at Ariane. "Oh, n-no, Ariane, please! I—I don't want you to go off and marry anyone and leave us."

"Then you should have thought of that before you stole Renard's horse," Gabrielle said. "I thought we had managed to be rid of the man and now you have drawn him straight back to our gates. Ariane will probably have to marry him just to keep you from being arrested."

Tears welled in Miri's eyes. "Oh, Ariane, I—I am so s-sorry. I didn't know. I didn't think—"

"You never do—" Gabrielle began hotly, but Ariane cut her off.

"Gabrielle, this isn't helping." Ariane wrapped her arm around Miri's shoulders. "Don't cry, dearest. I fear Monsieur le Comte would have returned anyway."

"But—if the comte tries to f-force you—"

"He will do no such thing." As Ariane hugged her sister, she concealed her own worried frown. The truth was she had no idea what Renard might be capable of. The Deauvilles had the reputation of being hard and ruthless. What if Gabrielle was right? What if Renard did try to use Miri's misadventure to coerce Ariane?

She was given little time to consider the matter. Their serving lad, Leon, suddenly burst into the barn, his thin face streaked with dust and sweat, his carrot-colored hair sticking up from his head.

"Oh, m-mademoiselle! Mistress Ariane." He panted. "Louise sent me to find you. There is a rider at the gates. 'Tis—'tis the Comte de Renard."

Ariane experienced a moment of blind panic. This was one of those times she wished her Papa had spent less money on the stables and invested in a good sturdy drawbridge instead. And a moat, preferably one with dragons.

Take hold of yourself, girl, she admonished herself. After all, no matter how intimidating he might be, Renard was only a man, the same as any other . . . wasn't he?

She certainly was not about to betray her nervousness, especially not to her younger sisters. Managing a weak smile, Ariane said, "Apparently, Monsieur le Comte wasted little time in acquiring himself another horse."

"He probably found one at Port Corsair. That fool at the inn would lend a horse to the devil himself as long as he had a title." Gabrielle's mouth pursed in a worried frown. "So what are we going to do, Ariane?"

Ariane rubbed her hand across her brow. Thinking swiftly, she began rapping out orders, "Fourche, fetch the rest of Monsieur le Comte's tack from wherever you and Miri have hidden it and saddle that horse. Gabrielle, I want you to take Miri up to your bedchamber and stay there until I send for you."

Fourche shuffled to obey, but Gabrielle said, "If anyone needs to hide, it is you, Ariane. I won't leave you to face that great ogre alone."

"And, what about Hercules?" Miri cut in. "I won't abandon him. I promised—"

"There is no time to argue," Ariane said. "Gabrielle, take Miri and go. I will deal with Renard."

Gabrielle cast her a frustrated look before flinging up her hands in resignation. "Oh, very well." Ignoring Miri's wail of protest, she seized the girl by the hand, half dragging her from the stables. Miri cast a piteous look back over her shoulder, pleading with Ariane not to surrender Hercules.

As the girl vanished from view, the horse thrust its head out of the stall, its lip curling back in a shrill whinny.

"I don't need to hear anything more from you either." Ariane reached out cautiously to stroke the stallion's muzzle, a little astonished when it allowed her to do so, regarding her with sad equine eyes.

If she had possessed one tenth of Miri's ability with horses, she would have been tempted to fling herself on the horse's back and bolt, ride far away from all her troubles, the arrogant Renard, the mountain of debts, the uncertainty of their future if their father did not return. Just run away.

Aye, exactly like Papa did.

It was that reflection more than anything that caused Ariane to steel her spine. Heading from the stables, she braced herself to receive her most unwelcome guest.

Chapter Two

ARIANE DASHED INTO HER BEDCHAMBER LONG ENOUGH TO strip off her damaged apron and make sure her hair was tucked neatly beneath her veil. By the time she emerged, she discovered that Renard had already been ushered into the great hall. Standing in the shadows of the musician's gallery, she peeked down into the chamber below, studying the man who had invaded her home.

When the comte had come to demand her hand in marriage, he had advanced upon her like a conquering prince, accompanied by a small army of retainers. This time, he appeared to be alone, but that didn't render Renard any less formidable. The broad span of his shoulders strained beneath a black leather jerkin opened to reveal a sweat-stained shirt and a vee of darkly tanned chest. With a large hunting knife strapped to his belt and his rough countenance, he could have passed for a wandering mercenary, which was exactly what many folk declared him to be.

There was something mysterious about this man who seemed to have sprung out of nowhere to claim his inheritance. His accent spoke more of Paris than the rougher Breton dialect. Some whispered that he might not be a Deauville at all. Others declared that he was a bastard, the product of a misalliance between the late comte's youngest son and a harlot and that was why the old comte had never acknowledged his existence.

Still others believed that in his youth, Renard had done some dark and terrible deed that caused him to be banished all this time. If that were true, Ariane shuddered to think what his crime must have been. None of the Deauvilles had ever been saints.

Renard's heavy boots rang out on the wooden floor as he paced across the great hall, stripping off his leather riding gloves and tucking them in his belt. Ariane scanned Renard's features, but it was frustratingly impossible to tell anything from Renard's impassive countenance.

His disposition would certainly not be improved if she kept him waiting. Fortifying herself, Ariane slowly descended the stairs to the gallery.

The chamber's most striking feature was the magnificent collection of tapestries that adorned the stone walls, beautiful and intricate weavings done by women right here on the island. Instead of the usual hunting or battle scenes, the tapestries celebrated remarkable ladies of the past, Eleanor of Aquitaine riding bare-breasted to the Crusades, Matilda of Flanders dispensing alms to the poor, the brilliant Anne of Brittany surrounded by her court of artists and scholars.

Renard had come to a halt before one of these tapestries, pausing to study it, his broad back turned toward Ariane. She did not think that Renard was even aware of her approach until he startled her by speaking.

"Hildegard of Bingen?" he asked, without turning round.

"W-what?"

Renard gestured toward the weaving. "The tapestry. I was

wondering if it was meant to depict the Abbess Hildegard, the noted German mystic and writer."

"No." Ariane was astonished that Renard knew anything of Hildegard or any other female intellectual. Most men would have only seen the portrait of a medieval woman wielding her quill when she should have been doing something more useful.

"The tapestry honors my Great-aunt Eugenie who was also something of a scholar. It was designed by my sister, Gabrielle," Ariane added. Back in the days when Gabrielle had still had faith in something besides bottles of perfume.

"It is a magnificent piece of work."

"Thank you," Ariane murmured, nervously twining her fingers together. She had anticipated anger over the theft of his horse, resentment because she had defied his plan to marry her. She had never imagined having a calm discussion about her sister's tapestry. But from the first moment of their acquaintance, Renard had made an art of the unexpected.

He turned to face her. There was no haste in Renard's movements. Heavy lids veiled eyes of deep forest green. Whatever else about him might be true, the man was no imposter. Ariane had known his late grandfather and Renard had the same eyes, that shuttered expression that gave so little away. They regarded each other in silence for a moment until Ariane recollected her manners. She sank into a respectful curtsy.

"Monsieur le Comte."

"My lady Ariane." He sketched her a brief bow. "I believe there is *someone* here who belongs to me."

"No, I—I don't," Ariane faltered in dismay. "I already told you that I wouldn't—"

"I was referring, of course, to my horse." Renard's brows rose in a look of mock surprise, but his lashes swept down, veiling a wicked gleam.

Ariane flushed over her error, a mistake she suspected he'd deliberately encouraged. She had never known any man who could fluster her as quickly as Renard. She owed him an apology and an explanation, at least about the horse. But it was difficult to think where to begin.

"Won't you please be seated, my lord?" she invited diffidently.

Renard lowered himself onto the wooden settle near the hearth. Even seated, he was a Goliath, resting one powerful arm along the back of the bench and stretching out long muscular legs. He gave the appearance of indolence, but Ariane suspected it was as deceptive as a powerful lion lazing in the sun moments before it pounces.

She had her entire household to come to her aid should the need arise and yet she had felt far more comfortable that day she had been alone with Renard in the woods. Despite the rumors surrounding him, she had been rather charmed by the new comte's self-deprecating wit and sense of humor. Of course, she had known he was in the market for a wife. He had assembled at his castle some of the loveliest and wealthiest noblewomen in Brittany from which to make his selection.

That was why when he had come to call upon her at Faire Isle, she had been surprised, but not the least apprehensive of his errand. She had even politely asked him if he had found himself a bride.

"Indeed I have," Renard had replied with one of his lazy smiles. *"You."*

Ariane had been so confounded that as she had backed up to sink into a chair, she had ended up on the floor instead . . .

Banishing the memory, Ariane settled herself stiffly opposite him. Drawing comfort from the familiar feel of her mother's chair, she folded her hands demurely in the folds of her gown.

"To begin with, my lord," she began. "I suppose I should explain why I—I felt obliged to take your horse—"

"To begin with, my lady, you should not attempt to lie to me," Renard replied. "You have neither the face nor the heart to make a good deceiver. I saw quite clearly who made off with my horse and it was not you. My horse was stolen by a petite blonde elf of a girl. Your youngest sister, I believe?"

"Yes." Ariane's hands tightened on her lap. "Miribelle is no more than a child, my lord. What she did was very wrong, but she gets these unusual notions in her head. She has a most tender heart toward animals and is forever rescuing some injured creature. For some reason, she had the impression that your horse was being abused."

"It was."

"It—it was?" Ariane stared, scarcely able to believe that Renard would so callously admit to such a thing.

"The stallion was being abused, but not by me. It had been handled badly by the drunken lout I bought the horse from. The young fool had already done considerable damage to the poor creature's mouth," Renard said. "But happily he had not managed to break the horse's spirit."

"I noticed that Hercules seems to have plenty of that."

"Hercules?"

"Er—y-yes. My sister, Miri, believes that is what the horse prefers to be called."

"That explains everything," Renard drawled. "Not perceiving any heroic qualities in the brute, I was calling him Lucifer. No doubt that is why he parted company with me before I was quite prepared to dismount. I thought at first he'd been spooked by a snake or a badger. That was before I realized there was a young sorceress hidden in the trees, enchanting him away from me."

His words sent a jolt of alarm through Ariane. "Oh, no, my lord. It was nothing like that. My sister's ability with horses must seem quite unusual in one of her age and size. But she is far stronger than she looks and she has been riding since almost before she could walk. There is nothing in the least unnatural about her ability and—and—"

"Easy, ma chère." Renard leaned forward to rest his hand on

hers to halt her panicked flow of words. "I was merely jesting. Do I seem to you the sort of man who would charge a child with witchcraft?"

"Well, I—I—" Ariane had no idea what kind of man he was. No one else seemed to know either.

Renard enveloped her fingers in a reassuring clasp. "When you know me better, you will realize I am not so alarming."

The unexpected gentleness of his tone disarmed her. For a fleeting moment, his eyes were so warm and kind, he coaxed a reluctant smile from her.

"I am not here seeking retribution for the theft of my horse," he continued. "The stallion is of little importance. I am sure you know I had another reason for coming to see you."

"O-oh." Ariane glanced down, surprised that her hand was still resting comfortably within his grasp. When she eased away from him, he made no effort to restrain her. He settled back in his seat, his heavy lids veiling his gaze once more. An uncomfortable silence fell.

"Are you not even going to ask me, ma chère?" he prodded softly.

"Ask you what?" Ariane faltered.

"About how magnificent our wedding feast was."

Ariane stared at him, aghast. "Our—our wedding feast? You *still* had it?"

"But of course. What else could I do? The feast was arranged, the musicians engaged, the bishop waiting, and all the guests assembled. Everything was perfect except for one small detail. When the bridal carriage arrived, it was empty."

"My lord, I—I—" Ariane tried to interrupt, but Renard flung up one hand to stay her.

"No, wait. I correct myself. The coach was not empty. There was a lady inside, most elegantly attired in the satin gown I had sent for a wedding gift. But when I reached for my bride's hand to help her alight from the coach, lo and behold! I discovered to my astonishment, she was made entirely of straw."

Ariane felt a hot flood of color surge into her cheeks.

"Not that I am complaining. This straw bride of mine, she was not much on conversation, nor was she passionate in bed. But when it came to dancing, she was light on her feet."

Ariane shot to her feet, pacing agitatedly before the fireplace. She heartily regretted now that she had not made more of an effort to stop Gabrielle from playing her prank with the straw bride. But she had been certain that substitution would be detected by Renard or his retainers long before the comte ever reached the church door. Although the man had brought it upon himself, Ariane cringed at the thought of his humiliation.

"I—I am so sorry, my lord. It was indeed a cruel and ill-mannered jest. But I *told* you I would never marry you. Why did you not listen?"

Renard fetched a mock sigh. "I have a very poor memory."

Ariane stopped pacing to eye him reproachfully. "I tried to refuse you politely. It was never my intention to—to hurt or embarrass you."

"Do not distress yourself, chérie. I have a very thick hide. I was more disappointed than embarrassed. However, I do now realize my mistake."

"By not accepting my refusal?"

"No, by not coming to claim you myself." Renard uncoiled himself from the settee with an alarming suddenness. As he stalked toward her with a purposeful gleam in his eye, she knew a craven impulse to retreat behind her mother's chair. But the Lady of Faire Isle was not supposed to permit men to chase her around the furniture.

Refusing to give ground, she tipped her head challengingly. "And so what now, milord? Do you propose to remedy your error by tossing me over your shoulder and carrying me off?"

Renard's green eyes glinted. "A tempting solution, ma chère. It would be the most direct way of getting what I want and I am usually a most direct man. I tend to forget how romantic you ladies can be. It is only natural you should wish to be wooed."

Ariane gasped when he stole his arm about her waist. No man had ever been so bold. She didn't know whether it was her dignity that kept men at bay or the fact that she was not alluring enough to tempt them. Compared to Gabrielle's delicate beauty, Ariane often thought herself far too tall and gawky.

Being hauled close to Renard's overwhelmingly masculine frame was not entirely disagreeable, but when he sought to kiss her, Ariane scrambled away.

"Please, monsieur!" she said. "I assure you I have not the least wish to be wooed. All I desire is for you to give over this madness."

"Madness?" Renard's brows rose in astonishment. "Without wishing to seem immodest, most women would deem me a good match. Your father's lands in Brittany border mine. You have to be familiar with my rank and holdings."

"I know your estate, my lord, but I know little of *you*. Only what I have heard whispered on the mainland and down in the harbor."

"Ah, no doubt you have gleaned some fascinating tales."

"They say that you spent your youth as some sort of—of pirate or bandit."

"I have also heard that you are a witch," Renard retorted.

"I am skilled in the arts of healing and the usage of herbs. That is a very different thing."

"Then it appears we would both be far wiser to pay less heed to idle gossip."

Ariane acknowledged the justice of his mild reproof with a gracious nod of her head. "You are right, my lord. I am sorry. But that still doesn't change the fact you are a stranger to me. I have only ever met you twice before. Once that day in the woods and then when you arrived on my doorstep, insisting that I marry you."

Renard closed the distance between them, brushing his fingers down her cheek in a light caress. "Ariane, many couples do not even meet until their wedding day."

"But in such cases, the match has usually been arranged by one's parents," she argued.

"Is that what is troubling you? Your father's absence? I hope the good chevalier will return soon, but I doubt that he would refuse to give you to me."

"I realize it is the established custom for fathers to dispose of their daughters, often against their will," Ariane said indignantly. "But the women of Faire Isle are not accustomed to being bartered off."

Renard's lips curled cynically. "Everyone is bartered off sooner or later."

"I don't see it happening to men."

"You'd be surprised." An odd look flashed into Renard's eyes, something akin to bitterness, although he continued to smile. "Alas, it would seem I have offended you again. I fear I have made a very bad beginning. I beg you to allow me to make amends."

"No amends are necessary, monsieur," Ariane said earnestly. "Please let us put this talk of marriage aside and part friends."

"Ah, how could any gentleman refuse such a charming request?"

Ariane brightened. "Then you agree—"

"No. I fear I have never been much of a gentleman."

Ariane stifled a frustrated sigh as Renard reached for a purse knotted to his belt. She eyed him warily, hardly knowing what to expect next. He unfastened the drawstrings of the small leather pouch and withdrew an object, which he held up for her inspection. It was a ring, an unpretentious circle of metal with unusual markings on it, large enough that a man could have slipped it upon his small finger.

"For you, milady. Just a small token of my esteem."

Ariane stared at the ring, completely nonplussed before shaking her head in protest. "My lord, I cannot possibly accept—"

"Oh, I realize it does not look like anything much, a mere trinket. But its worth is invaluable. It is a magic ring, you see."

"*Magic?*" Ariane did not trouble to hide her skepticism.

"You do not believe in magic, mademoiselle?" Renard clucked his tongue at her. "You? A sorceress of such great repute?"

"A healer, nothing more," Ariane corrected him flatly. "And yes, I do believe in magic, but you strike me as being far too much of a cynic to do so."

"When you know me better, chérie, you will find that I always try to keep an open mind."

"Well, I don't. Not when it comes to magic rings. The power of plants and herbs to cure, the miracle of the human spirit, phenomena of the mind too extraordinary to be explained. But as for charms and tokens like that ring, no, I fear not."

"Aren't you the least bit curious? Don't you want to know what this ring can do?" he coaxed.

Ariane studied him, trying to determine if he was in earnest or in jest. Whatever this new game was that Renard seemed bent upon playing, Ariane decided to humor him.

"Very well, my lord. What does the ring do?"

"This unusual ring is part of a set that I acquired—er—from an old gypsy woman during my travels abroad. You see that the companion to the ring now rests upon my own finger." Renard held up his hand. The rings were identical except that the band that Renard wore was wider, heavier.

"According to the legend, when you slip this ring upon your finger, we will be linked in a way that defies all distance and time. You will be able to summon me to your side with merely a thought."

"Forgive my frankness, my lord, but summoning you to my side is er—ah—not exactly high on my list of priorities."

Renard grinned. "You prefer to consign me to perdition?"

"Not quite that far. Comfortably back at your own castle will do."

"You can have your wish. Wear the ring and I will leave you in peace."

When Ariane eyed him doubtfully, Renard said, "I give you my solemn word of honor. Keep the ring and I will keep my distance. But if you ever find yourself in need of me, just hold your hand over your heart and think of me. I will come to you at once. You may summon me three times."

"Only three times? And then what happens? Do I turn into a newt or a toad?"

"No, you turn into my wife," Renard replied affably. "When you use the ring for the third time, you must cry forfeit and surrender. Marry me. Is it a bargain, ma chère?"

"Certainly not. I would never agree to anything so outrageous, even if I did believe in magic rings, which I don't."

"Then what have you got to lose?" Renard grasped the ring between his thumb and forefinger, dangling it temptingly before her eyes. "Keep the ring and you may be rid of me."

"And if I don't?"

Renard smiled his languid smile, but there was a steely glint in his eyes. "I fear I would feel obliged to fall back upon more direct methods."

"What do you mean by that?"

"Oh, perhaps I shall build a willow cabin at your gate or play the troubadour beneath your window." His teeth flashed in a predatory grin. "Or I might take a lesson from how the Romans dealt with those stubborn Sabine women and simply fling you over the bow of my saddle."

Ariane's eyes widened. Something in his voice sent a dark shiver through her. If she refused the ring, would he really attempt to carry her off? Force her to the altar and into his bed?

Ariane searched his gaze—a skill long practiced by wise women, the art of reading the eyes, those mirrors of the soul. Ariane was so adept at it, she could often take not only the measure of a man's character, but divine his very thoughts.

Ariane struggled to read Renard's mind, but it was frustratingly impossible. He stared fixedly back at her, as though he guessed what she was trying to do and it amused him. In the end, Ariane felt obliged to look away.

Renard held out the ring to her with a quizzical lift of his brows. She hated feeling backed into a corner, but compared to risking Renard's more "direct methods," the ring seemed by far the safer proposition.

"Very well," she said reluctantly. "Give me the ridiculous thing."

"And you agree to my terms? Use the ring three times and you are mine?"

Ariane nodded, but she could not help tensing when Renard slipped it on her finger. With the matching band adorning his large hand, it was as though they had already plighted their troth.

"There, you see," he said. "The ring fits you perfectly."

"It feels rather snug to me." But Ariane was astonished to realize the ring was indeed a miraculous fit, as though it had been destined for her hand. A disconcerting thought.

This was all nonsense, she reassured herself. The ring was not magic. When Renard came to his senses and married someone else, she would send the useless trinket back to him. Then why was she left with this uneasy feeling, as though she had just slipped her foot into a snare?

She thought she detected a flash of triumph in Renard's eyes. But the expression was quickly masked behind a look of the blandest innocence.

She drew away from him, saying, "And now, my lord, I don't wish to seem rude, but you did say if I took the ring you would leave me in peace. I am sure that Fourche has saddled your stallion so—so—"

"So why the devil am I not already gone?" Renard finished with a rueful chuckle. "You are right, mademoiselle. I promised I would go away until you use the ring and you will find me a man of my word."

He removed his riding gloves from his belt, preparing to leave. She did not ever expect to see Renard again, but there was one thing she needed to know.

"My lord, may I ask you a question before you go?"

Renard glanced up from smoothing on his glove, an inquiring lift to his brows.

"Is there a strain of insanity in your family?"

The inquiry surprised a bark of laughter from Renard. "I have a distant cousin who is perhaps a little addled in his wits. Why do you ask?"

"Only that I am at a loss to account for your determined pursuit of me. I am possessed of neither great wealth nor great beauty—" Ariane began.

"That is a matter of opinion, ma chère," Renard murmured.

Ariane refused to be distracted by his compliment or the provocative look that accompanied it. "If my father does not return from his voyage, everything we own may be swallowed by debt. You could look much higher for a wife, so why are you so bent upon having me?"

An odd smile touched Renard's lips. "I will answer that question, but only on our wedding night."

Ariane frowned, annoyed by his evasive reply, but she saw there was no hope of gaining a more sensible answer.

"Then it seems my curiosity is destined to go unsatisfied. I bid you adieu, Monsieur le Comte." She made a prim curtsy, holding out her hand in a gesture of farewell.

"Let us rather say, au revoir."

Renard took her hand. Ariane supposed he meant to carry it courteously to his lips, but before she could even blink, he hauled her off-balance, tumbling her into his arms. He stifled her protest by claiming her lips with a swift kiss.

A kiss? It was more like a heated collision, a dueling of lips, warm, fierce, and ruthless. Dazed by the unexpected assault, Ariane clung weakly to the front of his doublet. She had never been kissed before. Whenever she had imagined what it might be like, she had always pictured something tender and soul-stirring.

Instead, she felt the blood rush through her veins, making her hot, flushed, almost giddy. And for one insane moment, she experienced a mad urge to kiss him back just as fiercely.

When Renard released her, she struggled to come to her senses. She ought to box his ears for his impertinence, but it was all she could do to catch her breath. She finally recovered enough to cast Renard a reproachful look, but the villain was unrepentant.

"Forgive the liberty, milady." He smiled lazily down at her. "But I needed one sweet memory to last me until you use the ring to summon me back again."

He swept her a magnificent bow and turned to stride away. Ariane pressed a trembling hand to her mouth. The need to always have the final word was Gabrielle's habit, not hers. But something in Renard's swaggering step, his insufferable manner of self-assurance goaded her into shouting.

"Renard!"

He paused to glance back.

"I am never going to use that ring."

Renard's answer was an infuriating smile.

Chapter Three

TWILIGHT SETTLED OVER THE HOUSE, THE BARNYARD FILLED with the bleating of lambs settling in for the night. A soft breeze perfumed the air with lavender from the herb garden, wafting the sweet scent to Ariane through the open window.

But the tranquility of the evening was lost upon her as she sat hunched over the oak table, trying to balance the household accounts. It was difficult to render a good accounting when there were more debts to be settled than there was coin to go around.

Ariane sighed, pausing to light the candles as the day faded. The soft glow flickered over the room that had once been her mother's bedchamber. There in the massive bedstead with the rose-hangings, she, Gabrielle, and Miri had been born. And there was the jointed stool where all the girls had frequently sat while Maman brushed and braided their hair.

Ariane gazed bleakly around her. The room that had once seemed so warm and bustling with life felt cold even in the midst of summer. With Maman gone, it was as though the very heart had been cut from the house.

Everyone now looked to Ariane to take her mother's place as the Lady of Faire Isle, and she felt herself a poor substitute. Rubbing her tired eyes, she turned back to the household accounts, wiping the smudged slate to begin again.

Her task was made all the more difficult by the object lying upon the desk. The Comte de Renard's ring. She had slipped it off her finger because the thing kept distracting her. Just a plain circle of metal and yet it was decidedly older than she had first imagined. When she had polished it with her handkerchief, she had discovered engravings upon the exterior, ancient runic symbols as mysterious as the man who had given the ring to her.

Her thoughts kept returning again and again to her encounter with Renard this afternoon, the intimate feel of his mouth against hers, that ruthless kiss that seemed to have set the seal on the strange bargain they had made.

When you use the ring for the third time, you must cry forfeit and surrender. Marry me.

Such an odd proposition. The man must indeed be mad. But as Ariane's gaze strayed back to the coffer open before her, the pile of unpaid debts, she thought that perhaps she was the one who must be mad to spurn marriage with a man as powerful and wealthy as Renard.

But as the Lady of Faire Isle, she had a grave responsibility to choose her husband with care. That is if she ever married at all. She had been left guardian of ancient manuscripts that contained powerful knowledge, dangerous should they ever fall into the wrong hands. The man she wed had to be completely scrupulous and trustworthy and Renard's evasiveness, his inability to return a straightforward answer to the simplest question, troubled her deeply. If there was one quality she valued above all others in a man, it was honesty.

Renard's grandfather, the old comte, had been overbearing, ruthless, and cunning by turns, willing to do anything to gain his own ends. Renard showed signs of being cut from the same cloth.

Yet she could not help recalling how kind he'd been when he had soothed her fears about Miri. He had also been remarkably good-humored about the theft of his horse and the trick Gabrielle had played upon him. And he had provoked her into smiling when she was trying her hardest to be serious.

Ariane was resolved to think no more of him and yet . . . She turned his ring over in her hand. The thing could not possibly be magic, but it did serve Renard's purpose in one way. The ring's presence kept her thoughts focused on him. What, if anything, would happen if she ever did follow Renard's instructions and try to use it?

Her brow furrowed with concentration, she had the ring poised over the tip of her finger when a cry rang out.

"What are you doing, Ariane?"

Ariane started. She nearly dropped the ring, making a mad grab to catch it. Gabrielle stood on the threshold scowling.

"You shouldn't be fooling with that thing. It could be dangerous."

"It is only an old ring, Gabrielle." Ariane felt a trifle sheepish. But her sister stormed across the room to snatch the ring away from her.

Ariane had been obliged to tell Miri and Gabrielle something of what had passed between herself and Renard. After she found out that Ariane had surrendered Hercules to the comte, Miri had lost interest. But Gabrielle had badgered Ariane with questions until she had drawn out the entire story of the bargain Ariane had made over the ring.

Gabrielle perched on the edge of the table to study the ring herself, her bare feet dangling. She was already attired for bed in her soft linen night shift, her golden hair cascading down her back. It made her look younger, more like the little sister Ariane remembered.

They kept early hours at Belle Haven. Candles were dear and, as Gabrielle frequently complained these days, there was nothing to do on the island but sleep. However, her usual air of ennui was absent tonight, her blue eyes alight with curiosity as she turned the ring this way and that, appraising it as a jeweler might have done.

She bit down upon the circle of metal and pulled a face. "Humph! I don't know what it is made of, but certainly not gold. Where did the comte say he acquired this thing?"

"Somewhere during his travels. From an old gypsy woman."

"What gypsy woman? What travels?"

"I don't know," Ariane replied, carefully shifting some ledger sheets that were in danger of being crushed beneath Gabrielle's bottom. "Monsieur le Comte is not exactly the most forthcoming man. He smiles, he jests, and he tells one absolutely nothing."

"Didn't you try to read his eyes?"

"Of course I did! But it was like—like attempting to peruse a book whose pages are sealed together."

Gabrielle digested this information in disappointed silence before turning her attention back to the ring. She scrunched up her face as she examined the metal band more closely.

"What are these funny symbols?"

"Runic letters," Ariane replied. "Very similar to those in many of our old manuscripts downstairs."

"Can you translate what it says?"

"Perhaps. I am not sure." In truth, Ariane had been curiously reluctant to try. But Gabrielle leaped down from the table to fetch Ariane a magnifying glass.

While Ariane held the ring under the glass, Gabrielle hovered over her shoulder.

"Well?" she demanded, pressing closer while Ariane strained to make sense of the lettering.

At last, Ariane lowered the glass and said hesitantly, "I believe that it translates as something like *this ring to me doth bind you both heart and mind.*"

Gabrielle pursed her lips. "That sounds like a spell to me."

"Don't be silly. It is only a romantic inscription. Maman did not raise any of us to place credence in such foolish tokens as magic rings and amulets."

"All the same, I still think you should get rid of it. Toss it down the well."

Ariane shook her head. "I can't do that."

"Why not?"

"Because I promised the comte that if he would leave me in peace, I would wear the ring."

Gabrielle shot her a look of exasperation. "A promise coerced from you with threats! Why should you feel obliged to keep such a pledge?"

"It is a question of honor, Gabrielle."

"*Honor,*" Gabrielle scoffed. "That's a man's notion, the excuse that they give for killing each other in duels."

"Nevertheless, I gave my word and I won't go back on it."

"My God, Ariane!" Gabrielle rolled her eyes in disgust. "I vow you would feel obliged to play fair with the devil himself even if it meant your funeral. Or in this case, should I say your wedding?"

"It will never come to that, although . . . perhaps it should."

Gabrielle eyed her sternly. "Ariane Cheney! Never tell me you are thinking of giving in and marrying that odious man."

"No, I suppose not, although given our circumstances, it seems foolish of me to refuse."

Gabrielle reached past her and grabbed the pile of parchment. Ariane had never wanted either of her sisters to know the full extent of the straits they were in, but she felt too weary to stop Gabrielle from sifting through the notes.

The debts had mostly been incurred by their father in financing the three carracks for his grand voyage of exploration. Grand voyage. In bitter moments, Ariane had called it Papa's grand flight. Running from the wife he had betrayed and the reproachful eyes of his daughters.

Gabrielle came to the end of the stack, looking a little subdued. But she rallied, tossing the debts down, sending them cascading across the table.

"There is nothing there we cannot deal with ourselves. What about that potion you were trying to brew this morning? If we could improve the yield of our holdings in Brittany, given time—"

"Time is something we may not have." Ariane tidied up the mess Gabrielle had made, neatly restacking the pile. "Papa has been gone so long, his investors are growing impatient. And if he does not return, the Brittany estate will pass to our cousin, Bernard."

Gabrielle made a moue of distaste at the mention of Bernard Cheney.

"Bernard is a pig."

"He is a male pig and that gives him more rights under the law than we have, especially since Papa never saw fit to draw up a will."

"Papa has not been declared dead yet, Ariane. So I see no reason for you to rush into some noble sacrifice by marrying Monsieur le Ogre."

"Perhaps Renard is a little rough-hewn, but I would not call him an ogre," Ariane protested.

"He is an arrogant bully and a brute and—and what's more a wicked *Deauville*." Gabrielle seized hold of both of Ariane's hands and hunkered down in front of her. Her blue eyes were at once fierce and solemn. "You are so kind and wise and good.

You deserve only the very best of men, someone who will adore you, be absolutely devoted to you. And so does Miri."

It was a rare thing for Gabrielle to express herself this openly. Deeply moved by Gabrielle's concern, Ariane stroked back a wayward curl from her younger sister's brow.

"And what about you, child?"

A shadow passed across Gabrielle's lovely features, but she was quick to rally with a bright laugh. "Me? Oh, I will only ever tolerate a man of the greatest wealth and importance. I would never settle for a mere comte."

"Oh? I suppose you would prefer a duke."

"A duke?" Gabrielle rose to her feet with a scornful toss of her head. "I'll have nothing less than a prince, although a king would be better."

Ariane couldn't help smiling as her sister struck a pose of haughty self-assurance.

"Kings tend to require both royal blood and a considerable dowry of land when they wed."

"Who is talking of marriage? Everyone knows it is better to be a man's mistress. That is where the real power and wealth lie."

Ariane's smile faded. "That is nothing to jest about, Gabrielle."

"I was not jesting, Ariane." The soft contours of Gabrielle's flawless profile still spoke of youth and innocence, but her eyes took on that hard expression Ariane so dreaded. "If you have any doubts upon the matter, you should remember Papa's lady friend."

The pain and disillusionment of discovering that Papa had kept a mistress still weighed heavily upon Ariane. She had struggled for a long time to reconcile that fact with the image of the father she had trusted and adored.

"I suppose most men are unfaithful to their wives," she said in a hollow voice. "But I try to believe that in the end it was Maman who held Papa's heart."

"That must have been a great consolation to her. Having his heart while his money and jewels went to that woman in Paris." Gabrielle stared moodily out the window.

"Paris," she murmured. "That is where we should be instead of rotting away on this dismal island."

"Paris is the last place Maman would have ever wanted us to go."

"Maman is no longer here." For a moment, Gabrielle's voice constricted with grief. She shook back her hair, going on in a brooding tone. "Everything is so dull and hopeless here on the island. But Paris! There will be a royal wedding at Notre Dame this summer. The king's sister, Margot, is to marry the young prince of Navarre. Only think of the balls, the masques, the celebrations there will be.

"Given the right gowns, the right jewels, I would be certain to have some opportunity to catch the eye of the king."

"Gabrielle!" Ariane reproved gently.

Her sister's face was at once mutinous and pleading. "If you would only help me get to Paris, Airy. I could make all our fortunes. You and Miri would never have to worry about anything ever again."

"Enough, Gabrielle! I don't want to hear any more of this kind of talk." Ariane began cramming the stack of bills back into the coffer, hoping to put an end to this disturbing conversation.

But Gabrielle persisted. "You don't think I could capture the heart of the king, hold complete sway over him?"

"King Charles is half-mad and someone else already holds sway over him."

Everyone knew the real power behind the French throne was the king's mother, Catherine de Medici. Sometimes referred to as the *Italian Woman* or the *Dark Queen*. But more often called by a word that was only spoken of in hushed whispers.

Sorceress.

Ariane was loath to ever speak of her at all, but Gabrielle had no such compunction. She tipped her chin to a defiant angle.

"I am not afraid of the Dark Queen. She is just the same as we are, another daughter of the earth."

"Yes, but one who has devoted herself more to the darker arts than those of healing. She is a dangerous woman, Gabrielle, especially to anyone who challenges her power over the king."

"And yet our own mother was her friend once."

"Until she sought to thwart one of Catherine's evil schemes and then—" Ariane broke off, her throat constricting. "And then you know quite well what she did to Maman."

The reminder silenced Gabrielle for a moment, but she argued, "Maman was too good, too gentle and vulnerable. I am not like that."

She leaned up against the window frame, looking suddenly deflated.

"I am not like you either, Ariane," she added in a more subdued tone. "Charming men is all I am good for. It is the only magic left to me."

Ariane regarded Gabrielle in dismay. Gabrielle pretended to be so hard, so tough, but Ariane thought her sister had never looked more vulnerable than at this moment, her brittle expression a thin mask for the pain and confusion roiling just below the surface.

"What you say is not true, dearest," said Ariane. "Only look at the sculptures and paintings you have created. You breathe life into mere stone, and what you can do with a bit of paint and a yard of canvas—"

"That's all gone now. Whatever ability I had, I outgrew a long time ago."

"No, only last summer, I fear."

Gabrielle tensed, as she always did, at any hint of what had happened last June. The disillusionment of discovering certain truths about their father, his abandonment of them, the death of their mother . . . those things had been as hard on Gabrielle as on Ariane.

But something else had wrought this terrible change in Ariane's sister, the advent of a certain young knight, a man whose handsome profile had not been matched by his heart.

The Chevalier Danton had come to visit them one fair summer day, claiming to be a friend of their Cheney cousin. Etienne had been lively and charming, dispersing some of the gloom that had settled over Belle Haven after Maman's death. If only Ariane had not been so distracted, still struggling to assume her duties as Lady of Faire Isle. If only she had probed Danton's eyes more carefully, read his true character instead of just being grateful for the diversion that he offered to Gabrielle's grief.

Instead Ariane had received the knight into their home with all the courtesy Belle Haven had always extended to travelers. But when Danton had finally gone on his way, he had taken Gabrielle's innocence away with him as well.

Ariane had found her sister in the barn after the knight had gone. Gabrielle's hair had been disheveled, her dress torn, her shoulder bruised. But that had been as nothing compared to the bruised look in Gabrielle's eyes.

She had not wept. But Ariane had, cradling Gabrielle's stiff frame in her arms, torn between grief and outrage. If ever in her life Ariane had been tempted to employ the dark magic against anyone, it had been then. But Danton had already been well out of her reach.

All that had been left her to do was to take care of her sister. Gabrielle had regained her composure, perhaps all too quickly, and refused to ever discuss what had happened in the barn that day. It was a silence Ariane feared she had allowed to go on for far too long.

"Gabrielle," she began, but her sister shied away from her.

"No, Ariane! I know what you are going to say, and I don't want to talk about it."

"But at some time we must. What happened to you that day—"

"Nothing happened," Gabrielle snapped.

"When one has been—been injured as you have, you cannot begin to heal if you do not at least acknowledge you have been hurt."

"I was never hurt."

"Gabrielle—" Ariane reached out to her, but Gabrielle pushed her away, eyes blazing fiercely.

"I know what you think happened, but you are wrong. I am no man's helpless victim nor ever will be. Danton never forced me to—" She broke off, winking back savage tears.

"Get it through your head, Ariane. I—I seduced him and then I discarded him. Now let that be an end to the matter."

Gabrielle whirled about and stormed out of the room, but not before Ariane saw the tears streaming down her cheeks.

"Gabrielle!" Ariane called after her, knowing it would do little good to follow her.

From the time Gabrielle had been a child, she had been difficult to comfort whenever she was hurt. If only Maman were here, she would have found a way to soothe Gabrielle, to heal her.

But Maman would have never allowed Gabrielle to be hurt. Dragging her hand wearily through her hair, Ariane turned back to the task of locking up the household chest. She picked up Renard's ring. Somehow since translating that inscription, she felt uneasy wearing it and yet she had promised Renard. But she hadn't promised to keep it on her finger.

Fetching a silver chain from the chest, she attached the ring and fastened that about her neck. As she did so, she heard a footfall behind her and spun about, hoping against hope that Gabrielle had changed her mind and come back to talk.

Miri stood there, regarding Ariane with the stony expression she had adopted ever since Ariane had told her she'd given Hercules back to the comte. Ever since their mother's death, Miri had come to Ariane every night to have her hair brushed and braided.

But tonight Miri had done it for herself. It hung over her shoulder, moon-gold wisps sticking out of the clumsy braid like a length of rope that was about to come unraveled. She had grown so much taller this past year that her night shift was too short for her, reaching up to mid-calf.

Exhausted as she was, Ariane made an effort to smile at her sister. "Miribelle. I thought you might already have gone to bed."

"I would, but I can't sleep. I keep worrying about Hercules."

That infernal horse was the least of Ariane's worries, but she tried to summon all her patience. "Miri, we have been through this already. The comte was not the one who abused Hercules. He will take good care of the horse, I promise you."

"You didn't even let me say good-bye to him. Hercules wanted to stay with me and—and I needed him."

"You have a perfectly fine pony."

"Butternut is getting too old. It is very hard on him to make the journey up the cliffs of Argot."

"You have no business going up those cliffs yourself," Ariane told her little sister sternly.

"But it is only days away from the time when the sleeping giants must be honored and you have completely forgotten."

The event had slipped Ariane's mind, but such nonsense was not high on her list of priorities. Legend said that the menhirs on the isolated side of Faire Isle were in truth a pack of petrified giants, that upon the full moon once a year, the mammoth standing stones would assume their human form.

If one approached the menhirs at just the right moment, one might see the giants awaken. Of course no one ever had, but it was as good an excuse as any for a midnight revel.

"We have gone every year to pay respect to the giants," Miri said. "How could you forget?"

"I have had more important things on my mind, Miribelle. The giants will just have to excuse our absence this time."

"*You* don't have to go. I will go by myself—"

"No, you most certainly will not. After the way you behaved today, stealing that horse, I think you had better stay closer to home. Spend a little more time on your studies."

Miri's eyes filled with rebellion, but her lower lip trembled. "You are always so tired and cross these days, Ariane. And all Gabrielle thinks about is her gowns and dressing her hair. If Papa were here, he would not forget about the ceremony."

Yes, very likely. Louis Cheney was as big a dreamer as Miri. Maman had always done her best to teach them the difference between genuine magic and nonsense, but Papa had been ever ready to believe in legends of sleeping giants or wild tales of an El Dorado full of gold to be found across the ocean.

Ariane closed up the heavy chest and toted it over to the cupboard, wishing Miri would just take herself off to bed. Exhausted, she felt the niggling of a headache behind her eyes.

But Miri trailed after her. "When Papa comes home, he promised to bring me a monkey and a parrot from Brazil. He will come sailing grandly into the harbor, his ship loaded with such treasure, we'll have a stable full of fine horses again and he would never forbid me to ride anywhere. If Papa were here now—"

"Well, he isn't," Ariane snapped, goaded beyond endurance. "And when he does come back, it will likely be with an empty ship and a broken sail. That is if he ever comes back at all."

Ariane regretted the bitter words the minute they were out of her mouth. Miri's eyes flew wide, her face crumpling.

"You and Gabrielle don't believe in anything anymore. Not even P-papa."

"Miri, I am sorry," Ariane began, but her sister had already burst into tears and bolted from the room.

Ariane sagged against the bedpost. Within the space of minutes, she had managed to reduce both her sisters to tears. She felt like sinking down by her mother's bed, burying her face in the coverlet and weeping herself.

But she was denied even that small luxury. The little maid, Bette, poked her head into the room with an announcement.

"Please, Mistress Ariane, if you could come at once. Charbonne has ridden all the way from town with an urgent message for you from the mother abbess."

What now? Ariane thought in dismay.

But she wearily nodded her assent. "I shall be there at once."

Moments later, she trudged down the corridor to find Charbonne waiting for her in the great hall. She was a strapping peasant woman who did gardening and stable work and ran errands for the convent of St. Anne located near the harbor town. Her closely cropped milk-white hair and muscular frame often led her to be mistaken for a comely boy.

At the sight of Ariane, Charbonne respectfully doffed her cap. "Pardon the intrusion, Mistress Ariane, but Reverend Mother asked me to deliver this to you."

Charbonne handed over a folded piece of parchment sealed with the emblem of St. Anne's. Marie Claire, the head of the convent, had been a longtime friend of Evangeline Cheney's. A daughter of the earth herself, she had frequently consulted with Maman regarding the old healing potions and remedies.

Ariane broke the seal of the letter to find a few lines written in Marie Claire's elegant flowing hand.

Ariane, there is a man here from Paris asking for you. He will speak to no one else. I would beg you come to town as soon as may be.

Ariane frowned. There was no one she knew from Paris, or at least, she amended, no one that she wished to know. Ever since she had sent inquiries abroad, trying to gain some word of her father, she had been beset by wandering sailors and travelers, claiming to have information, hoping for some manner of reward.

She folded the note. "Very well. Tell Marie—I mean the Reverend Mother, I will come see this gentleman in the morning."

To her surprise, Charbonne shook her head vehemently. "Oh, no, mistress. That won't do. He may not be here."

"Where would he go at this hour?"

"To heaven or to hell, wherever someone tried to send the poor devil."

"What!" Ariane exclaimed.

Charbonne leaned closer, saying in a hushed whisper. "The man is dying, milady. He's been shot clean through."

Chapter Four

*L*IGHT SPILLED FROM THE WINDOWS OF THE PASSING STRANGER into the narrow street. On such a fine summer evening, the breeze was coming from the harbor of Port Corsair, enabling the inn's shutters to be left open with no dread of noxious odors drifting down from the tanner's shop at the next corner.

The Faire Isle was inhabited mostly by women, wives and daughters of sailors gone long months at sea. The women had become hardy and independent, disconcerting to male travelers to the island, accustomed to a more docile breed.

The Passing Stranger was this peculiar place's only male bastion. Tonight, the taproom was thronged with the usual collection of fishermen, sailors, and itinerant peddlers, the ancient Breton language mingling with more polished French accents and even a few English and Spanish ones.

All the tables were crowded, save one. Justice Deauville sat alone in one dark corner, the remains of his supper littering the table. Nursing a cup of good red wine, his heavy lids lowered to half-mast, he appeared indifferent to his surroundings. But he was keenly aware of the looks cast his way, and muttered conversations exchanged behind cupped hands.

"... 'tis the Comte de Renard ... from the mainland."

"Claims to be old milor' Robert's grandson."

"Still after marrying our Mistress Cheney, I s'ppose."

"A comte, you say? Looks more like some burly field hand."

Renard ignored the whispers. He was well accustomed to the kind of speculation he aroused everywhere he went. Even Ariane had attempted it, probing with those remarkable gray eyes of hers. But Renard had learned a long time ago how to mask his thoughts and emotions from the greatest enemy he'd ever had. His own grandfather.

Renard called for more wine. The serving girl who came to plunk the bottle down upon the table regarded him with a mingling of curiosity and disapproval. Perhaps the wench found it odd for such a powerful nobleman to be drinking alone in the tavern as though he were a peasant farmer.

It probably was an unlordly thing to do. Renard doubted that his late grandfather would have deigned to set one polished boot in such a humble establishment as the Passing Stranger.

But Justice was not about to change all his ways simply because he had become the Comte de Renard. Tossing a coin to the maid, he waved her away and refilled his glass.

Wooing was thirsty work, especially with a woman as obstinate as Ariane Cheney. But his triumph was all but assured now. He had gotten her to take the ring and he well knew the power of that harmless-looking circle of metal.

Had not the magic of the rings already worked for a simple peasant maid from the mountains, winning her the heart of a comte's son? Renard's romantic and rebellious father had been all too ready to fall in love with a pretty shepherdess.

Ariane, however, was full of suspicion, as well as questions about his life. Questions he was obliged to avoid until he had her safely wed. He could still hear her demanding in that forthright way of hers.

"You could look so much higher for a wife, so why are you so bent upon having me?"

He doubted that Ariane Cheney would have liked his answer if he had replied truthfully, if he had told her the real reason he'd made up his mind to have her on that very first day they had met . . .

༷ ༷ ༷

RENARD LAY SPRAWLED ON HIS BACK, THE WIND KNOCKED OUT OF him, the bank of thicket and tree root he landed upon providing no soft cushion. He drew in a ragged breath and managed to elbow himself painfully up to a sitting position.

The clearing in the forest was empty, that demon of a stallion nowhere to be seen. It had probably bolted all the way back to the stables by now. He couldn't believe it had managed to toss him yet again, Renard thought with a grunt of self-disgust.

But the stallion was as clever as the devil himself, which was why Renard had taken to calling it Lucifer. The young squire who had previously owned the horse had all but ruined the stallion's mouth with his rough handling of the reins. Renard had done the horse a favor by rescuing it from that young idiot, but apparently Lucifer failed to appreciate that fact.

Rolling onto his side, Renard struggled gingerly to his feet. As near as he could tell, the beast hadn't managed to break any bones—this time. He limped off a few stiff, bruised steps, taking stock of his surroundings.

The wood was quiet except for the twittering of a few sparrows. The massive oak trees were still black and dripping from last night's rain, the branches just beginning to bud with the first hints of spring. A fine haze curled across the forest floor, giving the silent woods a hushed, mystical atmosphere.

A hunting horn sounded faintly in the distance as the chase moved farther away from him. Apparently no one had noted his absence as yet and that suited Renard just fine. He was already wearied of entertaining his guests; a collection of empty-headed nobles who at one time would not have considered Justice fit to hold their horses.

But now they fell upon him with an acquisitive gleam, thrusting their unwed daughters into his path; for the most part, simple, blushing creatures who could not raise their eyes from their needlework.

Justice Deauville could go his own way, remain a bachelor to the end of his days. But the Comte de Renard would be expected to produce an heir. He had it in his mind to fix his interest with one of his lady guests by the end of the week.

Actually it didn't matter which of these young women he chose as long as she turned out to be a good breeder and possessed a decent dowry. Beyond that, she merely had to have the wit to leave him to his own devices.

He'd had far different ideas of marriage once, involving affection and respect, working alongside his bride by day, curling up safe with her in his arms by night. But those had been the simple notions of a boy, and that part of his life was long gone.

Brushing dead leaves and twigs from the seat of his trunk breeches, Renard strove to get his bearings. The mist had evaporated enough that he could make out a rough path that would doubtless take him out of the forest, back across the fields to the castle nestled in the heart of the estate.

The Château Tremazan, his grandfather's estate, lands that Renard had never wanted, but they were *his* now. The old man had gone through three wives in recent years, desperate to get himself another male heir, all to no avail. Renard had been told that his grandfather had died cursing the name of Justice Deauville, knowing that he'd failed to keep him from inheriting his property. The thought filled Renard with a certain savage satisfaction. He'd managed to win out over the old bastard in the end.

But the satisfaction was short-lived as Renard moved deeper into the forest. After what seemed like hours of trudging along, he had made little progress. He saw no sign of any fields or castle. Only more trees, the branches getting thicker, scratching at his face, tearing at his jerkin.

It might be his land, but he was lost. He was hot, he was tired, and his body felt like a solid mass of bruises. Renard's first impulse was to charge ahead like a frustrated boar, tramping down the brush and tearing the branches from his path.

But he forced himself to pause, reflect. He'd clearly spent too much of these past years on the decks of ships, or caught up in the roar of crowded cities. As a lad, he would have known exactly what to do if he found himself lost in the woods or up in the mountains.

Center himself to the earth. But it was a magic he had not practiced for ages. He was no longer sure he could do it. Closing his eyes, he forced himself to be still. He could almost hear the old woman's voice whisper in his ear.

"Concentrate, Justice. Don't fight the woods. Embrace them."

Renard flung back his head and extended his arms wide, breathing deeply in a slow steady rhythm, trying to root himself to the earth. But nothing happened, no heightening of his senses, no sharpening of his instinct. He opened his eyes and lowered his hands.

He was still lost.

He had no choice but to blunder on. After another frustrating ten minutes, he paused again to listen intently. A faint rushing sound . . . of a stream, not that far off. Perhaps about two hundred yards . . . to his left.

Heartened, Renard headed in that direction. The land began

to slope downward, silvery glimpses of water visible between the trees. He caught a soft equine whicker. Was it possible that his demon of a horse was idling by the river for a drink?

He crept forward. If he could catch the devil, he wouldn't have to walk all the way home after all. Crouching behind a thicket of trees, he parted the branches, peering down toward the brook.

To his disappointment, he saw a sturdy pony tied off to a large gnarled root protruding from the muddy bank. Renard craned his neck, looking about for the pony's owner.

He spotted her a little farther down the bank, wading in the stream. A tall woman, supple as a willow wand, her skirts hiked up to her knees, revealing a flash of white, shapely legs. Her dark blue gown and apron appeared to be of simple homespun fabric, her thick chestnut hair swaying down her back in a tight braid.

Yet this was no peasant maid. Her skin was too fair and there was a solemn dignity about her face that put Renard strangely in mind of a druid priestess.

Renard found himself seized by an unexpected flash of memory . . . something the old woman had foretold long ago.

"Someday, Justice, you will be lost. More lost than you have ever been. You will come upon the woman with the quiet eyes."

"Quiet eyes?" He recollected tormenting the old woman. "What sort of shade is that, Grand-mère? Something between muddy brown and hazel?"

Old Lucy had given him a whack with her walking stick. "Pay heed, Justice! The woman with the quiet eyes will be the one . . ."

Renard took great pains to block all memory of Lucy's fireside visions. Her predictions had never brought him anything but trouble.

Shaking off the memory, Renard parted the brush and started forward. The pony continued to chomp placidly at some ferns, taking no notice. The woman likewise was too absorbed in her task. She bent down, scraping some substance off the river rocks and transferring it carefully to an earthenware jar.

When a twig cracked sharply beneath Renard's boot, she froze. Renard was fully aware that both his size and the rough contours of his face made him an alarming sight.

He held out one hand in a reassuring fashion. "Don't be frightened, mistress. I mean you no harm—"

But she was already sloshing out of the water, scrambling to let her skirts down.

"I didn't mean to startle you," Renard continued. "I am not some bandit or wandering vagabond, so please, don't scream."

"I wasn't going to." She finished smoothing down her skirt and lifted her head. Though no beauty in the classical sense, her face was a curious blend of calm strength and femininity, a stubborn chin and prim mouth offset by the delicate arch of her cheekbones. Her dove-gray eyes were clear and direct.

"I have seen you out riding across your lands and I know who you are, Monsieur le Comte." Still clutching her jar, she dipped into a polite curtsy.

"Then you have an advantage over me, fair trespasser. For I have no idea who you might be."

"I am Ariane Cheney. My lands border yours, or rather my father's do."

Renard's breath stilled. Once again, he felt that strange tingling. Somehow he'd known who she would be even before she'd said it.

"Pay heed, Justice! The woman with the quiet eyes will be the one . . ."

Renard experienced a strong impulse to bolt back into the safety and sanity of the woods. Intrigued against his will, he managed to incline his head in a respectful nod. "I am pleased to make your acquaintance, mademoiselle. I—I have heard much of your father."

Louis Cheney was well known throughout France, a knight

famed for his courage in the wars against Spain as well as his wit and charm. But although Renard failed to say so, he had heard much more of Ariane's mother, Evangeline.

He'd passed many long winter nights in the cottage up in the mountains, staring idly into the peat fire while old Lucy told him tales about the Lady of the Faire Isle.

"A true daughter of the earth, she be, Evangeline Cheney. A sorceress beyond compare." Old Lucy's eyes had gleamed in the firelight. "The wisdom that lady is said to possess! Not like mine, gleaned by word of mouth, most of it half-confused or for-gotten, but learning from books!

"They claim the Lady Evangeline has a treasure trove of old parchments hidden away containing ancient secrets, knowledge beyond your wildest imaginings. And always remember, Justice, such knowledge is the only true power."

As a lad he hadn't been particularly interested in ancient knowledge or power. But the world had taught him far different since. So much so that he now scrutinized Evangeline Cheney's daughter with such intense interest, she shifted with obvious dis-comfort.

Renard lowered his eyes. "I am truly delighted to have en-countered you, Mademoiselle Cheney. I will be even more so if you take pity and decide to rescue me."

"You do not appear to me the sort of man who would re-quire rescuing, my lord."

"Ah, but appearances can be deceiving. I became separated from my hunting party and I fear that I am a trifle—er—how should I put it—a bit—"

"Lost? You astonish me, my lord. Few men are ever willing to admit such a thing."

Renard pressed a hand dramatically over his heart. "You cannot imagine how it devastates my manly pride to do so. How-ever, the alternative is to keep wandering these woods until I die of starvation, leaving my bones to be picked clean by scavengers."

"I doubt it would come to that." A faint smile tugged at her lips. "However, I should be happy to set you on the right path if you would give me a moment to put my shoes back on."

"Certainly." Renard noticed where she had draped her cotton stockings across a bush. He fetched them for her, saying with a hint of mischief in his voice, "Is there anything I can do to be of assistance?"

Ariane looked much shocked by the suggestion, a flush spreading across her cheeks. "Ah—ah, no, I thank you. I can manage."

She snatched the stockings away from him. Gathering up her shoes, she moved some distance away, casting a worried glance at him over her shoulder.

Renard was gentleman enough to turn his back. So the lady was not given to jesting or flirting. He wondered if Mistress Cheney always took everything so seriously.

While Ariane made haste to get her shoes and stockings back on, Renard noticed the collection of apothecary jars lined up near the bank, filled with some repellent green substance Ariane had been scraping from the rocks. He picked up one to study it more closely.

Behind him, Ariane called out, "I would like you to know that I was not trespassing, Monsieur le Comte. I pay your steward well for the privilege of collecting samples from your stream."

"My steward charges you for gathering slime?"

"It is a kind of mold that grows on the rocks, and Monsieur le Franc charges for everything. I much doubt that all the fees he collects end up in your coffers either."

"I will definitely have to have a word with Monsieur le Franc." Renard squinted at the contents of the jar, pursing his lips with distaste. "And what is so special about this slime—er, mold—that you are willing to pay to have it?"

"It has properties most useful in dealing with the pox." He heard Ariane give a last shake to her skirts as she moved to join him. She took the jar carefully, almost reverently, from his hands.

"Perhaps you have not heard, but there has been an outbreak in the village."

"When I passed the local doctor on the road last evening, he said he has taken care of the problem."

"I am sure Dr. Carre believes that he has. His notions of treating infections extend to prancing outside the sick person's house with bells on his shoes and a sponge tied to his nose while he boards up the door." Ariane's eyes darkened with the same sort of contempt Renard had often seen on old Lucy's face whenever she spoke of medical men.

"Fortunately I have better remedies than locking people in their homes to die." Ariane began picking up the jars to transport them over to the waiting pony. Renard grabbed up the last two and followed her.

"Ah! So then you *are* a wit—" he broke off, amending quickly. "A healing woman, yourself."

"I do my best." Ariane packed her jars carefully into the saddlebags strapped to the pony's sturdy back, then reached for the two Renard still held.

"Thank you, and now I will show you the way back to your château."

Gathering up the reins, Ariane led the pony up the bank, setting off with an air of confidence that showed her familiarity with his forest. Apparently without any fear of encountering wild boar, wolf, or snake, it was as though she belonged to this land as much as any woodland creature. Renard had seen that sort of assurance in only one other woman before . . . old Lucy.

He hung back just a little, his appreciative gaze roving over Ariane's lithe figure. Her hips swayed with a natural grace that could not be taught, her braid dangling down her back.

Renard had seen cords of rope that were not as tightly and precisely woven as Ariane's hair. He was beset by an inexplicable urge to undo it, test the silken texture with his hands, and send the dark waves cascading wildly about her shoulders.

"... for the entire past month, my lord."

Renard realized that Ariane was speaking to him. Mustering his wayward thoughts, he took a long stride, falling into step beside her.

"Ah-er, truly? The whole past month?"

"Everywhere one goes, all one hears about is the miraculous return of Master Justin Deauville."

"It wasn't all that miraculous. By ship and horse mostly. And it is Justice."

Ariane cast him a puzzled look. "I beg your pardon, my lord?"

"My name is *Justice*. Apparently, my mother had high hopes for me."

"A hope that I trust will be realized. Your lands could use a little justice."

"Is that a rebuke, milady?"

"I meant no disrespect, monsieur. The late comte had been ill for so long that he entrusted more and more of his affairs to his steward. Your grandfather could be a, a hard man—"

His grandfather could be the very devil, Renard thought, but kept the retort to himself.

"I don't like blackening any man's character, but Monsieur le Franc is a villain, grasping and unscrupulous. Extorting money from your tenants, tossing villagers out of their homes on the slightest pretext, charging some poor farmer with theft merely to seize possession of his last cow.

"And you have no idea how poorly he manages your farms. Constantly sowing and plowing, never giving the land a chance to lie fallow." Ariane suddenly bent down, scooping a handful of earth from forest floor.

She seized hold of Renard's hand and sifted the earth into his palm, the cool weight of it resting against his riding glove, the loamy scent rising to his nostrils.

"You are blessed to have such good soil, my lord, but it must have a chance to heal, to rest. Your steward is wounding the earth with his greed and you must put a stop to it. Monsieur le Franc—" Ariane bit her lip, coloring deeply as though it suddenly occurred to her that she had just given Renard a handful of dirt. She made haste to brush off his glove.

"Your pardon, my lord. I sometimes get carried away. You must think me quite mad or impertinent."

What Renard thought was that Ariane Cheney was unexpectedly lovely when she allowed herself to wax passionate.

"Do not distress yourself, mademoiselle. I welcome your opinions and advice and I promise you I will look into the matter." He flashed her his most charming smile. "Since my return, I have been surrounded by too many people inclined to tug their forelocks and mew 'yes, Monsieur le Comte' and 'no, Monsieur le Comte.' In fact, I would deem it a great honor if you would consent to sup with me . . ."

What the devil was he saying? Renard knew he'd be far wiser to stay clear of this woman. Yet his disappointment bit astonishingly deep when she refused him.

"Oh! N-no, I thank you." Ariane looked flustered by his suggestion. "I—I couldn't."

"But why not?" he heard himself persist. "It seems only proper that I should get to know my nearest neighbors."

"I am not truly your neighbor, my lord. Since my mother died and with my father gone on his voyage, my sisters and I spend most of our time at our house on Faire Isle. I come to the mainland only occasionally to check on the estate. We have an excellent steward."

"Unlike my foolish self, eh?"

Ariane looked horrified. "No, I never meant—"

"I was but teasing you, mademoiselle. However, you speak to me of injustice when you are guilty of a great one yourself."

"Me?"

"But certainly. Hiding yourself away on your island. To me,

that seems almost a crime. Especially when there are such lonely men in the world as myself who would welcome your fair company."

Most women would have been flattered by such words. Ariane merely pulled a wry face at him, setting the pony into motion again. "I doubt you are all that lonely. I have heard that your castle is fairly bursting with ladies at the moment."

"Ah, more gossip from the village, no doubt. I have forgotten how keen an interest country folk take in everyone else's affairs."

"Especially yours, Monsieur le Comte."

"And what are they saying?"

"Only that you have assembled the fairest and wealthiest collection of women in all of Brittany at your château to choose a wife from them. They are calling it the judgment of Paris."

"Are they indeed?" Renard drawled. "I must harbor a remarkably well-educated group of peasants on my land, to be so familiar with Greek myth."

"I suppose I am the one who has been calling it that," Ariane confessed sheepishly. "It just reminded me of how the prince Paris of Troy was called upon to choose the most beautiful goddess, awarding her the golden apple. Only the lady you select will end up with—with—"

"Me," Renard filled in.

"Exactly." Although Ariane gave him a fleeting smile, he caught the hint of a crease between her brows.

"And you don't find me much of a prize?"

"I am sure most women would deem it a great honor to marry Monsieur le Comte. It is only—" Ariane broke off.

"Only what?"

Renard prodded, "Oh, come now. You have been forthright enough with me so far. Why stop now?"

Ariane fidgeted with the pony's bridle. "Well, it does not seem to me a good way for you to be choosing a wife, although I realize that is how it is done by most noblemen."

"And how would you have me go about it?"

Ariane raised her face earnestly to his. "Marriage is not something to be undertaken lightly. The lady you choose will be by your side the rest of your life, the mother of your children. You should spend some time truly getting to know her, her thoughts, her opinions, looking deeply into her heart."

Or at least her eyes, Renard thought, staring fixedly at Ariane. He may have forgotten many of the other skills old Lucy had taught him, but he was still good at the reading of the eyes. It was a skill that he'd found most useful over the years, whether in dealing with his enemies or gaining what he wanted from members of the fair sex.

And Ariane's eyes were so open and honest, he was able to take full measure of her intelligence, the strength and wisdom she'd inherited from generations of women before her. She was a nurturer, a caregiver, but most of all a healer.

In those few moments, he could feel her tranquil spirit brush soothingly against his own far more restless one. His grandmother had been right.

There was such a thing as a woman with quiet eyes.

He lowered his gaze, feeling oddly unsettled by the contact between them. Before he could say anything more, he heard a distant shout.

"My lord? Justice? Where are you? God's teeth, answer me, lad!"

Renard recognized Toussaint, the old man's usually gruff tone sharpened by fear. Renard rushed toward the sound, plunging into a clearing. He cupped his hands around his mouth to shout back.

"Holla, Toussaint. Over here."

A crashing sounded through the underbrush. Toussaint appeared a few moments later, breaking through the line of trees. Drawing rein on his dark gelding, his weathered face lightened with relief at the sight of Renard.

"Ah, there you are, lad. Haven't you heard me shouting? We've been combing the woods looking for you ever since that demon horse of yours came limping riderless across the fields. Are you all right?"

"I am fine." Renard strode toward him anxiously. "But what is wrong with my horse?"

"Nothing. He merely threw a shoe." The doughty old man slid from the back of his mount. Toussaint's fierce blue eyes raked over him and he clapped both hands on Renard's arms as though to assure himself Renard was still in one piece.

"Blast your hide, I've been tearing about like a madman, picturing you lying helpless out here alone with your bones broke—"

"Nothing is broken, not unless it's my pride, and I haven't been alone. I—" Renard glanced behind him to where Ariane should have been. She hadn't followed him into the clearing.

He rapidly retraced his steps, seeking the spot where he had left her. He thrashed about, shoving aside branches, peering through the thick line of trees.

It was as though she had faded into the trees or the forest had opened up and swallowed her. More likely, seeing that he was safe, she had used the opportunity to slip away.

Toussaint came up behind him, leading his horse. "What in thunder are you doing, lad?"

"Looking for *her*. There was this lady—"

"A lady? In the middle of the woods?" Toussaint asked incredulously.

"I didn't find her in the woods. She was down by the stream."

Toussaint gripped him by the elbow. "What you need is a good lie down and I daresay some cold cloths pressed to your head."

"Damnation! I didn't hit my head," Renard said. "She was here, Toussaint. A most remarkable lady. Ariane Cheney. She was helping me find my way back."

Toussaint had been trying to propel him back toward the clearing, but the old man stiffened, his eyes flying to Renard's face.

"Cheney, you say? This lady wouldn't have anything to do with that other Cheney woman, would she? The one old Lucy used to talk about."

"Yes, Ariane is Evangeline Cheney's daughter."

"Then she also is a—a—"

"A witch? I have little doubt of it, and one possessed of an astonishing inheritance."

"From all I have heard tell, the Cheneys are rather poor these days."

"I am not talking about base jewels or coin, Toussaint, but a legendary store of books, ancient knowledge."

Toussaint looked uneasy. "I never saw where books did anything for a man except muddle up his brain. Especially books of *that* sort. Besides, if this lady had wanted to remain with you, she would have just stayed put."

Before Renard could argue further, the rest of the hunting party descended upon them. Tightening his grip, Toussaint tugged more insistently and Renard had no choice but to give over any hope of searching for Ariane.

He doubted he would have been able to find her anyway if she didn't want to be found. Toussaint was right in that respect. She had made it clear she had no wish to pursue the acquaintance and it should not have mattered to him either. But somehow it did.

One of the squires surrendered his horse to Renard and he mounted up, casting a reluctant look behind him. He was beset by an odd sense of loss the rest of the ride home, not even responding to Toussaint's teasing about Lucifer getting the better of him again.

The empty feeling persisted, even back at the château when he was surrounded once more by his glittering assemblage of guests, lords too eager to flatter, ladies trying too hard to charm.

It afforded him a certain grim amusement to think how most of these women would have reacted if he had surprised any of them out in the woods. They'd have shrieked or fainted, not stood their ground and regarded him with calm, gray eyes.

His great hall rang with feminine chatter. Renard wondered irritably why he'd never noticed what shrill voices women had. That is, all save one. The first opportunity that presented itself, he stole away, climbing to the topmost tower of the château to stare restlessly out across his fields.

The sun blazed, setting over the distant shadowy outline of the forest. The trees appeared to melt together, closing up like the gates to a dark, mysterious land that was both enticing and forbidding. As Renard leaned against the rough stone parapet, the rest of old Lucy's prophecy forced its way into his mind.

"You will come upon the woman with the quiet eyes. And she will be the one who will lead you safely back. Your destiny."

Destiny? It was like old Lucy to use such a grandiloquent word. Her predictions for his future had always been high-sounding and irritatingly mysterious. Her visions also had a disconcerting habit of coming true, no matter how hard one fought against them, and as a young man he had certainly fought when Lucy had insisted he would one day become the Comte de Renard.

Renard sometimes felt like one of those gnarled oaks in the forest, blasted by two powerful opposing forces, Lucy on one side, his Deauville grandfather on the other. Bending and twisting his life until it was far removed from the simple, direct path he'd meant to follow, until he scarcely recognized himself anymore.

And now even from her grave, Lucy's visions were reaching out to ensnare him. Ariane Cheney . . . his destiny? Renard didn't bloody well think so and yet . . . He knew the folly of trying to thwart Lucy's prophecies.

And why bother fighting anymore? He'd long ago lost Martine Dupres, the only woman who might have been the love of his life. He needed to marry someone. Why not Ariane Cheney, he thought with a cynical shrug of his shoulders. He was certainly attracted to the lady, her voice was blessedly unshrill, and she was far more intelligent than those chattering wenches down in his great hall.

True, she had certain peculiarities in her family background, but so did he. And while her fortune might not be substantial, she possessed a dower that he found intriguing. As the wind whistled past the parapets, once more Lucy's voice seemed to whisper seductively in his ear.

"Knowledge beyond your wildest imaginings. And always remember, Justice, such magic is the only true power."

And perhaps that was the only thing that mattered in the end, Renard reflected bitterly. Power, the ability to make sure one's life remained one's own, to never again dance to the tune of anyone else's piping.

Drawing away from the parapet, Renard wended his way down the tower stairs. By the time he sat down to sup that evening, he had made up his mind to be rid of his steward and his guests as well, all those simpering women. The judgment of Paris was over. He had made his choice of wife.

ּ ּ ּ

"MY LORD?"

The voice penetrated the hum of noise in the tavern and Renard's thoughts as well. Someone hovered over his solitary table, blocking his view of the room. Toussaint towered over him, his tall frame stiffer than many a man half his age. His white hair was windblown, his jerkin and cloak dusty from the road, his face lined with weariness and looking less than pleased with Renard.

Renard poured himself another glass of wine. "Toussaint, what the devil are you doing here?"

The pleasant inquiry only caused the old man's scowl to

deepen. "What I always seem to end up doing, searching for you. Although it was not hard for me to guess where you had gone, once I realized the fog was cleared off this cursed island. I had hoped that after that disaster of a wedding, you'd have sense enough to leave Mistress Cheney alone. I should have known better."

"You should indeed." Using the toe of his boot, Renard kicked a chair toward Toussaint. "So now you have found me. You may as well sit down and have a drink."

The old man's thick white brows drew fiercely together. "Is that a command, my lord?"

"I suppose you may consider it as such, for it does little good for me to request anything of you. I have asked you several times to stop 'my lording' me every time you turn around."

"It is the proper way for me to address you, Monsieur le Comte."

"Yes, but you only seem to remember to do it when you are annoyed with me."

Toussaint glowered at him for a moment before lapsing into the chair. Renard signaled for another glass. Pouring the wine himself, he shoved the cup across the table to Toussaint.

Despite the white hair thinning on top, Toussaint was still a redoubtable figure of a man, broad-shouldered and barrel-chested. He'd lived to an age few men ever hoped to see. Some speculated that he was past seventy, although Toussaint himself was not even sure.

Most of the time, Renard forgot that this distant cousin of his had to be old enough to be his grandfather. But as the candlelight from the wall sconces played over Toussaint's face, he could not help noticing the deep pockets of weariness gathered beneath the old man's eyes.

"I am sorry if I worried you," he said. "You didn't need to come haring after me. You should know I can look out for myself."

Toussaint gave a loud harrumph as though there were much doubt on the subject. "Damn it, lad, you can't just up and take off unattended. You are the Comte de Renard, a man with a great deal of responsibilities and a certain position to uphold. You're not even supposed to go to the privy without a herald to announce you."

"You are confusing me with my grandfather," Renard drawled.

"No, you are the one who has been doing that."

Toussaint knew well that Renard hated any comparisons with the late comte. "Exactly what do you mean by that?"

"It gives me no pleasure to say it, but you've been behaving more and more like that old devil lately, consulting your own will with no regard to anyone else. Trying to bully Mistress Cheney into marrying you—"

Renard frowned into his wine cup.

"You may be surprised to hear that I have reached an understanding with the lady."

Toussaint *was* surprised. "She has agreed to wed you?"

"She will . . . eventually." Renard took a large swallow of wine before confessing. "I unpacked the rings from the old chest and gave my mother's to Ariane."

He hadn't expected Toussaint to be pleased and he wasn't. When he noticed the ring glinting on Renard's hand, the old man actually paled and crossed himself.

"I thought you had tossed those cursed things into the sea a long time ago."

"Why would I? When they are all I have left of either of my parents or Lucy?"

"Those damned rings never brought anything but trouble to your family!" Toussaint's voice rose, causing a few heads to swivel in their direction. Lowering his tone, he leaned across the table.

"I am fair astonished you were even able to get Mistress Cheney to accept one of them. From all I have heard tell of the lady, she has the good sense to confine her skills to healing and stays well away from the sort of evil magic bound in those rings."

"The rings are not evil and as I told you before, Ariane and I reached an understanding. A pact."

"What sort of pact?"

"I have agreed to leave her in peace until she uses her ring three times. After then she is mine."

"And what makes you think she will ever use it?"

Renard's mouth tightened in a grim smile. "I think I know my Ariane rather well. She might never employ magic on her own behalf, but the first time someone else is in trouble and she can't handle it herself, she will be tempted to use the ring."

Toussaint regarded him for a long frustrated moment, then heaved a deep sigh. "Well, I suppose what is done is done. But I have to warn you. I have heard a disturbing report that the witch-hunters are on the move again. They have been practicing their hellish trade just south of here. This is not a good time, lad, to be playing with magic rings."

Witch-hunters. Renard froze at the sound of the word, but not with fear. He iced over with an anger so hard and cold, it was as though a blade of steel had been driven through his heart.

"If they should come into Brittany—"

"They won't," Renard said tersely. "They will never set up their inquisition upon my lands."

"How could you prevent it? If their commission comes from the king—"

"Not on my lands. Nor this island!" Renard banged the palm of his hand against the table. "I vowed that a long time ago. That none of those devils would ever come near me or mine again. Not my home and certainly not my bride. Do you hear me, Toussaint?"

"I hear you." The old man stole an uneasy glance around him. "I just pray no one else does. And you take a great deal for granted calling Mistress Cheney your bride. Ring or no ring, it is just possible she has already given her heart to someone else."

Renard laughed. "That is most unlikely. The woman practically lives like a nun, shut away here on her island."

"It's a strange sort of nun that steals out of her bed for a rendezvous at this late hour."

"What the devil are you talking about?"

Toussaint shrugged. "Only that on my way here, I saw your lady stealing through the streets, riding with another man."

"Impossible. I'd wager my last sou she is home safe in her bed. Your eyesight is failing you, old man."

"There is nothing wrong with my eyes." Toussaint bristled. "And you would lose your bet. I recognize Mistress Cheney well enough even when she is attempting to hide her face."

"But what in the world would she be doing abroad with some man at this hour?"

Toussaint arched his brows suggestively. "You tell me, lad."

There were times when Toussaint could be more than irritating. His suggestion about Ariane having a rendezvous with a lover was completely ridiculous.

Renard knew the woman better than that . . . at least he thought he did. He frowned, the first niggling doubt sifting into his brain.

Perhaps he had grown a trifle too arrogant of late. It had never even occurred to him that she might have other suitors.

Renard still didn't believe it, but it might be just as well to determine what the woman was up to. He shoved abruptly to his feet. "Let's go."

Toussaint, who had been in the act of pouring himself another cup of wine, glanced up at Renard with surprise. "Go where?"

"Show me where you last saw Ariane."

"Didn't you just tell me that you had agreed to leave the woman in peace?"

"*Now,* Toussaint. Unless you want me to march through town, kicking in doors to look for her."

Toussaint rose to his feet with a long-suffering sigh. "Yes, milord. As you wish, milord."

But Renard didn't even seem to hear him. He was already striding out of the inn and Toussaint had to make haste to keep up. As he had done so often of late, Toussaint searched for some trace of the openhearted generous boy he'd once known, but he found none in the grim, determined man he trudged after.

As he followed Renard into the night, Toussaint's heart was heavy with memories of the old days and regrets. He mused as he had done too many times before.

Ah, Lucy. Why couldn't you have set aside all the witchcraft and your cursed predictions and ambitions for the lad? You have done better to keep him safe atop your mountain.

Justice would have been the happier for it and Lucy . . .

His darling Lucy might still be alive.

Chapter Five

THE CONVENT OF ST. ANNE'S WAS SITUATED ON A MODERATE rise of land, a peaceful sentinel keeping watch over Port Corsair. The spire of the modest church strained heavenward, the snug house of the chaplain tucked nearby just outside the stout stone walls that sealed off the convent.

At the gates, Charbonne rang the bell. Beyond the iron bars, Ariane could see the shadowy outline of the cloisters, bathed in an aura of quiet serenity. On such a gentle night, it was difficult to believe that evil or violence could exist anywhere in the world.

That is until Charbonne pointed out to her the place where the wounded man had been found, the grass still stained with his blood. Ariane shivered as a ghost-like figure melted out of the darkness, carrying a lantern. The sister's flowing white robes brushed against the grass as she glided forward to open the gate.

It was the Mother Abbess herself. Marie Claire's wimple framed a face that one exasperated archbishop had described as being too strong and willful to belong to a nun. Marie Claire had retorted that a woman who sat back with her hands meekly folded in prayer did not always serve God best.

The daughter of a duke, Marie Claire Abingion had thwarted her family's ambition to marry her into the royal family, defying both her father and the late King Francis by choosing the veil instead.

A woman who had long been her mother's friend, Marie Claire beckoned Ariane inside and wrapped one arm about her in a fierce hug. "Ariane, child! Thank heavens you are come."

Ariane drew back, fairly bursting with questions, but she was hushed by a gesture from Marie Claire. The abbess had no wish to speak in front of Charbonne.

Marie Claire thanked the servant and dismissed her. As Charbonne led the horses off in the direction of the stables, the abbess murmured to Ariane. "I would trust Charbonne with my life, but I don't want to involve her further in this business until I know more myself about what is going on."

"What business?" Ariane whispered back. "Who is this man who has come looking for me?"

"I cannot tell you. He has adamantly refused to speak to anyone but you. He would not even give his name."

"Do you think it is possible that he could be someone with word of my father?" Ariane could not quite keep the quiver of hope from her voice.

Marie Claire shook her head. "No, my dear. I fear that whatever has brought this stranger to you, it is nothing good."

"Were you able to read his eyes?"

"I have always been too impatient to master that skill. I trust to my instincts instead and rely on other observations and—well, come with me."

The abbess's lantern lit the way across the silent grounds. At this hour, the other sisters were gathered in the refectory for the evening meal. The other buildings were all dark save for the glow from one long low building.

The infirmary was meant to treat the illnesses of the sisters. There were strict regulations regarding visitors to the convent, but those had long been ignored, the sisters frequently giving succor to the elderly and indigent of the town. Like many of the other women on the Faire Isle, the sisters of St. Anne's tended to live by their own rules.

Ariane saw that most of the infirmary's beds were empty except for one at the far end that had been cordoned off by a tall wooden screen. Nearby, the infirmarian tore and rolled bandages on a low stool before the empty hearth.

But at a few quiet words from Marie Claire, the elderly sister left. Marie Claire beckoned Ariane to approach the bed hidden behind the screen.

The stranger stretched out on the narrow cot looked harmless enough, but any man in his condition would. Unconscious, he was stripped to the waist, bandages wrapped tightly across his chest. Marie Claire moved the branch of candles closer so that Ariane could better view his face.

Thick lashes rested against cheeks that must have been deeply tanned, but his complexion was ghastly pale. His dark gold hair was cropped close, likewise his beard and mustache. Ariane judged him to be somewhere in his mid-twenties.

"Do you know him?" Marie Claire asked softly.

Ariane shook her head. Her gaze moved from his face down his sinewy body, his long muscular arms, the trace of old scars bisecting both his right shoulder and the base of his collarbone. This man was no stranger to hard physical labor or violence. He lay still, his breathing barely perceptible.

"Is he—will he be—" Ariane faltered.

"All right? I don't know," Marie Claire said. "I did my best for him, although I don't possess anything like your mother's healing skills. He had a crossbolt embedded in his side. Half-broken off. I suspect he did that so he could keep on riding and not weaken himself by removing it.

"I managed to get the rest of it out. But as you well know, his danger now will be from infection and loss of blood." Marie Claire's eyes rested thoughtfully on her patient. "I would say he has a good chance. He appears to be a strong and thoroughly de-termined young man."

"But *who* is he? Was there no clue about his person?"

"Unfortunately, yes." Marie Claire motioned Ariane away from the bedside, where she produced a battered leather saddle-bag.

"Our mysterious guest obviously parted company from his horse somewhere on the mainland. As near as I could determine, he came across the channel to Faire Isle in one of the fishing boats. Besides his sword, this is all he had with him."

Marie Claire perched the bag upon a wooden stool and undid the straps. She tugged out a white garment. The article was a white overtunic with a red cross stitched onto it.

"Do you know what this is?" Marie Claire asked.

"No."

"The uniform of a Huguenot soldier."

Of course, Ariane was aware that there had been unrest and trouble in much of France for years, a terrible civil war of reli-gion, Protestants and Catholics hell-bent upon murdering each other in the name of God. But that hideous conflict had always seemed far removed from Faire Isle.

"Do you think there has been a battle near here on the main-land?" Ariane asked.

"No, one of the few things our soldier did tell me is that he came from Paris, and I know a truce exists there at present be-cause of the proposed marriage of our Princess Margot to the Protestant prince of Navarre.

"And yet, that bolt did not lodge in this young man's side by accident. He is definitely a fugitive from something or someone. I fear we will learn nothing more until he recovers his senses."

Marie Claire folded the tunic and stuffed it back in the saddlebag. Ariane regarded her with troubled eyes.

"Pardon me, Marie, but is this not rather dangerous for you to be sheltering this man? If the archbishop were to find out . . ."

"His eminence would expect me to hand over this heretic at once, doubtless to be tortured for his salvation." Marie Claire smiled wryly. "Unfortunately, I fail to see how that would benefit this young man's soul. Or mine."

She patted Ariane's cheek. "Don't worry about me, child. With any luck we will have this soldier healed and on his way before anyone realizes he was here.

"Now it is almost time for Compline, so I must leave you. You will stay and watch over our young friend?"

Ariane nodded, although she saw nothing in this stranger to make her presume that he was a friend. Not that Ariane held the fact that he was a Huguenot against him. Some of her own beliefs and skills could easily have condemned her for a heretic and even worse. But Ariane had trouble sympathizing with anyone who practiced the unholy arts of war, especially in the name of God.

After Marie Claire had gone, the silence in the large, empty room seemed oppressive. Ariane paced by the bed, staring at the unconscious man almost as though she could force him to say what he wanted of her.

In the distance, Ariane heard the clang of the bell, announcing the hour of Compline. Tonight even that had a foreboding sound, more like the peal of an alarm than a call to gather the sisters for their evening prayer.

With nothing else to do but wait, her attention was drawn back to the stranger's saddlebag. She tugged out the tunic for another look at it, then dug deeper to inspect the rest of the bag's contents, even though she supposed Marie Claire must have already done so.

A hunk of molding cheese, a hard remnant of bread, a nearly empty flask of wine. A tinder box and a dagger that Ariane gingerly passed over. Wadded at the bottom of the bag was a small leather purse. It seemed light and woefully thin of coin.

Ariane realized it did contain something . . . something soft was stuffed inside. Was there any chance his initials might be embroidered on a handkerchief?

She undid the drawstrings to check, but instead of a handkerchief, the purse contained a pair of lady's white gloves. Ariane drew them out into the light. They were beautiful, delicate silk, softly perfumed.

"Don't touch those."

The sudden hoarse command almost startled Ariane into dropping the gloves. She glanced up to find the soldier with his eyes wide open, staring at her with a burning ferocity.

"Put—put those back," he rasped.

Embarrassed, she hastened to comply. Before she could say a word, he gasped out another command.

"Now . . . go wash."

"W-what?"

"Wash your hands!"

The order only added to Ariane's confusion and astonishment, but he was growing so agitated, she obeyed. Then she wet down a cloth and fetched a glass of water.

His eyes had closed again. Ariane feared he must be delirious, lapsing into a fever. But when she applied the cloth to his brow, she was surprised to find his skin cool to the touch.

His eyes fluttered open and he dashed the cloth from his forehead. But he seemed glad of the glass of water Ariane pressed to his lips. Ariane tried to get a fix on the brown eyes that stared up at her, but it was difficult.

The pain swirling in those dark depths blocked her efforts, making her unable to get past it to anything else. Pain and sorrow and not all of it recent, Ariane realized, not all of it stemming from his wound.

He pushed the glass away. "No more. I—I thank you."

He regarded his surroundings with confusion. "Where am I?"

"In the infirmary at the convent of St. Anne's," Ariane said. "On Faire Isle."

"Ah." He sighed, relaxing a trifle. "Yes, I remember now."

To Ariane's surprise and dismay, he kicked the blanket aside and struggled to rise from the bed.

"Have to—to get out of here. Must go."

"No, lie still." Ariane made haste to restrain him, but as she pressed her hands against his bare shoulders, she could feel the tension and power surging through him. Ariane feared she would not be able to stop him. He possessed an amazing strength of will.

"Please, you are safe," Ariane soothed him. "No one here means you any harm."

"I—know that," he said in taut breaths, fighting to rise to his feet. "But must leave . . . must find Ariane Cheney."

"I am Mistress Cheney," she informed him gravely.

He stared at her for a long moment before sagging back down onto the bed. His gaze roved over her, his expression torn between doubt and hope.

"So young," he murmured at last. "I was expecting an older woman."

"And I was not expecting you at all." Retrieving the blanket, Ariane tucked it firmly around him again. "Who are you, sir?"

"My name is Remy . . . Captain Nicolas Remy."

Ariane stiffened. The captain flinched, obviously paying the price for his recent attempt to stand, but he was still perceptive enough to notice Ariane's reaction.

"You have heard of me then?"

Ariane nodded grimly. "Your reputation has even carried here. You are a captain in the army of Navarre, are you not? Famed for your ferocity in battle against the Catholics. I believe they call you the 'Scourge.'"

Remy grimaced. "That is a title I despise and have never sought. I am merely a soldier seeking to defend my homeland and the right of any man to think and worship as he pleases."

"Very admirable. But I still don't understand why you have come to Faire Isle or how you even know of me."

"I learned of you from an apothecary's wife in Paris. She is one of your kind."

Ariane felt a warning prickle at the base of her spine. "What do you mean—*my kind*?"

"I—I mean . . . you know . . ." Remy hesitated, then said bluntly. "A witch."

Ariane flushed, squaring her shoulders back. "That is not a title *I* like. Anymore than you like to be called a scourge. And if that is why you have sought me out, you have wasted a great deal of effort."

"But mademoiselle, I—"

"I am a healer, nothing more. If you came to Faire Isle thinking to find some sort of—of dark magic or spells to aid you in your war, you are highly mistaken."

"No! I need your help, Mistress Cheney. But not for war. For justice." He attempted to rise again only to sink back with a stifled groan. "Please, will you not at least hear me out?"

Ariane frowned. She had never known any man who declared that he was seeking a witch to be after anything decent. But there was something in Captain Remy's eyes that arrested her, something open and earnest, something . . . yes, something good.

"Very well," she said. "I will listen, but only if you promise to lie still with no more of that thrashing about."

The captain nodded weakly.

Ariane settled herself upon the stool and folded her hands in her lap.

At length, he said, "As I told you before, I am a captain in the army of Navarre. I recently accompanied my queen to Paris as the head of her royal guard. You—you have heard of my lady Jeanne d'Albret?"

"Yes, my late mother spoke highly of her, praising her strength and intelligence. A good woman and a good queen."

"*Was,*" Remy said bleakly. "My queen is dead."

"Oh, I am sorry. I had not heard."

"She died only last week in Paris."

Ariane's mother had had a great admiration for Jeanne of Navarre. She was one of those rare instances of a woman who ruled by her own right, not through marriage. Like Elizabeth of England, Jeanne d'Albret had inherited her kingdom from her father and also like Elizabeth, Jeanne had governed with incredible sagacity and strength.

"I am truly sorry," Ariane said. "My mother always said that your queen was a truly vigorous, forceful woman. Was she struck down by a sudden illness?"

"Struck down?" Remy choked out. "Yes, but not by any illness."

He flung one arm across his eyes to conceal an unsoldierly display of grief. "She—she was murdered. *Poisoned.*"

Ariane stared at him, horrified. "Is that what the doctors determined?"

"Those court lackeys? They determined she died of natural causes, but I know better. When a woman is healthy one day and the next perishing in great agony, there can be only one explanation."

Ariane sighed. No, there could be several explanations. Ariane would have guessed that under ordinary circumstances Nicolas Remy was a practical and rational man. But grief could drive even the most sensible person into making wild accusations.

"Captain Remy," she began gently. "There are many diseases that seem to strike suddenly—"

"This was no disease!" Remy lowered his arm to glower at her. "My queen was poisoned and I managed to lay hands on the evidence. It is in my saddlebag. You have seen it for yourself."

"You mean that half-empty bottle of wine?"

"No, not the wine. The gloves! The god-cursed gloves."

"Poisoned gloves? Captain Remy . . ." Ariane let out a long breath, slowly shaking her head.

"Are you going to tell me such a thing is not possible, that such black magic does not exist?" Remy demanded.

"N-o-o," Ariane said. "But it is extremely rare. You have no idea how skilled one would have to be in the dark arts to brew such poisons that can penetrate the skin, bring about a violent death, then leave no trace on the victim.

"Fortunately, there are few daughters of the earth who possess that kind of knowledge, especially here in France. One was the witch Melusine, and she is long dead. The only other I know of is—is—" Ariane hesitated.

"The Dark Queen," Remy said, finishing the thought Ariane was so reluctant to complete. "Catherine de Medici. Is that not right?"

When Ariane didn't answer, Remy prodded, "Or perhaps you think that the Dowager Queen of France would not be capable of such a monstrous act?"

Ariane would not have put much of anything past Catherine when the woman felt her interests were threatened. She had only to remember what had taken place between her own mother and the Dark Queen. But it was one thing for Catherine to wreak havoc upon courtiers or someone like Evangeline Cheney. Would even Catherine de Medici dare employ her dark arts against another queen?

"But it makes no sense," she argued with herself as much as Remy. "Why would Catherine murder your queen? Jeanne of Navarre came to Paris to arrange for the wedding of her son to Catherine's daughter. The marriage was instigated by Catherine herself, was it not? Heralded as the beginning of a great truce between Catholics and Protestants."

"I will tell you something that only I know, mademoiselle," Remy said. "My queen had begun to suspect some sort of treachery, that there was something truly rotten about this so-called truce. While I was escorting Her Majesty to some of the shops in Paris, she confided to me that she was on the verge of calling off the wedding.

"Our last visit that day was to Queen Catherine's own royal glovemakers. My queen bought a pair that she was assured had been designed especially for her by the order of Catherine herself. As we left the shop, my queen, with all a woman's innocent delight, put the gloves on, never dreaming of such evil magic, of such treachery.

"By the time we returned to the palace, my queen was seized by the most agonizing spasms as though she'd swallowed an entire cup of hemlock. By the next morning, she was dead. So you tell me what happened, Mistress Cheney."

"I don't know," Ariane murmured. What Remy suggested could be true. That was much of the reason Ariane chose to keep herself and her sisters well clear of all the political intrigue that seethed in Paris, the dark schemes of Catherine de Medici, even though as the daughters of the Chevalier Cheney, they could have taken their places at court.

"If your suspicions are correct, monsieur, I am most grieved by it," she said. "But I do not know in what way I can be of assistance to you."

"By helping to prove the gloves were poisoned."

"How? By putting them on?"

"No, of course not," Remy said with an impatient toss of his head. "I was told you possess great knowledge in these matters."

"Not in the dark arts!" Ariane shoved to her feet, venting her agitation in small, useless tasks, smoothing out Remy's blanket, shifting the position of the candlestick. "I admit that I do have books that I could consult. Possibly there are solvents that might be brewed, methods of detecting poisons.

"But even if I could prove those gloves had been tampered with, if we could connect the crime to Catherine, then what? Would you like to march into the Palace of Justice in Paris and accuse the Dowager Queen of France of witchcraft and murder?"

"Yes!"

Ariane cast him a disbelieving look. "You are quite mad, monsieur. You still don't seem to understand the sort of woman you are dealing with."

"I understand perfectly, Mistress Cheney," Remy said somberly. "I only said that bringing the Dark Queen to justice is something I would *like* to do. That may not be possible . . . yet."

"Or ever. Do you realize Catherine may be aware that you suspect something and that you have those gloves? Who has been shooting at you?"

"The queen's private guard," Remy admitted.

"Then you may well have endangered everyone on this island by coming here."

"No, I managed to elude pursuit and it will be expected that I will head west, back to Navarre, to warn my prince—" Remy paused to sadly correct himself. "I mean my king now. And that is what I should do except that I fear my king will be determined to go through with this marriage and the truce, unless I can offer him solid proof of what Catherine did to his mother."

"I wish you all the luck in the world, monsieur, but I don't think I can help you."

"But I was told you are the daughter of one of the greatest wit—" Remy caught himself and amended quickly. "One of the greatest wise women who ever lived."

Ariane traced her fingers wearily across her brow. Yes, she was Evangeline Cheney's daughter. But what Remy and no one else seemed to understand was that she did not possess a tenth of her mother's skill, strength, and courage.

"I am sorry," she began, but Remy cut her off.

"Please, mademoiselle." Remy dragged himself up onto one elbow to plead with her. "If Catherine did this to my queen, I am terrified of what else she might be plotting. Against my countrymen, against my young king. He is all that remains of the house of Navarre. You must help me to save him."

Ariane turned away to avoid his imploring eyes. Why did she feel so cold? Because she did not want to become involved in any of this. She had troubles enough of her own. All she desired was to take care of her sisters, keep them safe, live quietly on her island, and tend to her herbs. She wanted nothing to do with poisoned gloves, Dark Queens, or desperate Huguenot soldiers.

Yet she was a daughter of the earth, a seeker of wisdom and knowledge, a defender against superstition and darkness, a healer and a caregiver. These roles had been bred into her very bones. To turn her back on Captain Remy would be to fly in the face of everything she had been taught.

After a long tussle with her conscience, Ariane faced Remy.

"All right," she said. "I cannot promise anything, but I will at least take the gloves back to my workshop and examine them."

"Merci, mademoiselle." The captain was so grateful, it was all Ariane could do to keep the earnest young man from tumbling from the bed to his knee, to take her hand and express his gratitude.

She once more forced him back to his pillow, but it was not so difficult this time. Having made his case, the captain seemed thoroughly drained and it was not long before he fell into an exhausted sleep. As Ariane tucked the blanket across his shoulders, she was astonished to see the grim set of his features relax in a deep repose. But then why not? Ariane reflected. The captain had just managed to ease the weight of the world from his shoulders and shifted it squarely onto hers.

⚜ ⚜ ⚜

CANDLELIGHT FLICKERED OVER THE ROUGH STONE WALLS, THE AUSterity of the abbess's quarters broken by touches of Marie Claire's own forceful personality, a colorful braided rug, a tapestry of St. Joan making war on the English, and a large cage holding her pet bird, a raven with brilliant black feathers and a long bill. It greeted Ariane with a harsh quork, tipping its head to study her with curious brown eyes.

The fierce-looking bird was positioned well away from the shelves bending under the weight of Marie Claire's books. Many of these were traditional texts, the Bible, orthodox scripture interpretations, the canons of the Church. And many were not, writings of female mystics, the articles of Martin Luther, even a copy of the Koran. As Marie Claire had once told the horrified convent chaplain, if one's faith could not bear the test of reading a few forbidden books, well, then, it was a paltry faith indeed.

Even though Ariane admired Marie Claire's thirst for knowledge, she did not think the abbess wise to flaunt it. It was dangerous even here with the security of the island.

But Ariane doubted that anything could prove more dangerous than what she had brought to Marie Claire's attention tonight. Even with the shutters firmly closed, sealing off the room from any prying eyes, Ariane still felt a strong sense of unease with the contents of Captain Remy's purse spilled out across Marie Claire's table.

Yet the gloves were so harmless looking, costly white silk, exquisite workmanship, apparel truly fit for a queen. Marie Claire studied them, prodding one fingertip with the tip of her quill pen.

"Quite beautiful," she pronounced. "Trust our dear Catherine to find a way to convey death in so charming a fashion."

Ariane felt her stomach knot. "Then you do think the gloves are poisoned? That Catherine used them to kill the queen of Navarre?"

"Knowing what I do of Catherine, I think it highly probable. It would not be the first time she has employed such methods and I doubt it will be the last."

"Someone should have stopped her a long time ago."

"Your Maman tried, my dear, and you know how that turned out."

Ariane did, to her sorrow. Not that she could accuse the Dark Queen of killing her mother. Perhaps in some way that might have been more merciful. Instead Catherine's vengeance had taken a more cruel and diabolical form. She had found the one sure way of breaking Evangeline's heart, of shattering the peace and happiness of the Cheney family forever.

"Maman was always reluctant to talk to me about what she had done to incur Catherine's anger," Ariane said. "All I know is that she prevented the Dark Queen from using her poisons on someone."

"Not just any someone," Marie Claire replied. Folding her handkerchief about the gloves, she carefully tucked them back inside Remy's purse. "Evangeline stopped Catherine from killing Diane de Poitiers, an intelligent and fascinating woman. She was also the king's mistress.

"In those days, Catherine was queen in name only, ignored by her husband. It was Diane who held the king's heart and ear, making her the most powerful woman in France. Catherine had good reason for wanting her gone. She had actually succeeded in administering the poison and Diane would have died."

"Except for Maman," Ariane said with quiet pride.

"Yes, Evangeline was able to counteract the poison and save her. The ironic thing was that she intervened for Catherine as much as Diane. Catherine was not as subtle with her poisons way back then. She would have been the first one suspected, and not even her position as queen could have protected her from the king's wrath.

"Your mother very likely saved Catherine's life." The abbess sighed. "Unfortunately Catherine did not see it that way."

"So she set out to destroy my mother." Ariane had often wondered why the Dark Queen had not simply chosen to kill her mother. Perhaps in some strange way it had amused Catherine to strike in another way, at the place where Evangeline Cheney had been most vulnerable, her love for her husband.

The romance between Evangeline and Louis Cheney had been the stuff of legends, the Lady of Faire Isle and France's most valiant knight. Few noblemen wed for love or remained faithful even when they did so. But even after years of marriage and the birth of three daughters, the Chevalier Cheney had remained devoted to his Evangeline—that is, until the Dark Queen had set that creature loose upon him.

Marguerite de Maitland, one of Catherine's infamous *Escadron Volant*. The Flying Squadron, a collection of some of the court's most beautiful ladies. Ladies? Ariane thought contemptuously. No, women of the night, courtesans, skilled in every unholy art of seduction and betrayal.

"Papa should have been stronger, Marie Claire. If—if he had truly loved Maman, he should have resisted that evil woman."

Marie Claire only shook her head and gave Ariane's shoulder a sympathetic squeeze. "Child, you have no notion how devastatingly irresistible those creatures of Catherine can be. Beautiful and voluptuous. I have heard that the Dark Queen even further enhances their charms with mind-stealing lotions and perfumes that she brews."

"At least I will never have anything to fear from the Flying Squadron," Ariane said fiercely. "I don't ever intend to be in love and I don't have a husband to lose."

"No, you have only your life to lose. And your sisters."

Ariane felt herself grow a little pale at the mention of Miri and Gabrielle. "So then you are advising me to have nothing more to do with this business, Marie? You think I am being too reckless?"

Marie Claire gave a dry laugh. "All I am saying is that we must proceed with great caution and a clear head while we consider the alternatives.

"And in aid of that . . ." Marie smiled at her and went to a small cupboard to fetch two fine crystal glasses and a dust-covered bottle. Like the inhabitants of many other convents, the sisters of Saint Anne would have had to close their gates and disband a long time ago for lack of funds. But St. Anne's had managed to remain self-sufficient by means of the currant wine they distilled and sold on the mainland.

Ariane eyed the glass of ruby-colored liquid Marie pressed into her hand with some misgiving. The wine was a heady brew and Ariane doubted it would contribute much to clarity of thought.

But she took a polite sip, the ruby-colored liquid sweet and heavy upon her tongue. A warmth spread through her, dispelling some of the chill that seemed to have settled in her veins ever since she had heard Captain Remy's tale. She leaned back in her chair, some of the tension melting from her shoulders while Marie Claire settled opposite her.

"To begin with, the captain is certain that he managed to elude his pursuers?" she asked.

"Fairly certain," Ariane said. "Although as soon as he seems well enough, it might be wise to move him to a safer hiding place."

Marie Claire nodded in agreement.

"And I will set to work on the gloves."

Marie Claire sipped her wine, peering thoughtfully into her glass. "And if you can prove they have been poisoned, then what?"

"I honestly don't know," Ariane confessed. "In ancient times, we used to have the council to deal with matters like this. Elected daughters of the earth who met twice a year at the circle of standing stones on this island, to consult, to govern, to discipline."

"Alas, my dear, nowadays, women are quite simply too afraid that if they left their homes and husbands to hold a great assembly, they would be deemed a satanic coven and all of them burnt at the stake."

Ariane acknowledged Marie Claire's words with a rueful sigh.

"And yet . . ." Marie Claire lightly traced one fingertip around the rim of her glass. "The Council of the Earth may be long gone, but the daughters have not entirely been scattered to the four winds."

Rising from her chair, Marie Claire glided over to her bedstead and knelt down. Ariane watched, mystified as Marie Claire dragged a heavy iron box from beneath the bed. Producing a key she kept hidden beneath her robes, the older woman unlocked the box and rummaged through the contents.

She struggled to her feet with a thin leather-bound manuscript clutched in her hands. Ariane shuddered to think how dangerous this book must be that was kept locked away. Curiosity drove her to rise and peer over Marie Claire's shoulder as the older woman thumbed through the crackling parchment.

The words were inked out in the old runic symbols, but the writing did not look that ancient. In fact, it looked remarkably like Marie Claire's own elegant flowing style.

"What is that?" Ariane asked, straining to translate some of the words, but the abbess flipped through the pages too quickly.

"It is a listing of the daughters of the earth."

When Ariane gawked at her in astonishment, Marie Claire chuckled. "Well, not *all* the daughters of the earth. Only the ones who are known to me. As you are well aware, too many of our number have been reduced to the state of peasant women, unable to read or write.

"But the ladies set down in my book are well educated and determined to stay connected as in the old days. We correspond frequently to share knowledge and—ah, here we are."

Marie Claire paused at last on one particular page long enough to allow Ariane to read the heading.

Paris.

Ariane watched as Marie Claire skimmed her finger down what was obviously a list of names. "Marie, what or should I say who are you looking for?"

"Someone who may be able to help us," Marie Claire murmured. "They say that the Dark Queen has eyes everywhere these days. Well, we may need some eyes of our own and . . . and yes!"

Marie Claire jabbed her finger down hard on a particular entry. "I believe this may be our woman."

Ariane translated slowly. "Louise . . . Louise Lavalle?"

"Yes, a bold and accomplished woman. A noted courtesan in her own right. She has always preferred being a rich man's mistress than a poor man's wife."

"I don't understand. How is such a woman to help us?"

"By letting us know what is really going on in Paris. Louise could help us find out by insinuating herself at court, perhaps even become a member of Catherine's Flying Squadron."

"Spy on the Dark Queen? Catherine de Medici is not so easily fooled. Maman said she had never met anyone better at the reading of the eyes."

"Ah, you don't know Louise. I have never known anyone better at masking their thoughts."

"Then it is obvious you haven't spent much time with the Comte de Renard." Ariane retorted.

Marie Claire cast her a sympathetic glance. "I heard that he returned to the island today. He is still after you to marry him?"

Despite her weariness and tension, Ariane bit back a smile. Marie Claire missed little of what took place on Faire Isle, and she certainly seemed to be better versed in the doings of the world than Ariane.

Pouring out the entire tale of Renard's visit, Ariane displayed the ring fastened to the chain around her neck. To her astonishment, the abbess was completely fascinated with the small metal band.

"Mon Dieu," she said. "I have not seen one of these for years."

"You've seen a ring like this before?"

"But certainly. *Le cercle d'amour.* They always come in pairs. There should be a mate to yours."

"Yes, Renard is wearing it."

"These special rings are love tokens fashioned from the metals of the earth to bind two souls together across space and time. I don't know what gypsy sold the rings to Monsieur le Comte, but no doubt she was a wise woman well versed in the old ways."

Ariane shook her head. "Maman put no faith in such things as charms or tokens. You cannot possibly believe this ring really is magic, Marie."

"I don't know." Marie Claire held the ring up to the light for one last look before returning it to Ariane. "I have always tended to be a bit more credulous than your wise maman. I would take good care of that ring. If its magic does work, it might prove quite valuable in the days ahead. A powerful man like Renard could be useful in fighting off any minions Catherine might send against us."

"Yes, at a price! What if I ended up having to marry the man?"

"Would that be such a terrible fate? From what I have seen of him, this Renard appears a lusty specimen."

"Marie!" Ariane exclaimed, much shocked.

A wicked twinkle sparkled in the abbess's eyes. "Just because I chose the celibate life doesn't mean I don't appreciate the sight of a fine, strapping man."

"Well, I will admit that Renard does appear rather—rather vigorous." Ariane blushed a little when Marie Claire laughed. "But that would be no good reason to marry a man, especially one so mysterious. I know nothing about him except that he is a Deauville and that is certainly not to his credit."

"Surely you are too wise to hold the sins of a man's grandfather against him. Renard may prove to be quite different from the old comte. He certainly has a finer pair of thighs."

Ariane frowned. "Marie, are you trying to persuade me to accept this man's suit?"

"No, child. I was only teasing you. You are always so solemn on the subject of men. You don't have to end up married to Renard simply because you employed the power of his ring. If you were only to use the thing once or twice, then lock it away . . ."

"Your pardon, Marie, but that strikes me as being slightly deceitful. To call upon Renard's services twice, and then discard him."

The abbess shrugged. "Monsieur le Comte set the rules for this game. If he falls victim to his own conditions, it will be no fault of yours."

But such a course seemed more than deceitful to Ariane. It struck her as being downright dangerous.

"Ah well," Marie Claire said. "I daresay you are right and this business about a magic ring is all nonsense anyway. Let us go back to more practical means of obtaining help."

She turned to her weathered book, tapping her finger against the name of the Parisian courtesan. "Sending Louise to spy on

Catherine will be a better way of uncovering information than you meddling with those gloves. I can get word to Louise by morning."

"By morning?" Ariane exclaimed. "All the way to Paris? What have you got, Marie? A flying horse?"

"No, something better." Marie Claire startled Ariane by emitting a low strident sound at the back of her throat. The raven, which had appeared to be asleep, puffed out its feathers and echoed the cry. To Ariane's astonishment, the bird plucked open the door to its own cage, hopped out and glided across the room to settle on the abbess's wrist. Marie Claire bent close to the bird, cooing and stroking its glistening black plumage. Ariane shivered to see Marie Claire draw her face so near to that dangerous-looking beak, but the bird only fluffed out its feathers and nibbled playfully at her fingers.

"Your little Miri is not the only one who has a way with the creatures of the earth, although my skill has always been greater with birds. I have an especial fondness for ravens."

"Wolf birds?" Ariane protested. "But they are predators, Marie, feasting on the flesh of dead beasts."

"Do we not do the same?" Marie Claire caressed the raven's sleek head. "I have always found these so-called wolf birds to be amazingly loyal and intelligent. I have trained my Agrippa to carry messages for me in a small band attached to his leg. That is how I have always safely managed to communicate with other daughters of the earth.

"Agrippa has been taught to fly to a certain house in Paris, to the wife of one of the doctors at the university. Madame Pechard will get word of what we need to Louise."

Ariane regarded her friend in frank amazement. "Marie, I have known you all my life and I never had any idea you possessed such links to other wise women."

"Now it seems right that you should know. Your mother was

well loved, child. Though there are many daughters of the earth who long ago gave up and lost all courage, there is still a great number out there who would willingly offer up their lives to aid the Lady of Faire Isle. And now that Evangeline is gone, that title belongs to you."

Ariane stared at Marie Claire, both touched and daunted by what she was offering her. She scarcely felt capable of governing her own affairs, let alone commanding some legion of nameless women. She certainly didn't want anyone offering up their life for her.

"No, Marie," she said quietly. "I appreciate you telling me all this, but please put your wolf bird back on its perch. If there is to be any risk taken in defying the Dark Queen, it should be mine." Ariane stiffened her spine, drawing herself up to her full height. "If I am to be the lady of the island, it is my province to protect the people of Faire Isle and that includes you, the sisters of this convent, even the women in that little book of yours. Besides, it was to me that Captain Remy came seeking help and I am the one who gave him my word."

"No one would blame you for breaking such a promise."

"I would blame myself. Because it is high time the Dark Queen was brought to justice and not only for the poor queen of Navarre.

"But for what she did to Maman as well," Ariane added softly. "Like it or not, the task seems to have fallen to me and to me alone."

Marie Claire studied her for a long moment, recognizing the futility of continuing the argument. She fetched a deep sigh and returned her raven to its cage. Her eyes misting with sudden tears, she hugged Ariane.

"Ah, child, you are indeed your mother's daughter."

Ariane wondered. Despite all her brave words, she felt as though a hollow core of fear and doubt had embedded itself deep in her heart. As she returned Marie Claire's embrace, she stared over the older woman's shoulder, trying to draw some inspiration from the tapestry mounted on the wall.

Joan of Arc, one of the most courageous daughters of the earth who had ever lived. Caught forever in the intricate woven threads, she valiantly raised her sword.

But St. Joan had an entire garrison at her back. Ariane had only one lone soldier, already wounded. And St. Joan had only been setting out to defeat the entire English army, Ariane thought with a shudder.

Not the Dark Queen.

Chapter Six

THE GREAT SALON AT THE PALACE OF THE LOUVRE WAS SILENT, only a few candles illuminating the vast recesses of a chamber usually thronged with glittering courtiers. Bartolomy Verducci crept across the tiled floor, a gaunt scarecrow of a man with his thinning hair and straggling beard. Bartolomy shuddered as he inched forward for his private audience with the queen.

Bartolomy had more reason than most to be afraid. He had failed his mistress and the Dark Queen seldom tolerated failure.

For a moment, Bartolomy thought the chamber truly was empty. He experienced a brief sense of reprieve until he spotted a dark shadow behind the throne.

"Y-your Majesty." Bartolomy's voice sounded strange and hollow, echoing round the salon as he deeply bowed.

Catherine de Medici slowly emerged from the shadows, her plump bejeweled fingers folded before her. She was not a tall woman, but she carried herself with all the regal assurance of one who had been born a duchess in the most powerful family in Italy. Her once fair hair was now streaked with silver, her sallow face round and heavy like the rest of her body. But no one ever mistook the Dowager Queen for a matronly figure. Her dark Medici eyes precluded that, cold and piercing, set beneath razor-thin brows.

The queen stared down at Bartolomy from the edge of the dais. He held his velvet cap before him like a shield, his thin fingers fretting the plume.

"Well?" Catherine asked.

Bartolomy tried to keep his voice from cracking. "If—if it please Your Majesty. The problem is well in hand."

"Truly?" Catherine's brows lifted slightly. She crooked one finger, beckoning him closer.

Bartolomy cringed, suppressing an urge to bolt. He shuffled forward until he stood within arm's reach of the Dark Queen. She fixed him with a basilisk stare. It was said that Catherine possessed the ability to read eyes, to compel the truth from men. Bartolomy could not seem to tear away from that cold, steady gaze until Catherine abruptly released him.

"Liar." The single word was spoken softly. "You have allowed Captain Remy to escape," Catherine said.

"Well, Y-your Grace . . ." Bartolomy realized it was useless to deny it. His eyes had already betrayed him.

"Remy has escaped," Catherine went on inexorably. "And taken away with him the evidence that *you* should have recovered."

"It was not my fault, Your Grace," Bartolomy whined. "There were so many people attending the queen of Navarre when she died, Captain Remy, her ministers, her ladies-in-waiting. I could not get close enough. I—I—"

"You fool."

Catherine's voice was calm. One seldom knew the full extent of her anger—until it was far too late.

Bartolomy prostrated himself before her, clutching at the folds of her gown and pleading for her forgiveness. The queen endured this for several moments before plucking her stiff brocade away from him with an expression of impatience.

"Oh, do get up, you imbecile, and cease your sniveling. This helps nothing."

Bartolomy rose trembling to his feet, while the queen demanded, "So what is being done to rectify this situation?"

"The soldiers are still hard after the captain. He'll not get far. He has been wounded and we do know where he is going."

"Any dolt could guess his destination. He will race back to join his young king in Navarre."

"No, Your Grace. We have reason to believe he is headed elsewhere. One of our spies discovered that before he left Paris, he consulted the wife of a certain apothecary, a Madame Belvoir.

"She was reluctant to give us any information about the captain, but a few hours on the rack loosened her tongue. She confessed that the captain plans to seek help from some Cheney woman who lives on the Faire Isle."

"The—the Faire Isle," Catherine breathed. If it had been anyone else but the Dark Queen, Bartolomy would have imagined he saw a flicker of fear in her eyes.

"Yes, Your Majesty. Though I cannot imagine what help the captain imagines he shall find there. It is only a small island, inhabited mostly by women and—"

"Only an island of women?" Catherine glared. "Yes, only insignificant women. Many of them just like me."

Bartolomy's mouth fell open in dismay. Women like the Dark Queen? He knew full well what she meant.

Sorceresses, he thought with a shudder.

"Yes," the queen said as though he had spoken aloud. "And Ariane Cheney is likely the most dangerous of them all. Her late mother, Evangeline Cheney, was once a friend of mine."

Bartolomy could not conceal his surprise.

"It astonishes you, does it, my dear Bartolomy?" Catherine asked dryly. "That I ever had a friend?"

"Yes, I—I mean no, Your Grace. I—I—mean," Bartolomy stammered into incoherence, flushing a hot red.

"Frankly, it surprised me, too," Catherine said. "But I developed an unusual kinship with Evangeline. Perhaps because we were both new brides and felt like foreigners at the French court, she, the lady from Faire Isle, I, 'that accursed Italian Woman.'"

Catherine swept past him to the diamond-paned windows. She stared into the night, a faraway look settling in her eyes.

"We became great allies, Evangeline and I. But unfortunately she never understood the necessity for employing the darker arts available to us. She even sought to thwart me when I did so. Of course, I could not allow that."

Catherine sighed. "Oh, what I was obliged to do to my poor dear friend."

The queen fell silent, but at length she appeared to rouse herself from her reflections. She turned her attention back to Bartolomy. "Now thanks to your ineptitude, I may have Evangeline's daughter to deal with."

"Oh, n-no, Your Majesty."

"You *will* stop Captain Remy from ever reaching that island."

"Oh, y-yes, Your Majesty." Bartolomy nodded.

"And recover the evidence."

Bartolomy nodded even more vigorously.

"Stop bobbing about like an idiot and get to it! And for mercy's sake, continue your hunt with some discretion. I want no hint of anything suspicious reaching Henry of Navarre. I need the young fool here in Paris for the wedding."

Bartolomy started to nod again, then checked himself. He bowed, backing away, thankful to make his escape. He had almost gained the safety of the door when Catherine's voice floated after him.

"Bartolomy."

"Yes, Your Grace?"

"Do not fail me again," the queen said quietly.

Catherine pursed her lips as the trembling servant all but tripped over his own two feet in his haste to quit the room. She remained stiff and rigid until the door closed behind him. Only then did Catherine allow her weariness to show, the weariness of a woman who had long battled to maintain her position in a land where she was frequently mistrusted and despised. Fighting to keep her half-mad son secure in his throne, threatened by other noble French families with claims to royal blood, by uprisings of Huguenot rebels, by the king of Spain stretching his greedy fingers toward France.

Most days, Catherine felt more than equal to the struggle for power. At times, she even relished all the intrigue. But tonight she was feeling strangely tired and alone.

It was the mention of Faire Isle, stirring up memories of Evangeline and all those conflicting emotions her dear friend had stirred in Catherine. Love and hate, admiration and the bitterest of envy. In the end, the hatred and envy had won out.

Evangeline with her perfect marriage, perfect love, daring to thwart Catherine's attempt to rid herself of her husband's mistress. Evangeline had been right to stop her, of course, but that had not made her interference any more tolerable.

Catherine had resolved to show Evangeline exactly what it felt like to be the scorned wife of a faithless husband.

"Pain for pain, my dear Evangeline," Catherine whispered.

It had been so pathetically easy to set one of her ladies loose upon the Chevalier Cheney. Despite all his passionate avowals of adoration for his wife, he had proved as weak as any other man.

Catherine could recall quite clearly that exquisite instant when Evangeline had first learned of her husband's betrayal. Evangeline had always had such incredible eyes, as though a light burned behind them, strong and steady.

But in that moment, Catherine had watched the light flicker and dim, never to fully rekindle. The memory should have been so sweet, yet somehow it had become aching and empty.

Catherine rubbed her eyes, trying to grind out all thoughts of her friend. But she could not help wondering. What if the captain did manage to reach the Faire Isle and solicit Ariane's help?

Catherine's mouth set in a grim line.

"Oh, my dear Evangeline," she murmured. "I pray Ariane has better sense than you ever did, the wisdom not to meddle in my affairs. I truly should not like to have to destroy your child."

Chapter Seven

ARIANE LED HER PONY AWAY FROM THE CONVENT AS CHAR-
bonne locked the gates behind her. Ariane doubted that Marie
Claire would be pleased if she knew that Ariane had dispensed
with Charbonne's escort, but it was late and the woman would
need her sleep, having a full day of chores awaiting her in the
morning.

Ariane felt bone-tired herself, wanting to swing into the saddle and gallop for home. But that was scarcely possible with
Butternut. Miri was right. The pony was getting old. Ariane
would have to spare him as much as possible, even if it meant
leading him through the streets until they gained the road that
wound inland away from the harbor.

She would not likely reach home until the small hours of the
morning, but it would not be the first time Ariane had been
abroad that late. She had frequently ridden out alone after sun-

set, hastening to the bedside of someone desperately ill. She had always felt safe enough here on her island.

At least until tonight.

As she tugged Butternut down the moonlit hill, she huddled close to the pony's side, all too conscious of the secret burden she carried strapped to her side, Captain Remy's leather purse with its deadly contents.

When she had ridden to the convent only hours ago, Faire Isle had seemed the most peaceful place in the world. Now even the herb garden outside the apothecary's shop bore a sinister aspect, too many corners to lurk in, too many bushes to hide beneath.

They say the Dark Queen has eyes everywhere.

Marie Claire's words drifted back to Ariane. Her hand crept to her neck and she nervously fretted the chain holding Renard's ring. Her skin tingled with the eerie sensation that somewhere out there in the darkness, someone was watching . . . waiting. Ariane fought a fierce urge to bolt back to the safety of the convent.

"Stop it!" She would not allow Catherine to fill her with fear, tarnish the way she viewed the world, even her own island.

Butternut came to a halt, the pony resting his weight against her, threatening to fall asleep right there in the middle of the road. Ariane gave him a brisk pat, grumbling with a wry smile. "That's right. Go ahead and lean on me. Everyone else does. I wish just once I had someone's shoulder to lean upon."

"Will I do?" a deep voice rumbled from the darkness ahead of her.

Her heart leaping into her throat, Ariane dropped Butternut's reins as a hulking figure stalked toward her, all enormous shoulders and powerful arms. Ariane drew breath to scream only to have a callused hand clamp firmly over her mouth.

"It is all right, ma chère. It is only me."

Pulse racing, she stared up at the Comte de Renard, moonlight throwing the rough angles of his countenance into sharp relief. He removed his hand from her mouth slowly, his fingers sliding across her lips like a caress. Where the devil had he sprung from? It was as though he'd been conjured up out of the earth itself by a wizard's dark spell.

Or a magic ring?

Ariane's eyes widened as she realized she had been toying with the metal band when she had made her wish. Could she have inadvertently—No, the idea was ludicrous, impossible . . . wasn't it?

She stumbled a step back from Renard, gasping, "M-monsieur le Comte. Where did you come from? I—I didn't summon you."

She added weakly, "Did I?"

"Not this time," Renard replied with a trace of amusement.

"But then what are you doing here?"

"Looking for you," he said as calmly as though they both had been attending some summer fair and he'd lost track of her in the crowd.

Ariane's initial alarm faded, giving way to anger at the fright he'd given her. "Then it was you who I sensed watching me. You have been following me."

Renard hunched his broad shoulders in a dismissive shrug. "What else would you have me do, when I thought my claim on you was being threatened by a rival?"

"A rival? What on earth are you talking about?"

"My friend Toussaint reported that he saw you out riding with another man and I feared that you might be stealing off for a tryst in the moonlight."

The notion was so ludicrous she laughed in spite of herself. "I was with Charbonne, the woman who works at the convent. She is a strong and strapping female to be sure, but if she heard that your friend had mistaken her for a man, she would likely break his nose. She frequently escorts me when I visit St. Anne's."

"I realize that now. I saw the, er, young woman letting you out of the gate."

"And you have been out here all this time, lurking, waiting for me?"

Renard rubbed the back of his neck, looking sheepish. "I fear I have been behaving like a jealous fool."

"You certainly have been," she said sternly. "And quite absurd besides. One has to be in love to be jealous."

"No, only to want someone very much and be determined to protect what is mine."

Ariane could only shake her head, finding Renard's continued pursuit of her more mysterious than ever. "But I am not yours," she said. "And you have no right to be spying on me. What would you have done if I had been meeting another suitor?"

"Discouraged him. Would you not expect me to fight for you?"

"Certainly not. I am not the sort of woman men battle over."

"Then what sort are you?"

"The sensible kind that patches up broken heads when the fight is over."

"You underestimate your own charms, chérie." Renard stroked his fingers along the curve of her cheek. His touch was gentle, but Ariane shied away from him.

She turned her back upon him, tensing when Renard's large hands closed upon her shoulders. He leaned closer, his breath warm against her skin as he murmured in her ear, "Forgive me. I have behaved very badly."

Ariane tried to remain proof against the contrite note she heard in his voice. But it was difficult, even more so when he turned her to face him. His eyes for once were completely open and sincere.

"I am sorry if I offended you," he said gravely. "And gave you such a fright. Terrifying you is the last thing I wish to do."

"I wasn't terrified so much as startled," she admitted grudgingly. "In fact, it is rather strange but I find you more alarming when you are prowling about my great hall." Her gaze roved over his towering height, the powerful expanse of his shoulders. "Somehow you don't seem tame enough to be kept indoors."

"Why don't you domesticate me?" he murmured, drawing her closer.

She peeled away from him with a shaky laugh. "I doubt that I would be up to the task, my lord."

To her relief, Renard accepted her rebuff with a good grace. "And so if you have not been stealing off for a romantic rendezvous, what have you been up to? I didn't think convents usually allowed visitors, especially not this time of night."

Ariane lowered her lashes demurely. "Well, I have this extremely persistent suitor, so I was thinking of taking the veil."

"Ariane." Although Renard chuckled at her playful retort, there was an undercurrent in his voice that warned her he would not be satisfied with such an evasive answer.

To buy herself time to think, she slipped away from Renard, feigning a need to check on her pony although Butternut had scarcely stirred a step from where she had left him. She went to his head, stroking his nose, pretending to soothe him. Quite ridiculous, Ariane realized. If the pony had been any calmer, it would have been asleep.

She heard the crunch of Renard's boots behind her and braced herself. But as he pulled her around to face him, his hands were as gentle as his voice. "Ma chère? Are you in some kind of trouble?"

The very softness of his question disarmed her. His eyes were so kind and warm that Ariane felt her breath hitch in her throat.

"Tell me what is wrong," he coaxed. "Let me help you."

Ariane had to swallow hard to contain a mad impulse to

confide everything to him. There was something world-weary and wise in Renard's battered features. She doubted anything could daunt the man, not even the Dark Queen.

Ariane had to force herself to remember how little she really knew about the Comte de Renard. She had no idea what his views on politics or religion or even dark magic might be. It was the thought of that ring more than anything else that kept her silent, a reminder that any help from Renard would not come without a price.

Avoiding his compelling gaze, she said, "N-nothing is wrong. I am often called to the convent, even at night. Marie Claire, the mother abbess, opens her infirmary to anyone who needs help. There was a traveler who was injured on the road and I came to offer my assistance."

That was the truth as far as it went. Ariane risked a glance at Renard. She could not tell whether he believed her or not, but her answer clearly displeased him, for he frowned.

"You should not be rushing to the aid of every wounded stranger. You are too damned reckless, Ariane."

"I am generally considered by most people to be prudent and sensible. You call it reckless to try to heal someone?"

"It can be . . . for a woman. There is often a fine line between a woman being proclaimed a witch or a saint. You must learn to be more cautious. When you are my wife, I will insist upon it."

"But I am not going to be your wife, my lord."

His eyes darkened, his face so rife with frustration and impatience, Ariane's heart missed a beat. But then he forced a smile, his rugged features smoothing into his imperturbable mask.

"Ah, yes," he drawled. "I do seem to keep forgetting that."

"You also appear to have forgotten the terms of our agreement. You promised to return to your castle."

"I don't ever recall saying *that* precisely."

"You did. Or something very like it. You pledged to leave me in peace if I wore your ring."

"And are you still wearing it?"

Ariane tugged back her cloak enough to reveal the ring attached to her chain.

Renard sighed. "Very well. I will keep my side of the bargain. That is, as soon as I have escorted you safely home."

"That will not be necessary, my lord," Ariane began, but Renard interrupted her with a laugh.

"Oh, I think it will be." He gestured toward Butternut. Head drooping, eyes closed, the pony emitted a series of soft wheezes.

"It appears, milady, that your trusty steed has fallen asleep."

﷼ ﷼ ﷼

THE ROAD BACK TO BELLE HAVEN WOUND THROUGH THE TREES LIKE a silver ribbon discarded by some careless young beauty, the still of the night unbroken except for the steady thud of Hercules's hooves.

Whatever trouble he'd had with his mount earlier, Renard appeared to be in control now, one hand looped firmly around the reins, the other holding Ariane in the saddle before him. Ariane had never been as comfortable with horses as Miri. She would have felt more at ease upon Butternut, but she had been regretfully obliged to leave the exhausted pony in the stables at the inn.

Now as they reached the darkest and loneliest stretch between the harbor and her home, Ariane could not help being glad she had accepted Renard's offer, grateful for his strong presence, even if it was a little like being tucked under a mighty dragon's wing.

Ariane shifted in the saddle, stealing a glance at him. She could scarcely believe that he had followed her tonight, so determined to have her that he was prepared to wrest her from the arms of another man.

She knew she was not the sort of woman to inspire such desire or jealousy. Renard's pursuit of her could only be set down to his strange determination to take her for a wife.

But why? She had heard so many ugly stories about his grandfather, the number of unwilling maids dragged off to the old man's bed. It had been said the greater the woman's reluctance, the greater the old comte's pleasure. And yet she could not help recollecting Marie Claire's admonishment. *Surely you are too wise to hold the sins of a man's grandfather against him.*

Ariane hoped that she was, but Renard's efforts to coerce her into matrimony reminded her far too much of the old comte. Still she detected strains of a gentleness and humor in Renard that the old man had lacked. But smiling good humor could often be a mask for something darker. If only she knew more about Renard . . . if only she could read his eyes.

The road narrowed ahead and Renard drew rein, slowing Hercules to a walk. As he did so, he must have become aware of Ariane's intent scrutiny because he cast an amused look from beneath his heavy lids.

"Don't worry, chérie. I truly am taking you home, not attempting to run off with you. At least not tonight."

"How would I know that for certain?" she asked. "You Deauvilles do not have the best reputation when it comes to dealing with women. Your grandfather dragged his last poor bride to the altar after he had already ravished the girl."

Renard forced a smile. "Ma chère, I don't like being compared to my grandfather. There was little affection between me and the old man."

Ariane waited, hoping he might say something more. Sometimes the best way to get a man to talk was to be silent. But it didn't work with Renard. He merely settled back in the saddle, his mask fixed firmly in place. The silence stretched out so long Ariane was obliged to continue.

"I have heard—that—that is, on the mainland, they say . . . they say your grandfather banished you because you—you—"

"Committed some dark and terrible crime?" Renard finished when she hesitated. "The mere fact of my existence was a crime as far as the old man was concerned. He disapproved of everything that I ever was, everything that I ever did."

Renard spoke with his usual languid drawl, but Ariane detected a hint of bitterness behind the words.

"He would likely have disapproved of your wish to marry me," she said.

"I have no doubt of it." A trace of grim satisfaction played across Renard's face. So was that then the reason Renard was so determined to marry her? Ariane was surprised to feel a sense of disappointment.

"If I had been aiming to please the old man," Renard went on. "I'd have chosen one of those ladies whom I had gathered at my castle."

"And why didn't you? What happened to your judgment of Paris?"

"I put an end to it. After all, you were the one who told me that it was a foolish way to select a wife."

"It hardly seems any wiser to select a woman you met once while lost in the woods."

"But I have always tended to know what I want as soon as I clap eyes upon it."

"Especially if it is something that would have infuriated your grandfather?"

Renard shot her a keen glance. "Ah, so you are worrying that I chose you for a bride merely to hurl one last act of defiance at a dead man. I might have done so when I was eighteen, but I believe I have gained a little more wisdom over the years."

"Then why, Renard? And don't hand me any more of that nonsense about telling me on our wedding night."

Renard lapsed into silence for a moment, his expression unreadable. Then he shrugged. "I don't know. There was just something . . . strange about our meeting that day. Like finding you was a matter of fate."

Ariane studied him with pure frustration. Could he truly believe in such things as magic rings and fate? It didn't matter even if he did because she most emphatically did not.

"Our destinies appear to be at odds with each other, my lord," she said. "I almost consider myself past marriageable age."

"You are a mere babe."

"Then do allow me to introduce you to some older wealthy widows whom I know."

Renard merely laughed. "No, I already found my bride. At least if you have made up your mind to remain a spinster, I can assume that there are no other suitors for me to worry about?"

He attempted to make the question sound light, but there was an edge to his voice that told her he was not entirely indifferent to her answer.

Ariane almost wished she could have told him she had several other admirers, handsome and dashing, but she answered with her usual frankness. "Yes, unfortunately I do have other suitors. There is old Monsieur Lecloud, who suffers badly from the gout and is in love with my poultices. Then there is Monsieur Bonair, the provost who would like to improve his standing in the world by wedding the daughter of a knight. And lastly we have Monsieur Taillebois, a merchant banker from Saint-Malo, to whom my father owes a great deal of money and who would be happy to settle the account by having me instead."

"And these men have been plaguing the heart out of you?" Renard asked softly, his eyes keen upon her face.

Monsieur Taillebois certainly had been, becoming so persistent Ariane dreaded venturing onto the mainland. He was a large part of the reason she neglected visiting her father's estate.

Ariane forced herself to shrug. "I can handle them."

Leaning closer, Renard murmured in her ear, "You don't have to, chérie. Only use the ring and I will rid you of all three of these nuisances."

His breath tickled her neck, rousing sensations that were warm, intimate, enticing her to melt closer to him, making her wonder what it would be like if his lips actually brushed her skin . . .

Embarrassed by her wayward thoughts, she concealed her confusion beneath a light laugh. "I thank you for the offer, monsieur, but I can look out for myself. I am not one of these helpless damsels who needs a knight to come riding to the rescue every time she drops her handkerchief."

"Alas, I am beginning to perceive that, mademoiselle." His eyes glinted with amusement, but a certain admiration as well that brought a warm blush to Ariane's cheeks. She was startled to realize how much she enjoyed bantering with Renard.

She finished the rest of the journey in a bashful silence, relieved when they rounded a bend and she saw Belle Haven's square tower etched against the sky.

The gate was left open, as it always was when Ariane was abroad late. Renard guided Hercules through it, but instead of heading toward the stables, he made for the open court in front of the house.

Candles had been left burning in the hall windows, no doubt by Agnes or one of the other maids waiting up for her. Just as she had done so often for Maman, Ariane thought with an ache.

Renard reined Hercules to a halt and swung down from the saddle. He reached up, lifting Ariane down as easily as though she had weighed no more than a child. She staggered a little, trying to regain the feel of solid earth beneath her feet. But when

Renard's hands tightened on her waist to steady her, she backed shyly away from him.

"I thank you, monsieur, for bringing me home, but it is far too late. I cannot invite you in—"

"I did not expect you to do so. I only wanted to bid you farewell."

He caught her hand, preparing to carry it to his lips.

"I am wise to that trick, my lord." She drew her fingers away, recalling all too well what he'd done the last time, the tumult of her ruthless first kiss.

Renard frowned, his eyes honing in sharply on hers.

"Oh, ma chère," he murmured, his voice full of genuine remorse. "Your first kiss? I do crave your pardon. I was a clumsy brute. If I had realized, I would have been more gentle. Do allow me to make amends."

Before she could escape, his arms enfolded her.

"No, Renard!" Her protest sounded faint, even to her own ears. His gaze fixed on hers as he bent nearer. His breath was warm upon her face and she could not seem to look away. His eyes held her as much as his arms. Glinting from beneath his heavy lids, the green depths were intense, almost mesmerizing.

His lips over hers, his gentleness caught her by surprise. His mouth moved caressingly over hers as though she was as fragile as spun glass.

His arms felt so strong and sure. It had been such a dreadful day, between the quarrels with her sisters, her worry over the mounting debt, and now this alarming business with Captain Remy and the Dark Queen. Renard's mouth was warm, tempting her to forget her problems.

He coaxed her lips apart until she tasted the full sweet heat of his mouth, her breath mingling with his. Shivers of excitement rippled through her as he molded her to him, the softness of her body seeming to fit so well with his muscular frame. She stole her arms around his neck, pressing her lips to his shyly at first and then more eagerly, staggered by the new sensations coursing through her, the wild rush of her pulse, the mad pounding of her heart in rhythm with his.

Renard's lips claimed hers with increasing hunger, a passion that seemed to invade her entire being. Now gentle, now more insistent, now pulling teasingly back, now mating with her tongue in a fiery dance. It was as though . . . as though he was making love to her with no more than a kiss.

Her cheeks were flushed, her blood on fire, and she crushed closer to him, as though she could not get enough of the hard feel of him. Ariane at last understood how a woman could be seduced.

Shakily, she drew her mouth from his. Still she did not seem to have the strength to pull away from Renard. Her breath coming quick, she stood trembling in his arms.

Renard smiled down at her. "Was that better this time?"

Ariane could only stare up at him, not knowing how to answer. He bent toward her again and her heart lurched. She was not sure if she was more disappointed or relieved when he only brushed his lips against her forehead.

"You look quite . . . overwhelmed, ma chère. It has been a long day. You should go into the house now. Go to bed."

She gave a dazed nod, scarcely hearing his soft "good night" as she stumbled away from him and through her front door, closing it firmly behind her.

Agnes had nodded off while waiting up for her, the older woman snoring softly in Maman's chair. Ariane was glad of the fact. It gave her a moment to compose herself, for her flaming cheeks to cool.

She leaned up against the door, drawing in a deep breath. It was only then that the full import of Renard's words struck her.

"Oh, ma chère. Your first kiss? I do crave your pardon. I was a clumsy brute."

Her first kiss? How could Renard possibly have known? It

was as if—as if he had been reading her thoughts, *reading her eyes.*

Impossible. She had never known anyone but a daughter of the earth to possess such a skill. Surely no man ever could.

Heart thudding uncomfortably, Ariane cracked the door open to peer out. But Renard was already gone, both horse and rider vanished as though the night had simply swallowed them up.

Ariane fingered the ring fastened around her neck, studying it with a renewed sense of unease.

"Who the devil are you, Renard?" she whispered.

※ ※ ※

THE PASSING STRANGER APPEARED DARK AND SILENT, LANDLORD, servants, and guests having long ago sought their beds. All save one. A light flickered behind one of the windows of a second-story bedchamber.

It was a well-appointed room for such a humble inn. The bed with its thick feather tick mattress looked comfortable and inviting, but Renard showed no inclination to sink down beneath the coverlets. Moonlight spilled over his massive form, etching his intent features as he bent over the table he had positioned before the window, lighting the five candles, one by one. Four glowing wicks to invoke the four elements, fire, air, earth, and water. One to represent the soul of man.

Five candles arranged in the shape of a pentagram beneath the moon will enhance any spell, old Lucy had always declared. *Five candles to dispel the darkness . . . or to invite it in.*

The darkness of temptation.

Renard's mouth set in a grim line, hesitating as he lit the last candle, but he already found himself staring into the tiny flames as though mesmerized.

Except that it wasn't the candles that he was seeing, but the fire in Ariane's wide eyes after that kiss. Truth be told, he'd been shaken by it himself. Renard could not remember the last time he had found such passion in a mere kiss.

When he'd read in Ariane's eyes how badly he'd bungled her first kiss, he'd been determined to do it right. He'd never expected to find such pleasure in sampling her mouth, giving his prudent witch her first taste of desire and arousing in him such an unexpected hunger.

He'd ached to spend the night with her, holding her in his arms, teaching her how to kiss, his body growing hard with the need to teach her even more. It had taken all his will to let her go, but he'd seen clearly that he'd already given her enough of a lesson for one night.

He'd played the gentleman, allowed her to flee to her house, a decision that he now regretted, for Ariane had not been the only one receiving a lesson. That kiss had taught him a few things as well, that his witch was neither as prim as she seemed nor as transparent.

Ariane had an unsounded depth of passion he longed to explore. She also had an unexpected capacity for concealment that disconcerted him. The lady was keeping a secret from him and he had been completely unable to read her eyes.

Fortunately there are other ways, Justice. Lucy's voice seemed to whisper slyly in his ear.

Renard shook out some of the contents of a small leather pouch into his hand. Dried jasmine petals, fragrant, sweet, harmless in themselves, but when combined with certain other ingredients—.

The door to the inn room wrenched open, cutting off Renard's dark reflections. As Toussaint stomped into the room, Renard dropped the pouch and spun about to face him, attempting to conceal the pentagram of candles arranged on the table.

But Renard could have been conducting a witch's sabbath in the room and he doubted Toussaint would have noticed, the old man was in such an ill humor. He cast Renard a surly glance before slamming the door behind him, grumbling under his breath.

"Fine thing for a man of my years to be spending half his night in the stables."

"It was your own idea," Renard reminded him. "I rubbed down Hercules, gave him water. He didn't need any more coddling."

"But I never saw the poor brute in such a lather. I don't think he likes having that pony in the stall next to him. He was *upset*."

"The pony will be gone, returned to Mistress Cheney in the morning. And I daresay that devil horse was only upset because he didn't manage to dump me on my arse again. We had a rather heated dispute about the route we were going to take after I left Ariane at Belle Haven."

Whatever had inspired Hercules's brief lapse into docile behavior, it was over. Old Lucy had always said that four-legged beasties were more clever and sensitive than men gave them credit for.

Renard frowned. "I know this is going to sound ridiculous, but I almost think that horse believed I was returning him to Ariane's sister. I didn't have any problem until I tried to ride away from Belle Haven. He kept tossing his head and whinnying as though he was actually calling out to the girl."

"That's because the both of you are bewitched by those Cheney women." Toussaint sagged down onto a jointed stool and yanked off one of his boots. "Only you, my lad, should have better sense than a beast. Haring about town at all hours, chasing after—"

The old man broke off, his eyes narrowing as he at last caught sight of the candles on the table behind Renard.

Toussaint froze in the act of removing his second boot. "What—what the devil have you been doing in here, lad?"

Renard affected a yawn. "Waiting for you so I can finally get to bed."

One boot left on, Toussaint rose from the stool and hobbled toward the table. Renard knew a guilty urge to block his way, then felt annoyed with himself.

Shrugging, Renard stepped aside. Toussaint stared at the carefully arranged candles and released a shaky breath.

"Mother of God! How—how could you—? Damnation, Justice. You swore you would leave this stuff alone."

Toussaint shot him a reproachful look. His fingers actually trembled as he snuffed all the candles but one. Then his hand fell upon the leather pouch, the dried leaves scattered across the table.

"J-jasmine," he quavered.

"To perfume the room. The air in here is rather stale."

"Don't take me for a fool, boy," Toussaint growled. "I know what jasmine can be used for. Brewing up an aphrodisiac. Lucy made them often."

"Ah, my grandmother used one on you, did she?"

Toussaint flushed bright red. "No, but she sometimes traded them down in the village for some bit of livestock or an extra bushel of potatoes. Sold the potion to unscrupulous men who would stick at nothing to get round a lass's virtue."

"The women were just as bad, seeking out Lucy's potions to seduce some hapless male," Renard pointed out.

"Perhaps they did, but never did I think to see *you* resort to such vile trickery." Toussaint's old eyes were no longer angry but filled with such disappointment that Renard squirmed.

"Damn it, Toussaint. Don't look at me that way. All an aphrodisiac does is enhance what passion is already there. If a woman despises a man, it cannot work. But if she feels a mutual attraction, deny it though she will, the potion merely—"

Toussaint broke in flatly. "The consent of the body is not always the same as the consent of the heart. God's truth, lad. Is that how you'd win the lady?"

Renard glared at him defiantly for a moment, then felt himself flushing with shame. "Brewing up the aphrodisiac was only an idle thought. I wasn't really going to do it."

At least, he hoped that was true. Sometimes Renard harbored such dark thoughts, he felt like a stranger even to himself, and it frightened him. He marched over to the table, brushed the dried jasmine back into the leather pouch, and pulled the drawstrings tight as though temptation could be neatly cinched away.

Renard offered Toussaint a rueful smile. "I am sorry. I have always had an unfortunate fascination with the darker side of magic."

"I know," Toussaint said sadly. "That is why I wish you would leave Mistress Cheney and whatever hidden store of books she possesses well alone."

"Don't let us have that argument again. I have already told you, Toussaint. She is my destiny. I *will* have Ariane for my wife."

While the old man sank back down on the stool to finish removing his boots, Renard continued, "I am not without worries. While I may not have any serious rival for Ariane, there is something else afoot. I don't believe she told me the truth about why she felt impelled to visit a convent in the middle of the night."

"Couldn't you do that thing that Lucy taught you?" Toussaint asked. "I never saw any harm in the reading of the eyes."

"Nor do I, but alas, it does not always work. Usually I can employ it quite successfully with Ariane, but not tonight. She is hiding something from me."

"Well, you might try the method the rest of us mere mortals use. You could just ask the lady what is wrong."

"Ariane Cheney would never confide in me. She doesn't trust me."

"Astonishing! I wonder why that would be." Toussaint stroked his grizzled chin. "If you want my advice, lad—"

"Not if it is going to be irritating."

Toussaint scowled at him but continued, "If you must give

your lady that infernal ring, at least take the conditions off it. Win her confidence. Tell her the truth about yourself."

"Even about old Lucy?" Renard asked tersely.

Toussaint met his gaze levelly. "Especially about Lucy."

Renard shook his head. "I don't believe that would be a good idea. In my experience, truth can be vastly overrated in dealings between men and women."

"Oh, there is a sentiment truly worthy of your late grandfather."

Renard's lips thinned dangerously. If this conversation continued, he knew that he and Toussaint were only going to end up in another of their quarrels.

He snuffed out the candle and flung himself down upon the bed. He was aware of Toussaint standing motionless for a long moment. Then the old man heaved a wearied sigh and settled down upon his own pallet.

Long after Toussaint started to snore, Renard remained awake, fretting over the old man's words.

Despite what Toussaint said, he wasn't like his grandfather, plotting to drag Ariane off by her hair. Perhaps he had waxed a trifle ruthless when he had considered using the aphrodisiac, but if a man could be hanged for having wicked thoughts, the entire male population of the earth would be wiped out by now.

He would just have to school himself to be patient. He did not know what Ariane had gotten involved in tonight. Whatever it was, Renard had a strong presentiment that Ariane Cheney would be tempted to make use of his ring. And very soon.

Chapter Eight

DESPITE THE SOFTNESS OF MAMAN'S GREAT BED AND HOW exhausted she was, sleep continued to elude Ariane, her mind churning with questions about the man who had so recently vanished from her doorstep.

If she was ever so foolish as to suspect a man of practicing sorcery, that kiss alone would be enough to condemn Renard. For surely there must have been some sort of wicked magic in an embrace that had left a lingering fire in her veins, making her still feel as though she wanted more, imagining his long, clever fingers undoing the laces of her gown, caressing her skin, cupping her bare breasts. He had such large, strong hands . . .

"Oh, stop it, Ariane," she muttered, thumping her pillow, shocked by the direction of her own thoughts.

It had only been a kiss. No doubt the embrace had seemed more potent to her than it really was, merely because of her lack of experience and . . . and she had been very tired. Exhaustion could do strange things to a person. It could even be used as a kind of torture, playing tricks with the mind, compelling one to behave in ways most unlike oneself. Just like Renard's kiss.

Although if Renard's kiss had been torture, Ariane reflected with a soft sigh, women all over France would be rushing to fling themselves into dungeons.

There were other far more disturbing things about the comte than his kiss, she reminded herself. What about the fact that he wielded those glinting green eyes of his like weapons, shielding his every thought, while at the same time seeming to pierce her clean through? And then there was the question of his strange ring.

Even now, she could feel Renard's ring nestled beneath her night shift, a cool, but oddly reassuring weight resting against her skin. It was strange, but she had already grown accustomed to wearing it.

Tugging on the chain, she drew the ring out, barely able to make out its shape in the night-darkened room. Somehow she did not believe Renard's tale about acquiring it from a gypsy woman. What if . . . what if Renard had forged it himself?

Perhaps all the speculation about Renard was wrong, the wild rumors that he'd existed all these years as a pirate or roving bandit. Perhaps there was something even more sinister about his past.

She had heard of a few instances where daughters of the earth, lacking female offspring, had passed their knowledge to their sons. A few men had actually managed to learn, to master the old ways, the late Nostradamus for one.

But for the most part men who claimed to be sorcerers either turned out to be charlatans or credulous fools. So what did that make Renard?

Tucking the ring back inside her night shift, she closed her eyes, determined to will herself to sleep. Closing her eyes, she concentrated on her breathing, deep, slow, rhythmic, forcing herself to relax, to grow drowsy.

She was wrenched wide-awake by the sound of a muffled cry. Ariane lay still for a moment, heart thudding, wondering if she had imagined it or had merely started to dream.

The cry came again. Faint, but unmistakable and coming from the direction of her sisters' bedchamber. Ariane flung off the covers and was out of the bed and moving, not even pausing to light a candle.

She made her way down the corridor more by feel and memory than by sight. Of course there was no reason to suppose that either of her sisters could be in danger. None, other than the tension and anxiety that had been coursing through Ariane ever since her meeting with Captain Remy.

She rushed toward their room, nearly tripping over her nightdress in the process. Easing the door open, she called anxiously, "Miri? Gabrielle?"

She was met with silence, the chamber seeming as calm as when she had checked in upon her sisters earlier and found them both asleep. Miri had left the shutters wide open, no doubt. Moonlight spilled across the small chamber Ariane had once shared with her sisters before her mother's death, before she had become the Lady of Faire Isle.

The bedchamber was still filled with Gabrielle and Miri's treasures, evidence of girlhood that Ariane had long ago put behind her. Gabrielle's precious apricot silk lay tumbled across a chair, a small table laden down with her perfumes and hair ribbons. Nearby was stacked a pile of wood, hammer, and nails for the small boxes Miri was forever building to house the smaller woodland creatures she rescued.

On the wall opposite the bed hung the painting Gabrielle had started for Miri, a silvery unicorn bounding out of the forest.

Only the mythical beast's powerful head and shoulders were complete, its mane whipping in the wind.

It was the last canvas Gabrielle had ever worked upon before that terrible afternoon in the barn. Now the painting seemed destined to remain unfinished. Ariane turned sadly away from it to tiptoe closer to the bed. Gabrielle's burnished gold hair fanned across the pillow as she sprawled out, as usual taking up more than her share of the bed.

The cry must have come from Miri. The coverlet had been kicked off onto the floor and the girl lay shivering, curled up like a frightened field mouse. As Ariane crept round to Miri's side of the bed, she saw that her little sister's eyes were wide open, staring. That did not necessarily mean that Miri was awake. Ever since she had been a little girl, Miri had been known to talk, sometimes to even walk in her sleep. One had to take great care not to terrify her by jarring her suddenly awake.

Ariane hunkered down by her sister, gently rubbing her thin shoulder. "Miri. Miri, sweetheart. Wake up."

Miri trembled beneath her touch, but did not otherwise stir.

"Miribelle. You are having one of your nightmares."

Miri blinked rapidly, the glazed look fading from her eyes as she focused on Ariane crouching over her. She startled Ariane by suddenly sitting bolt upright, moonlight framing her pale face.

"Maman?" The girl called eagerly. "Is it really you?"

"No, dearest," Ariane said. "It is me, Ariane."

Ariane knew the moment her sister came fully awake. Miri's hopeful face crumpled under the crushing weight of her disappointment, a disappointment that echoed in Ariane's own heart.

Miri gave a muffled sob, then flung her arms around Ariane's neck, hugging her so tightly, Ariane could scarcely breathe. But Ariane cradled her little sister close, rubbing her back.

"It's all right, babe. Everything is all right," she crooned in Miri's ear.

"B-but Ariane. I—I had 'nother one of—of my bad d-dreams."

"I know, dearest. I know."

Miri began to sob in earnest and Ariane noticed Gabrielle stir, sound sleeper that she was. Ariane lifted Miri from the bed and carried her over to the window seat.

Despite her twelve years, Miri still weighed little more than a child. Ariane settled onto the seat with Miri on her lap. The girl buried her head against Ariane's shoulder, weeping. Ariane cradled her close, rocking her back and forth, saying nothing for a very long time until at length Miri's sobs grew quieter.

Then using the sleeve of her own shift, Ariane dried her little sister's eyes. "Now tell me, dearest. What was the dream about?"

"Oh, Airy! It—it was awful." Miri paused to collect herself with a deep gulp. "There was this town, but—but not our town. It was bigger, with all these towers. And there were bells in these towers. They kept ringing and ringing. They wouldn't stop."

Miri shuddered. "And a terrible mist seeped through the town, driving everyone mad. The men rushed into the streets. They wanted to paint the palace red, but a beautiful princess didn't want them to. She begged them to stop but no one would listen.

"Then the mist grew darker and suddenly everyone started to choke, to die, and—and that was when I realized it wasn't red paint splashed everywhere at all. It was b-blood."

Miri tunneled her face back against Ariane's shoulder as though by doing so she could blot out the memory of her nightmare. Her braid had come completely undone and Ariane stroked her fingers gently through the tangled strands of moongold hair.

"Hush, angel. It was only a bad dream."

Miri wrenched her head back to stare reproachfully at Ariane through her tears. "How can you say that, Ariane?" she cried. "When you know what has happened other times?"

Ariane did know. Miri's nightmares often had a frightening way of coming true. She had dreamed over and over again of their mother vanishing into the forest, a week before Evangeline Cheney had died. Then there had been her peculiar nightmare about battling pieces on a chessboard, the black knight cracking open the white king's head. Shortly thereafter King Henry of France had been killed, pierced through the eye with a splinter from a lance during a mock tournament with one of his own knights.

But Ariane kept her alarm to herself. "Perhaps this time it will turn out to be nothing more than a strange dream."

Miri shook her head. "No, it won't. I can always tell when the nightmare is this bad, I am going to have it again and again until something dreadful happens."

She clutched desperately at the front of Ariane's night shift. "You have to help me, Airy. Tell me what my dream means and maybe this time we can stop it."

Ariane regarded her sister helplessly. "I don't know how, dearest. I have never had the ability to interpret dreams."

"Then stop me from having it again. Maman could do that, at least for the rest of the night. She'd brush her fingers over my forehead and take the bad dream out of my mind."

Miri caught Ariane's hand and pressed it to her temple, staring at Ariane with wide, beseeching eyes. "Make it go away, Ariane. P-please."

Ariane caressed Miri's brow, her heart aching. "I am so sorry, Miri," she said, her voice thickening. "I don't know how to do that either."

Miri's lip quivered, then she flung herself back onto Ariane's shoulder, commencing to weep all over again.

"Oh, A-ariane. I want Maman!"

Ariane hugged her little sister close, her own eyes burning with tears. "I know, dearest," she whispered. "I want her, too."

※ ※ ※

ARIANE STRETCHED ON TIPTOE TO LIGHT THE WALL TORCHES IN THE hidden workshop, the red flame flaring over her face, hard and grim with determination. It had taken her a good hour to soothe Miri back to sleep. All during the time she had comforted and rocked her sister, a dread resolution had formed in her heart.

Perhaps thought of this deed had always lurked somewhere in her mind, ever since the day her mother had died. But she had lacked the courage or perhaps the desperation to act on it before.

Now she moved quickly, as though she feared that if she hesitated for an instant, she would change her mind. Shifting the ladder, she climbed up to the topmost shelf and brushed aside cobwebs, dragging down the black candles, the copper basin, and the book whose contents were so dire, it did not even bear a title.

Evangeline Cheney had almost burned the heavy leather-bound volume a score of times, but could never quite bring herself to do so, perhaps out of respect for the memory of her predecessors. But Evangeline had always insisted the book be considered as no more than an heirloom, part of their family history. The dark contents of those pages were never to be consulted or employed.

"Forgive me, Maman." Ariane wiped the dust from the book's cracked leather cover. "But I don't know what else to do."

Her trembling fingers rifled through the yellowed parchment pages until she found the exact one she needed. She scurried to make the preparations, filling the copper basin with water, lighting the black candles. As she fetched the small iron burner and set incense to burning, her heart hammered in her chest.

She did not know if this was going to work, but she kept going, refusing to allow herself time to think. The workshop was soon thick with the sweet, heady smoke of the incense. Using the mortar and pestle, Ariane worked to grind up the right proportion of dried herbs and wine before adding the last ingredient, pieces of the strange wild mushroom that grew at the heart of Faire Isle.

The potion mixed, she hesitated a moment before downing a large swallow of it. The mixture was so vile, so bitter, she choked, fearing she was going to be ill, but somehow she managed to get it down.

Then she waited, drawing in quick, nervous breaths. The effect was almost immediate, a fire that seemed to spread up from the pit of her stomach, like a dark smoke slowly curling its way to her brain.

Her head swam and for a moment the workroom seemed to shift and tilt around her. Her eyes blurred and she had to grab the edge of the worktable for support. Just when she feared she was about to faint, her vision cleared and everything came into focus with a vivid clarity that was almost painful.

Her hands stopped trembling and she felt suddenly calm, filled with a sense of power that was nigh intoxicating. She moved the black candles until their glowing wicks reflected over the darkened surface of the water in the basin.

Ariane closed her eyes and wrapped her arms tightly about herself. The superstitious imagined that witches cast spells by chanting strange incantations, but Ariane had always known that true magic came from the power of the mind, the strength of the will.

She delved through the corridors of her own mind, striving to bring an image of her mother into focus. It was more difficult than she had imagined. Ariane was distraught to realize that her mother's face had already started to blur in her memory and for one panicked moment, she feared she would be unable to do it.

She forced herself to breathe more deeply of the incense, allowing the potion to do its work. Slowly, one by one, Evangeline Cheney's features came sharply into focus, the strong but gentle face, the clear gray eyes, the soft brown hair.

Oh, Maman. Come to me. I need you.

Ariane launched her thoughts into the night, shining them like a beacon across space and time, through the mysterious barrier that was death itself. A gravelike hush seemed to settle over the hidden workshop, over the entire house.

Then Ariane felt a chill. A brisk draft tore through the workshop, flickering the candles and rippling the water's surface.

Ariane's heart pounded uncontrollably as she watched an image form in the basin. Shadowy at first, then ever clearer until Ariane found herself gazing at her mother's face. Not the way Evangeline Cheney had looked during those last terrible days of her illness but when Maman had still been well and strong, her glossy brown hair pulled back from her vibrant features, her calm gray eyes feathered with those tiny lines Ariane remembered so well.

The wrinkles so dreaded by other women, Evangeline had taken great pride in. Her creases of wisdom, she had called them, a woman's greatest beauty.

As her mother's beloved face shimmered before her once more, Ariane's breath caught in her throat.

"Oh! M-maman."

A tender smile hovered on her mother's lips, but her eyes were so sad.

"Ariane, my dear. What have you done?" Maman's voice seemed to resonate from a great distance away.

"I—I am sorry, Maman," Ariane said. "I know you would not have wanted me to—that I should never have—but—"

The water rippled almost as though Evangeline issued a faint sigh. Then her voice came again, clear and strong.

"What is it, my child? Tell Maman what troubles you."

The words were so comforting and familiar to Ariane, spoken by her mother so many times before, even up to the moment of Evangeline's death. Ariane felt a tear cascade her cheek and she stretched out her hand, longing to touch her mother. She was only stayed by the knowledge that even one brush of her hand against the water would be enough to end the magic.

"Everything is going wrong, Maman," she cried. "I—I don't seem able to manage anything properly. The estates, the debts, and Papa still has not returned. Is he—is he—"

Ariane dreaded to ask the question, but her mother understood her well enough.

"No, your father has not crossed over. I cannot tell you where he is or even when he will return. But you must keep faith that he will do so and take care of yourself and your sisters until then."

"I c-can't," Ariane said. "I am even making a disaster of that. Miri is having nightmares again and—and Gabrielle—. There was this dreadful man who came to our island, Maman, and I—I didn't protect her."

"My dear child. Do you remember the time when you were little and you stumbled by the fire and burned your hand on the cauldron?"

"Y-yes."

"I was right beside you and still I could not move quickly enough to catch you. We cannot always protect those we love."

"But since I became the Lady of Faire Isle, everyone looks to me to do so, expecting me to be like you and I am not. And now I may even be called up to fight the Dark Queen."

"What?" Evangeline's voice rang out sharper.

In halting breaths, Ariane poured out the story of Captain Remy and the gloves, the likelihood that the Dark Queen had murdered Jeanne of Navarre. At the end of Ariane's tale, Evangeline looked even sadder.

"My poor Catherine."

Ariane was aghast. "Maman, you cannot possibly have any sympathy for that horrible woman, especially not after what she did to you, to our entire family."

"Ariane, any wise woman who gives over her soul to the darkness is much to be pitied."

"But it is what she may be up to right now that concerns me. She needs to be stopped, brought to justice."

"Just make sure that it is justice you seek, my daughter, and not revenge. Whatever course you pursue against Catherine, do it carefully. Avoid her darkness."

"But that is just the problem, Maman. I am not sure how to proceed. I don't have your wisdom. Or—or even your courage and strength."

Her mother smiled sorrowfully. *"Ah, my dear child. That is because you have always confused being strong and independent with being alone."*

"But I am alone, Maman," Ariane quavered. "I miss you so terribly sometimes I can scarcely bear it and there is still more I must tell you. I am being pursued by this—this man. Justice Deauville, the old Comte de Renard's grandson. He is determined to claim me for his wife.

"But there is something so strange about him. I—I have almost come to fear he might be some manner of sorcerer."

"You must take care whom you marry, child. You are the Lady of Faire Isle, heiress to a legacy of powerful secrets. An unscrupulous man might make ill use of them."

"I know that, Maman. I have no intention of wedding Renard, but he—"

Ariane hesitated, far too embarrassed to confess to her mother about Renard's kiss, the desire that he had aroused in her. "He is so persistent and—and only look at this strange ring he has given me."

Ariane wrenched hold of the chain and bent forward. But in her eagerness to display the ring, she bumped against the side of the basin, disturbing the water. To her horror, her mother's image rippled.

"Oh, no," she cried, placing her hands on either side of the basin, attempting to steady the bowl. She fought hard to concentrate, keep her mother's face etched clear in her mind, but it was too late. Evangeline's image faded before her eyes.

"Maman! P—please, no. Stay with me. Don't leave."

Evangeline's voice came to her in broken snatches, fainter, like someone trying to call out over crashing waves.

"Must go . . . You should not have . . . great risk, this dark magic even for good. Promise me . . . won't do it again."

"I won't, Maman," Ariane said desperately. "Please just stay long enough. I feel so frightened, so alone, so powerless against everything. Tell me what to do."

"You must rely . . . rely upon—"

But her mother's voice faded along with her image in the water. Ariane dashed her hand into the basin as though somehow she could grasp hold of her mother, but the moment Ariane's fingers touched the water, a terrible weakness washed over her.

Her head reeled, the room started to spin. Her knees buckled and she grabbed wildly for the table's edge, just managing to break her fall before she sank to the ground, losing consciousness.

When next she stirred, her eyes fluttered open in confusion. She blinked, trying to get her bearings, recall where she was. Shifting a little, she winced at the feel of hard flooring beneath her. She was flat on her back, looking up at gray light pouring through a hole in the ceiling.

No, it was not a hole, but the trapdoor leading down to the hidden workroom.

"Gabrielle," Ariane muttered thickly. "How many times do I have to tell you . . ."

A foggy recollection sifted through her mind. It had not been Gabrielle, but Ariane who had forgotten to close the secret door when she had come down here last night.

Her tongue seemed as thick as a wad of cotton and she had

the vilest aftertaste in her mouth. The air in the workroom that was usually musty smelled even worse, stale with the tang of smoke, of—of—

Incense.

Recollection of last night's events slammed back into Ariane's consciousness. She tried to sit up, only to fall back with a low groan, her head aching as though it had been split open with an ax. Her stomach lurched and she was certain she was going to retch.

By taking deep breaths and concentrating hard, she managed to stave off the wave of nausea. She struggled to a sitting position by dint of proceeding very slowly. Clutching the table, she dragged herself to her feet.

Her legs trembled beneath her as she stared uncertainly at the littered worktable, the evidence of her proceedings last night. The open book, the melted pools of black wax, the basin of water.

Had she succeeded in doing what she'd set out to do? Had she truly summoned forth her mother's spirit, spoken with her? Ariane rubbed her throbbing head, no longer so sure in the cool light of morning.

Perhaps the entire conversation had been nothing more than her wistful imaginings, a mad dream born out of meddling with wild mushrooms and breathing too much incense.

Ariane's eyes filled with tears. All she knew for certain was that her brief foray into the occult had neither provided a solution to her problems nor assuaged her grief.

Whether she had contacted Maman or simply imagined it, losing hold of that dream was somehow as bad as losing her mother all over again. And Ariane wept silent tears, feeling more bereft than ever.

Chapter Nine

ORT CORSAIR BASKED BENEATH THE AFTERNOON SUN, THE houses and shops presenting a cheery face, many of the timber facades ornamented with bright-colored molding, red, blue, and green. The morning shopping done, most of the island wives turned their attention to other tasks, washing linens, beating rugs, and weeding gardens.

The entire island bore such a peaceful look, making Ariane's fears of last night seem foolish. As she alighted from the farm cart that had fetched her to town, she felt ashamed of what she had done, meddling with the dark magic in an effort to disturb her mother's peace.

Whether she had actually succeeded in raising Evangeline's spirit or merely imagined it, Ariane had puzzled out the meaning of her mother's last, fading words . . . *"You must rely upon . . ."*

It was something Maman had often said to her: *"You have good sense, Ariane. You must always remember to rely upon it."*

From here on, Ariane would be the strong and wise woman she was expected to be as the Lady of Faire Isle.

The first task she had set for herself this morning was seeking out the Comte de Renard. A stable lad had returned Miri's pony to Belle Haven this morning with Monsieur le Comte's compliments. When Ariane had inquired after Renard, asking if he had left the island, the boy had been able to assure her that milord had not.

As the farm cart lumbered away, Ariane adjusted her marketing basket over her arm and marched toward the Passing Stranger. Although traces of a headache lingered behind her eyes, she felt far more in command of herself today. She meant to have the truth from Renard, regarding his murky past and his reasons for wanting to marry her. And if he evaded her questions, she was going to remove his ring, hand it back, and firmly inform him their pact was at an end.

But as she strode into the taproom, and inquired after the comte, she was met by the unwelcome intelligence that Renard was out. He had gone into the town and no one knew when he would return.

Ariane struggled to conceal her chagrin. Not because she was that eager to see Renard. She merely wanted this confrontation over with while both her courage and resolve were still high.

Leaving a message requesting that the comte should call upon her at Belle Haven later that afternoon, Ariane strode off in the direction of the main street. Many of the shops were nearly a century old, sagging against one another. The bottoms of horizontal shutters were let down to form counters displaying wares while the upper ones formed awnings. Through the open windows, both apprentices and masters could be seen hard at work in their shops. Or more often *mistresses.*

Many of the artisans were widows or daughters who carried on their husband's crafts, while others were spinsters who had found in Faire Isle a strange unique place where a woman might practice some trade other than being wife or prostitute. As Ariane progressed down the street, she was greeted warmly.

She was heartened as always by the affection and respect she received from the folk of Faire Isle, but her own replies were a trifle distracted. When she traversed the entire street with no sign of Renard, she was rather astonished by the depth of her disappointment.

Ariane at last reached a squat cottage that appeared at odds with the other, taller buildings. A sign creaked in the breeze, the three gilded pills proclaiming it as an apothecary's establishment. At least that was what Madame Jehan dared to call herself. But with her straggling white hair and the wart on her chin, she fitted the image of what most mainlanders would have called a witch.

Madame Jehan took full advantage of the fact, doing a brisk trade selling love ointments and virility potions to credulous sailors. Adelaide Jehan was in fact a wise woman, well versed in the ancient science. She would have certain ground powders that might be useful to Ariane in deciphering the mystery of the gloves and in brewing a restorative medicine for Captain Remy as well.

Beside being a skilled herbalist, Madame Jehan was a master storyteller. Her shop was often crammed full of the island children clamoring for her tales. Ariane and her sisters had been no exceptions when they were young. She could remember how eagerly they had looked forward to visiting the apothecary shop. While Maman had made her selections, they had all been held spellbound by Madame Jehan's stories.

Gabrielle had been particularly fond of hearing the bloodcurdling adventures of the legendary Melusine. Madame Jehan's voice had always dropped to a sinister whisper as she recounted the witch's evil deeds.

"And Melusine was right beautiful to look at, but her heart was colder than the murky dark bottom of a well. She had made

up her mind, you see, that the daughters of the earth should rule over France. Not men or kings."

"What is wrong with that?" Gabrielle had piped up. "It sounds like a grand idea to me."

"Ah, but Melusine went about pursuing her dreams in the cruelest, wickedest way, my pretty one. She sought to bring the great lords to their knees by attacking their lands, putting a blight on their crops, cursing their livestock."

"Even the—the little lambs?" Miri had quavered, her eyes waxing large in her small face.

"Oh, especially the poor little lambs, my pet. It was a terrible sight to see what that wicked Melusine did to them." And Madame Jehan would commence to twitch, baaing plaintively and lolling out her tongue in a terrifying imitation of a sheep perishing in mortal agony.

Her eyes filling with tears, Miri would shudder and bury her face in Ariane's skirts. At this juncture, Evangeline Cheney would intervene, gently but firmly requesting Madame Jehan to stop before her girls were afflicted with nightmares.

Although Madame Jehan's horrific tales of Melusine had often frightened them out of their wits, Ariane reflected ruefully, that certainly had never stopped her or her sisters from begging Madame Jehan for more. Nor had it deterred any of the island children since.

But when Ariane entered the shop, she found the place empty this afternoon except for the old woman herself. When she placed her order, Madame Jehan nodded and bustled to fetch several vials from her well-stocked shelves. Powders for detecting poison or powders for healing, it was all one to Madame Jehan. That was what many people found so comforting about dealing with the old woman. She never asked awkward questions.

As she tucked the small bottles inside Ariane's basket, she

inquired pleasantly instead, "How are those two pretty sisters of yours, dearie?"

"Oh, er—quite well," Ariane murmured, although she feared Gabrielle and Miri were anything but. Miri had been pale and withdrawn this morning in the wake of her nightmare, not touching a bite of her breakfast. She had disappeared at once into the barn to take solace from her animals. As for Gabrielle, she had been cool and aloof, cutting off any reference to the words that had passed between her and Ariane the night before. But despite Gabrielle's chilly demeanor, Ariane had seen the unhappiness shading her sister's eyes.

As she paid for her purchase, pressing a few coins into Madame Jehan's withered hand, she felt the old lady's shrewd eyes upon her.

"What all three of you girls need is a little romance, a lusty young lover."

Ariane rolled her eyes, having heard this opinion before. Madame Jehan voiced it every time Ariane entered the shop.

"Now, madame," Ariane scolded. "I hope you are not trying to sell me one of your love potions."

"I should say not. Fancy me attempting to impose such nonsense on the Lady of Faire Isle. All I am saying is that a woman's bed can be a lonely place at night without a man to warm it. I should know. I've outlived four husbands, rest their souls."

"F-four?" Ariane exclaimed. She knew the apothecary had been widowed, but she had never guessed as many times as that.

"Aye, fine strapping fellows the lot of them. Guess I just wore them out. But I did adore each and every one of them."

"So . . . so many loves," Ariane could not help murmuring.

Madame heaved a gusty sigh. "Aye, and I wouldn't say no to a fifth if the right man ever came wandering into my shop, some bold fellow with a ready laugh, quick hands, and a roving eye."

The old woman tweaked Ariane's chin, peering affectionately into her eyes. "I fear you will never love so easily, but when you do fall, it will be hard, deep, and forever. You will give your heart but once, just like your dear maman."

And just like her mother, she might well end up with a broken heart. Ariane gave a stubborn shake of her head.

"I don't intend to surrender my heart at all. I have too many duties as the Lady of Faire Isle to go searching for a lover."

"Maybe he'll find you," the old woman suggested slyly. "I hear tell the Comte de Renard has returned to Faire Isle."

"He has." Ariane tried to look supremely indifferent.

"Now there's a man for you. All brawn and bone, but nobody's fool either. Not handsome perhaps, but I have always preferred a man with a lived-in face and a bit of the devil about him."

"Too much of the devil perhaps," Ariane replied. "Madame, you have so much experience of men. Have you ever met any of them who had mastered the old ways? Who were skilled in sorcery?"

The old woman's eyes twinkled up at her. "Well, my third husband was a bit of a wizard between the sheets."

Ariane gave a wry laugh, but persisted. "*Seriously,* madame, one hears so many troubling rumors about the present comte. He could be a complete scoundrel, plotting who can imagine what sort of mischief."

Madame Jehan shrugged. "So marry the man and keep him out of trouble."

"I doubt I would be up to the task. I cannot even read Renard's eyes. I never know what he is thinking."

"Oh, likely what most men think about. How soon he will be able to get you into bed and what's he going to be served for dinner."

Ariane was assailed by a sudden image of Renard tangled in her sheets, lean, hard, and naked. She drew in a sharp breath and fought down a blush.

"There are other ways of discovering what a man has on his mind," Madame Jehan said. Rummaging beneath the counter, she produced a small vial of a rust-colored liquid. When Ariane's brows rose questioningly, Madame leaned closer, speaking in a conspiratorial tone.

"*L'essence de verité.*"

"A—a truth potion?" Ariane exclaimed.

Madame nodded. "When the reading of the eyes fails, this is the next best thing. Place a few drops of this in Monsieur le Comte's wine and I guarantee you he will tell you anything that you want to know. I had to use this potion frequently on my second husband, the rascal."

Ariane touched the vial, both intrigued and appalled. "But madame, this—this is black magic."

"Not black magic, dearie," Madame said soothingly. "Only a little *gray.*"

"Maman considered anything dark magic that tampered with another person's mind or threatened his free will."

"Your maman, bless her, was too much of a saint, far too good for this world." Madame Jehan closed Ariane's fingers around the vial. "Take the potion and use it on your young man, dearie. With my compliments."

Ariane stared down at the small bottle and for a moment, she was horribly tempted. She was holding in her hand the one thing that might finally give her an advantage over Renard.

But Ariane knew Evangeline Cheney would have disapproved. Bad enough what she had already done last night, dabbling in the forbidden realms of necromancy.

With a heavy sigh, Ariane returned the vial to Madame Jehan. "Thank you, madame, but no. I admit there is much I am anxious to discover about Renard, but I will stick to more straightforward methods."

Madame Jehan shrugged. "Suit yourself, dearie. I only hope Monsieur le Comte plays as fairly with you."

Ariane fingered the ring, already having doubts on that score. She watched as Madame Jehan squirreled the potion away again, then bade the old woman farewell and hastily quit the shop, removing herself from any further temptation.

As she emerged into the sunlit street, she walked head-on into Monsieur Taillebois. He emitted a startled oath. But as Ariane staggered back, the man's lean hands shot out to steady her.

As Ariane regained her balance, she stared up at the merchant, her stomach dipping to her toes. He was a tall man, with black hair, a blade-like nose, and high cheekbones. Most women found him handsome and Ariane supposed that he was in a lean, arrogant sort of way. The fur-trimmed robe that draped over his slender shoulders bespoke all the trappings of a wealthy burgher. He had a soft insinuating smile, but his eyes always seemed to Ariane as hard as the business that he practiced.

"Monsieur Taillebois. I—I do beg your pardon." Ariane forced a polite smile to her lips. "I fear I was not watching where I was going."

"No need to apologize, Mistress Cheney. It is always a great pleasure to see you, even when you tread upon my toes." Taillebois made an effort to jest, but unlike Renard, he was far too stiff about his teasing.

"You so seldom grace the mainland with your fair presence these days." Was that a faint trace of accusation? His fingers lingered on her shoulders and Ariane squirmed away.

She felt the beginnings of a flush steal into her cheeks. Monsieur Taillebois was perhaps justified to voice some complaint. Ariane had been steadfastly avoiding him.

"I am sorry, monsieur. There—there has been so much to do at Belle Haven. I have been most preoccupied, but I have been meaning to come speak with you about my father's note."

"No need to worry yourself about that, milady," Taillebois said. "Although I must admit I had expected repayment long ere now."

"Yes, well I am sure my father is going to return any day—"

"I have no wish to shatter your hopes, mademoiselle, but many have been known to make the voyage to Brazil within six months. Chevalier Cheney has been gone over two years. One must begin to assume the worst."

"If you thought my father's voyage so perilous, I wonder that you ever advanced him the money for it."

But when Taillebois's eyes narrowed, his brows snapping together, she hastened to amend her tone. "Your pardon, monsieur. But I have not given up hopes for my father yet and if you could just be generous enough to allow me a little more time—"

"I could be very generous, Mistress Cheney," Taillebois interrupted, his hand resting lightly on her arm. "I believe I have made it quite clear that the debt would be entirely forgotten if only you would—"

"Marry you or else you will take legal action against me?"

"Ariane," he chided gently. "It is only that I worry so much about your welfare. I care for you deeply, my dear. If only you would allow me to show you."

Taillebois bent closer. Usually, Ariane would have discouraged his boldness, but this time she found herself appraising him with a surprising detachment. Physically, he was not repellent and she studied the smooth outline of his lips with frank curiosity. She thought back to last night, her overwhelming response to Renard's kiss, and wondered again if it might all simply have been owing to her own lack of experience.

Consequently, instead of wrenching away, she forced herself to remain still. Taillebois's eyes widened with surprise and gratification at this unexpected compliance. Leaning closer, he pressed his lips to hers. Ariane felt the warmth of his mouth, but that was all she felt.

Monsieur Taillebois drew back, smug and pleased with himself. Ariane doubted that he'd even noticed her lack of response. Renard would never have settled for such a tame reaction.

"My dear Ariane," Taillebois began, then stopped, inhaling his breath sharply at a strange harsh sound. The metallic scraping noise made Ariane flinch as well and want to cover her ears. Seeking the source of it, she twisted to glance behind her.

The Comte de Renard leaned against the side of Madame Jehan's shop, idly sharpening a large sword. How long he had been there, how much of her conversation with Taillebois he might have overheard, Ariane had no idea.

Certainly he had been present long enough to have witnessed the kiss, Ariane thought, her face flooding hot with dismay. Damn the man. How like him to turn up now at the worst possible moment.

Monsieur Taillebois looked as disconcerted as she. Only Renard appeared unperturbed. He made a great show of inspecting the steel, testing it for its sharpness before giving a satisfied nod.

Straightening away from the fence, he ambled toward Ariane, in his usual lazy fashion. Although smiling, there was a dark glint in his eyes.

"Good afternoon, Mistress Cheney. A fine fair afternoon for visiting the shops, is it not?"

"Well, I—I—yes," Ariane stammered. Yet it was none of Renard's affair whom she kissed. Still, she had a sinking feeling that the comte would not see it that way.

Resting the hilt across his palm, Renard displayed the formidable weapon. "Observe the magnificent workmanship, especially on the blade. Who would have ever imagined I would find such a splendid sword here on your tiny island? And fashioned by a woman, too. Mistress Paletot also makes some fine needles and pins."

"Yes, I—I am aware of that," Ariane said.

"I know most men these days prefer the rapier, but there is nothing like an old-fashioned broadsword for properly lopping off heads or any other body part one finds inconvenient." Renard added with a significant glance at Taillebois's hand, still resting upon Ariane's arm.

The merchant made haste to withdraw it as Renard stepped closer.

"And what about you, monsieur?" Renard asked. "Do you not think this is a most splendid weapon?"

"I have little interest in swords."

"What a great pity, Monsieur . . ."

"Taillebois." The man managed a stiff nod. "Andre Taillebois."

"Ah, the moneylender," Renard purred.

"Certainly not. I am no usurer." Taillebois drew himself up indignantly. "I consider myself a merchant banker."

"A fine distinction, monsieur. I would also wager the tax collector prefers to think of himself as a civil servant rather than a thief."

Taillebois quivered with outrage. Ariane hastened to intervene.

"You must not mind Monsieur le Comte. He is fond of making jests. Er—have you met the Comte de Renard?"

"No, but I have heard of him." Taillebois attempted a sneer. "The reputation of the Deauville family precedes him."

Renard's mouth flinched, the expression so slight Ariane was certain only she had noticed. She experienced a curious urge to fly to his defense.

Not that he needed it. As he loomed over Taillebois, Renard's heavy eyelids lowered to dangerous slits. "I am glad you have heard of me, monsieur. That saves so much time. Then you must be aware that I am the man who is going to marry Mistress Cheney."

"Renard!" Ariane's protest went ignored as he closed in on Taillebois. He continued to smile at the merchant, but it was difficult to say which looked more deadly, the blade in Renard's hand or the glint in his eyes.

Taillebois made an effort to hold his ground. "The entire island knows of your intentions, my lord. But you should know that Mistress Cheney has other suitors."

"Indeed. Anyone that I need worry about?" Renard asked softly.

"Well, I—I— Let me make myself perfectly clear on this point, milord—"

"No, let me make myself clear." Renard abandoned all pretense at amiability, raising his sword until it all but rested at Taillebois's throat. "If I ever catch you embracing my lady or hounding her again, you will end up kissing steel. Understand?"

Taillebois struggled to summon the courage to make some reply. He gave up the effort, spun on his heel, and fled down the street as though the devil was at his heels.

A ripple of laughter followed him. The little scene had drawn a crowd, apprentices leaning out shop windows, housewives and artisans pausing in their tasks. Monsieur Taillebois had never been a popular visitor to the island and Renard's routing of him actually drew a burst of enthusiastic applause.

Renard flourished the sword and swept all the onlookers a magnificent bow, while all Ariane wanted to do was sink beneath the nearest bushes. Another woman might have enjoyed being the center of a dispute between two men, but all she felt was foolish and embarrassed.

As the comte sheathed his sword, she choked, "Renard, how—how could you! Monsieur Taillebois was not even armed."

"A real man would have been or at least he'd have made haste to fetch himself a weapon instead of running away."

"Some men choose to conduct their affairs more reasonably than brawling like a street ruffian. Monsieur Taillebois is my father's chief creditor. I really cannot afford to have offended him."

"You didn't. I did." Renard cast her a grim look. "In fact, milady, your conduct toward him was quite the opposite. You told me last night I had no serious rivals."

"You don't. That—that is—it is none of your affair. And I am quite capable of chasing off my own suitors."

"You can certainly *try,* ma chère," he retorted. "Although you didn't make much effort with that fellow. What sort of coin did you decide to pay him with?"

Ariane's face flamed. She already felt ashamed enough of the mad impulse that had induced her to let Monsieur Taillebois kiss her. Renard's harsh words only added to her mortification. Swallowing hard, she spun away from him and charged off down the street.

She was dimly aware of people drawing respectfully back, the curious glances cast her way. Behind her, she heard Renard calling her name, but she only quickened her pace until she was all but running. He still caught up to her easily by the blacksmith's shop and drew her out of view behind the shed. His massive frame blocked any escape.

She employed her basket as a shield, fighting the prickling sensation behind her eyes. She would not complete her humiliation by crying, not after only this morning resolving to be stronger and wiser. She always had prided herself on maintaining a certain dignity. Now she had kissed two men within a span of twenty-four hours and made a public spectacle of herself as well.

Renard's voice was gentle. "Ariane, I—I am sorry. That was a rotten thing for me to have said to you about Taillebois. I didn't mean it. I—" He blew out a gusty breath, dragging his hand back through his hair.

Ariane struggled to maintain a stony profile, refusing to be beguiled by the warmth in his eyes, the coaxing note in his voice.

"Forgive me. I have little to offer in my defense except even you must admit it is a jolt for a fellow to come across his betrothed kissing another man in broad daylight."

"I am not your betrothed," she snapped. "And—and if I did kiss him, it was your fault."

"My fault?" Renard echoed, looking thunderstruck.

She tipped up her chin defiantly as she blurted out, "It is because of that kiss you gave me last night. I—I never expected. I have so little experience in these matters. I was only wondering . . ."

She trailed off, feeling more foolish than ever when Renard's eyes widened incredulously.

"You kissed Monsieur Taillebois to compare him to me?"

Ariane nodded, then cringed, bracing herself for Renard's laughter. But although a glint of amusement appeared in his eyes, all he did was smile at her tenderly.

"Ma pauvre chère, kisses are like sweetmeats. If one suits your palate, there is no need to sample all the rest."

Before she could prevent him, he plucked the basket from her hands and set it down in the grass at their feet. When he gathered her into his arms, she made no effort to resist, her heart tripping over itself. She was dismayed to realize that a part of her was more than willing to experience the dark magic of Renard's lips again.

She had to fight hard to remind herself of her vow, not to allow Renard to distract her before she obtained some answers regarding her troubling questions about the man. She turned her head at the last minute so that his mouth grazed her cheek.

Renard's lips whispered against her skin. "Ah, don't be angry, Ariane," he coaxed. "I am sorry if I displeased you by warning off Taillebois. But watching that jackal touch you made my skin crawl."

"Just tell me one thing," she said. "Do you intend to frighten off all my other suitors from now on?"

"Yes, if they be cowards or curs like Taillebois. No man could be worthy of you, my lady, who would give up so easily." The customary drawl was gone from Renard's voice, his words vibrating with a passionate sincerity.

He was like a battered knight, fully ready to fight for her, to defend her honor at any cost. The image was more appealing than Ariane cared to acknowledge. She tried to draw away from Renard, but his arms only tightened.

"Let me go, my lord," she said quietly. "I am hardly worth the effort of your championship. I will never have the kind of suitors who will merit the use of your steel."

"You would have if you did not hide yourself away on this island."

"Oh, yes," Ariane said dryly. "I daresay I would have scores of dashing men fighting over me."

"Not scores perhaps. You are like a quiet stream with hidden depths. But once a man discovers your beauty, he must find you unforgettable."

Renard's lips caressed her chin, then continued trailing kisses down the column of her throat. Ariane shivered, discovering that he did not need to claim her mouth to arouse her.

"Oh! P-please don't," she begged.

"Don't what?" Renard asked huskily. "Kiss you? Pay you compliments?"

"S-sound as if you meant them." Ariane managed to peel herself shakily out of his arms. "That—that is too much like Andre Taillebois. He is by far the worst of my suitors."

Renard managed to smile. "What? Even worse than me?"

"Oh, by far. Because he pretends to be in love with me. At least you are honest enough not to do that."

"No, I would never pretend that. But I do like and admire you, Ariane, more than any woman I have ever known. Is that not enough?"

At one time, Ariane might have thought so. She had convinced herself that she was not romantic, that if she ever did wed, she would be well satisfied with liking and respect. But Renard's words left an empty ache inside her.

Studying his face closely, she continued, "Monsieur Taillebois is both a greedy and foolish man. He did not propose to me merely in hope of being recompensed for his loan to my father, but the man actually harbors some stupid notion that I might know the alchemist's formula for turning lead into gold.

"What an imbecile! If I could do that, I would have paid off Papa's debts long ago. There could not possibly be any more reprehensible reason for wanting to marry a woman than believing she is a witch in possession of some secret knowledge."

Renard made no reply, but Ariane thought a strangely uneasy expression crossed his face. Ariane's stomach knotted with apprehension.

"That could not possibly be your reason, milord?"

"No, I have no interest in gold," Renard replied smoothly.

"And I don't suppose you are feeling ready to share with me what your particular reason might be for continuing to pursue me?"

Renard's shuttered expression became more pronounced. "When we are wed. That will be soon enough to bare my soul."

Before she could press him further, Renard countered by saying, "You are so keen to know my reasons for marrying, chérie. I might just as well ask why you are so determined to remain unwed."

"I am not." Ariane bent down to retrieve her basket. "But I do have to be more cautious than most women. I am the Lady of Faire Isle. Do you have any idea what that means?"

"It is a title of courtesy, bestowed upon the wives and daughters of the most prominent family on this island. As the eldest daughter of the Chevalier Cheney—"

"My father has nothing to do with it," Ariane interrupted. "Our laws here are different than elsewhere in France. Our land has been passed down through the women in the family for generations. I am respected, not because my father was a famous knight and soldier, but because of who my mother was."

"Let me show you something." She impulsively tugged at his hand.

Looking mystified, Renard followed her toward the center of town. Ariane led him into the open market area; once a pasture, it was now ringed in by shops and the imposing stone building that housed the merchants' guild and the public scales.

On fair days, the grassy area was thronged with visitors to the island, stalls set up by merchants who traveled from everywhere. But this afternoon, the square's only occupant was the towering stone statue of a lady in flowing robes, her arms outstretched in a gentle, welcoming gesture.

Towns in Brittany frequently had such memorials, but mostly honoring long-dead kings or warriors. The Faire Isle was the only place Ariane had ever known to pay such tribute to a woman.

The pedestal was as usual piled high with floral offerings. Many of the petals had fallen, partly obscuring the inscription. Setting down her basket, Ariane bent down to brush the dried blossoms aside until the words were fully revealed.

Evangeline, it read simply. *Our Lady of Faire Isle.*

Ariane remembered how outraged the local archbishop had been when the island people had erected the statue. Such a memorial had made Evangeline Cheney seem as though she was a holy martyr, the indignant prelate had groused, and only the church could confer such a distinction. But his protests had gone ignored.

She glanced up to find Renard close to her side, staring up at the memorial.

"Your maman?" he asked.

Ariane nodded proudly.

Renard studied the statue for a long moment, then his gaze shifted to Ariane.

"And this is a good likeness of her?"

"I—I believe so. As much as anything carved of stone could

be like the vibrant woman that my mother was. In a way, this memorial does not just represent her, but the long line of strong and noble women who came before her."

Ariane turned earnestly to Renard. "Like the rest of Brittany, we pay taxes to the king of France. And it is his provost who administers petty justice and conducts the business of the harbor. But there has always been a Lady of Faire Isle, a wise woman who devotes herself to the protection of the people of this island. Most often she remains unwed, passing her title on to a niece or a cousin. My mother inherited Belle Haven from my Great-aunt Eugenie."

"But your mother married."

"My mother was the exception."

"And this is why you are so determined to remain unwed? Because of some ancient tradition?"

"Partly. A husband is not always a blessing to a woman, Renard." Ariane glanced up at the statue, her heart constricting with the thought of all her mother had endured.

She started when Renard's hand suddenly closed on hers, his callused palm warm and rough against her skin.

"What happened with your parents is an all-too-familiar tragedy, but it would never be that way with us, milady," he said. "I am no longer a callow youth. My wild days are behind me. I know it is the custom for many men to take a mistress, but I would not wed you if I was not prepared to be true to one lady."

Ariane stiffened. He had just read her thoughts and this time there was no mistaking the matter. She stared up at him, her eyes wide with accusation. Renard apparently realized his mistake, for he released her hand, looking both vexed and uncomfortable.

"You just did it again."

"Did what?" Renard did his best to appear innocent.

"You read my mind."

"I—I *guessed* your thoughts."

"It was more than that! How else would you know about my father and—" Ariane flushed with shame. "His—his mistress?"

"I lived in Paris for a while. Regrettably I learned there about the Chevalier and the woman that he kept—"

"No, Renard, you didn't. You just learned of it from me. You *read my eyes.*"

"I have no notion what you are talking about, ma chère."

"Where did you learn such a skill?" Ariane demanded fiercely. "Who taught you the old magic?"

Renard flashed her a tentative smile. "Chérie, look at me. I am a simple fellow. It was a miracle that my tutors could get the mere rudiments of reading and writing through my thick head.

"There is no magic involved in my guessing your thoughts. You have a transparent face and—and I have learned to become a good observer during the course of my travels."

"What travels? Where?"

"Everywhere. Here and there."

"Damnation, Renard!"

Her swearing clearly took him aback, but Ariane had had all of the uncertainty and evasion that she could endure. She tugged the chain from beneath her gown. Practically wrenching it off her head, she slapped the ring, chain and all, back into Renard's palm.

"Here. Take your ring back right now."

Renard's heavy brows drew together in a warning frown. "You are breaking our agreement, chérie?"

"I most certainly am. You can scowl at me all you wish, but I refuse to have anything more to do with a man who is so secretive about his past that he will not answer the most simple question or part with any hint of the truth."

Their eyes met. Locked in a collision of will, this time Ariane refused to back down. It was Renard who shifted his eyes first, his lips tightening in exasperation.

"Very well," he said. "What is it you wish to know about me so badly?"

"Any small fact would be a good beginning. For instance, exactly where have you been all these years?"

"Traveling. To Paris, Italy, Greece, the Holy Lands. Anywhere but here."

"Why? What caused the estrangement between you and your grandfather? What did you do?"

"Nothing. I told you. My crime was in my birth." Renard dragged his hand down his face, the gesture rife with weariness. Then as though the words were wrung from him, he said, "My mother . . . was a shepherdess. My father fell in love with her and married her anyway. But in the eyes of my grandfather and his friends, I was considered base-born, a peasant. Very likely that is how you will now see me as well."

"No," Ariane said slowly. "I believe that nobility lies in character rather than the blood."

Renard gave a harsh laugh. "I am not sure I possess much of either. At any rate, now you know the great mystery behind Justice Deauville. Not nearly so romantic as if I'd turned out to be a pirate or some cutthroat bandit, but I trust you are satisfied?"

Was she? Ariane believed he was telling her the truth, but Renard was leaving something unsaid. She searched his face and for one startling instant, she was actually able to read his eyes. The man before her dwindled into a boy who despite his strength and overpowering size had no defense against the cruel wit of his grandfather, the slights and scorn of other nobles.

Renard was quick to hood his eyes and Ariane was almost glad of it. What she'd glimpsed had been too private, too painful. She felt somewhat ashamed for prying.

"I am sorry, my lord. When a man pursues a woman with such determination as you have done, it is only natural she should want to know, but I—I never meant to cause you any pain."

"If you wish to ease my suffering, you only have to resume our agreement. Take back my ring."

But when he held the ring out to her, she backed away.

"No, milord. And it is not because of what you told me about your mother," Ariane added hastily. "But this peculiar bargain of ours is very one-sided. I keep my promise to wear the ring, but you have not honored your pledge to leave me in peace."

"I only lingered in hopes of seeing you one last time. But I plan to leave the island this very day."

"Truly?" Ariane eyed him doubtfully.

"I swear it. I will not return again until you send for me. Indeed I have little choice. I have received word of some trouble I acquired back on my estate, due in part to you."

"To me?"

"Yes, I took your advice about dismissing my steward. It appears Monsieur le Franc has taken his revenge by stealing one of my horses and burning down a few of my laborers's cottages as he prepared to leave. The man has been captured and now it becomes necessary for me to live up to my name and administer a little justice."

"Oh, I am glad."

"Glad that Monsieur le Franc will be punished? Or glad that I am going?"

Ariane hardly knew how to answer that, especially as Renard drew closer. Before she could protest, he settled the chain back around her neck. His fingers lingered against her skin, slowly sliding to cup the nape of her neck, draw her forward.

Her heart hammered against her ribs as she realized he meant to kiss her.

"*No, milord,*" she said firmly so that he would know she really meant it this time.

"But ma chère, if you do not intend to use my ring, this will be the last time you will ever see me. Can you not find it in you to grant me just one brotherly kiss?"

His eyes held hers fast, his gaze warm and coaxing.

"Well, I—I—" Ariane faltered. She stole a furtive glance around to ascertain that no one was looking. "All right. Take your kiss. But do it quickly."

She closed her eyes, but she should have remembered that Renard seldom ever did anything quickly. He settled her into his arms and his mouth fastened over hers by slow degrees, starting gently, then flaring to an intensity that robbed her of breath. Her lips parted in a soft gasp, allowing him to deepen the kiss, the thrust of his tongue sending a flush of heat through her.

He kissed her, long and lingering, as though it truly was the last time they would ever meet, his mouth hot and hungry, caressing and bruising her with the force of his passion. Her blood pounding through her veins, her heart racing, Ariane issued a low moan and kissed him back just as desperately. It was like being caught up in a strong undertow. But before the man could entirely sweep her senses out from under her again, Ariane pulled her head back.

"N-no." She sighed. "You—you really must go."

"But I can't, ma chère." Renard whispered, his breath warm against her ear.

"Why not?"

Renard peered down at her, his green eyes narrow slits, simmering with heat, but a hint of mischief as well. "Because you have your arms wrapped so tightly around my neck."

"W-what?" Dazed, Ariane was mortified to realize it was true.

Flushing, she took a trembling step back, locking her arms firmly across her breasts as though to suppress any further temptation. The gesture appeared to amuse Renard, but there was a certain tenderness in his look as well as he reached out to stroke her cheek.

"Stay safe, my lady," he said. "And remember, you have but

to slip my ring on your finger to send for me. I will only ever be a thought away."

Then he strode away without looking back.

⚜ ⚜ ⚜

RENARD TRUDGED BACK TOWARD THE HARBOR, THE WARM GLOW FROM kissing Ariane already starting to fade, his boots growing heavier with every stride that took him farther away from her. He'd spent the better part of the morning trying to turn up some hint of what had really been going on at the convent last night, but to no avail. He'd almost begun to believe he was fretting over nothing until he had come across Ariane outside the apothecary shop.

His lady had appeared on the surface as though she had little more to worry about than her unwanted suitors. But she had been more pale than usual, faint shadows beneath her eyes telling him she had not slept well. Renard would have liked to believe it was thoughts of him keeping her awake last night, but he feared otherwise.

No, there was something else afoot, and every instinct he possessed, every desire, every wish dictated that he remain here on Faire Isle, keep a close watch over her. But there were the pressing matters of his estate that required his attention. He had no choice but to go.

Trying to shake off his sense of unease, Renard continued toward the Passing Stranger. He found Toussaint waiting beneath the creaking inn sign, the old man in a lather of impatience.

"Saints be praised. You have finally decided to come strolling back, have you?"

Renard quirked one brow in haughty fashion. "I wasn't aware I was keeping you waiting. When I left, you didn't seem interested in much else beyond wolfing your way through that partridge pie."

"Ah, don't be giving me any trouble, lad. I've already more than enough of it from that devil horse of yours."

"Hercules? Now what is wrong with the infernal creature?"

"He's been kicking all hell out of his stall this morning, to say nothing of biting two stable hands. I consider myself lucky to still be in possession of all my fingers." Toussaint held up one hand and frowned, as though checking that a thumb had not gone missing. "That great brute truly is bewitched. I could swear that he senses we are about to leave the island and doesn't like it."

Renard gave a vexed sigh, feeling in little humor for another battle of wills with his horse. "To tell you the truth, I am not very keen on leaving Faire Isle myself."

The old man's sharp eyes flew to Renard's face. His gruff voice softened a little as he asked, "What's wrong, lad? Did you find out there was something amiss at that convent last night?"

"No, and that is what is worrying me. I walked all the way up to the gates of St. Anne's, but I never saw any place appear more serene. I couldn't persuade any of the sisters to let me in, so I tried to exercise my charms upon some of the good wives of the town. I have never met so many ladies so good at keeping their thoughts to themselves. They are especially close-mouthed when it comes to any question from a stranger that involves Mistress Cheney."

"Women who won't gossip?" Toussaint asked in astonishment.

"Shocking, isn't it?" Renard said dryly. "It's enough to shatter all of a man's most cherished beliefs about women. Even Ariane. I thought when I met her by daylight, when I could see her face clear of shadows, I could read her easily, but she was still able to hide something from me. Even when I kissed her."

"She let you kiss her? Er, you haven't been using—"

"No, nothing but my own natural charm. The lady enjoys my kisses, although she'd probably jump into the harbor before she would admit that. I have never seen anyone so stubborn."

"You obviously haven't spent much time looking into a mirror."

Renard cast the old man a disgruntled look. He was astonished when Toussaint responded by clapping him heartily on the back.

"Well, congratulations, my lord. It appears you are on the verge of winning. Not only did you succeed in getting kissed, but if your suspicions are correct, your lady will soon be in some mortal peril. She'll be forced to use your ring and you can come charging to the rescue. I just hope you manage to get to her in time."

"If Ariane needs me, I'll be there. And who said anything about mortal danger to my lady? If there is any sort of problem, it belongs to someone else. Ariane would never be taking such pains to guard her own secrets."

"Ohhh, I see. Someone else's life will be at risk. Well, that makes everything all right then."

Renard glared at him. "You are being deliberately provoking, Toussaint. No one will be at risk. Ariane has my ring. All she has to do is use it to send for me."

"As long as the lady is not too obstinate to do so."

Renard stalked away from the old man. He wondered exactly when Toussaint had developed this truly annoying habit of telling him just what he didn't want to hear.

Renard hesitated outside the stable door, stealing one last glance at the sunlit town and harbor. Very likely he was conjuring up trouble that didn't exist, as old Lucy used to say. He had never seen any place appear more peaceful than the Faire Isle on this bright summer afternoon. How much difficulty could his lady possibly get into before he managed to return?

☙ ☙ ☙

ARIANE MADE HER WAY BACK UP THE STREET TOWARD THE CONVENT, balancing her basket on her arm. Renard was truly gone this time. Lingering near the blacksmith's shop where she had had a good view of the Passing Stranger, she had watched Renard mount his horse to ride away. For a moment, the issue had seemed doubtful, Hercules putting up quite a fight, rearing and plunging in the stallion's efforts to unseat Renard.

It had been a battle of titanic proportions between two mighty male creatures of strapping size and equally stubborn will. But Renard had won in the end, bearing down with his knees, tightening his grip on the reins. He had forced Hercules toward the road leading back to the mainland, closely followed by a fierce-looking old man on a dark gelding.

Ariane certainly had enough to contend with in her life without dealing with Renard's unsettling presence. And yet it was most strange . . . The street around her still bustled with its customary color and noise, but somehow her island already felt an emptier place.

Ariane tried to shrug off the melancholy sensation, but her heartbeat quickened when she heard the clatter of hooves approaching behind her. *Renard,* she could not help thinking. She might have known he'd never keep his promise to stay away. But her anticipation died when she saw that it was not the comte, but a troop of some half-dozen riders.

She shrank back as they passed, the lathered horses looking as though they had been ridden long and hard, the riders in little better condition, their cloaks travel-stained. The leader of the troop suddenly held up one hand, bringing the retinue to an abrupt halt. He twisted in the saddle and as he did so, his cloak fell back to reveal the bright blue tunic of the royal guard.

Ariane's mouth went dry. She possessed just enough presence of mind to draw farther into the shadows between two of the shops while the captain of the group wheeled his horse around, scanning the street with sharp eyes.

He beckoned imperiously toward a cluster of women who were goggling at him and his men. Most of them huddled near the apothecary shop, but Madame Elan, the potter's wife, had ever been a flirtatious creature. She sauntered over to flutter her eyes up at the leader of the guard.

Strain as she might, Ariane could only catch snatches of what was being said.

"Searching for . . . escaped convict. Dangerous man. Young, powerful stature, dark blond hair, beard, likely wounded . . . wanted dead or alive by warrant of the king."

Ariane pressed her hand to her lips. Despite all this talk of escaped murderers, she was certain these men were in pursuit of Captain Remy. Equally, she had no doubts about who had sent them. Not a king, but a queen. A dark queen.

Trembling, Ariane backed slowly away until she reached the alley behind the shops. And then she ran, bolting toward the convent of St. Anne's as though her life depended upon it.

Chapter Ten

*O*PEN IN THE NAME OF THE KING!"

The convent bell clanged, followed by the thunderous sound of a fist pounding against the convent gate. The impatient summons sent nuns scattering across the courtyard like a flock of frightened chickens.

"Stay calm, my daughters," Marie Claire commanded.

Ariane wondered how Marie Claire could manage to sound so calm. Her own heart was tripping in her chest as she watched Captain Remy plunked over Charbonne's shoulder, his arms dangling limply down her back. Straining under his weight, the burly woman carried him to the waiting farm cart and eased the captain down upon the makeshift bedding hastily assembled on the rough wooden planks.

Ariane sprang up beside Remy on the back of the wagon, praying his wound had not been torn open. The captain had taken a feverish turn during the night, but there was little to be done about it now, with the royal guard clamoring for admittance to St. Anne's. Perhaps it was a mercy that the young man was unconscious.

"We are going to kill him," Ariane said, pressing a vinegar-soaked cloth to his heated brow as the mother abbess came up behind her, fetching a blanket.

"Nonsense. He's a tough man." Marie Claire tucked the blanket around Remy carefully. "And what would happen if he stayed here? Even with my authority, those buffoons may very well ransack St. Anne's."

"They are telling everyone he is an escaped convict, Marie. If the soldiers capture Remy, they likely have orders to kill him on the spot."

"Very likely. So we must make sure he doesn't fall into their hands. If Charbonne takes the cart out through the vineyard onto the path through the woods, it will be rougher and longer, but you'll have a better chance of avoiding the soldiers."

"And what about you, Marie?" Ariane asked.

"Bless you, child. I am a tough old dragon. It won't be the first time I have breathed the fire of defiance. What are a few paltry soldiers compared to an archbishop? Besides, St. Anne's will be safe enough once Captain Remy is away."

Marie Claire carefully arranged the hay in the cart over the captain's inert form. Ariane moved to help her.

"I will do my best to delay the guard here in town as long as I can," Marie Claire said. "I did hope we would have more time to find the captain a safer hiding place. I never wanted you to have to bring him to Belle Haven."

Ariane hated the prospect of involving Gabrielle and Miri. But there was no sense fretting over what could not be helped.

"We have no other choice, Marie," she said. "Besides, no one has ever been able to locate our hidden workshop and there is a small room down there where I can place a pallet. It will not be the first time it has been used as a hideaway. Great-aunt Eugenie frequently used to offer sanctuary to poor women fleeing the abuse of their husbands."

"Hoodwinking a few drunken louts is not the same thing as routing a company of the royal guard. I wish your Renard was here with that new sword he bought."

"He is not *my* Renard and how did you hear about that?"

"When one creates that kind of stir in the town market, it does not take long for the tidings to spread. You know, this might not be a bad time to try out the power of that ring."

Marie Claire gave a grim smile, as though she were jesting, but only partly so. Ariane's hand closed reflexively over the outline of the ring beneath her gown, then she shook her head.

"The comte has left the island. Besides, it will not improve matters if Renard rushes in brandishing his sword and bashing heads."

"Perhaps not. Although occasionally a little bashing can be most useful, my dear Ariane."

As Charbonne clambered up onto the seat of the wagon and gave an impatient signal that they needed to be gone, Marie Claire reached up and pressed Ariane's hand.

"Go with God, my dear." She added in low urgent tones, "There is one other thing I must tell you and you may not be pleased. But I went ahead and sent word to Louise Lavalle in Paris requesting her help."

Marie Claire rushed on, "I know you did not want to spread the risk to others, but we desperately need information. If we are going to fight Catherine, it is far too dangerous to do it in the dark."

Ariane sighed. It was pointless to remonstrate now. And there clearly was no more time. As the pounding at the gate grew more insistent, Marie Claire signaled Charbonne to go.

Ariane did her best to keep the captain as comfortable as she could as they lurched away from the convent. With each jolt of the wagon, Remy uttered a low moan. Ariane bit down on her lip, torn between anxiety for him and her fear of seeing a squadron of soldiers come galloping across the vineyard after them.

She felt somewhat easier when they reached the crude path leading through the forest, but she continued to peer tensely behind her. Scarcely thinking what she did, she tugged the chain from beneath her gown, fretting with the ring.

When she realized what she was doing, she peered down at the ring. Small as it was, it felt like a warm, comforting weight in her hand. She had been so determined to be rid of the thing and Renard as well.

But somehow the man had once more persuaded her to keep to their strange pact. And not through threats and bullying this time. She had not been able to withstand the gentleness in his eyes, the warmth of his parting words.

"You have but to slip this ring on your finger to send for me. I will only ever be a thought away."

A thought away. There would have been a time she would have been completely convinced that she did not want Renard that close. He had alarmed her yet again with the fear he might be able to read her eyes.

But his explanation had seemed reasonable when he had finally been induced to tell her the truth about himself. He was the son of a peasant woman. Such a simple explanation, yet Ariane could well understand why he had felt the need to keep that part of his past hidden. It also might explain his faith in magic rings. Shepherdesses and other such people of the earth often cherished such notions. Renard very likely inherited some of his beliefs from his mother's people.

Still . . . Ariane felt oddly disappointed that there was not more to it than that, that the ring truly did possess some magic. She held the ring poised over her finger, overcome by an inexplicable temptation to try it. If the ring were magic, she could summon Renard back to her . . . just this once.

Ariane had the ring halfway down her finger, when she paused, amazed at what she was doing. The cart had lumbered deeper into the forest with no sign of any pursuit. She didn't need Renard, and considering the effect his kisses had on her, the man already seemed in danger of gaining enough power over her.

Ariane tucked the ring firmly back inside her gown.

K K K

THE SMALL ROOM OFF THE DOWAGER QUEEN'S BEDCHAMBER WAS forbidden to all, even her son, the king. The closet had been set aside for the queen's most private devotionals, complete with a gold-trimmed altar, crucifix, candles, and kneeler. But it had been a long time since Catherine had done any praying.

The kneeler shifted easily, becoming a lever that when pulled caused the entire altar to swing out, revealing a dark chamber beyond not unlike the hidden cellar at Belle Haven. The Dark Queen's workshop was of necessity smaller, the walls cramped with well-stocked narrow shelves. Ancient books to give Catherine access to forbidden knowledge, jars of herbs and powders to aid her with her brews, and the skull of some long-vanquished foe . . . simply because it amused the Dark Queen.

Lights from dozens of votive candles flickered over her determined features as she bent over her worktable, intent upon the formula she was mixing. She wore an apron over her stiff brocade to protect her gown, her plump fingers stripped of her costly rings. But that was more to protect the formula. Some of the mixtures she brewed were so delicate that the merest contact with any sort of metal might contaminate her efforts.

Seizing a small glass vial with a pair of tongs, Catherine waved it over the flame of a large candle, until the liquid turned bright red, bubbling like overheated blood. She held the vial closer to inspect it before giving a satisfied nod.

The brew would help her son Charles retain his sanity, and keep Catherine's grip upon the throne of France secure. But even with her potions, Catherine was not certain how much longer she could stave off his descent into complete madness.

All her children were proving a disappointment. Her first-born, poor Francis, had been of a sickly constitution and had died only a few years after his coronation. Charles showed signs of faring little better, although the weakness was in his mind rather than his body.

Catherine pinned most of her hopes of retaining power on her third son, Anjou, clever, ambitious, and charming. If only she could keep the boy from gaming, drinking, and whoring himself to death before it was his turn to ascend the throne.

And then there was her daughter, Margot, wild and rebellious, vowing she would not go through with Catherine's plans to wed her to the king of Navarre. She was in love with the duc de Guise, a handsome, greedy nobleman who would be only too pleased to use a union with Margot as an excuse to lay claim to the throne himself.

Margot was not the only one raising objections to her approaching marriage to the Protestant king of Navarre. His Most Catholic Majesty of Spain had raised an outcry against it. Phillip had been warning Catherine for some time that she had better find an effective way of suppressing the spread of heresy in her country or he would do it for her. Of course, everyone knew the wretched man was merely hungry for any excuse to invade France.

There were rumblings among the Huguenots as well, suspicious and uneasy about the proposed wedding, even more so since the sudden death of the queen of Navarre. It didn't help matters that Captain Remy was still out there somewhere, roaming loose with evidence of Catherine's crime tucked in his purse.

She needed matters to proceed smoothly. That wedding had to take place. It was her surest way of dealing with both the threat from Spain and further Protestant rebellion. All she had to do was make sure she prepared a proper reception for all those wedding guests.

Catherine turned her attention to the second bottle on her worktable, a large glass flagon filled with a cloudy liquid, a mixture she had been steeping for weeks. Catherine shook the flagon, the sediment shifting, becoming even more viscous until it looked like mist captured in a bottle. Almost ready.

Catherine smiled, contrasting the bloodred of her son's medicine to the cloudy liquid in the other bottle.

One potion to prevent madness. Another to induce it . . .

Catherine was startled from her thoughts by a light tapping sound. It came from the outer door to the altar room. Her lips thinned with displeasure but she supposed the interruption scarcely mattered since she was finished here . . . for the present. Removing her apron, she pocketed her son's medicine and locked the other brew carefully away.

Extinguishing the votive candles, she emerged into the outer room. One tug on the kneeler and the entire altar shifted back in place, concealing the hidden room just as the knocking sounded again.

Catherine composed herself to appear as though she had just risen from her knees and was mighty displeased to have her prayers disrupted.

Swinging open the door, she peered coldly at the young woman who sank into a deep curtsy. A petite blonde beauty, the chit's courage far outstripped her size. Gillian Harcourt was by far one of the boldest members of Catherine's elite Flying Squadron.

"What do you want?" Catherine demanded. "You know well my orders that I am never to be disturbed when I am at my devotions."

The beauty mark at the corner of Gillian's lip quivered as though the woman suspected how little praying went on in the queen's closet. But one basilisk stare from Catherine was enough to wipe the smirk from her face.

"Forgive me, Your Majesty," Gillian said, kneeling before her. "But you asked to be informed at once when Louise Lavalle arrived for her audience."

"Yes, I suppose that I did," Catherine said, frowning. "Very well. I will receive Lavalle in the antechamber, but do not make a habit of this impertinence, mademoiselle."

"No, Your Grace." Gillian made haste to kiss her hand.

By the time Louise Lavalle was escorted into the Dark Queen's presence, Catherine had arranged herself carefully so that the light spilling through the antechamber windows would fall full upon the face of the young courtesan and not on hers. The chair that Catherine occupied was high-backed and intricately carved. Although not as elaborate as the king's throne, all of Paris knew which was the true seat of power.

Louise Lavalle seemed suitably aware of it. The red-haired beauty sank into a deep obeisance before Catherine, her eyes swept down. Catherine did not immediately give her permission to rise, her gaze narrowing as she studied the girl.

Louise possessed a voluptuous figure, her gown cut low to call attention to her generous décolletage. She had enhanced her charms after the current court fashion by rouging her nipples, but otherwise she employed no cosmetics. She had a fresh face, her nose and cheeks dusted with a smattering of freckles that gave her an impression of innocence men seemed to find attractive.

She was a witch of course, but Catherine did not hold that against her. Most of the successful women whom she knew were, and Louise was an accomplished seductress. In the past Catherine had attempted to recruit Louise's talents for her own use, an offer that Louise had politely but steadfastly refused.

After a lengthy scrutiny, she finally said, "You may rise, Mademoiselle Lavalle."

The girl straightened in one graceful fluid movement. "Thank you, Your Majesty. You do me great honor to grant me an audience."

"I was intrigued when I received your request for a private interview. I wondered why mademoiselle should make such a request."

Louise folded her hands meekly before her and peeped at Catherine through the thickness of her lashes. They seemed ridiculously long, actually casting shadows over her eyes. "Your Majesty once made me an offer that I was unwise enough to decline. An offer to join your elite squadron of ladies. I was hoping— That is, I was wondering if it was too late for me to reconsider."

"Perhaps not. But I confess I am astonished to hear you say so. When you refused my offer, you made it quite clear you were doing well enough on your own."

"Alas, not any longer. My protector, the duc de Penthieve, cast me off in favor of a new mistress."

"Truly?" Catherine murmured. "I had heard that it was quite the other way round, that you had grown bored with His Grace."

"Oh, no, Your Majesty. The fault was mine. I have been doing a poor job of managing my own affairs."

Catherine leaned forward, doing her best to engage the young woman's eyes. But Louise had a frustrating way of fluttering her lashes as she spoke, keeping her expression quite blank. Catherine's attempts to probe yielded nothing.

Of course it was quite possible that there was little to read, that Louise's mind was that empty.

"I realize now that any possibility for real advancement lies only in Your Majesty's service," Louise said with an ingratiating smile.

"I never thought you were that interested in advancement or wealth or power, Mademoiselle Lavalle. Only in your own pleasure."

"At some point, a girl has to give thought to the future, Your

Grace. I am not getting any younger. And once beauty fades, well!" Louise hunched one pretty shoulder. "I have never placed much faith in those tales of women holding a man spellbound by wit and conversation alone."

"Indeed," Catherine replied dryly. She rose slowly to her feet and paced around Louise, studying the girl from every angle.

Mademoiselle Lavalle remained quite calm and composed during this intent inspection. It was just possible the girl was telling the truth.

"Very well," Catherine said. "You may become one of my ladies, Louise."

"Oh, thank you, Your Grace." The girl started to sink into a curtsy, but Catherine's hand flashed out to stop her.

Cupping Louise's chin, she forced the girl to look up. Louise lowered her lashes.

"Only understand one thing, mademoiselle. Once you enter my service, I require complete loyalty, unquestioning obedience no matter what I ask you to do. There will be no turning back. Your soul will become mine. Do you understand?"

Her soft words produced the reaction Catherine desired. A ripple of fear coursed through Louise and her eyes fluttered open wide. The briefest flicker, but it provided Catherine with all the window she needed inside the girl's head.

"Y-yes, Your Majesty," Louise said.

"Good," Catherine replied, reading the courtesan's eyes. She released Louise abruptly, turning away before the courtesan could guess that with that single stare Catherine had drawn out all her secrets, Louise's real reason for coming to her, and even more important than that . . . who had sent the girl.

Catherine tensed with a surge of anger and fear, but before she shifted back to face Louise, her more turbulent emotions were already controlled beneath a bland smile. "Then I shall direct that quarters be prepared for you here at the palace with my other ladies."

Louise was profuse in her thanks and Catherine offered her hand to be kissed. Both of them wearing their best masks, Catherine thought dryly. Only Louise's had slipped. As she backed away, Catherine detected the hint of triumph in the girl's smile.

The little witch was good, Catherine had to give her that much credit. Just not good enough to be sent to spy on the Dark Queen. As the antechamber door closed behind Louise, Catherine uttered a vexed oath.

"Mon Dieu, Marie Claire, was this the best you could do?" she muttered scornfully. "When you were at court, you used to be a little more adept at handling intrigue. You have clearly been at your rosaries too long."

It might have been almost amusing except that Catherine's brief glimpse into Louise Lavalle's mind told her that her worst dread had come to pass. Captain Remy had reached the Faire Isle and spilled out his story to Ariane Cheney.

It would do no good now for her royal guard to track the man to the island. Neither the captain nor the gloves would be found. It would take more than a company of soldiers to match wits with the women of Faire Isle.

She needed aid from a different source, a far more ruthless weapon to wield. Summoning Gillian Harcourt to her, Catherine said, "I want you to locate a certain man here in Paris for me."

Gillian stretched languorously. "And seduce him."

"No, fool. Just find him and fetch him here to the palace under the cover of darkness. I need to see Vachel Le Vis."

"Le Vis?" Gillian was unable to conceal her horror at the mention of the name. "The—the witch-hunter?"

"Yes, you have some objection?" Catherine demanded with an icy lift of her brows.

"N-no, Your Highness," Gillian said. "It is only that—that—well—Le Vis. He is a dangerous fanatic, Your Grace. It would be like seeking to deal with the devil himself."

"Nonetheless, I want him brought to me and secretly. No one else is to know of his visit, do you understand?"

"Yes, Your Grace," Gillian said, although it was clear she didn't. Her usual pert manner was markedly absent as she left to carry out Catherine's command.

Catherine fully comprehended the woman's revulsion. To have dealings with a witch-hunter was the worst thing any daughter of the earth could do. But Catherine had broken nearly every other commandment thus far. She could hardly stick at this one.

There was one fact of life her lady-in-waiting did not understand that Catherine had grasped a long time ago. Sometimes it was necessary to deal with the devil in order to survive.

Chapter Eleven

CAPTAIN NICOLAS REMY STAGGERED THROUGH THE NARROW BY-ways of Paris, pain knifing in his side. He felt dazed, unable to remember what he was doing here, filled with a sense of urgency, a need to escape. But the streets twisted and turned like a maze.

No matter how hard he ran, he ended up back at the glove-maker's establishment. The proprietress loomed in the doorway, her teeth glinting as she held out to him his leather purse.

But as he stumbled closer, he reeled back in horror. It was not a pouch at all, but the head of his queen, Jeanne of Navarre. The shopkeeper assumed the shape of the Dark Queen. Catherine de Medici's cold eyes taunted him.

"The Great Scourge," she mocked. "Did you ever truly think to defeat me?"

Laughing, she tossed the head at his feet. When Remy bent, trembling, to retrieve it, he saw that it was not Jeanne at all. The sightless eyes of his young king, Henry, stared back at him.

Remy groaned and forced his eyes open. Heart thudding, he lay still for a moment, shaking off the last wisps of his nightmare. He tossed his head on his pillow, fighting to regain his bearings.

Wherever he was, he was certainly no longer at St. Anne's. He was shut up in a small room, cramped and confined as a cell, the darkness only broken by a single torch flickering over the rough stone walls.

It was like being in a tomb. Remy shuddered. With shaking hands, he touched his own face, half-dreading to feel the cold rigor of a corpse.

"Am—am I dead?" he whispered.

"Not quite," a voice replied.

Remy twisted toward the sound, realizing that someone watched him from the doorway of the room. Gazing directly at the torch hurt his eyes and he squinted, able to make out no more than the silhouette of a woman.

"Who—who is there?" he rasped fearfully. "M-mistress Cheney?"

"Yes," she said.

But it was not Ariane who emerged cautiously from the shadows. Remy's breath caught painfully in his throat as a vision in blue approached him, a young woman whose beauty was beyond a mere soldier's ability to imagine.

Long golden hair spilled in shining ringlets around a face of alabaster perfection, fine arched brows, a slim straight nose, and full carnelian lips. Her every movement whispered of silk and some sweet elusive perfume.

She peered down at him with a tentative smile and he still didn't know whether he was in heaven or hell. The lady possessed the beauty of the brightest seraphim, but her blue eyes held the haunting sadness of a fallen angel.

"You—you are not Ariane," he said hoarsely.

"No, I am her sister, Gabrielle."

Gabrielle . . . she even had the name of an angel. Remy stared, too dazed to speak. When he attempted to moisten his parched lips, she moved to pour him a cup of water from a pitcher that had been left on a crude table.

He was too weak to lift his head from the pillow and she was obliged to support his neck to press the goblet to his lips. Remy swallowed, the liquid cool and soothing upon his throat, but he was equally conscious of the feel of Gabrielle Cheney's fingers against the nape of his neck.

Remy's experience with women was that of a soldier, limited to the simpler, coarser class of female. He had never realized a woman's touch could be so warm and soft. Even as he sipped at the water, he could not tear his eyes from her face.

"So . . . you are Mistress Cheney's sister. Then you also must be a witch. I—I beg your pardon. I mean a wise woman."

A ripple of amusement crossed Gabrielle's face. "You needn't be so tactful with me. I don't mind being called a witch, but unfortunately I have misplaced my magic."

"Where did you lose it?"

Gabrielle's smile turned brittle. "In the hayloft of a barn."

The conversation only added to Remy's confusion and he struggled to focus on something that would make sense.

"Where am I and—and how did I get here?"

"I have no idea how you got here, but you are now hidden in one of the dungeon chambers beneath our home at Belle Haven."

Remy frowned. So he had been moved from the convent to Ariane Cheney's own home. The Dark Queen's soldiers must have traced him to Faire Isle.

A jolt of alarm surged through Remy and he made an effort to rise. A sharp pain bit through his side, leaving him gasping and his head spinning. Gabrielle placed her hands upon his shoulders to restrain him.

"Lie still," Gabrielle commanded.

"But—but, I must go. I put you all at risk by staying here."

"I don't know who is after you, but they will never find you here. At Belle Haven, we are very good at keeping things hidden."

Remy made another futile effort to sit up that only left him feeling dizzy and frustrated. "I should have been long gone from here. I need to return to my king."

"Your king?"

"Yes, I—I serve Henry of Navarre."

"Truly?" Gabrielle's remarkable eyes shifted over him as though she doubted he could be of much service to anyone. Remy suddenly felt acutely conscious of how he must appear to this elegant young beauty, weak and bedraggled, haggard, and totally naked beneath the thin layer of blanket. He had never worried a day in his life over how he appeared to any woman, but now he tugged the blanket higher across his bared chest.

"Could—could you possibly fetch me my clothes?"

"Yes, but I doubt it would do you any good. You don't even have the strength to lift your trunk hose, let alone put them on." She dimpled with a mischievous smile. "And I certainly am not going to help you."

"No, of course not, mademoiselle. I would never expect that, but—but I endanger you every moment I linger. The soldiers—"

Gabrielle touched his brow lightly. "You still seem to be a trifle feverish. I am not that skilled in the healing arts. I had better fetch Ariane."

"No, wait!" Before she could pull away, Remy caught her hand and held it to him. He felt strangely loath to let Gabrielle Cheney go, although he scarcely knew what he wanted with her. Perhaps just to look at her a little longer.

Her bright blue eyes softened as she promised, "Don't worry. I will be back to sit with you later."

She eased her hand away with another dazzling smile and then she was gone. Remy stared weakly after her, feeling light-headed. Ariane Cheney might choose to call herself a wise woman, but Remy had no doubt that her sister was an enchantress of the most dangerous kind.

※ ※ ※

ARIANE BENT OVER HER WORKTABLE, GRINDING MADAME JEHAN'S powders in the bowl, hurrying to brew another dose of medicine for Captain Remy. She had one ear cocked for any untoward sound above stairs. Leon had been posted on the road, instructed to alert her if there was any sign of a mounted troop approaching Belle Haven. Thus far all remained quiet.

Adding a splash of wine to the powder, Ariane stirred the brew, then proceeded to measure out a dose into a small vial.

"Ariane?"

Ariane jumped at the sound of Gabrielle's voice. Besides Captain Remy, she had thought herself quite alone in the catacombs beneath the house. Her hand shook so badly, she was obliged to set down the vial before she dropped it.

"Gabrielle! You frightened the wits out of me. What—what the devil are you doing here?"

"I thought I lived here," Gabrielle replied with a faint arch of her brows.

"You know what I mean. I believed that you and Miri were in the orchard. What are you doing down here?"

"Well, among other things, I was trying to discover why we are hiding a man in our cellars."

Ariane had counted it a fortunate thing that Miri and Gabrielle had been out of the house when she had returned with Remy. The less her sisters knew of this dangerous affair the better, especially if the soldiers did come. But she had been foolish to hope she could keep anything concealed from Gabrielle for long.

"My dear, this is nothing for you to worry about," she began.

"Nothing to worry about?" Gabrielle cried. "Ariane, you have a naked man lying barely conscious in the next room."

"You have been back there to look at him?" Ariane asked in dismay, then the import of her sister's words registered. "He is stirring at last?"

"Yes, he is awake. Or at least he was when I left him."

"Then I must go to him at once."

"Not until you tell me what is going on, Ariane."

"Gabrielle, please. I have no time for explanations. Just go back upstairs. I don't want you and Miri involved in this."

Gabrielle cast her an exasperated look. "Miri is so occupied right now in nursing an injured fox she found, I doubt she will even notice you have a man hidden in the house. As for myself, it is hard for me to become involved, since I don't have the vaguest notion of what *this* is."

She peered suspiciously at the remains of the medicine Ariane had been mixing. Unfortunately her gaze lighted upon the small wooden box where Ariane had stored the de Medici gloves.

"What's this?" she asked, reaching to open the lid.

Ariane slammed her hand down upon the box. When her sister stared at her in surprise, Ariane grimaced, realizing her nervous behavior would only rouse Gabrielle's curiosity further.

"What have you got in there?" Gabrielle demanded.

"Nothing to interest you." Ariane shifted the box farther away from her sister. "Just some—some powders I got from Madame Jehan, very sensitive to—to the light so they must be treated carefully. I needed them to brew medicine for Captain Remy."

"And just why are we hiding *Captain Remy*?"

Ariane was going to have to offer her sister some sort of explanation. "Nicolas Remy is a great hero of the Huguenot army. They call him the Scourge or some such. He serves the king of Navarre."

"He mentioned something about that."

"You spoke to him?" Ariane asked in alarm. "What else did he tell you?"

"Not a great deal, and when he started talking about his king, I thought he might still be a bit delirious. Is he highly placed in the king of Navarre's service?"

Gabrielle's voice sounded light, but something about the question caused Ariane to study her sister's face. Gabrielle's lashes swept down, blocking Ariane's effort to read her eyes. But given Gabrielle's avowed ambition to find herself a king, any interest she displayed in Navarre could not be good.

"Never you mind," Ariane told her sister sharply. "Neither Captain Remy nor his king are of any concern to us."

"Then why are we helping him? I don't even understand why this Captain Remy is a fugitive. Isn't there supposed to be a truce between Huguenots and Catholics because of the proposed marriage between Princess Margot and King Henry?"

"Apparently, there are—are complications, too lengthy to be explained."

"Do try, Ariane." Gabrielle said, folding her arms with a stubborn smile. "I have all the time in the world."

"Well, I don't. It doesn't matter why Captain Remy needs our help. Here on Faire Isle, we have never refused aid to any honest man. So Gabrielle, if you would please just . . . just . . ."

"Run along and play?" Gabrielle's lips thinned. "I am not Miri, Ariane. I think when you choose to hide some dangerous stranger in our cellar, I am old enough to be told about it."

Ariane realized there might be another reason behind her sister's questions than mere curiosity. "Oh, dearest, forgive me," she said, ashamed of her own insensitivity. "I never thought what it would mean to you to have some stranger beneath our roof. But I promise you Captain Remy is a good man. You don't need to worry that he would ever offer you the least insult or—or—"

Gabrielle regarded her blankly for a moment, then as comprehension dawned, she flushed. "My God, Ariane. I wasn't worried about anything like that. In his current state, Captain Remy couldn't ravish anyone and I fully know how to look out for myself."

"Yes, but I fear the mere presence of a strange man here must stir painful memories—"

"Any wound I have ever felt is long since toughened over," Gabrielle said. "Or at least it would be if you would stop probing."

Gabrielle's haunted eyes told Ariane otherwise, but when she attempted to press her sister's hand, Gabrielle shied away from her and flounced up the circular stair. Ariane winced as the trapdoor slammed closed behind her.

Well, Ariane sighed, she had managed to get rid of her sister, but not in the way she would have chosen. Why couldn't she seem to make Gabrielle understand that all she wanted to do was to take care of both her sisters, protect them?

The wooden box containing the gloves remained in full view, perhaps not the wisest place to leave it, knowing how determined Gabrielle could be when her curiosity was aroused.

Ariane's gaze roved around the workroom, seeking an adequate hiding place. Shifting the ladder, she carried the box up to the topmost shelf, shoving it far back behind some cobwebs. Gabrielle might claim to be undaunted by men, but she had a deathly fear of spiders.

※ ※ ※

FOR THE NEXT THREE DAYS, THE DARK QUEEN'S SOLDIERS PROWLED Faire Isle, searching for Captain Remy. The royal guard descended upon Belle Haven, poking and prodding through every corner of the estate, even tossing through the hay in the barn. But they were eventually obliged to depart in frustration to continue the hunt elsewhere.

By the third day, word reached Belle Haven that the soldiers had given up and left the island. A sense of relief settled over the household, shared by everyone except Miri Cheney.

She wandered through the house like a disconsolate shadow. No one even remembered what day it was, Miri thought resentfully, that the time had come to pay homage to the stone giants at the cliffs of Argot.

The ceremony appeared in danger of being forgotten with Papa still away at sea and her mother gone. Not that Miri was sure Maman had entirely believed in the ancient ritual, but she had always paid honor to the old ways. At the moment, Ariane seemed able to think of nothing but that wounded soldier she was hiding and whatever mysterious work kept her busy in the workroom below stairs.

Miri's only hope for a companion on the pilgrimage to the giants rested with Gabrielle. And that, she feared, was a slim hope indeed. But she trudged upstairs in quest of her sister.

She was disgusted to find Gabrielle lying abed in the middle of the day, her golden hair wrapped up in a veil. Her elegant gown discarded, she was stripped down to her shift, some glistening white concoction patted on her face.

"What on earth are you doing, Gabrielle?"

Her sister popped open one eye. "Treating my skin to keep it fair, which is something you might give some thought to instead of always running around in the sun like a little gypsy."

Miri's eyes roved over the mess Gabrielle had made in mixing her ointment, her frown deepening when she saw the cracked eggshells.

"The hens are not going to like you wasting the fruits of their labor for something so frivolous."

"Pardon me if I am not overly concerned about the opinion of someone who is eventually going to end up on my dinner plate. If anyone is distressing the hens, it is likely you, bringing home that fox."

"Renard is quite healed. I already released him."

"*Renard?* You named the fox after Ariane's suitor?"

"No, the name belonged to the fox first. I daresay the comte stole it from him."

Gabrielle started to smile, then froze as though any movement would be enough to disrupt her skin treatment.

Miri drew up a stool close to the bed. She could not help recalling how differently things had been other summers. By this time Papa would have already herded all of them into the wagon to make the journey to the cliffs of Argot. The wood for the bonfire would have been loaded, the supper they would share with the giants packed up into the basket. She and her sisters would have been laughing and chattering with excitement, Maman smiling with indulgence.

Miri suddenly felt very lonely. She cast an aggrieved glance at Gabrielle, who appeared on the verge of drifting off to sleep.

"I suppose you are trying to look beautiful because of that Captain Remy we are hiding," Miri said scornfully.

That caused both of Gabrielle's eyes to pop open. She eased up onto her elbows to scowl at Miri. "How do you know about him? I am surprised you even noticed he was here."

"I am indifferent to men, not *oblivious,*" Miri replied with dignity. "It would be difficult not to notice something was amiss when those soldiers came tramping through the barn and stables looking for the captain, upsetting all my poor animals."

She added grudgingly, "However I did feel a little sorry for the man. When I sneaked down to the dungeon to peek at him, he looked very old and sick."

Gabrielle plunked back down upon the pillow, closing her eyes. "I am astonished you were allowed to see him at all. Ariane guards the man like a dragon. But if you had been able to obtain a better look, you would have seen that Captain Remy is far from old. I suppose it was his beard and his pallor that fooled you. He is quite young, and when he is not recovering from a wound, I would imagine he is also rather vigorous."

Miri stubbornly shook her head. "His body might be young, but his soul is not. If you look at his eyes, it seems he has seen too many bad things. Sometimes I am afraid your eyes are getting like that."

With obvious effort Gabrielle forced a placid expression. "I can't read eyes and if I did have that ability, I wouldn't waste it on Captain Remy. He is only a common soldier."

She paused, then asked in a softer tone, "Er—but what else did you read in Remy's eyes? Perhaps you noticed something in his eyes about—about—"

"About what?"

"About . . . about his king."

Miri had a feeling that was not at all what Gabrielle had meant to say. Her sister rushed on, "I am only interested in the captain because he serves the young king of Navarre."

"A king." Miri sniffed. "What about the giants?"

"I beg your pardon?" Gabrielle drawled, shifting to a more comfortable position.

"*The stone giants.* The ceremony."

"Oh, that."

"Am I the only one who recalls the respect due to the old ones? I cannot even get Ariane to take the time to speak of it."

"Our older sister is much preoccupied these days, with weighty matters that appear to be far too taxing for we *children* to understand," Gabrielle said with an acid bite to her voice that told Miri her two sisters must have been quarreling yet again. Small wonder she preferred the company of her animals.

"Even if Ariane will not take time for the ceremony, you and I must go," Miri urged her sister.

"Tramp all the way up those cliffs to prance around in the moonlight before some huge blocks of stone? You have to be jesting."

"But Gabrielle—"

"You need to concern yourself with something more important, like brushing out your hair once in awhile."

"You brush your hair quite enough for the both of us and—" Miri bit down hard on her lip to swallow the rest of her retort. "Oh, *please,* Gabby. This is so important. Come with me, just this one last time."

"No, Miribelle. Visiting the giants is pure foolishness. Now go away and stop bothering me. I cannot keep talking. The pomade is starting to harden."

The pomade wasn't the only thing, Miri thought, studying the taut set of her sister's mouth. Gabrielle twisted onto her side, turning away from her, and Miri gave up her pleading with an unhappy sigh. But as she stood up and trudged toward the door, Gabrielle called after her.

"And don't you even think of sneaking up there alone either. Ariane will have your hide if you go off by yourself. Until we are sure those soldiers aren't coming back, she wants all of us to stay close to the house."

Miri stalked out of the room. Neither Gabrielle nor Ariane could understand. *She* had to go and for a reason too frightening to discuss with either of her sisters.

Her nightmare of the blood-soaked city and its terrible bells was growing worse, presaging some great evil that was drawing steadily closer. An evil that might be placated if she paid proper respect to the stone giants. Perhaps attending the ritual would not work, but it would certainly be better than another night of tossing upon her bed, sleepless and afraid.

Miri crept back downstairs, fearful that Ariane might come upon her and read from her eyes what she was about to do. Stealing a furtive glance behind her, she didn't breathe easy until she was safely out of the house. Then she raced to fetch her pony for the journey to the one place where she was sure there was still some magic left.

✺ ✺ ✺

THE LIGHT WAS FADING AS MIRI LED HER PONY UP THE STEEP HILL-side, murmuring encouraging words in Butternut's ear. The path ahead was rugged, most of the vegetation stripped away from the rocky surface of the cliffs, forcing her to proceed carefully.

Below, the dark ocean lashed against the cove, its foam breaking against the defiant rocks in a wild slash of spray. The sight was dizzying and Miri tried not to look down, fighting back the tangles of hair that the wind whipped into her eyes.

Somehow she had forgotten how wild and remote this part of the island was, far different from the sheltered valley that housed Belle Haven. Or perhaps the journey up the cliffs of Argot had not seemed nearly so daunting other years with Papa's strong hand clasping hers.

She hugged close to her pony and trudged onward until she could see the summit of the rocky hill, the massive circle of dol-mens silhouetted against the twilight sky. Miri paused to catch her breath, heartened by the sight. Her Maman was lost to her, perhaps her Papa as well. Her sisters were acting different and strange. Her beloved pony was growing old. But at least this was something she could count upon never to change . . . the stone giants standing as fixed and immutable as ever.

The rising moon bathed the ring of towering stones with a solemn and mysterious beauty. Ariane claimed the dolmens had been erected in a time long ago when the arts of engineering had been better understood, and that the circle was in fact some an-cient way of charting the movement of the heavens. But Ariane always tried to find a logical reason for everything.

Miri put more faith in the old tale of a race of gentle giants who had once inhabited the island. When superstitious fools from the mainland had threatened them, the Earth Mother her-self had worked her magic to shield them, turning them all to stone. Miri wondered how anyone could doubt the story. This was not a place of science and reason, but magic and legend.

Urging her pony onward, Miri ascended higher up the hill. She caught the first tang of wood smoke, telling her that someone had already lit the bonfire.

While the thought pleased her, it caused her eager steps to slow as well. Although she had known most of the people from Port Corsair all her life, she still felt shy around anyone not from her immediate circle of family and servants. Other years, she had had the comfort of her father to cling to, or she could fall back to stand in the shadow of Maman and her sisters.

When she heard the hum of voices, she halted completely. The wind carried the sound to her, a high-pitched intoning of some odd guttural words she did not understand. The chanting had an eerie quality to it that caused the hairs at the back of Miri's neck to prickle. She didn't recall any such strange song ever being part of the ceremony before.

"What do you make of that, Butternut?" she whispered.

The pony whickered, clearly wanting to return to the bottom of the hill. But Butternut had never liked high windy places. The chanting increased in pitch and intensity, rendering Miri uneasy, but she had come too far to retreat now.

She led Butternut to where he would receive some shelter from the widest of the standing stones. Miri had never in her life had to tether any creature to keep it from straying. Patting the pony's mane, she looked deep into Butternut's eyes and murmured, "You stay here, please."

Then she crept round the side of the stone giant, determined to investigate before she revealed herself. A bonfire illuminated the clearing in the center of the stones, a cluster of strapping girls dancing around the crackling and leaping flames.

These girls were none she recognized from the town. The

faces reflected by the firelight seemed coarse and frightening to Miri.

She was being silly again. No doubt they were only peasants from some of the isolated cottages dotted beyond the cliffs, a wild breed of folk who scratched out a living by fishing the rougher waters on this side of the island.

The young women undulated their hips, beat at their breasts, and tore at their hair in a frenzy. One buxom wench with a heavy bosom and an unkempt mane of dark hair raised her thick arms to the heavens and gave a piercing shriek.

"Oh, great Comte Ashtoreth. Look down and find favor with your handmaidens. Choose one of us to be your bride."

Miri frowned. Who was Ashtoreth? What was this nonsense about taking a bride? Everyone knew that the giants were all women.

The other girls fell to their knees before the flat altar stone in the center of the ring. They moaned as though in some strange ecstasy, while the buxom one swayed and brandished a knife.

"Oh, come to us, great horned one. We offer a sacrifice in your honor."

A sacrifice? Miri craned her neck for a better look and her blood ran cold. The altar stone, usually laden with floral offerings to the giants, was bare . . . except for something dark bound to the flat rock. Something living. It struggled and stirred, lifting its head, enabling Miri to make out the form of a small black cat.

Its amber eyes seemed to pierce the darkness, sensing Miri's presence in the shadows. The cat set up a plaintive yowl that she understood as clearly as if the creature had called out to her.

Help me. Please.

Even as the cat yowled, the dark-haired girl loomed over the altar, raising the knife.

"No!" Miri cried, charging forward.

Her shout caused all the girls to freeze, the chanting dying abruptly away. Miri hurled into their midst, shoving the dark-haired girl out of the way. She flung herself in front of the altar stone.

"Get back," she shouted. Snatching up a stout branch, she brandished it at them. "You leave this poor creature alone. You—you wicked barbarians."

Miri's unexpected appearance stunned them all for a moment, even the dark-haired one hesitating before she demanded, "And just who would you be, foolish mortal? Who dares to interrupt our witches' sabbath?"

Before Miri could reply, one of the other girls tugged urgently at the dark-haired one's elbow.

"Berthe, that's the Cheney girl from across the island," she said fearfully. "She's a real witch."

Berthe's eyes slid uncertainly over Miri, then she sneered. "Bah, she is only a weak little girl."

"I'll show you weak," Miri said, raising her stick like a club. "Come a step closer and I'll break your stupid head open. And—and put a curse on you besides."

Her fierce words caused most of them to draw back, but Berthe cast a contemptuous glance at her companions.

"What? Will you be frightened by a child? Seize her!"

Most of the girls hesitated, but urged on by their leader, a few of the bolder ones inched forward, trapping Miri against the rock, ringing her in on all sides.

A lump of fear rose in Miri's throat, but she was determined to go down fighting. Curling back her lip, she emitted a savage snarl. She lashed out from side to side with her branch, but the girls only leaped back laughing and taunting her.

Then they fell on her like a pack of jackals. Miri fought desperately, biting, kicking to no avail. She was dragged to her knees, her arms pinioned roughly to her sides. Berthe strode forward and seized her so brutally by the hair, Miri's eyes watered.

She wrenched Miri's head back, gloating down at her.

"So you wanted to save the cat. Well, perhaps we don't need him any longer. Maybe it is you we should sacrifice."

With a wicked grin, Berthe laid the knife alongside Miri's throat. Heart pounding, Miri closed her eyes and braced herself.

"Hold! You daughters of darkness."

The voice came like a call on the wind. For a moment, Miri believed she had imagined it, then she heard the indrawn hiss of Berthe's breath. The hand holding the knife at her throat seemed to waver, as did the others that were holding her down.

"Heaven save us," one of the girls muttered. "Who is that?"

A surge of hope rushed through Miri, but as her eyes fluttered open, her relief died. She felt as daunted as any of her attackers by the sight of her rescuer.

Firelight caused his shadow to loom up against one of the rocks, but he seemed scarcely more than a shadow himself as he glided closer across the grass. Tall and thin, he was robed entirely in black, his cowl pulled far forward, obscuring his face.

"Let that girl go," his voice rasped from the depths of his hood.

After a brief hesitation, Miri felt herself abruptly released. Even Berthe's hand fell to her side as the phantom loomed closer, his long robe rustling across the grass.

"By the order of the Malleus Maleficarum, I command you to cease your hellish practices here at once."

"He—he's a witch-hunter," someone shrilled.

Girls screamed, and stumbled, colliding with one another in their haste to flee. Berthe dropped her knife, nearly trampling over Miri as she bolted to escape. The weapon fell inches from Miri's knee.

Miri reached out to seize the knife. Although her own heart was hammering with fear, she scrambled to her feet and bent over the altar stone. The cat emitted a plaintive cry.

Even as she feverishly sawed at the ropes, Miri tried to

soothe the little creature. "Don't be afraid. I am not like those other foolish girls. I am a true daughter of the earth."

The cat blinked up at her. *I know.*

As the last of the bonds fell free, the cat staggered to its feet. It was not entirely black as Miri had at first supposed, its paws as white as though they had been dipped in snow. Miri scooped the cat gently into her arms, the poor thing so thin, she could feel the ridge of its bones beneath its matted coat of fur.

"Don't worry," she whispered. "You will be safe, but we have to get out of here."

But as she turned to flee, she collided with a wall of black, the hooded phantom who had crept up behind her far more solid than he had appeared from across the grove. A terrible silence ensued, broken only by the crackling of the bonfire and Miri's own frightened breathing.

She was alone with the witch-hunter. Her eyes took in the details of the flames embroidered on the hem of his robes, the fiery crosses emblazoned on the sleeves that signified his dreaded trade. Shrinking back against the altar stone, she cradled the cat protectively in her arms. As the witch-hunter reached up to draw back his hood, she sucked in her breath, bracing for some truly hideous visage.

But the face revealed was that of a boy. Although about a foot taller than Miri, he did not appear much older than she. Lustrous black curls tumbled over his brow, his smooth cheeks as yet showing no hint of beard. His skin was milk white, providing a startling foil for his dark brows, thick lashes, and intense dark eyes. All she could do was stare at him, spellbound. He was quite the most beautiful creature she had ever seen walk upright on two legs.

"Are you all right, mademoiselle?" he asked gruffly.

Miri released a long breath and managed to nod. "Who—who are you?"

"Simon Aristide," he said proudly. "A servant in the order of Malleus Maleficarum."

Malleus Maleficarum . . . the Hammer of the Witches. Miri shivered. Even she knew this was the most fanatic of orders, their sole purpose to track down and destroy sorceresses. Yet as Miri's gaze roved over the handsome boy standing before her, those dreaded crosses embroidered on his sleeves made no sense.

"You . . . you truly are a witch-hunter?" she faltered. "But I thought all witch-hunters were old and ugly."

"Odd. I have always believed the same about witches."

"But I am not a witch."

"I never said you were," he said gravely. His smile broke free in spite of himself, softening his face and lighting his eyes. Miri stared deeply into them.

She had never been as good at reading human eyes as she was with animals. She was not foolish enough to believe she could trust any creature simply because it walked on all fours and bore fur. Sadly, some became irreparably damaged by contact with the world of man.

Simon's eyes sparkled like the distant stars. Besides, it was clear the little cat trusted him. The creature actually purred as Simon stroked it beneath the chin.

"And so what is a little girl like you doing out here alone at night?" he asked.

"I am not a little girl," Miri protested. "I would wager I am as old as you."

"I am fifteen," he said, puffing out his chest a little.

"Well, I am . . . am fourteen," Miri replied, stretching the truth by a few years.

"You don't look much more than eight."

Miri bridled, starting to indignantly refute the claim when they were interrupted by a distant shout.

"Simon? Simon Aristide?"

The boy's smile fled. He stiffened away from Miri like a soldier called to attention. Whirling around, he shouted back into the darkness. "Over here, Monsignor."

Miri heard a footfall, the sound of heavy boots dislodging stone. Another figure emerged into the grove, an older man, shorter and stockier than Simon, but far more alarming. His robes were of blood-red satin, his hood flung back to reveal a rough-hewn visage and bristle of white hair.

Miri's pulse skittered and she felt the cat tense in her arms. It reached up one white paw to tap urgently at her chin, its eyes glowing up at her.

You must flee, daughter of the earth. Now!

But as though sensing her fear, Simon glanced back to offer her a reassuring smile. "It is only my master, Monsieur Le Vis. You needn't be afraid of him. You've done nothing wrong."

Miri smiled back at him, trying to draw comfort from his words. But she watched anxiously as Simon stepped forward to make deep obeisance to the older man.

Monsieur Le Vis stared at Simon, his heavy mouth twisting in displeasure. "You there, boy! I told you not to march so far ahead of the rest of us."

"Forgive me, Monsignor. I saw the smoke from the bonfire and was too eager to wait."

"Yes, these islanders have been at their hellish rites tonight just as I supposed. It would have been a good place to begin our hunt except now you have given them all a chance to flee with your clumsy barging in."

Simon ducked his head. "I am sorry, master, but—"

"Silence. I need none of your excuses. Well, at least you have managed to capture one of these daughters of darkness."

Miri shivered, realizing that the man was staring directly at her. Simon positioned himself in front of her.

"Oh, no, Monsignor. This is a child who I managed to save from the witches."

"I am not a child," Miri cried. Although she trembled, she tilted up her chin proudly and continued, "I am not a daughter of darkness either. My name is Miribelle Cheney and—and I am the daughter of the Lady of Faire Isle and the Chevalier Louis Cheney, the greatest knight in—in . . ."

Miri's voice faltered, realizing at once she had said something terribly wrong. Even Simon was regarding her strangely, his look somewhere between wariness and disbelief.

Monsieur Le Vis thrust Simon out of the way, stalking closer.

"Well, well, Miribelle Cheney, is it?" he rasped. "It is the wrong sister, but she will serve our purpose. Excellent work, Simon, my lad."

Miri swallowed hard, shrinking farther away from him as Le Vis's face was more fully revealed by the firelight. Deep pit-like scars were embedded in his skin, one eye drooping slightly lower than the other.

Far worse was the blank expression in his eyes. They were empty and flat as murky glass. As Le Vis stalked closer, the cat's fur bristled and he hissed at Miri.

Run.

Heart leaping into her throat, Miri whirled to do so, but it was already too late. More shadowy figures were emerging into the clearing, the circle of stones suddenly alive with robed phantoms.

Miri glanced wildly about her for a route of escape but there was none. As the witch-hunters closed in on her, she shrank down. Clutching her cat, she closed her eyes, sending up a fervent prayer for the Earth Mother to turn her to stone.

❦ ❦ ❦

ARIANE RUBBED HER EYES AS SHE TRIED TO STAY AWAKE. SHE HAD no idea what time it was. Shut up in the workroom, it could be nearly dawn for all she knew. The candles certainly had burned far lower in their sockets and were in danger of guttering out.

She had been laboring for hours and with no success. The beautiful white gloves were laid out before her like an elegant mockery, refusing to yield their secrets. A half-dozen chafing dishes lined up in a row, filled with the fibers she had carefully removed from the garments and the various solvents she had brewed to test them.

She had uncovered nothing malevolent so far. Whatever poison Catherine had employed, all the science in Ariane's ancient texts was proving useless in aiding her detection. Either the Dark Queen knew of some substance older than anything recorded by a daughter of the earth or she had developed her own.

This was one of the few times in her life when Ariane actually wished she was better versed in the dark arts. She scarcely knew what to try next.

As she turned over the possibilities in her mind, her hand crept toward the ring on the chain around her neck. She frowned, realizing she'd developed a habit of fidgeting with Renard's ring every time she felt tense or worried about something.

Four days had passed since she had parted from Renard in the market square, four days in which she constantly expected him to turn up on her doorstep, or spring at her from out of nowhere.

He had kept his word this time. The man was truly gone, but Renard's own words kept coming back to haunt her.

"No man could be worthy of you, my lady, who would give up so easily."

But that was ridiculous. She didn't care if he gave up. After all, she was the one who had wanted him gone, wasn't she?

Then why did she feel this hollow sense of disappointment when another day slipped by with no sign of him? It was almost as though . . . as though she missed Renard, which was quite absurd.

And yet she was constantly beset by memories of his wicked, teasing smile, of the banter they had shared, of the way he could make her laugh even when she tried so hard not to, coaxing her out of her solemn, serious self, even if only for a little while. Most of all, she kept remembering the dark, sweet heat of his kisses that had stirred such unexpected fire within her. She could not stop herself from wondering where those passionate embraces might have led if she had not insisted upon sending him away . . .

Into trouble, that was where, Ariane reminded herself firmly. Despite the tug of attraction she felt, the comte was still a stranger to her. A seductive smile and a devastating ability to kiss were not good enough reasons for any woman to marry, let alone the Lady of Faire Isle, who had to be so careful of her choice.

Besides, it was not a husband she needed, but answers to the riddle of those wretched gloves. Ariane tucked the ring and chain back inside her gown and turned her dispirited gaze back to her experiment. Yawning, she packed the gloves away, resolving to make further tests after she had obtained a few hours sleep.

But as she started to rise, Ariane was alarmed by thumping at the hidden entrance above. Before she could respond, the trap door was wrenched open.

One of the older servants all but stumbled down the stairs in her haste. Agnes's face was as white as her nightcap and for a moment the woman was too breathless to speak.

Ariane rushed to the stairs, peering up at her. "What is it, Agnes? What's wrong?" she asked sharply.

"Oh, m-milady. You . . . must come at once. Ch-charbonne is here to fetch you."

Ariane's heart went still. There was no good reason Marie Claire would have dispatched Charbonne to her.

"Dear Lord! The soldiers have not returned, have they?"

"No! F-far worse." Agnes pressed her hand to her heart, the old woman looking like she was going to drop from sheer terror on the spot.

"*Witch-hunters!* Here on our island, milady. And they have taken Mistress Miri."

Chapter Twelve

THE PALLOR OF A GRAY MORNING HUNG OVER PORT CORSAIR.
Shop windows remained closed, doors were locked, even the
customary bustle of the harbor seemed muted, the men going
silently and grimly about their work.

A cluster of frightened women gathered about the notice
nailed to the door of the market hall. They fell back respectfully
when Ariane arrived. She passed through the group, closely followed by Charbonne and Gabrielle.

Several of the women curtsied and Ariane did her best to
calmly return the greetings. But as she drew closer to that piece
of parchment fluttering in the wind, she felt a chill sweep through
her that had nothing to do with the brisk morning air.

Mounting the steps of the hall, she trapped the paper against
the door with her fingers and read.

NOTICE TO THE PEOPLE OF PORT CORSAIR

You are hereby directed, commanded, and required, that if anyone knows of any person reputed to be a witch, that it should be revealed to this tribunal, especially if that person is suspected of such foul practices that cause injury to men, cattle, or the fruits of the earth. The withholding of such evidence shall be deemed to be a crime punishable by death.

VACHEL LE VIS
Grand Master, Order of the Malleus Maleficarum

Ariane stared at the notice, a cold lump of fear settling in her throat. Vachel Le Vis . . . there could have been no more dreaded name to any wise woman. A merciless fanatic, Le Vis had already cut a swath through the south of France with his torturing and burnings. By the time he had finished practicing his hellish trade, there had scarcely been a daughter of the earth left alive.

Swallowing hard, Ariane tore the notice from the door and rent it slowly to pieces. She heard an awed gasp from the crowd of women behind her and was glad no one could see the way her hands trembled as she tossed the bits of parchment into the wind. She needed to appear calmer than she ever had in her life as she turned back to face the women of Port Corsair.

A throng of faces gazed up at her, many of them plainly terrified, some merely anxious, and a few, like Gabrielle, bristling with defiance. Ariane wished she could have forced her sister to remain behind at Belle Haven, but short of chaining Gabrielle in the old dungeon, there would have been no way to do so.

She looked up at Ariane, her chin resolute, her blue eyes as fierce as a soldier waiting the order to attack. Ariane directed her attention to the crowd instead.

"So where are these foul creatures?" she called out. "Does anyone know what they have done with my sister?"

Her questions produced a barrage of shouted replies, some of them verging on hysteria.

"She's being held prisoner at the church."

"They'll torture her, make her give up other names. We'll all be arrested and burned," someone shrilled. Madame Elan, the potter's wife, began to sob. Others appeared in danger of joining her when a gruff voice called out.

"Oh, stop that caterwauling. It won't help a thing."

Madame Jehan shoved her way to the front of the group. At least one woman in town did not appear to be losing her head, although the elderly apothecary had more reason to fear than anyone.

She was the epitome of what the witch-hunters would be looking for, with her wild white hair tangling in the wind, rheumatism gnarling her fingers in the chill morning air.

But her eyes were calm as she informed Ariane, "This is all the fault of those ignorant chits on the far side of the island. From what I have learned, they were turning the old ceremony of the giants into some sort of witches' Sabbath when little Miri tried to stop them. That is when she was arrested."

"Witches' Sabbath!" Madame Jehan rolled her eyes and snorted. "I don't know where these young girls today get such nonsense."

"From those superstitious fools over on the mainland," Mistress Paletot, the swordmaker, piped up.

"The next thing you know we'll have these idiot girls attempting to ride broomsticks," someone else called out.

"The world would be a far better place if wise women were in charge," said Madame Jehan. "No more foolish wars, no more ignorant suppression of ancient learning, and best of all no more witch-hunters. Melusine had the right idea when she mounted her rebellion to restore power to the daughters of the earth. Maybe we should take her example."

"And would you have us adopt her methods as well?" Ariane

admonished. "Poisoning wells, blighting crops, cursing cattle with infectious disease. We are daughters of the earth, madame. We are meant to use our knowledge to heal, not destroy."

Madame Jehan folded her arms stubbornly across her scrawny chest, but the old woman looked somewhat abashed by Ariane's solemn reminder.

"For all her knowledge of the dark ways, Melusine failed in the end. Her peasant army was defeated by the king's soldiers, but not before a good many innocent people had died. Melusine's excesses only gave the authorities more excuse for the persecution of other wise women. She was as much a danger to our kind as any witch-hunter."

"Nor was she all that clever." Madame Paletot spoke up. "I heard tell that the witch-hunters got her in the end. She was burned the same as any poor old helpless woman."

Madame Elan quavered, "So—so what are we to do, milady?"

Anxious faces turned toward Ariane, a score of expectant eyes asking the same question. Ariane's heart sank, for she didn't have an answer. The situation was far worse than she had thought. Girls attempting to hold a black Sabbath, giving the witch-hunters an excuse to cut a swath through Faire Isle.

I should have known such nonsense was going on and been the one putting a stop to it, not Miri, Ariane thought. As the Lady of Faire Isle, it was her responsibility to be aware of all that was taking place on the island, to be vigilant, to protect these women, even from themselves.

Ariane looked out over the circle of tense faces. "The best thing that you can all do now is go home, go about your daily tasks, show these witch-hunters we are not afraid."

Madame Elan cried, "Are y-you certain we should not flee now? While there is still time?"

"Trying to run would be the worst thing you could do. It will only be taken as a sign of your guilt and you will be tracked down. Besides, where would you go? The Faire Isle is your home. Will you be so easily frightened away?"

"Mistress Cheney is right," Madame Jehan said. "We must not give way to panic. Now all of you be off to your homes and allow the Lady to handle this matter."

The group began reluctantly to disperse, many saying to each other in comforting tones, "Yes, let the Lady deal with the witch-hunters. The Lady will find a way to protect us."

The murmurs carried back to Ariane, falling heavily upon her ears. The level of trust these women placed in her was almost terrifying. What if she failed not only Miri, but the rest of the island as well? She feared that she already had, by allowing these witch-hunters to ever set foot upon Faire Isle in the first place.

The square slowly cleared, leaving only herself, Charbonne, and Gabrielle. At least her sister didn't look as though she expected Ariane to perform some sort of miracle, Ariane thought.

As she descended the steps of the market hall, Gabrielle challenged, "So what *are* you going to do, Ariane?"

"Well . . . to begin with, I had better see this Vachel Le Vis and discover where Miri is being held. I want you to return with Charbonne to the convent and—"

"Oh, no, I am going with you, Ariane."

"I think it would be best if I had a chance to speak with Le Vis alone."

"Speak with him? To what end? You can't reason with a witch-hunter, Ariane. There is only one sort of persuasion those devils will understand and it is *this*."

Gabrielle wrenched open her cloak. For once her elegant sister had abandoned her fine silks for a plain workaday gown. But what truly alarmed Ariane was the sword that Gabrielle had strapped about her waist.

"Sweet Jesus!" Charbonne exclaimed.

"Gabrielle, where did you get that thing?" Ariane cried.

"From Captain Remy."

"He *gave* it to you?"

"Not—not exactly."

Gabrielle tried to avoid her eyes, but Ariane cupped her chin and read the truth with a single piercing glance. "Oh, Gabrielle! You took it from him and left him struggling to get out of bed to stop you?"

Gabrielle tossed her head with an air of angry impatience. "I had no time for any display of foolish male heroics. Agnes will look after him. I am more worried about my sister."

"And so are we all, but you rushing about brandishing a sword will help nothing. Now keep that thing hidden until you leave town." Casting a nervous glance around her, Ariane tugged Gabrielle's cloak closed.

"Do you think I don't know how to use it?" Gabrielle asked fiercely. "I remember all that Papa ever taught me."

"Yes, just enough to get you killed. I already have one sister in danger. I don't want to risk another as well."

"But I should be the one to pay, not Miri." Gabrielle's eyes blazed up at her. "Don't you understand? What has happened to her is all my fault. I refused to go to the cliffs with her. I should have known she would go off on her own. I didn't even notice when she failed to come to bed last night. When I fell asleep, I thought she was out in the barn with her animals, still sulking."

A tear splashed down Gabrielle's cheek and she dashed it furiously aside. Ariane longed to envelop her in a tender hug, but she knew how little Gabrielle would welcome such comfort.

Instead she attempted to soothe, "Dearest, it is more my fault than yours. I have been so preoccupied lately. Unfortunately, deciding who is to blame won't help Miri now."

Ariane ventured a light touch to her sister's hand. "Please, Gabrielle, do as I ask. Go with Charbonne to St. Anne's and at least give me time to assess the situation before you go rushing in ready to lop off heads. Who knows? I may require you to rescue me as well."

Ariane tried to smile, make it sound like a jest, but they both knew it wasn't. Gabrielle regarded her for a long moment, then muttered in grudging tones, "Very well. But if you are not back with Miri in one hour, Ariane, I am coming after both of you."

Ariane watched as Charbonne led her reluctant sister toward the main street leading up to the convent. But it was not until the two women vanished from sight and Ariane found herself utterly alone in the middle of the usually bustling square, that she allowed her rigid mask of control to slip. Her shoulders sagging, she pressed a trembling hand to her lips.

Witch-hunters here on Faire Isle, preparing to set up their tribunal! Such a thing had never occurred in the island's entire history under the rule of any other Lady. And the first victim could well end up being her own sister.

"Oh, what am I going to do?" she whispered, giving way to a moment of pure despair.

She stumbled over to the memorial to Evangeline Cheney. Ariane needed her mother's counsel so desperately, she felt as though she could have risked attempting to invoke Evangeline's spirit again, right then and there in the middle of the town. But no doubt the witch-hunters were already busily gathering evidence against the women of Faire Isle. She didn't need to offer them any more.

Instead she stared up at her mother's statue, her eyes raised in mute appeal.

Oh, Maman, give me the strength and wisdom to deal with this.

༓ ༓ ༓

THE CHURCH DOOR CREAKED AS ARIANE THRUST IT OPEN AND slipped inside. She blinked, the interior more dark than usual on such a gray morning, the stained-glass windows appearing muted with no sunlight flowing through them.

St. Anne's was a plain stone church, with high vaulting arches and a long nave that stretched up to the altar. During mass, the interior was usually crowded with the stools of the parishioners, the nuns cloistered behind a screen.

But this morning the church appeared empty except for the glow of candlelight coming from the direction of the altar. But as Ariane moved deeper into the nave, a man in a long black robe emblazoned with fiery crosses suddenly blocked her path.

"Halt! State your name and purpose for being here," a youthful voice demanded.

Ariane's gaze swept over the witch-hunter, arrested by the sight of his face, young and handsome, dark curls spilling over his brow.

"Since this is a church, I would have thought my purpose in being here was obvious."

"In case you have not heard, this holy place has been temporarily commandeered for our prosecution of those involved in the crime of witchcraft."

"*Persecution* would be a better choice of word. More shame to you."

Her rebuke clearly took the boy aback. But he stiffened, repeating more sternly, "Your name and purpose, mademoiselle."

"I am Ariane Cheney, and I want to see Monsieur Le Vis. I have come to demand the release of my sister, Miribelle."

"O-oh." The boy's bravado faded like a puff of smoke, a hot tide of guilty color surging into his pale cheeks.

The boy knew something about Miri, Ariane realized. She stepped closer, capturing and holding his gaze. The boy's eyes were so clear, it was an easy matter to read his thoughts.

"You were there," Ariane accused. "You were with Miri when she was taken and you know that she is innocent."

The boy's gaze skittered away from hers. "I—I am only an apprentice. It is not my place to determine innocence or guilt."

"Then you should never have promised Miri she would be safe."

"But—but how could you possibly know?" His face paling, the boy stumbled away from her. "I—I will just go tell the Grand Master you are here."

Ariane stalked after the boy, heading toward the front of the church and saw that a table and chair had been placed directly below the dais. A pair of gold candlesticks had obviously been confiscated from the altar. They rested near a stack of books perched on the table's gleaming mahogany surface.

A man with a stubble of white hair sat behind the table, scratching away with a quill pen, his bloodred robes in startling contrast to the earnest youthfulness of the boy in his jet-black attire.

The lad bent over the table, whispering urgently, but the older man never looked up from the parchment he was working on. He gave an impatient nod, then lifted one hand in a dismissive gesture.

The boy beckoned Ariane, as though he was half-afraid to say another word. As she came closer, the young witch-hunter melted into the shadows, disappearing through the side door.

She approached in an unnerving silence, broken only by the relentless skritch of the pen. She was given full leisure to study the Grand Master of the Order of Malleus Maleficarum.

So this was the dread Vachel Le Vis. He had a harsh face, deeply pitted, but Ariane had seen men scarred by the pox before. His thin mouth hinted at cruelty and intolerance, but there was nothing especially alarming about that either.

Only when she stood directly before the table and he at last glanced up at her did she understand how Vachel Le Vis was able to inspire such fear. It was his eyes, one drooping slightly below the other, so cold and soulless, Ariane was afraid to attempt to read them, to delve beyond that glassy expression.

They measured each other for a long moment. Then Le Vis

tossed down his quill and said, "I am Vachel Le Vis, the Grand Master of—"

"I know who you are," Ariane cut in. "I have heard of you. I am Ariane Cheney."

"I have also heard of you, mademoiselle," Le Vis interrupted softly. "You are the one they call the Lady of Faire Isle."

Le Vis made her title sound like an accusation. He might as well have called her a witch.

Le Vis leaned back in his chair, folding his hands across the front of his robe. "And exactly what is it I can do for you, Mistress Cheney?"

"I have come about my sister Miribelle, whom you have wrongfully imprisoned. I demand that you release her at once."

"I regret that that is quite impossible, mademoiselle. Your sister has been detained on suspicion of witchcraft."

"My sister is no witch," Ariane replied coldly. "Nor is she like most of your usual victims, monsieur, some poor nameless peasant girl. Our mother was Evangeline Cheney, a noble lady well loved on this island and respected in much of Brittany. Our father is a heroic knight, much decorated for his service to France during the Spanish wars."

"Ah, yes, the Chevalier Louis Cheney. A good man, but alas long absent from these shores. No doubt it would grieve him mightily to learn that one of his daughters has sold herself into the service of Satan."

"Miri has done no such thing."

"She was caught near the old ring of pagan stones preparing to take part in a witches' Sabbath and animal sacrifice."

"That's ridiculous. Miri would never harm so much as a hair of a single living creature."

"We have evidence. We have the cat in our possession."

"Oh?" Ariane arched one brow sardonically. "And are you planning to persuade this cat to offer up testimony against her?"

Le Vis forced a light laugh. "Contrary to what you might

think, mistress, I am not a superstitious fool. No, I have a human witness. Young Simon Aristide."

"That boy who was here awhile ago? If he speaks the truth, he will tell you Miri had no part in any witches' Sabbath."

"Aristide knows his duty. He will say what is appropriate."

"Or in other words, whatever lie you put in his mouth," Ariane retorted angrily.

Le Vis's eyes flashed. "Have a care, mademoiselle, or you may soon find yourself up on charges yourself."

"Knowing the way that you and your kind work, I am surprised that I'm not already." Ariane compressed her lips, knowing that she was being foolish to provoke Le Vis.

"Gabrielle was right," she muttered. "It was a waste of time my coming here. Any trial you hold will be pure farce. You decided upon my sister's guilt the moment you arrested her."

Pivoting on her heel, she started to stalk out of the church.

"Wait!" Le Vis shouted after her.

Ariane faltered halfway through the nave, her pulse thudding. She expected that at any moment Le Vis would summon his guard and have her seized. But she refused to run. It was too undignified, and it would not do her any good.

Instead she forced herself to turn and stare imperiously back at him. He was poised before the altar, but he did not look as though he was preparing to have her arrested. A strangely speculative expression had settled over his coarse features.

"Your sister's situation is indeed grave, Mistress Cheney. However, I acknowledge that she is scarcely more than a child who has possibly been led astray by bad influences. A pardon might yet be obtained with true repentance on her part . . . and some cooperation on yours."

"If you think I am going to give you names, accuse other innocent women in order to—"

"No, I have no interest in that. I was speaking of compliance of a different sort."

A thin smile carved Le Vis's lips and suddenly Ariane feared what he might be hinting at.

"No, not that either." Le Vis sneered, apparently comprehending her reaction. "I was not speaking of cooperation of a carnal nature. I have never tainted myself with the feel of a woman's flesh nor do I ever intend to do so."

"Then what is it you want from me?" Ariane asked.

Le Vis leaned closer. He had colorless lashes that fluttered over his cold eyes like pale sickly moths.

"Captain Remy," he whispered.

"W-what?" Ariane said, her heart going still.

"Surrender the captain to me, and the property that he stole, and your sister will be set free."

Ariane gaped at Le Vis, stunned into speechlessness. How could he possibly know about Remy and the gloves? Unfortunately there was only one way that he could, only one way that made sense.

She was a fool not to have made the connection sooner.

"My God," Ariane said hoarsely. "Catherine sent you."

"If you are referring to our good and glorious queen, yes, I do have the honor to serve that great lady."

"Great lady." Ariane all but choked. She shot the Grand Master a look of complete contempt. "You are either a hypocrite or a fool, Monsieur Le Vis. You come here prepared to trap and torture innocent women while at the same time, you are being employed by one of the worst sorceresses France has ever—"

"Silence! It is treason to speak of Her Majesty that way. I could have you arrested at once."

"Why haven't you? Isn't that what Catherine sent you to do?"

Le Vis seized her wrist. "There is only one thing saving you or any of the women on this wretched island and that is the queen's mercy. Give me Captain Remy and the stolen gloves and my tribunal will depart and leave in peace."

"I have no idea what you are talking about." Ariane attempted to pull away from him, but Le Vis tightened his grip.

"Don't try my patience, witch. You have until sunset to comply."

"And if I don't?"

"Then I will march your sister into the square to administer my first test to prove she is a witch."

"The first test?" Ariane faltered.

"The ordeal by water."

Ariane felt herself pale. "The—the ordeal by water? But that test is never used here in France."

"A fact I intend to remedy. I'll admit our English brethren have little to teach us, but some of their methods in dealing with witches are to be admired. Your sister will be taken to the pond in the square, her hands bound. She will be thrown into the water. If she floats, that is proof she is a witch."

Le Vis continued, clearly relishing every detail. "However, if your sister sinks to the bottom, as any honest woman would, she will be proclaimed innocent."

"But she will also be drowned."

"Then we will accord her a Christian burial."

"Damn you! This is no test of anything. It is a death sentence."

"Your sister's fate is entirely in your hands, mademoiselle, not mine. You can put a stop to these proceedings right now. Just give me Remy and the gloves."

Le Vis released his crushing grip and Ariane fell back. She rubbed her throbbing wrist, daunted by the choice that Le Vis offered her, Remy's life for her sister's. How could she ever agree to such a hellish bargain . . . and then again, how could she not? But even if she did betray the young captain, could the witchhunter truly be trusted to keep his word?

Although repulsed by the prospect, she forced herself to stare into Le Vis's eyes. Ariane shuddered. It was like plunging into an icy lake, murky and fathomless. She felt pulled deeper and deeper into a dark place that held no room for reason or compassion.

She realized it would not matter to Le Vis if she did surrender Captain Remy. The Dark Queen's command had given the witch-hunter the opportunity he longed for, to ferret out every last wise woman on Faire Isle. He meant to destroy them all and there was nothing Ariane could do to stop him.

⚘ ⚘ ⚘

AN HOUR LATER, ARIANE PACED THE SNUG CONFINES OF THE ABBESS'S room, still shivering. Even here, safe behind the convent walls, she felt chilled by her recent encounter with Le Vis. She paused in her agitated motion, to peer out the window, catching sight of her sister.

While several alarmed nuns watched her from behind the pillars of the refectory, Gabrielle practiced lunges with Captain Remy's sword. Gabrielle's lovely face was filled with such grim purpose, it frightened Ariane.

She had sworn to her mother on her deathbed that she would always look out for both Miri and Gabrielle. Now she had one sister in the hands of witch-hunters and the other armed with a sword, preparing for who knew what rash and desperate action.

Ariane's shoulders sagged. "How did I ever allow any of this to happen, Marie?"

Marie Claire bustled up behind her to wrap her arm around Ariane's shoulders. "What do you think you could have done to prevent witch-hunters from descending on us?"

"Perhaps I should have refused to help Captain Remy. I should have at least been more cautious, more vigilant about looking after my sisters."

Marie Claire sighed. "My dear child, you cannot hold yourself responsible for everything. Sometimes I fear you confuse yourself with—with—"

"With Maman?" Ariane said.

"No, I was going to say with God almighty himself." Forcing Ariane to sit, Marie pressed a glass of wine into her hands. Ariane held the cup without tasting it, staring bleakly into the empty hearth.

"When you agreed to help Captain Remy, you believed you were doing the right thing," Marie Claire said.

"Unfortunately, doing the right thing may get us all killed."

"Is there no way of bargaining with this Le Vis?"

Ariane shook her head. "The man has no intentions of keeping any agreement he makes with us. I read his eyes, Marie. Never have I encountered such malevolence, such unreasoning hatred. He has long wanted to destroy all the wise women on Faire Isle and now Catherine has given him license to do it."

"I can hardly believe that even Catherine would set such a creature upon us," Marie Claire said. "She is still a daughter of the earth. God's teeth! Has the woman been completely consumed by her own darkness?"

Marie Claire frowned, steepling her fingers beneath her chin. "I don't understand it. Why did we receive no warning from Louise? The last word I had from her was that she was installed in the palace and keeping a close eye on Catherine. Louise said that so far she saw nothing amiss."

"I feared it would be impossible to spy on Catherine. She is far too cunning. No doubt Louise herself is in great danger. You should warn her to leave Paris while she still can."

"Perhaps you are right, but at the moment I am more concerned about Miri." Marie Claire stole an anxious glance toward the window. The leaden gray sky made the light seem as though it had already begun to fade. "We don't have that many hours until sunset."

"I realize that," Ariane replied tersely. "We are going to have to devise some plan to rescue Miri and I fear it will have to involve some armed resistance. It would seem that Gabrielle was wise after all to take the captain's sword."

"It is not Gabrielle's sword arm that is needed," Marie Claire said, with a thoughtful glance in Ariane's direction.

"What do you mean?"

"Have you given no thought to Renard? I know you are reluctant to call upon the comte for help, not wanting to place yourself further in his power—"

"Oh, Marie, do you think I would care about that?" Ariane cried. "I would conjure up the devil himself to save Miri, but surely it is far too late to send for Renard now. No messenger would arrive in time."

"Why do you need a messenger when you have this?" Marie Claire bent over her. Tugging on the chain fastened around Ariane's neck, she pulled Renard's ring out into the light. Ariane reached up, closing her hand over the strange metal circle.

"I have no doubt Renard is a brave man, Marie," she said. "But when we made our pact, he likely envisioned deeds like— like frightening away my other suitors or paying off my debts. Do you think that even he would be willing to battle witch-hunters for me?"

"I think he would do anything that you asked."

"And—and you believe that I can use this ring to summon him? That it would truly work?"

"What have you got to lose? I don't know about you, my dear, but I am desperate enough to try just about anything."

Ariane stared at the ring, hesitating a moment longer. Then she eased the metal circle off the chain, hating the flicker of hope that sprang to life inside of her. This was nonsense. But she was indeed desperate enough to try anything.

Her hand trembled a little as she slipped the ring on her finger. Now what? His instructions had been brief and simple.

"When you slip the ring upon your finger, we will be linked

in a way that defies all distance and time. You will be able to summon me back to you with merely a thought."

Closing her eyes, Ariane pressed her hand over the region of her heart, concentrating hard, sending her thoughts out into the void like a fervent prayer.

Renard, if there is any magic in this ring at all, please hear me. You must return to Faire Isle at once. I need your help.

She felt foolish at first, but she persisted. *Renard, please. Witch-hunters have come to my island. They have taken Miri. I need you.*

Then she felt it, a strange tingling in her finger, followed by a rush of warmth that spread through her entire body. She trembled as she heard Renard's voice whisper in her ear.

"Hold on, ma chère. I come."

Chapter Thirteen

SIMON PAUSED OUTSIDE THE CRYPT DOOR, THE TRAY WITH ITS meager contents balanced on his hand. A little bread, a little cheese, some water, and a slice of currant cake. The latter had been Simon's addition and he felt a twinge of guilt. Somehow he doubted that Monsieur Le Vis would approve of him feeding cake to a witch.

He peered through the bars of the locked gate that led into the crypt, looking for the prisoner. Miri was huddled on the stone floor, her back resting against the sarcophagus carved with the image of some long-forgotten knight. Her knees drawn up, she rested her chin upon them, her fine gold hair falling forward like a curtain to shield her from her grim surroundings. She looked so small and wretched, Simon's own shoulders slumped at the sight of her.

"She would have run away but for you."

Ariane Cheney's accusation lingered in his mind. He felt a sharp stab of conscience, which he fought to set aside. Master Le Vis had done right to arrest Miri Cheney. When Simon had given his assurances to the girl, he had not known who she was. One of the Cheneys, the very women their order had come to this island to seek.

Simon could well believe it of the older sister. He had sensed the strange and terrible power of Ariane Cheney's eyes. But Miri reminded Simon painfully of his own sister, or how Lorene might have been if she had lived. If she, his mother and father, and the rest of his village had not been destroyed by witches . . .

When he began to feel too tenderhearted toward Miri Cheney, he needed to remember that. Unlocking the gate to the crypt, he shuffled inside the small stone vault. He saw Miri tense, but she did not lift her head.

"Mademoiselle?" he said sharply.

She only shrank deeper into her corner.

"I have brought you some food." He plunked the tray down in front of her.

One silvery-blue eye peeked at him through the curtain of her hair. "I am not hungry."

He could see the tip of her small, straight nose. It was quite pink. She had obviously been crying. Simon felt all his resolve to remain stern and aloof melting away.

"You should try to eat something," he said, more gently. "Look, there is cake. I brought it especially for you."

He picked up the small slice and held it out coaxingly. "Please take it."

Miri hesitated, then her hand shot out, accepting the gift. She retreated with the cake behind her fall of hair and Simon was forced to repress a tiny smile. She reminded him of a little mouse nibbling away in her corner. He longed to brush back those shining white-blond strands from her face and had to ball his hand into a fist to suppress the inappropriate urge.

Between mouthfuls of cake, Miri mumbled, "How—how is the cat?"

Simon stared at her in amazement. She was worried about the cat?

"Your cat is fine," he told her. "It is tucked away in a cozy cage and I gave it a saucer of milk."

"He is not my cat. You can't own creatures of the earth and he won't like being caged. He needs to be set free."

He touched her knee lightly. "You should worry more about yourself. You are in a serious situation, mademoiselle, but there is hope. If you would but confess, repent."

Miri lifted her head to regard him reproachfully. "Repent of what? You said yourself I was doing nothing wrong."

"That is before I knew who you were. You come from an entire family of witches, do you not?"

"Ariane says we are wise women."

"Your sister has misled you."

Miri scowled at him, dusting cake crumbs from her fingers. "Ariane would not do that. She is exceedingly wise, just like my Maman was. My father is a great knight. If he were here, you would all be terribly sorry."

"But he isn't. Monsieur Le Vis has sworn you may go free, just tell him what he needs to know. Where is the heretic you and your sisters are hiding?"

"I don't know anything about any heretic," Miri said, looking genuinely confused.

"The Huguenot soldier, Captain Nicolas Remy."

"Oh." Miri bit down on her lip, her eyes dropping to the floor. "I—I don't know anything about him either."

The girl was clearly lying.

"Miri, I don't believe you are wicked. But you are very confused—"

"You are the one who is confused. Go away and leave me alone."

Simon studied the stubborn set of her lips with exasperation. The foolish child had no idea what she was up against. He
had seen the implements Master Le Vis used to extract confes-
sions from witches, the irons that could be heated red hot, the
thumbscrews, the iron boot that could so easily crush a full-
grown man's leg, let alone the slender one of a girl.

All grim and cruel, but necessary in the war against sorcery.
He knew that Master Le Vis had something special planned for
Miri Cheney, the ordeal by water. The thought caused a tight
knot of apprehension in Simon's gut. But before he could attempt to reason with her further, he heard the tramp of boots.

Two others from the order appeared at the door to the crypt,
the lean ascetic Brother Jerome and Brother Finial, with his constant sour expression and shock of peppery hair.

Brother Finial frowned. "What are you doing in here, boy?"

Simon hastily got to his feet. "I was just feeding the prisoner."

"A waste of food," Finial sneered. "A full stomach will not do
this witch much good by the time Master Le Vis finishes with her."

As the two men marched into the crypt, Simon moved instinctively to stand in front of Miri, but Finial brushed him aside.

"Stand up, wench. It is time for your testing to begin."

Simon said, "But Master Le Vis promised that the Cheney
women would have until sunset to produce the heretic."

Jerome, who could be more kind than many of the other
brothers, explained patiently to Simon. "The master grows tired
of waiting. There is a storm moving in and he believes it best that
we proceed for the good of all the innocent folk on this island.
The longer we allow witches and heretics to remain among them,
the more their immortal souls will be endangered."

The two men crowded around Miri. Finial hauled her roughly
to her feet. She looked terrified to death, but she made no sound.
It was Simon who had difficulty suppressing his outcry.

He forced himself to stand aside, knowing this was the way things had to be, reminding himself of all that he owed to the memory of his family, to Master Le Vis. After his village had been destroyed, Simon would have been naught but a beggar lad with nowhere to go.

The master had taken him in, given him a home, his education, his livelihood. But as Miri was dragged from the crypt, she cast Simon such a look of mute appeal, he was obliged to close his eyes and turn away.

※ ※ ※

THE SKY HAD DARKENED, HEAVY STORM CLOUDS ROILING IN FROM the harbor. Thunder rumbled in the distance, but the sound was nowhere as ominous as the beat of the drum emanating from the town square. The relentless tattoo summoned people out of their homes and shops.

The crowd slowly began to gather. Master Le Vis had made it plain that any who refrained from bearing witness to the trial would be suspected of being as guilty as the accused. And no one was particularly eager to be the next to fall victim to the witch-hunters' brand of justice.

Word of the proceedings had reached Ariane at the convent. She flew down the street, not waiting to see if Marie Claire, Gabrielle, or Charbonne followed. She lifted up her skirts and ran, not pausing to draw breath until she reached the edge of the crowd in the square.

Anxiously scanning the cluster of faces, she caught a glimpse of the grim features of Madame Jehan and Mistress Paletot, little Madame Elan hiding timidly behind her husband. Many of those in attendance were male, rugged sailors and fishermen from the harbor, the proprietor of the Passing Stranger, stable hands, and apprentice lads.

But the one face Ariane most sought was not there. Renard. She whipped about to stare down the road leading to the square from the harbor, praying for some sight of a powerful man astride a rebellious gray stallion.

The road was becoming obscured by the gathering clouds. The way from the mainland would soon become impassable.

"Oh, where are you, Renard?" she murmured, twisting the ring on her finger. After that initial burst of warmth, that strange giddy sensation when she had first attempted to use the ring, she had felt nothing, except a growing sense of despair.

The ring had not worked. She needed to have worked out some other way of rescuing her sister, but Le Vis had not given her enough time. The man had broken his word to wait until sunset.

Ariane pressed forward. When her presence was known, the crowd fell back, clearing her a path, many drawing away as though she now carried the plague. The drum sounded louder in her ears and Ariane's heart thudded fearfully in time with it as she saw the witch-hunters.

They were lined up before the pond like a flock of black-winged scavengers, their hands tucked within the sleeves of their robes, their pallid faces concealed beneath their dark cowls.

Only one seemed human. Simon Aristide banged out the rhythm on the drum, his shoulders rigid, but beneath his hood, the boy looked wretched. Le Vis stood nearby, in his fiery robes, gripping a tall crosier like some unholy shepherd presiding over his flock.

Ariane looked frantically for her sister, but Miri appeared to be swallowed up somewhere behind that sea of black robes. Someone shoved against her and Ariane realized that the others had caught up to her at last. Gabrielle pressed close to Ariane's side, close followed by Charbonne and a breathless Marie Claire.

Gabrielle glowered at Le Vis. "That bastard! So much for ever trusting the word of a witch-hunter." She drew Remy's sword and would have rushed forward immediately if Charbonne had not restrained her.

"Where is Miri?" Marie Claire asked.

Gabrielle paused in her struggle as they all craned their necks. The line of witch-hunters shifted and Ariane's throat constricted as she spotted her little sister imprisoned between two of the men. Miri's hands were bound in front of her, a halter fastened around her neck. She looked dazed and bewildered, her eyes wide and staring as though she sought retreat into some inner kingdom because the world in which she found herself had suddenly turned senseless and cruel.

Ariane had seen that numb expression of shock on her sister's face once before—the night that their mother had died.

"Miri," Ariane cried, moving instinctively toward the girl, but a wall of witch-hunters swiftly barred her way.

Le Vis signaled to Simon and the relentless beat of the drum stilled at last. The boy moved to the side, hanging his head, while Vachel Le Vis mounted the steps of the market hall. As he looked out over the crowd, his gaze honed in on Ariane. His cowl thrown back, he made no effort to hide his twisted pleasure. Raising his crosier for silence, he addressed the crowd.

"Citizens of Port Corsair, as you are by now aware, we come amongst you as deliverers, to rid your island of the terrible influence of the Evil One. This wretched girl you see before you, Miribelle Cheney, is accused of the crime of witchcraft. We call upon you to witness our justice as we test her guilt, using the most righteous ordeal by water."

An uneasy murmur rippled through the crowd. Her mouth thinning, Ariane positioned herself at the foot of the steps below Le Vis, her own voice ringing out.

"Don't listen to this man. Good people, you have known me and my sisters all your lives. The only evil here resides with Master Le Vis and these unholy wretches who serve him. There is nothing just or righteous about this tribunal. Le Vis comes only to spread superstition and terror amongst us. But we can put a stop to his cruelty right now if you will only come forward to stand with me against him."

Ariane's plea was greeted with a deafening silence, only a few like Madame Jehan and Mistress Paletot brave enough to step forward to join Marie Claire, Gabrielle, and Charbonne.

The rest sullenly hung their heads or steadfastly avoided Ariane's eyes. She understood the fear that caused the rest of them to hang back, but had somehow hoped for better. It seemed a cruel irony that many of them even now stood beneath the shadow of the statue they had erected to the memory of Evangeline Cheney.

"There is often a fine line between a woman being proclaimed a witch or a saint," Renard had once warned her. Ariane had not fully appreciated the bitter truth of those words until now.

She started as Le Vis stepped up behind her to murmur in her ear. "Mistress Cheney, you are the only one who can save your sister. Give me what I want and the child shall go free. You have my word."

"Just like you kept your word to wait until sunset—" she began angrily, only to check in alarm as she saw Gabrielle break free from Charbonne.

Trying to take advantage of the momentary distraction when all eyes were on Le Vis, Gabrielle drew her sword and rushed at the two witch-hunters who held Miri. One of them met her advance, drawing his own weapon. The two swords met in a clash of steel.

Gabrielle parried and lashed out fiercely, but she never stood a chance. A second witch-hunter brought a heavy cudgel down on her arm. She cried out, losing her grip on the weapon. Ariane watched in horror as the witch-hunter felled Gabrielle with another blow.

The man raised his cudgel to strike again. Hurtling forward, Ariane flung herself over Gabrielle. The blow fell hard upon her shoulder and Ariane gasped in pain. Gabrielle struggled to thrust her aside, but Ariane pinned her, using her body as a shield.

The next few moments were a chaotic blur. She was vaguely aware of Marie Claire and Charbonne trying to come to their aid, only to be repulsed. With a low curse, Gabrielle shoved Ariane off, but neither of them could move. Resting on her elbows, Ariane peered upward to find they were hemmed in by witch-hunters, the steely tip of several swords leveled at her and Gabrielle.

"Enough of this folly," Le Vis growled. The Grand Master towered over Ariane, his lips pulled back in a contemptuous smile. "So this is your answer to my demand, Mistress Cheney? Then so be it. Perhaps you will be in a more reasonable frame of mind when I pull your sister's lifeless body from the pond and then start in on this one."

He prodded Gabrielle savagely with his crook. Ariane tightened her arms around the girl, but she was flooded with a sense of helplessness and despair.

Oh, Maman, forgive me, Ariane thought as Le Vis turned to the witch-hunters holding Miri.

"Proceed."

As they began dragging Miri toward the edge of the pond, Ariane struggled to rise, only to be held back by the steel pressing against her.

"No!"

Frantic as Ariane was, the cry didn't come from her, but another quarter. Simon Aristide clutched at Le Vis's robes, his face a tortured mask. "Master, please don't. There must be some other way."

"Silence, boy!" Le Vis snapped, striking his hands away. "Get back—"

He broke off as another commotion arose, this time from the crowd. Shrieks and shouts. For a wild moment, Ariane hoped her speech might have done some good, that others were rushing to the rescue.

From her point on the ground, all she could see was that the crowd was breaking up, people colliding as they scrambled for safety, and not in terror of the witch-hunters. The cluster of black-robed men seemed to have frozen in place, even Le Vis wide-eyed and staring.

It was as though the dark roiling clouds had opened up to spew forth a giant astride a powerful gray stallion. The horse's mane whipped back as wildly as did that of the man as they charged toward the square.

"Renard," Ariane whispered, her chest tightening with a hope that was almost painful.

Renard loomed closer until he had to rein in to avoid trampling fleeing members of the crowd. Hercules reared up on his haunches, letting loose a shrill whinny like a battle cry.

"What—what—who the devil?" Le Vis faltered.

And well might he ask, Ariane thought. Even after Renard brought Hercules to a halt, the stallion snorted and pawed at the ground, looking as though it was about to breathe fire.

Renard's own nostrils were pinched tight, his mouth a grim slash in his rough face and any fool could have read his eyes. They were dark with a rage that was implacable as the storm-ridden sky.

Ariane was reminded of something Renard had once said to her. *"If I am ever angry, ma chère, you will know it."*

She was left in no doubt of the fact as Renard leaned forward in the saddle and snarled at Le Vis. "Release those women."

The witch-hunters who surrounded Ariane and Gabrielle wavered. Ariane struggled to her feet, tugging Gabrielle with her.

Le Vis confronted Renard furiously. "What is the meaning of this, monsieur? Who are you to interrupt the procedures of this tribunal?"

"Justice Deauville, the Comte de Renard."

The title appeared to take Le Vis momentarily aback. He spoke in milder tones. "Well, milord comte, you clearly do not understand what is happening here. I am Vachel Le Vis, Grand Master of the Order of Malleus Maleficarum and—"

"I know who you are, you bastard, and what you are doing. I am commanding you to desist at once and leave this island."

Le Vis's mouth opened and closed, his jaw working with indignation. "My orders come from Queen Catherine herself. These are not your lands, milord. You have no authority here."

"This is my authority!" Renard unsheathed his sword in a hiss of steel.

Le Vis's eyes widened in alarm. He had just enough time to dive out of the way as Renard urged his horse forward, charging into the line of witch-hunters. They closed in on him but many were forced back as Hercules reared and snapped.

Ariane scrambled to a safe distance, pulling Gabrielle after her. She watched with dazed eyes as Renard beat down the swords striking up at him. Bringing his hilt down hard on the head of one witch-hunter, he disarmed another and slashed the arm of a third.

Gabrielle clutched at Ariane's arm, her one eye near swollen shut. But she gawked at Renard through her good eye. "M-monsieur le Ogre. Where the devil did he come from?"

Ariane said nothing. Mutely, she held up her hand bearing the ring.

"Oh, Ariane, you didn't!" Gabrielle cried.

"Apparently I did," Ariane murmured, still lost in her own amazement. She was unable to wrench her eyes from Renard.

He sent another witch-hunter flying to the ground with a kick of his boot as he fought his way through to the edge of the pond. The witch-hunter who guarded Miri bolted, leaving the trembling girl standing alone. Renard swooped in and gathered the child up on the saddle before him.

Ariane choked on a glad cry, but her relief was short-lived as the witch-hunters regrouped for another attack. They fanned out, surrounding him on all sides, swords drawn.

Hercules shifted restively while Renard tightened his grip on his sword. He would never be able to fend off all the witch-hunters, especially not with Miri clutched in front of him.

Ariane twisted the ring on her finger.

Ride, she pleaded silently. *Just put spurs to Hercules and get Miri out of here.* But she knew that Renard would never abandon her and Gabrielle.

Renard wheeled about, bracing himself as the first witch-hunter charged. The man came within inches of Hercules when suddenly he jerked sharply, his sword flying from his hand. The witch-hunter fell back, clutching at the crossbolt embedded in his shoulder, blood blossoming between his fingers.

The other witch-hunters froze at the sight and suddenly the entire square seemed to swarm with mounted horsemen, the riders wearing Renard's gold-and-black livery. They bore down on the witch-hunters, led by the formidable-looking old man Ariane had seen with Renard before.

The old man edged his mount closer, leveling his crossbow. "None of you move. I never miss what I aim at, nor do the rest of these lads. Now throw down your weapons."

Slowly one witch-hunter complied and then another, swords clattering to the ground. Choked with rage, Le Vis couldn't speak. Renard ignored him. Sheathing his sword, he guided Hercules over to Ariane and lowered Miri gently down to her.

Ariane removed the halter from her little sister's neck and flung it to the ground while Gabrielle fumbled with her bonds. Ariane laid her hand tenderly on Miri's cheek. The child felt so cold, her face ice white. She still looked dazed and frightened. The child had never been able to comprehend the violence of men and she appeared as terrified of Renard's retainers as she was of the witch-hunters.

"Everything is all right. You are safe now, Miri," Ariane crooned, hugging the girl close. Even as she sought to reassure her little sister, Le Vis bore down upon them.

Renard wheeled his mount in between. Le Vis clutched his crosier in a white-knuckled grip.

"You are going to answer for this, monsieur. We are servants of the crown. To attack us is treason."

Renard's mouth tightened, his hooded eyes narrowing to dangerous slits as he slid off the back of his horse. Any man less crazed than Le Vis would have had sense enough to run.

The Grand Master stood his ground, quivering with outrage. "You have no idea what you are interfering with."

"Oh, I understand too well," Renard grated. "You intended to torture a child."

"Torture? No, the ordeal by water is merely a test for witchcraft."

"Then maybe we should try the test on you."

"What!" Le Vis gasped. "How—how dare you. I am no witch."

"We'll know soon enough. When you sink like a stone." Renard advanced closer.

Le Vis paled, making a desperate attempt to fend Renard off with his crosier. But Renard tore the crook from his hands and tossed it contemptuously aside. Seizing Le Vis by the front of his robes, he dragged him toward the edge of the pond. The witchhunter emitted a choked protest as Renard heaved him into the water.

Le Vis hit the pond with a loud splash and someone gave a loud cheer. Ariane believed it was old Madame Jehan. Flailing in sheer panic, Le Vis propelled himself even farther from the safety of shore. The water swiftly weighed down his robes and he vanished beneath the surface, only to bob up again, his face a grotesque mask of terror.

Simon Aristide had retreated with his drum, observing the entire fray in alarm, but now the boy rushed forward to appeal to Renard. "Please, Monsieur le Comte. The master—he cannot swim."

"Good," Renard snapped.

Flinging down his drum, Simon peeled off his robe and dove into the pond. He reached Le Vis in several swift strokes, but Le Vis grabbed wildly for him, pulling the boy under.

Miri gave a stricken whimper, burying her face against Ariane's shoulder. Horrified herself, Ariane watched the desperate struggle taking place, Simon no match for Le Vis's frantic strength. She certainly had no love for Le Vis, but it was clear that if someone didn't intervene, the man was going to drown and take the boy with him.

Easing Miri away from her, Ariane raced toward the comte.

"Renard, please," she began, tugging at him, but he didn't even seem to hear her. He stared at the pond, watching Le Vis and the boy sink from sight. Renard's expression was so cold and implacable, it frightened Ariane. For once she could read his eyes and she saw that he had disappeared down some dark corridor of the past.

Ariane shook him harder. "Renard!"

She appeared to reach him at last. Renard blinked, shifting his gaze toward her.

"Please," she said. "We—we can't just let them die. Master Aristide . . . he is only a boy."

Renard compressed his lips together. His gaze shifted back to the pond, then he muttered an oath. Turning away, he summoned two of his retainers, barking out a sharp command.

The pair dismounted, racing swiftly to plunge into the water. Ariane watched anxiously as the men dove once, twice, beneath the surface before they emerged, bringing up Le Vis and Simon.

Renard waded in himself to help retrieve the boy, while the other two dragged Le Vis out, flopping the Grand Master onto his back. Simon sank to his knees, choking and sputtering. But Le Vis's eyes were closed, his face pale and still.

"M-master?" Simon quavered, shaking him.

Renard relented enough to rest one hand on Simon's shoulder. "I am sorry, boy. There is nothing to be done for him. He's gone and good riddance."

Simon wrenched away from Renard, tears splashing down the boy's cheek to mingle with the droplets of pond water.

"Ahhh!" he groaned. "I—I know you all think him hard and cruel. But the m-master only sought to do his duty and—and he was ever g-good to me."

As the boy dissolved into bitter weeping, Ariane bit down hard upon her lip. If Le Vis had survived, he would be even more implacable, a relentless enemy, hell-bent on destroying her and her sisters, likely Renard as well. And God knows she despised the witch-hunter. It frightened her how much she wished him dead, but she could hear the echoes of her mother's voice.

"Hatred can be the worst sort of black magic, Ariane. It shrivels the heart and turns it cold. Never surrender to that sort of darkness."

Ariane hesitated only a moment longer. Hunkering down, she thrust Simon aside. There was a certain white magic her mother had performed. Ariane was not certain she possessed the skill to administer the Breath of Life, but she had to try. Locking her hands together, Ariane pumped the heels of her palms hard against Le Vis's wet chest. She felt nothing. Although she sickened at the prospect, she forced the man's lips apart and administered several quick breaths.

Time seemed to stand still as she labored over Le Vis. She was on the verge of surrendering the effort when the man's chest heaved. He choked to life, his eyes flying wide. Le Vis twisted onto his side, shuddering and spewing pond water from his mouth.

Ariane stood up, scrubbing her hand across her lips. A heavy silence descended, broken only by the sound of Le Vis dragging gulps of air back into his lungs. Ariane turned away to find herself surrounded by faces regarding her with a kind of dazed wonder, Simon, the other witch-hunters, Toussaint, the men at arms. Even Renard stared at her with awe.

He was the first to recover himself and began barking out commands. He nudged Le Vis with the toe of his boot.

"Get his carcass out of here," he snapped at Simon. "Before I change my mind and toss him back in again."

"Y-yes, monsieur," the trembling boy said. "Th-thank you."

"Save your gratitude for the Lady. If it had been left to me, both you and your pig of a master would still be at the bottom of the pond." Renard turned sternly to the other witch-hunters. "The rest of you. Pack up and be gone. You have one hour to leave this island and never return. Any witch-hunter attempting to return will not find himself as fortunate as Monsieur Le Vis."

The black-robed men hastened to obey, two of the witch-hunters helping Simon to cart off Le Vis, who still managed to throw a malevolent glance in Renard's direction.

Renard seemed impervious, but Ariane shivered. This was not the last she would hear from the man or the one who had sent him. But for the moment the danger had passed.

Miri was safe, surrounded by a cluster of rejoicing women, Marie Claire's motherly arm wrapped around the child. Ariane knew she should join them, but the strain of the entire ordeal seemed to overtake her at once.

She felt weak and trembling, her knees beginning to shake. She almost sagged to the ground, but suddenly Renard was there, shoring her up. He wrapped her in his strong arms, straining her close. Ariane leaned gratefully against the hard wall of his chest, her throat constricting, several tears squeezing past her lashes.

"Ah, don't cry, ma chère." Renard cradled her as though she were a child no bigger than Miri. His jerkin and trunk hose were soaked, but the terrifying look was gone from his face; his voice was all gentleness as he comforted. "It is all over now and those devils shall never come near you or your sisters ever again. I swear it."

Ariane buried her face against his damp leather jerkin, the events of the past hours seeming like some strange and terrible dream. Even Renard's rescue did not seem quite real. If he did not feel so solid beneath her touch, she still might have believed she was just imagining him here.

She tipped her head to blink wonderingly up at him. "You came. I—I summoned you and you—*you came.*"

He brushed a tender kiss across her brow. "But of course. Did you ever doubt that I would?"

She made no demur when he kissed her lips, the feel of his mouth sending a welcome rush of warmth through her. She stole her arms shyly around his neck. Renard's breath came quick and warm against her ear as he whispered, "One time, chérie."

"What?" Ariane murmured, nestling closer to him.

"You have now used my ring one time. You are one step nearer to becoming my wife."

"Oh. Oh, yes," she said in a subdued voice, wondering how she could have allowed herself to forget the reason for Renard riding to the rescue. Not out of any heroic chivalry or devotion.

He had come because of their peculiar bargain of the ring. She should not have needed him to remind her of that fact or been so strangely disappointed when he did. Ariane eased out of his arms, wiping her eyes with the back of her hand.

Whatever Renard's motives, he had saved Miri and very likely all the rest of the wise women of Faire Isle. She could not but be grateful to him for that.

"My lord, I—I do want to thank you for—for—"

Renard silenced her with a light touch to her lips and a firm shake of his head. "Do not thank me, chérie. There is no need. You called for me and I came. Just as we had agreed, although I must admit performing this particular service was a pleasure for me. I take a keen enjoyment in breaking the heads of witch-hunters and I am only glad that I was able to arrive in time."

Not like the last time. The thought flashed into Renard's eyes, so painful, for once he was unable to conceal it.

So . . . this was not the first time Renard had had an encounter with witch-hunters, Ariane realized. She supposed she should not be surprised by that. Any man who dealt in magic rings and wrapped himself in a cloak of mystery would be bound to be an object of suspicion.

And there had been the way Renard had looked at Le Vis, with that dark hatred that went far beyond the dislike an ordinary, rational man might feel.

Ariane tried to probe deeper, but Renard had already hooded his eyes, sealing off his thoughts as he strode over to retrieve his horse. Hercules appeared strangely docile as Renard reached for the reins, as though man and horse were in accord for once.

"Now that I have done what you summoned me to do, I expect you will want me gone."

Was that what she wanted? Considering that the ring actually did work, Ariane supposed that she should perceive Renard as more dangerous than ever. But to simply allow him to go away again, after all that he had done for her, with no more than a clumsy word of thanks, seemed so . . . so wrong.

"There is a storm coming," she said. "It might be dangerous for you to try to leave the island just now."

Renard paused in checking the cinch on his saddle to assure her. "Don't worry, chérie. I plan to quarter myself at the inn. I don't intend to leave Faire Isle until the danger is past."

"Then if you are going to stay, perhaps you would—I mean—you will not allow me to thank you, but the least I could do—that is, I would be very honored if you would consent to dine with me and my sisters at Belle Haven this evening."

The invitation that she blurted out astonished Ariane as

much as it did Renard. When he stared at her, she added awkwardly, "If—if you would like . . ."

Renard's rough features softened. "I should like that, ma chère. Very much indeed."

※ ※ ※

THE SQUARE STOOD EMPTY AS THE DAY FADED, THE ONLY THREAT to the peace of Faire Isle a natural one as the sky continued to rumble with the impending storm.

Renard lingered, like a conqueror surveying an abandoned battlefield, seeking to assure himself that a victory had truly been won. He had commanded his retainers to gather up the weapons that the witch-hunters had discarded, but he saw that one had been overlooked.

A sword lay forgotten in the grasses near the edge of the pond. Renard strode over to retrieve it. As he stared down at the hated symbol of the flaming cross engraved on the hilt, he felt the familiar surge of anger and the cold breath of fear as well.

A few minutes later and his mad race would have been to no avail. When he thought of what could have happened to Miri Cheney, to her sister Gabrielle, but most of all to Ariane, Renard felt a chill ice through his veins.

He would have been too late . . . just like the last time. The rippling waters of the pond blurred before his eyes. The entire square seemed to fade, and he was seeing the green of another village high up in the mountains.

Renard had traveled hard from Paris, pushing his horse to the point of collapse only to arrive the morning after. He had never witnessed what had happened that long-ago night, but the terrible event was as etched in his mind as though he had stood by helpless and watched the whole thing.

Renard only had to close his eyes to see the burning pyre, the grim gloating faces of the black-robed men as they had bound the old woman's frail wrists, lashing her to the slats of the crude ladder.

Those who had dared to speak to Renard of what had happened told him his grandmother had been unbelievably brave when the witch-hunters had come for her, almost resigned. But Renard had known the truth.

By that time, Lucy simply had not given a damn whether she lived or died. And Renard had long cursed both the old woman and himself for that. She had let those devils take her, let them build their fire, let them tie her to the ladder.

Those bastards had not even had the decency to bind her to the stake, give her the chance to suffocate on the smoke. Oh, no, they had made sure that his grandmother had been fully alive.

They had raised the ladder parallel to the blazing fire, forcing Lucy to stare straight into the hellish reflection of her own death. Renard had been told that the old woman had not struggled as the ladder had been released, as she had pitched face forward into the flames.

"My lord?" A voice tugged at him, a heavy hand clamping down on his shoulder.

Renard's eyes fluttered open and he experienced a sharp sense of relief to find Toussaint at his side.

"Are you all right, lad?" Toussaint asked gruffly. He could not read eyes, but he could obviously tell where Renard had been. It was a dark road into the past the old man had traveled himself once too often.

"Yes, I'm fine," Renard said. "I was just—just making sure all was secure. Here." He handed the witch-hunter's sword to Toussaint. "Take this infernal thing and get rid of it. Break it apart, melt it down. I don't care how you do it. I don't want any trace of those bastards left on this island."

Toussaint nodded grimly. "I'll see to that. But shouldn't you return to the inn and tidy yourself up a bit for your supper with the ladies? You should at least comb your hair before they crown you with your hero's laurels."

"I am not a hero, Toussaint," Renard said irritably. "I never claimed to be. I made it quite clear to Ariane why I came to the rescue, because she used the ring."

The old man eyed Renard fiercely. "You might spout such nonsense to your lady, but you should know better than to try it on me. You'd have come to save that little girl, ring or no ring."

"Yes, but Ariane doesn't need to know that."

"Why the devil not? I should think you would want her to."

Renard frowned, because part of him did long for just that. Some soft corner of his heart urged him to kneel at her feet and vow on his sword like some idiot knight errant, that he would never allow any harm to come to her or her sisters. And he would not demand so much as a kiss in return.

But those were the thoughts of a romantic young fool and he was hardly that anymore.

"Telling Ariane that I would have helped her without the ring certainly won't further my cause," Renard said. "If she thought that, she would never use the ring again."

"Which would be a mighty good thing." Toussaint shot him an exasperated look. "Damnation, boy, I can't believe you plan to continue playing this game after what nearly happened here today. I've been talking to one of the stable hands about what has been going on these past few days. First the queen's soldiers tearing apart the place and now witch-hunters. There is something amiss on this island."

"I realize that," Renard replied tersely. "I was far too complacent ever leaving here. It is a mistake I won't make again. I intend to remain right here on this island until—"

"Until what? Someone else is almost killed?"

"That won't happen!" Renard glowered at the old man, then vented a wearied sigh. "Lord, Toussaint, do you think I like this game either? But how else am I going to win Ariane? With my pretty face?"

"The lady appears to be softening toward you. She has finally trusted you enough to invite you to her home."

"Only out of gratitude, and that won't be enough to get the lady to the altar. The ring is still my only chance of claiming a woman like Ariane. She is—is completely amazing. You saw for yourself what she did today."

"Yes, the Breath of Life," Toussaint said in awed tones. "I remember Lucy speaking of it, but never did I think to see such an astonishing feat. A pity your lady had to waste such a miraculous gift upon a witch-hunter, but what an incredible thing to witness."

"Then perhaps now you start to comprehend why I am so determined to marry Ariane. A woman possessed of such remarkable power. To say nothing of her dowry of ancient books. I want her and I mean to have her."

"I would feel a deal better about all this if you said you loved her."

Renard shrugged. "You know that is one kind of magic I leave well alone." He had learned a long time ago that all love did was render a man too vulnerable.

Toussaint turned sadly away. Renard watched the old man's retreat with a stubborn set to his jaw. A part of him knew that Toussaint was right. The bargain with the ring had seemed so simple when Renard had first made it. He had not counted on there ever being any real danger. Nor had he counted on the gratitude that shone from Ariane's eyes when he had saved her sister, making him wish that he deserved it.

But she had used the ring. Renard was one third of the way to getting what he wanted.

Chapter Fourteen

RIANE CUT OFF ANOTHER ROLL OF LINEN FOR FRESH BAN-
daging while Captain Remy watched her through eyes half-closed
in pain. The man was paying a price for his desperate effort to go
after Gabrielle. When Ariane had returned to Belle Haven, she
had learned from Agnes that the captain had actually managed
to dress himself and make it as far as the great hall before he had
fainted and been returned to his bed.

Ariane moved the candle closer, the light flickering over the
rough walls of the old dungeon cell. She peeled away the old
bandage from Remy's side. The wound looked raw and seeped
blood, but it was nowhere near as bad as Ariane had feared. She
bathed the afflicted area, then applied some of her healing salve
and placed a fresh pad over it.

"You are a fortunate man. And a very foolish one," she told
the captain, but she softened the severity of her words with

a slight smile. "It would not have done us much good to hide you if you had staggered out of here, only to lose consciousness somewhere along the road."

Remy winced as Ariane wrapped the bandage tighter about his midriff. "I never meant to cause more trouble for you. But when I saw Gabrielle charge out with my sword, I—I could not just lie here while she—while you were all in danger."

"The danger is past . . . for the time being," she said.

Remy must have caught her hesitation, for his deep brown eyes fastened on her. "It was most strange, was it not? Witch-hunters descending on the island so suddenly."

"Yes." Ariane avoided his gaze, busying herself with removing the basin and the old bandages, but Remy was far too perceptive.

"Those men did not come here by chance, did they? *She* sent them. The Dark Queen sent those witch-hunters after me."

Ariane could not lie to him. "She dispatched Le Vis to coerce us into surrendering you and the gloves."

"My God! You should have done so before risking all your lives."

"One cannot make bargains with a fanatic like Le Vis. My sisters and I would still have ended up tried for witchcraft and you would have been turned over to the Dark Queen, dead or alive."

"But if she was desperate enough to send a man like Le Vis, she won't give up. She'll try again—"

"Which is why I must work quickly to solve the mystery of the gloves and you must heal so you can return to Navarre and warn your king. The sooner we put a stop to Catherine's evil schemes, the sooner we will all be safe."

Remy shifted one arm across his eyes. Even in the short time she had known him, the gesture had become familiar to Ariane. Remy did it every time he was seized by some strong emotion.

He said in a stricken voice. "I should have never come here.

I thought only of my cause, my king. But you ladies of Faire Isle have been so wonderful, helping me, and all I have done is put you in danger."

"We have always run a certain risk here from the threat of witch-hunters."

"No, they would have never come except for me. When I think of what could have happened to *her*—"

"Don't torment yourself over it. Miri was badly frightened, but she is fine now."

"Miri? Oh . . . oh yes," Remy said, a faint hint of red creeping into his pale cheeks.

Ariane stared at the captain, suddenly realizing the captain's thoughts had been centered on Gabrielle.

The unfortunate captain would not be the first to be dazzled by her beautiful sister or, Ariane feared, the last. She felt sorry for him. Ariane doubted that a solemn Huguenot like Remy could ever touch Gabrielle's wounded heart and perhaps that was just as well. As a hunted man, Remy's current prospects were rather bleak. The captain's growing fascination with her sister provided only one more spur for Ariane to hasten his recovery and get him away from Faire Isle.

She tucked the coverlet gently around his shoulders. "Try to rest now. I regret that we cannot move you to more comfortable quarters upstairs. But there is a man coming to the house to dine tonight and I think it best he does not know you are here."

"A man?" Remy asked anxiously. "What man?"

"The Comte de Renard. He is the one who came to our rescue today."

Remy frowned, looking confused. "Your pardon, mademoiselle, but does not that make him a friend?"

"Frankly, I have never been able to determine exactly what Renard might be," Ariane replied with a rueful smile.

When she passed through the hidden workshop, she realized

that in her haste to fly to Miri's rescue, she had forgotten to put away both the heavy tome on dark magic and the de Medici gloves.

Using tongs, Ariane gingerly picked up the gloves, scowling as she recalled all that these innocent-looking garments had nearly cost her. Part of her wished she had never seen the accursed things and part of her was more determined than ever to find a way to use them against the Dark Queen, to make that woman pay . . .

A dark, vengeful thought, and Ariane knew her mother would never have approved. She quickly returned the gloves to their box. As she did so, she became aware that she was still wearing Renard's ring. In all the excitement, she had neglected to take it off and return the metal band to the silver chain around her neck.

Small wonder that she had forgotten. The ring felt like it had become part of her hand. Now that she fully realized the power of the ring, she regarded it with a mixture of awe and a little fear.

Impulsively she turned to the heavy book at her elbow, leafing through it, but this time skimming past all the sections dealing with poisons, looking for any mention that had to do with charmed rings.

Absorbed in her reading, she barely noticed when the trap door leading down from the kitchens opened. But as Gabrielle began to descend the stairs, Ariane hastily closed the book.

Gabrielle trudged down slowly with none of her usual grace. She was clearly still experiencing the aftereffects of their battle with the witch-hunters. Ariane's own shoulder was stiff and sore from the blow she had taken and although the swelling had gone down around Gabrielle's eye, her sister had an ugly bruise.

As Gabrielle reached the foot of the stairs, Ariane saw that she had left the lid on the box with the gloves cracked open. She closed it as surreptitiously as she could. Fortunately Gabrielle's attention was focused elsewhere.

Her sister's eyes darted in the direction of the corridor leading to Remy's cell. She asked hesitantly as though fearing the answer, "So—so how is the captain?"

"He tore open his wound. It will take him a little longer to mend, but I believe he is doing well enough."

Gabrielle's eyes clouded with a mingling of guilt and defiance. "I only wanted to borrow his sword. I never asked the noble idiot to try to come to the rescue."

"Given the sort of man Remy is, what else did you expect?"

"That he would show some good sense. Just as I wish my older sister would." Gabrielle folded her arms across her bosom and regarded Ariane accusingly. "Agnes told me that you ordered her to lay an extra place for supper for the Comte de Renard. I could scarcely believe it. Whatever possessed you to invite that ogre to come here?"

"For mercy's sake, Gabrielle. That *ogre* risked his life today, without even really knowing what was going on."

"That makes two of us," Gabrielle muttered darkly.

Ariane continued, "Renard very likely saved most of the women on this island. Asking him to dine seemed the least we could do."

"Before you start feeling too grateful to the man, you should stop and remember why he came racing to the rescue. He is trying to trap you into marrying him. Or have you entirely forgotten that?"

Ariane hardly needed Gabrielle to remind her of Renard's true motives. And yet when she thought back over the rescue, the image that stood out most clearly in her mind was the gentle way Renard had lifted Miri down from the saddle and into her arms.

"He saved our little sister," Ariane said. "I am not altogether sure I care why he did it."

"And that is exactly what is starting to worry me."

"What do you mean?"

"You have not been acting like your usual prudent self, Ariane. Inviting the comte to dinner, using his accursed magic ring—"

"Our sister's life was at stake. I had no other choice. It was necessary to summon Renard."

"And was it also necessary to let him kiss you right there in the square in front of Marie Claire, Madame Jehan, and—and everybody?"

A hot tide of color washed into Ariane's cheeks. Somehow in the rejoicing over Miri's rescue, she had hoped that her brief interlude with Renard had gone unnoticed.

"I was a little overcome at that moment, Gabrielle. Having one's sisters nearly killed by witch-hunters does that to a woman."

"To another woman, maybe, but not to you. I have never seen your calm and reason overset by any man, at least not until Renard came along. It's that infernal magic ring of his. You need to get rid of it right now and him as well. Send him word not to come."

"I can't do that. It would be intolerably rude and perhaps tonight might afford me the opportunity to learn more about the man, find out exactly where this ring came from."

Gabrielle arched her brows. "Or it could be the perfect opportunity for him to draw you deeper into his power."

"I have no intention of falling into any man's power. And now if you will excuse me, I have much to prepare before the comte arrives."

Ariane was chagrined to realize that for once she was the one stalking away from one of their quarrels.

As she disappeared through the trap door, she completely missed the worried light that sprang to Gabrielle's eyes.

"Not fall into any man's power? Oh, my dear sister, I fear that you are nearly halfway there. But not if I can prevent it," Gabrielle said grimly.

❧ ❧ ❧

THE WIND LASHED AGAINST THE WINDOWPANES, THE RUMBLE OF THE threatened storm drawing closer. The world beyond Belle Haven seemed ominous and dark, but inside, an array of candles shed a soft light over the oak table set in the small alcove off Evangeline Cheney's bedchamber.

The table was modest, nowhere near as grand as the long mahogany one that rested upon the dais in the great hall below stairs. But that imposing banqueting table had never been used except on those rare occasions when the Cheneys had feted some of the chevalier's high-ranking acquaintances from the French Court.

Family suppers had always taken place in the cozy atmosphere of Evangeline's private chambers and it had been here that the Lady of Faire Isle had preferred to play hostess to her own respected guests, such as Marie Claire.

Ariane wondered if she was making a grave mistake in entertaining Renard here. Anxiously, she paused in front of the mirror to check her reflection one last time. The rose silk gown clung to her willowy frame, the square-shaped bodice filled in with a light modesty vest, decorated with beaded embroidery. The sleeves fell in tiered puffs down to fit snugly at her wrists.

The gown had once belonged to Evangeline Cheney and stirred a flood of poignant memories in Ariane, remembrance of Maman stealing away from the hall full of noble guests Papa had assembled, slipping upstairs to bid her girls good night, the rose silk whispering and shimmering about her.

Ariane had never touched the gown before, although it had been bequeathed to her. Gabrielle would have found the cut too old-fashioned and Miri was as yet too small. Ariane felt a little strange wearing it herself, as though, like the title of Lady of Faire Isle, the gown did not quite fit.

And yet she did not appear quite like her usual prim self tonight, with her dark hair arranged beneath a light veil held in place with a simple circlet of pearls. Her eyes looked softer, a glow of expectancy mounted high in her cheeks.

"Mistress Ariane!" The little housemaid, Bette, burst into the bedchamber. "He's here. Monsieur le Comte is here."

Ariane turned away from the mirror, her heart giving a nervous flutter. Before she could compose herself, Renard appeared. Bette presented him as breathlessly as though she was announcing the king of France himself. Ariane could fully understand why the girl was so awe-stricken.

Renard was very much Monsieur le Comte tonight, an imposing figure in his slashed doublet of green velvet, with dark trunk hose, a short cape falling arrogantly off one shoulder. His golden-brown hair had been recently trimmed, his square jaw freshly shaved. He looked magnificent and yet Ariane thought she preferred him in his rough leather jerkin and worn hunting boots. This Renard seemed more remote, inaccessible.

Renard's hooded eyes concealed the fact that he too was a bit overwhelmed. He had seen Ariane in many guises before, the affectionate sister, the simple knight's daughter, the healer in her plain apron gathering herbs. The tall stately woman standing before him suddenly reminded him that he was standing in the presence of the Lady of Faire Isle.

Ariane glided forward, dipping into a solemn curtsy. "Monsieur le Comte. Welcome to our home."

"Thank you, milady. I am well pleased to be here," Renard said, bowing over her hand.

Their eyes met and the absurdity of such formality after all they had been through today seemed to strike both of them at once. Renard gave a soft laugh and Ariane's lips quivered in a wry smile.

She still looked a trifle nervous as she hastened to explain, "We no longer use the great hall downstairs. We haven't ever since . . ." A shadow crossed Ariane's face.

Ever since Papa abandoned us. Renard read the thought. Her lashes swept down. "We have so few guests these days we tend to dine more informally. I—I hope you don't mind."

Mind? He was astonished that she would trust him enough to admit him into this inner sanctum. And humbled as well because he knew how little he deserved such trust.

Ruthlessly quashing his inconvenient pang of conscience, he replied, "I am deeply honored, milady."

His eyes roved with interest over the chamber that had obviously been the private reserve of the ladies of Belle Haven for generations. A decidedly feminine room, from the soft-hued bed hangings to the rose-patterned carpet. Renard's gaze came to rest on the wooden cupboard mounted into the wall and he wondered if it was there that Ariane kept them.

All those wondrous books old Lucy had told him about with a wistful glint in her eyes. Feeling ashamed of his speculation, Renard wrenched his gaze back to Ariane.

"You look beautiful tonight," he murmured.

"It is because of the gown, I expect. It belonged to my mother, although I am not sure the gown fits me any better than her title does."

"They both suit you very well, ma chère." Renard carried her hand to his lips. Ariane's fingers trembled in his.

They were interrupted by a loud "harrumph" coming from the golden-haired beauty poised in the doorway, attired in a fashionable gown studded with tiny seed pearls, a small white ruff accenting her slender neck. Even her black eye did little to dim the haughty perfection of Gabrielle's features.

Ariane snatched her hand guiltily away from Renard. "Oh, er—Gabrielle. Monsieur le Comte, you—you remember my other sister, Gabrielle?"

"Yes, indeed," Renard said with a polite bow. Although he hadn't taken much note of Ariane's middle sister on his other visits, he doubted that he would soon forget the hostility that radiated from those cool blue eyes.

She looked him up and down with all the disdain of a princess suffering a large and ugly troll to invade her kingdom. Renard had dealt with the scorn of women far more highborn and sophisticated than Gabrielle Cheney. As he held her eyes, he saw that there was still much of the child about Gabrielle and a hurt one at that.

He attempted to offer her a charming smile. "Mademoiselle, I am pleased you have joined us. I have a gift for you."

"Oh?" Gabrielle conveyed an impression of icy indifference.

"Not a gift precisely, but something I believe you might have misplaced today." Renard unbuckled his sheath, and drew forth a sword. It was a plain serviceable blade with a battered hilt that looked as though it had seen its share of action, a soldier's weapon.

"This definitely does not belong to any of the witch-hunters. I was told that you were seen wielding it?" Renard said with a questioning glance at Gabrielle.

The girl's haughty composure vanished, a flush mounting in her cheeks as she reclaimed the sword from Renard. "Er, ah, yes."

"It belonged to your Papa?"

Gabrielle exchanged an uncertain glance with Ariane, who had likewise tensed.

"Yes," Ariane said swiftly. "It—it was my father's."

Ah, Renard thought, studying both women, who were taking great pains to avoid his penetrating stare. So the sword obviously was not Papa's. Interesting. Then whose was it?

"You should never have taken the sword, Gabrielle. Later, you must make sure it is returned to—to where you found it."

Some silent communication passed between the two sisters, but before Renard could probe further, Miri Cheney slipped into the room. The child was doing her best to hide behind her fall of long, shimmering, white-blond hair.

When Renard greeted her, she mumbled something and ducked to the shelter of Ariane's skirts. If Ariane was the Lady, and Gabrielle the princess of the family, Miri was definitely the fairy child, a little wild, a little fey, and rather fragile.

Ariane draped her arm protectively around her little sister's shoulders and said, "You must excuse, Miri, my lord. She is rather shy of strangers."

Almost painfully so and Renard doubted that her recent ordeal had helped much. When she peeked at him, he saw that she was still very pale, shadows haunting her eyes.

He gentled his voice as he said, "Mademoiselle, I have something for you as well."

Striding to the door, Renard summoned the maid to fetch the wicker basket he had brought. He hunkered down in front of Miri, setting it at her feet. "There was something found at the church. Something that was left after everyone else had departed. A friend of yours, perhaps?"

Renard popped back the lid to reveal a scrawny black cat with white paws, who hissed, looking less than delighted with its confinement. As the creature leapt out of the basket, Gabrielle shrank back with a cry of alarm.

The cat looked slightly feral, obviously not domesticated to any home or barn. Renard wondered if he had made a mistake by bringing it here, but the transformation in Miri was miraculous.

"Ohhh!" Her eyes brightened, her cheeks flooded with color.

The cat had taken refuge beneath a chair, but Miri knelt down before it, murmuring something in coaxing tones. The cat crept slowly forward, allowing her to gather it up.

As she rose to her feet, the cat seemed to melt, going boneless in her arms, rubbing its head beneath her chin with a rumbling purr. Miri crooned in its ear. "I am so glad you are safe. Everything will be better for you now. You shall live in our barn, and you won't have to trouble the poor mice. I shall feed you a saucer of cream and a bit of fish every day. And you shall make the acquaintance of my other friends, like Hercules."

Her shyness all but forgotten, she paused to cast a timid glance up at Renard. "You did ride him here, monsieur?"

"But of course, mademoiselle. It seems difficult to keep him away from Belle Haven. And you."

"I should like to see him later. To thank him for coming to rescue me today."

"Yes," Renard replied with admirable gravity. "Wasn't it splendid of him?"

His wry humor was not entirely lost on Miri. She blushed and ducked her head. "It was splendid of you too, monsieur."

Gabrielle's snort was so audible, it shifted Renard's attention in her direction. The girl's nose crinkled with complete contempt but he scarcely took heed of that, arrested by the expression on Ariane's face.

She stared at Renard, her quiet gray eyes almost luminescent with gratitude.

"Thank you," she said.

"For what?" he said gruffly. "Alas, I have brought nothing for you, ma chère."

"You have already given me the greatest gift possible," she said with a significant glance at Miri. "My sister's life."

Renard gave a shrug as though to remind her that his rescue had been motivated purely by self-interest. But Ariane reached out to press his hand. Although surprised by the gesture, Renard smiled at her and for a moment it was as though they were the only two people present.

But Gabrielle was there to quickly remind them they were not alone. She thrust herself in between Renard and Ariane.

"Is it not time we dined? I'm about to perish from lack of food, and I have heard that it is dangerous to allow an og— I mean, a man, to go unfed."

Ariane shot her sister a reproving frown, but fortunately Renard only appeared amused by Gabrielle's rudeness.

As they all settled around the small table, Ariane's initial feelings of awkwardness returned. It had been a long time since they had entertained a man at Belle Haven, not since those long-ago summers when her restless father had set aside his court manners and they had all dined together as a simple family here in her mother's chambers.

Those days had been among the last times that Ariane could remember when they had been truly happy. . . . She tucked her napkin on her lap, forcing the poignant memory from her mind. When she looked up, she became aware that Renard was studying her across the table, his rough features softened with sympathy. Once again, Ariane was beset with the suspicion that the man could read eyes.

She kept her gaze focused mainly on her plate as the first course was served, wondering if this supper had been a mistake. The meal was a tense affair. Miri was quiet, absorbed in feeding tidbits to the cat. Gabrielle sullenly pushed her food about her plate as though waiting for this ordeal to be over. Although he ate with a hearty appetite, even Renard was strangely silent.

Recollecting that part of her hope this evening was to draw Renard out a little more, Ariane pressed him for tales of his travels and he opened up enough to discuss a journey he and his friend Toussaint had once taken to London.

"Oh, London," Ariane cried. "I remember going there myself as a little girl. My mother was half-English and we went to visit her grandmother. She and my Great-aunt Eugenie used to get into some fearsome arguments over whether the site of the legendary Avalon was in Glastonbury or here in Brittany. Great-aunt Eugenie maintained that no magic could possibly endure in a cold damp land such as England."

Renard smiled, sipping his wine. "The English would not agree. Their poets have even taken to calling their ruler the Faerie Queen."

"I have heard that Elizabeth is an astonishing woman, ruling her country as well as any king."

"They also say her mother, Anne Boleyn, was a witch," Renard replied.

Gabrielle stiffened, glaring at him. "Oh, and I suppose you are like most men, monsieur. Believing that the only way a woman could govern as well as a man is if she is using witchcraft."

"You mistake me, mademoiselle. I was only repeating idle gossip. I have the greatest respect for the intelligence, strength, and courage of women. Like the Lady of Faire Isle."

As Renard said this, he raised his glass in salute to Ariane, his eyes caressing her in a way that brought heat flooding to her cheeks. Gabrielle scowled, upsetting her wine, deliberately, Ariane was certain. Renard scooted his chair back just in time to avoid being doused.

Summoning Bette to clear away the mess, Ariane used the opportunity to administer a warning kick to Gabrielle under the table. Unfortunately, she got Miri instead.

"Ow!" Her little sister gazed at Ariane with a look of bewildered reproach. To Ariane, the tension at the table only grew worse after that. Renard could scarcely open his mouth to make any remark without Gabrielle taking offense or hotly contradicting him. Ariane feared if the comte had commented on the rain that was now lashing the house, Gabrielle would have stubbornly declared it to be the fairest night they had had all summer.

As the final course was being served, Miri drooped in her chair and begged to be excused. Ariane immediately seized upon the opportunity to be rid of Gabrielle as well.

"Of course, you must head off to bed, dearest," Ariane said to Miri. "And I am sure Gabrielle will be happy to help you into your nightdress and braid your hair."

Gabrielle showed no signs of budging. "Agnes can do that."

"I am sure after all she has been through today, Miri would by far prefer to have one of her sisters tend her than a servant," Ariane insisted.

"Oh, yes, please, Gabby." Miri fixed Gabrielle with a tremulous smile and large eyes.

Gabrielle could hardly refuse. She struggled to her feet with an obvious ill grace, flinging down her napkin. Renard rose respectfully to bid both girls good night, but Gabrielle ignored him, shepherding Miri out of the room. She paused on the threshold to cast a pointed look at Ariane.

"Ariane, could I have a word with you in private?" she said through clenched teeth.

Excusing herself to Renard, Ariane followed Gabrielle out into the hall. Miri had already disappeared into their bedchamber.

Gabrielle faced Ariane with arms locked furiously in front of her. "Are you out of your mind? Do you truly want me to leave you alone with that—that ogre in your bedchamber?"

"Stop calling him that," Ariane shot back in a low voice that would not carry to Renard. "I won't be alone. The servants are all nearby and I am sure the comte can be trusted to—"

"Since when? You don't know any more about that man than you ever did."

"Nor do I have much chance of knowing him better with you trying to dump your dinner over him and insulting him. Maman would have been so ashamed. Such discourteous behavior to a guest and one to whom we have much cause to be grateful."

"You had better take care how far your gratitude leads you, Ariane Cheney. There is some part of herself that a woman surrenders to a man she cannot get back again." Swallowing thickly, Gabrielle lifted her skirts and stormed after Miri.

Ariane gazed sadly after her, thinking that she needed no such reminder. If she was ever in danger of forgetting, she had only to look into Gabrielle's wounded eyes.

But as Ariane returned to Renard, she was acutely aware of being alone with the man, of the intimacy of their surroundings, the close proximity of the bed.

Renard rose courteously at her entrance. He was a titanic figure, easily able to overpower another man, let alone a woman. But his hooded eyes were his most alarming feature, those eyes that seldom revealed his thoughts.

When he held her chair for her, Ariane remained where she was, nervously entwining her fingers, feeling both awkward and slightly embarrassed by her sister's recent behavior.

"I—I must apologize for Gabrielle's rudeness," Ariane began.

"She doesn't trust me and warned you to beware of being alone with me," Renard said smoothly.

When Ariane flushed, he added with a grim smile. "It is all right, ma chère. I know that even when I don these ridiculous fine clothes, I still look like an alehouse ruffian, as my grandfather frequently pointed out to me. And your sister has reason to be wary of men. She suffers from a bruised heart."

Renard's expression turned grave. "I fear I can be all bully and bluster sometimes. And I did once threaten to carry you off if you refused to wed me, something I am now deeply ashamed of. I didn't mean it, Ariane."

"I know that." Ariane was surprised to realize that for all of his intimidating appearance and manner, there was an astonishing streak of gentleness in Renard, one that perhaps he was not aware of himself.

And he had betrayed himself again. There was only one way he could know about Gabrielle's bruised heart. He had the ability to read eyes, as Ariane had long suspected.

Renard was more unguarded tonight than Ariane had ever seen him. If she could get him completely relaxed, perhaps she could finally learn the truth about this enigmatic man.

Instead of settling into her chair, she hastened to refill his wineglass to the very brim. Renard made no demur, but his half-closed eyes glinted with amusement.

"That will not work, ma chère," he said softly.

"W-what won't?"

"Trying to ply me with wine. I have a hard head. Getting me drunk never loosens my tongue to give away secrets. I will be far more likely to regale you with bawdy songs."

"I wasn't . . . that is, I didn't mean—" Flustered, Ariane nearly tipped the bottle over as she plunked it down. "All right, perhaps I do hope you might mellow enough to let something slip, but you can hardly blame me after today. When I used that ring and then you appeared, you seemed to thunder out of those clouds as though you truly were some sort of sorcerer—"

"I am no sorcerer."

"But you *do* read eyes. You looked at my sister, Gabrielle, and you saw the pain she allows no one to see. You read the sorrow in her eyes."

"No."

Ariane frowned, frustrated that he could still persist in denying his ability. He continued in tones of quiet resignation, "I can read of her sorrow in yours."

At long last. She had finally gotten him to admit it, that he possessed skills and knowledge no ordinary man could possibly have. She sank weakly down into her chair and raised her eyes to his with a desperate earnestness.

"Please, Renard, you have got to tell me the truth. *Who are you?*"

※ ※ ※

CLAD IN HER NIGHTDRESS, MIRI PERCHED ON A LOW STOOL, TEASING the cat with a hair ribbon while Gabrielle brushed out her hair. Gabrielle dragged the brush ruthlessly through the moon-gold tangles, angry with Ariane. Angry with herself as well, for betraying to Ariane the existence of a wound that Gabrielle wanted to believe long healed over.

"Ouch!" Miri shot a reproachful look up at her. "You are pulling."

"Sorry." Gabrielle began to twist the shining strands into a braid. She tried to focus on the task and subdue all the unwanted emotions and memories churning through her. She didn't know why this evening should have triggered so many thoughts of her painful interlude with Etienne Danton.

Perhaps it was observing the soft light that had started to creep into Ariane's eyes when Renard was present, the innocent blush stealing into her cheek, an innocence Gabrielle no longer possessed.

A man didn't need a magic ring to seduce a woman and Renard seemed to know just the right way to get round Gabrielle's prudent sister. Bringing Miri that damned cat, drawling out his clever compliments.

Smooth-tongued villain, spouting the sort of flattery that Ariane would be most eager to believe! But perhaps she was merely jealous, Gabrielle reflected miserably.

Gabrielle snatched the ribbon away, disrupting Miri's game with the cat. She gave a last twist to the braid, then secured it with the now slightly frayed bit of silk.

Miri reached around to pat the braid, frowning. "It is too tight. I like the way Airy does it better."

"I did the best I could and unfortunately our older sister is a bit preoccupied tonight."

Miri scooped up the cat and regarded Gabrielle with a troubled look. "Is Ariane going to have to marry the comte now because she used his magic ring?"

"No, she has to use it three times. That is their ridiculous agreement."

"And . . . and do you think Ariane will ever use the ring again?" Miri asked anxiously.

"I hope not. If she does, I will find a way to get rid of that cursed thing, myself."

"Good. I don't want Ariane to go off and leave us to marry the comte. Even if we become dreadfully poor."

"That won't happen," Gabrielle said, briskly turning down the covers on the bed. "I will find a way to take care of all of us."

"But I don't want you to go away either. I wish all three of us could remain here on Faire Isle together, just as we are, and never change."

"I am afraid that is impossible." Gabrielle sighed. Change came to a woman whether she wished for it or not. The important thing was not to be powerless when it did.

"At least nothing will change right now." Miri comforted herself, cuddling the cat. "Monsieur Renard will go away again . . . although he does not seem quite as bad as I first thought him."

Gabrielle rolled her eyes. "Do not be imagining that a man is some sort of hero just because he gives you a cat."

"He can't give me what he doesn't own." Miri nuzzled her nose against the cat's dark fur. "But the comte did rescue me and Necromancer, and for that we are grateful."

"*Necromancer?*" Gabrielle stared at her little sister in disbelief. "Miri, considering you have already been suspected of witchcraft, do you really think that is the wisest thing to be naming that cat?"

"That is what he wants to be called."

"Fine," Gabrielle muttered. "Far be it from me to argue with a cat. Now show Monsieur Necromancer the door and give him directions to the barn."

Miri clutched the cat closer in her arms. "B-but he wants to stay with me."

"Oh, no. I am not going to tolerate any of your creatures here in our bedchamber. I have always made that plain."

Miri said nothing, just continued to regard Gabrielle with wide, beseeching eyes. She looked suddenly so small and fragile standing there in her nightdress and bare feet. Gabrielle's heart twisted with the thought of exactly how close she had come to losing her little sister that day.

Her eyes misted. She swallowed hard, then surprised both

Miri and herself by enveloping the girl, cat and all, in a fierce hug, until Necromancer let out a yowl of protest.

"All right. He can stay," Gabrielle said. "But he's not sleeping on the bed."

"No, indeed. Necromancer wants to mount guard on the window seat and keep watch in case the witch-hunters try to return."

"Oh, good," Gabrielle drawled. "I feel so much safer."

"Yes, me too," Miri replied seriously. She settled the cat on the window seat, with much fussing and petting until Gabrielle ordered her to come to bed.

For someone who had almost been nodding off at the supper table, Miri now fidgeted about the room, picking up discarded clothing, pausing to straighten the half-finished painting of the unicorn.

"That stupid thing," Gabrielle groused. "We should burn it."

"No!" Miri cried. "You gave the painting to me and I love it."

"A portrait of a legless unicorn?"

"Don't you think you will ever want to finish it?"

Gabrielle stared at the canvas. The dream-ridden girl who had been able to lose herself in the world of paint, canvas, and vivid imaginings seemed just that to Gabrielle. Lost.

"No," she said, abruptly turning away. "I don't have that kind of magic anymore."

Miri tiptoed around her, then reached up to plant a timid kiss on Gabrielle's cheek. "That's all right. I like the painting just as it is."

"And I would like it if you would stop delaying so we could go to bed. I am exhausted." But Gabrielle softened her complaint by tugging playfully on her sister's braid.

Miri clambered reluctantly into bed. Gabrielle extinguished the candle and settled down by her in the darkness. Gabrielle rolled over, punching her pillow into the shape she liked it.

"Gabrielle?" Miri whispered.

"Mmm?" Gabrielle replied, stifling a yawn.

"Do you think you will ever see a real unicorn?"

"No, because—"

Because according to the legend, any maiden who captured a unicorn was supposed to be pure, innocent, untouched. Gabrielle suppressed the bleak thought.

"Because I don't believe in them," she mumbled.

"I still do," Miri said. "And I still believe that Papa will come back someday too. That is what helped me when I was facing the witch-hunters. I tried to remember how brave Papa always was."

Gabrielle had her own opinions regarding the courage of a man who would abandon his dying wife and three daughters, but she said nothing. Apparently Miri found her silence equally as damning, for she asked, "Don't you believe that any men are good, Gabby? Not even Papa?"

Gabrielle was far too tired to get into any discussion with her innocent sister regarding their errant father. "Of course I still believe some men are good."

For some inexplicable reason, Captain Remy's image sprang to mind. She added, "However, the good ones are usually insufferably noble and earnest."

"What about witch-hunters?"

"What?"

She heard Miri struggling up onto one elbow to peer down at Gabrielle. "Do you think any witch-hunters could possibly be good?"

"How can you even ask such a thing? All witch-hunters have rotten black hearts. Now will you please stop asking me silly questions and go to sleep?"

Miri sighed and sank back down onto her pillow. After a moment her small voice came again. "I—I can't sleep, Gabby. I have been having some of my nightmares again and—and they keep getting worse."

Gabrielle rolled over. Even in the darkness, she could make out the glint of Miri's wide frightened eyes.

"Come here, then," she said gruffly. "The nightmares can't get you if you stay close to me."

Miri scooted gratefully closer, nestling her head against Gabrielle's shoulder. She asked in a wondering voice, "Have you become like Maman, then? Able to banish bad dreams?"

"No, she was a wise woman." Gabrielle gave Miri a squeeze and said in mock-fierce tones. "Me . . . I intend to be the most wicked witch the world has ever known. Even nightmares will be afraid of me."

Miri giggled. "My brave and bold sister. I will never forget the way you charged those witch-hunters with your sword."

Yawning, she snuggled down farther beneath the blankets and closed her eyes. Long after Miri had fallen asleep, Gabrielle held her close, listening to the even rise and fall of her breathing.

She was grateful Miri had fallen asleep, grateful for the darkness, glad that Miri had been unable to see her face. Otherwise the child might have realized that her brave and bold sister was just as afraid of bad dreams as she was. Nightmares of a certain sunlit afternoon in the hayloft of a barn.

Chapter Fifteen

THE STORM HAD DIMINISHED INTO A MONOTONOUS PATTER OF rain against the windows. Renard doubted that Ariane even noticed, her earnest gray eyes fixed on him, offering him no escape this time, her question hanging in the air between them.

"Who are you?"

Renard sipped his wine, resting his hand atop the table, the candlelight glinting off the metal surface of his ring. Ariane placed hers alongside, her fingertips falling just short of touching his, her hand in slender contrast to his own large, ungainly one.

Her brow furrowed in perplexity as she studied their matching rings.

"How could these rings possibly work?" she asked. "I know from my books on ancient science that a well-developed brain may possess the power to transfer thoughts. Do these rings act as some sort of conductor because of the metal they are made of?"

Renard regarded her. "You are a funny sort of witch, ma chère, always looking for logic rather than magic."

"I am not a witch," she replied. "And yes, I do prefer rational explanations, so tell me where you acquired these rings and no nonsense this time, please."

After a long, drawn-out sigh, Renard confessed, "The rings were . . . were a legacy. I inherited them from my mother."

"So she was *not* the simple shepherd lass you claimed her to be."

"Oh, yes, she was that. But she was also a daughter of the earth. The same as you."

Ariane had begun to suspect as much. "And your maman . . . she was the one who taught you to read eyes?"

"No, I learned nothing from my mother. I never knew her." Renard fortified himself with a swallow of wine. "I was raised by my grandmother, a wise woman of the mountains. It was she who taught me the arts of reading the eyes and other ancient lore. She is also the one who forged the rings for my mother and father. Powerful magic to bind them together forever.

"Unfortunately, forever didn't last that long. My mother died giving birth to me and my father perished shortly thereafter, struck down by a sudden inflammation of the lungs. Though I suppose there are some romantics who would have said he died of a broken heart."

"I am sorry," Ariane said quietly.

Renard shrugged. "It is hard to grieve for people one has never known. My parents seemed to me no more than a sad and sweet fairy tale my grandmother spun for me beside the fire on chilly evenings. Our cottage on the mountain, my kinsman Toussaint, and old Lucy . . . those were all that was real to me."

"Old Lucy?"

"That was what the folk of the mountain called my grandmother and I grew to do the same. She was not book-learned like your Maman. She could not even read her own name, but she was exceedingly wise—"

Renard checked himself as the serving maid, Bette, appeared, bearing more wine and a dish of comfits. Ariane was quick to dismiss the girl, telling her not to come again unless called. Gabrielle would hardly have approved, but Ariane feared he would attempt to close himself off again.

As soon as Bette had gone, Ariane leaned forward in her seat. "But what of your grandfather Deauville? Were you entirely forgotten by your father's people?"

Renard's lips tightened with that grim look he always assumed at any mention of the old comte. "For a long time, mercifully yes, the comte did forget about my existence. My grandfather had entirely cut my father off after his marriage to—as he scornfully put it—a filthy peasant, the daughter of an old witch.

"But my grandfather's rejection did not matter to me. I was quite content growing up on my mountain, tending our small garden and our flock of sheep. Exploring the hills with the other lads of our village, indulging in rough-and-tumble games."

Renard gave a rueful smile, rubbing the bridge of his nose. "That is how I broke my nose the first time, in a wrestling match with Timon the Trickster. A small but wiry boy, who could not be trusted to play fair. But for that matter I suppose none of us lads from the mountains could. We were a rather unruly lot, ma chère."

"I can well imagine," Ariane said.

Renard's eyes waxed a trifle wistful. "Don't mistake me. It could be a hard life up in those hills, the winds at times cruel and unforgiving. But old Lucy's knowledge of the earth, her skills in the ancient lore made certain we never went hungry. It was a good life, clean and simple until—"

"Until?" Ariane prompted softly when he hesitated.

The dark look crept back into Renard's eyes. "Until the day my grandfather ran out of other heirs. They died off one by one until his only remaining kin was the grandson of the witch, the oafish peasant boy. So in the summer of my sixteenth year he came to fetch me away."

Renard paused, taking a swallow of his wine.

"And what happened?" Ariane asked anxiously.

"I resisted him. After all, I didn't even know the old bas—" Renard checked himself with an apologetic grimace. "I beg your pardon, lady. I didn't even know my grandfather and I had no wish to ever become Monsieur le Comte. All I wanted was my own small piece of the mountain, a cottage with a fine stone hearth and feather-tick bed. A place to raise both a flock of sheep and a herd of boisterous children, with a sturdy, cheerful wife at my side.

"I had already fallen in love, with a comely miller's daughter. Martine Dupres was quite plump and pretty, with cornflower eyes and hair the color of wheat."

Renard's voice softened at the memory. From his description, Ariane had no difficulty imagining a more rustic version of Gabrielle. She touched the ends of her own somber brown hair and experienced an odd, sharp pang.

"You—you were betrothed to this girl?"

"Yes, but Monsieur le Comte was not interested in my desire to rut with some peasant wench, as he so delicately put it." Renard scowled. "He brought forth a horse and ordered me to mount up without even time to bid Martine farewell.

"When I told him to go to—er, that is, declined his offer to come live with him, my grandfather had me taken by force. That is how I broke my nose for the second time, or was it the third? I put up the devil of a fight, but I was dragged off to my grandfather's chateau and our tussle of wills began. He, attempting to make what he called a proper Deauville of me, me doing my damned best to spit in his eye and escape. I would run, but he would hunt me down and have me beaten."

"Oh, how could he!" Ariane cried. She had known the old comte could be a hard man, but to treat his own grandson thus . . .

Renard merely patted her hand and smiled. "Do not let my tale distress you. My hide is as thick as my head. The whippings only made me the more stubborn in my resolve, until one day I managed to get clean away, all the way back to my mountain. I was a ragged, filthy beggar by the time I collapsed at Lucy's door. Even you with your steady calm and courage, you would have recoiled."

Ariane blushed, pleased with his compliment.

"Lucy took me in, fed me, bathed my sore feet and then . . . then she told me that she would help me no further. I would have to go back to my grandfather. In fact, she had already sent for him. I—I was surprised."

Renard's fingers tightened around his wineglass. "I had trusted Lucy. I had been so sure she would help me escape from him, help me to fight."

"Your grandmother was only one old woman," Ariane reasoned. "What could she have possibly done to thwart the will of a powerful nobleman like your grandfather?"

"Lucy would not have helped me even if she could have," Renard said bitterly. "She insisted it was my destiny to become the Comte de Renard. It was another of Lucy's skills, or so she claimed, the ability to obtain glimpses of the future by staring into the fire. Do you believe in such visions?"

"My mother did not put much store by them. She said most times such visions were merely the product of imagination or so vague, they could be interpreted any way the seer wished. And yet, Miri often has disturbing dreams that cannot be explained, nightmares that seem to herald dire future events."

"Lucy had complete faith in her visions, although there were times I suspected that her predictions had more to do with things *she* wanted to have happen, and she did her best to ensure that they came true. After all, she was the one who helped my mother win the love of a comte's son. I was a fool not to have realized it sooner, but it was my grandmother's dearest ambition to see me become this great and powerful lord."

"Can you truly blame her for that?" Ariane asked. "You have surely seen for yourself how hard the life of a peasant can be. It is scarcely surprising that your grandmother would have wished something better for you."

"But they were *her* wishes, not mine, and I never forgave her for it."

He still hadn't. Ariane could see the ages-old resentment banked in his eyes as he continued, "Especially when I found out that she had arranged for *my* Martine to be married to another man in my absence."

His Martine. But for the interference of his grandfather, Renard would be long ago wed and raising his herd of children somewhere up in the wilds of the mountains. His path and Ariane's would never have crossed that day in the forest. It was somehow strangely hard to think of that.

"Were you very broken-hearted?" she asked.

Renard hunched his shoulders. "Hearts mend quickly enough when you are young. Far better to discover the folly of love when you are but sixteen and have time to live the rest of your life with greater wisdom.

"But losing Martine did rather take the fight out of me. When my grandfather arrived to reclaim me, I turned my back on my mountain and Lucy forever. I tried to fit into his world.

"However, I couldn't ride properly, couldn't wield a sword, couldn't wear my doublet and cape with the proper panache. It is difficult to swagger along in one's boots when you have feet the size of blacksmith anvils."

His wry description coaxed a smile from Ariane.

"You should have been there the first time I was obliged to attend a masked ball and tournament. But no, it is far better that you were not, because I made a poor spectacle of myself. I held my sword like a butcher trying to hack up a side of beef. I was easily disarmed. I pretended to yield, then when I had my opponent off guard, I rushed him, pinned his sword arm, and laid him out with a single blow. Then I stood, flinging up my arms in triumph."

He gave a dry laugh. "Unfortunately, instead of the applause I expected, I was greeted by jeers. My grandfather was livid, calling me a disgrace to the Deauville name.

"Great dolt that I was, I didn't even understand what I had done wrong, all their niceties about rules of engagement, the courtesies of battle. How can there be any courtesy in battle? When I fight, I fight to conquer. When I play, I play to win. The result, I suppose, of too many afternoons engaged in rough hurly-burly, learning to protect my poor nose from Timon the Trickster."

Renard smiled at Ariane, but she did not respond. She could see beyond his jesting to all the pain, the humiliation that awkward boy had suffered.

Feeling somewhat discomfited by her sympathy, he lowered his eyes. "I fear you may have succeeded in making me a little drunk after all. I cannot remember the last time I have droned on this way, boring a pretty lady."

"I am not bored," she murmured. "Please go on."

It was an invitation he would have refused from anyone else. It was those quiet eyes of Ariane's. Every wise woman he had ever known had had compelling eyes like that. But old Lucy's had been more shrewd, demanding. Ariane's eyes were gentle, calm, asking nothing . . . asking everything. Only that one be no less than honest with her.

Renard shifted guiltily in his chair and took another swallow of wine. "There is little more to tell, ma chère. When my grandfather despaired of teaching me anything himself, he packed me off to Paris, hoping I would acquire some polish there. If nothing else, it would keep the pair of us from murdering each other, which we might have done, had we continued under the same roof."

"Then, tell me about Paris."

"Have you never been there yourself?"

"Only once or twice when I was quite young. My father kept a house there. He was fond of city life and following the court. But my mother did not care for it, especially not for her children."

"I should fancy not. The French court can be a treacherous place, full of intrigue. Especially these days."

"Y-yes." Ariane steadfastly regarded the napkin on her lap, but not before Renard caught a flash of her eyes, reading just the merest glimpse, the barest insight into what—or perhaps it was more apt to say who—had been troubling the peace of Faire Isle.

Oh, ma chère. What have you been doing to incur the enmity of the Dark Queen?

Renard doubted she would answer him even if he voiced the question aloud. She was already blocking her thoughts. All he could do was remain alert, watchful until she lowered her guard again.

Pleating her napkin, she turned the conversation back to him. "So what did you do in Paris? You were not at court?"

"No, I was sent to attend the university. My grandfather's tutors had finally managed to drill the rudiments of reading and writing into my thick skull, the one accomplishment for which I am grateful to the old man."

"The university?" Ariane said wistfully. "I should have loved to be able to attend. There was a time long ago when some noble women were permitted to study medicine there."

"Chérie, there is nothing those fools could have taught you. The chief occupation of the students seemed to be rioting, drinking, and whor—er, gaming. I came to excel at all these skills.

"I suppose I would have continued on in this empty fashion except that one day Toussaint arrived in Paris. He is my grandmother's cousin, but he always felt more like my brother, uncle, or father. I was exceedingly glad to see him until I realized why he had come."

This was one part of Renard's past he would definitely have been content to forget, to leave well alone. Ariane rested her fingers lightly on his sleeve, and Renard continued reluctantly, "Toussaint brought me word that witch-hunters were combing our mountains, looking for Lucy."

Renard felt the sudden tension in Ariane's fingers and he covered her hand with his own. "Toussaint wanted me to come back with him. I am ashamed to confess that I nearly refused. I was still angry with her. But in the end, I rode out with him.

"You talk of premonitions. I was seized with a sense of urgency that pushed me to ride faster, harder until my horse was nigh on the brink of collapse. And still it did not matter—"

"You came too late," Ariane said.

Renard nodded grimly. "I found little left of our cottage or my grandmother. Only a pile of rubble and broken beams, scorched earth."

Ariane's fingers tightened on his arm, a myriad of emotions chasing through her eyes, horror, sorrow, and comprehension.

"So that is why you went after Le Vis with such hatred. Was he the one who—who—"

"No," Renard replied tersely. "I never set eyes on the villain until today. Witch-hunters are all alike to me. As for those who burned my grandmother, I dealt with them long ago. The only fires they will ever kindle again are in hell."

A hard cold light crept into Renard's eyes and Ariane shivered, drawing her hand away.

Renard cast her a taut smile. "The thought of my retribution disturbs you, doesn't it? You, with your all-too-kind and forgiving heart. You even saved Le Vis after all the vile things he tried to do, wasted your most precious magic upon him, the Breath of Life. Why did you do it, Ariane?"

"My mother always taught me to beware the darkness of vengeance. To heal, not to kill. To try to save life, not allow it to slip away. That is why I saved Le Vis and—and also partly because of you."

"Me?"

"I did not want you succumbing to darkness either. After all you had already done for us, you could have been in far greater peril if you had been accused of murdering Le Vis."

"Then you would be rid of both of us."

"I don't want to be—" Ariane checked herself.

Renard reached out to touch her cheek, but Ariane drew nervously away. She twisted the ring on her finger and wondered if Gabrielle was right, if this strange talisman was somehow pulling her deeper into Renard's power.

"So tell me what happened next," she said. "After the death of your grandmother."

Reluctantly accepting her rebuff, Renard leaned back in his chair. "After my actions against the witch-hunters, it was deemed wise that I should leave the country for a time. My grandfather was quite glad to have me go. Our enmity had worsened after Lucy's death.

"I could never prove it, but I strongly suspected the old comte had had a hand in setting the witch-hunters after Lucy. He believed that she had cursed him, that that was why all his other sons and grandchildren had died, leaving only me to inherit.

"My grandfather and I parted with mutual loathing. In fact, we each vowed to kill the other if our paths ever crossed again. Happily they did not. I set out on my travels with Toussaint. My grandfather took to ravishing young women in a desperate effort to get himself another heir.

"I did not set foot back in Brittany again until I received word of his death. I think I only came then partly out of spite to have bested the old man at last, and partly at Toussaint's urging. He seems to have this strange notion I might make a tolerable comte."

"He is right," Ariane said. "More than tolerable if you put your mind to it. You have seen so much of the world, my lord, and not just the world of wealth and power. You know the ways and cares of humbler, simple folk. You have such rare abilities to offer the people of your estate, such gifts of compassion, under-standing and—and—"

"I might make an excellent comte . . . with the right wife," he added, seizing possession of her hand. "Now that I have told you so much about myself, surely I deserve some sort of reward."

"What did you have in mind?" Ariane asked warily.

"Marry me. Tonight."

Ariane laughed. "That is quite a reward for a few confi-dences, my lord. Especially since there is one thing you still have not told me."

"Oh?" Renard's eyes narrowed. "And what is that?"

"Why you are so determined to wed me."

"Ah, that." Was it her imagination or did Renard seem a tri-fle relieved that that was all she wanted to know?

"After all, you do not pretend to be in love with me. Any more than I am with you," Ariane added quickly.

"No, we are both too wise for that. And yet there does seem to be some undefinable force drawing us together. I believe you feel it too, ma chère. Some inexplicable fate."

Fate? Ariane frowned, an unwelcome thought piercing her. "Oh, Renard, please. Never tell me that—that I formed part of one of old Lucy's predictions for your future."

Renard smiled and quoted, *"Someday, Justice, you will be lost. More lost than you have ever been. You will come upon the woman with the quiet eyes and she will be the one who will lead you safely back. Your destiny."*

"Oh Lord," Ariane groaned. "What nonsense."

"Ah, but Lucy's other predictions came true, did they not? I am now the Comte de Renard."

"Yes, but you said she helped to arrange that and besides, even if the prediction is true, I already rescued you from being lost in the woods. My part in your destiny is fulfilled."

"Not quite," Renard murmured, carrying her hand to his lips with a simmering look that caused her to shiver.

He was back to wooing her again, his hooded eyes too intent upon her face. Ariane had been more comfortable with him when he was simply seated at her table, being open, forthright, sharing confidences. At least then, she had not felt so warm and flustered.

Withdrawing her hand from his, she attempted to recover her composure. "There is only one place I should lead you and that is to your horse. It is growing late."

"Will you cast me out into the storm, chérie?"

"The rain has nearly stopped." Ariane rose to her feet. As she did so, her napkin cascaded from her lap. She moved to retrieve it, unfortunately at the same time as Renard. Their heads collided with a resounding thunk that sent her staggering back.

"Ow." She straightened, rubbing her throbbing brow, blinking away pinpoints of light. She saw Renard was doing likewise.

"You know, ma chère," he complained. "It is all right even for strong and wise women to occasionally allow a man to perform a trifling service for them such as fetching a napkin."

"I—I am sorry."

"Are you all right? I did warn you. I have an excessively hard head." He brushed her hands aside to examine her temple for himself. "My proud, independent Ariane. Was it so very hard for you to use the ring and send for me today?"

"The hardest thing I have ever done," she admitted. "And not just because I doubted the magic of the ring or my wariness over our agreement. But because I am the Lady of Faire Isle. It is my responsibility to protect this island. Yet when the witch-hunters came, I could do nothing. You were the one risking your life to save them."

"I broke a few heads with my sword, but you put yourself constantly at risk to help these people. Your eyes carry the burdens of your sisters, these islanders, and any stranger who chances across your path, asking your help. And you try to do it all alone. I wish you would trust me enough to allow me to help you."

Ariane wished that she could too when he looked at her that way, his eyes so warm and open, his hand so sure and steady as he cupped her neck, coaxing her closer. She made no effort to resist as his mouth settled over hers, soft and lingering.

Faint echoes of Gabrielle's recent warning chased through Ariane's mind, but another less sensible part of herself whispered, *It's only a kiss.*

His arm stole about her waist before she even realized what he was doing, gathering her closer. She raised one hand in a feeble effort to ward him off. But as he continued to kiss her, he placed his hand against hers, palm to palm, their matching rings striking against each other.

Something most strange happened. It was as though the ring grew warm upon her finger, sending a glowing current through her. Sensations of heat rushed through her, shattering her reason, her sense of control like fine spun glass.

Their hands entwined, rings locked together, Ariane kissed him back feverishly. She did not even seek to stop him when he fumbled with the fastening of her gown. She tugged urgently at his doublet, their lips never breaking contact, kiss after eager kiss.

The chamber around her whirled, blurred, and disappeared in a fiery haze. She was naked in his arms and never had anything felt so right. The heat and strength of his sinewy body pouring into her like some golden light, the tender globes of her breasts pressed to the coarse golden mat of Renard's bare chest. She flung back her head as his lips caressed her throat, his huge hands warming her wherever he touched.

She had been so cold and alone for so long. She scarcely realized how much until this moment when her fingers entwined with his, their rings nearly striking off sparks until the metal seemed to fuse and burn. Become one ring, one hand.

Ariane clung to Renard, almost weeping with the urgent need to be closer to him still, to be bound to him in the most intimate way possible between woman and man. One heart, one body. He felt raw with a primitive heat, strong and powerful, promising her far more than passion, promising her shelter from all the storms, all the Dark Queens, all the witch-hunters of this world.

And that was perhaps the most dangerous seduction of them all. This promise to protect and care for her forever. All she had to do to obtain such security was to . . . surrender.

"There is some part of herself a woman surrenders to a man she can never get back again."

Gabrielle's warning rang out stronger in her mind. Even as Renard urged her toward the bed, Ariane found the will to resist.

She stumbled back, panting as the fire burning inside her began to cool, the room shifting back into focus. Flushed, embarrassed, she crossed her arms in front of her in an effort to conceal her nakedness.

Her nakedness? Ariane blinked in confusion as her fingers closed over the soft silk of her bodice. Gazing down, she was stunned to see that her gown was not even disarranged. She was still fully clothed.

And so was Renard, his chest rising and falling quickly beneath his doublet. He looked a little dazed as well. He raised his hand to stare at his ring.

Ariane's gaze dropped to hers, the metal still curiously warm.

"What—what just happened?" she asked hoarsely.

"I am not sure. But I believe that when we touched hands and pressed the rings together, it was as though—as though it bound our minds together as well, intensifying all our wishes, our imaginings, our secret passions and desires."

"So we were about to make love . . . *inside our heads?*" Ariane cried. She stared at the ring on her hand with alarm. Shaking, she nearly clawed her own finger in her frantic effort to remove the metal band. She cast it down upon the table and backed away trembling.

Renard had already recovered himself enough to soothe, "Ah, chérie, please, don't be frightened. I'll admit that was a trifle unnerving—"

"I have threats enough in my life from debt collectors, unwanted suitors, and witch-hunters. But at least I have always felt safe inside my own head. Why didn't you warn me the rings could do such a thing if we brought them together?"

"I did not know myself."

Ariane regarded him with deep suspicion. "You were certainly quick enough to use the power once you discovered it," she accused. "Seducing me with—with your passionate imaginings."

"All those heated thoughts did not come entirely from me," Renard retorted.

Ariane's face burned. She wrapped her arms tightly around herself. But she realized it was more herself she feared, a wild, wayward part of her heart that she had scarcely recognized existed before tonight.

Renard stepped toward her. His fingers were gentle as he forced her to unlock her arms and gathered her hands into his own.

"Chérie, there is no need for you to be so distressed and embarrassed over what happened. As a daughter of the earth, you should know that the desire to mate is the most natural thing in the world. Why does it frighten you so?"

Because I don't want to end up like Maman, breaking her

heart over a faithless husband. Or even worse, like Gabrielle, wounded, embittered, my magic gone, Ariane thought desperately.

"But I am no ravisher or betrayer. Your magic would be safe with me." Renard replied as though she had spoken aloud.

Ariane started, then groaned, trying to pull away from him. "Renard, you have got to stop doing that. Stop invading my thoughts."

"Then tell your eyes to stop speaking to mine," he said, brushing a light kiss across her brow. "Why cannot we bring an end to this foolish game we have been playing? Just forget about rings and bargains and marry me."

"You were the one who set the rules for our contest, not I. I have only used the ring once and don't mean to ever again." She raised her hand wearily to her brow. "Now, please, it is very late and I am so tired and—and confused. If you want to remain until morning, I can supply you with a bed. Just not mine."

Renard regarded her for a long moment, his own eyes simmering with a mixture of regret and frustration. "No, it is likely for the best that I go," he said quietly. "But until I am certain all danger is past, I don't intend to be that far away."

Picking the ring up from the table, he folded it back into her hand. And then he was gone.

Chapter Sixteen

SHADOWS LENGTHENED ALONG THE WALLS OF THE STONE HOUSE in the countryside just beyond the suburbs of Paris. The place bore a gloom-ridden aspect and was shunned by its nearest neighbors. Monsieur Vachel Le Vis might be deemed a great and holy man, appointed by God to rid the world of witches, but even honest citizens dreaded to have his dark eye turn in their direction. Especially when he was in one of his black moods, as he had been ever since his return yesterday.

At such times only the boy Simon Aristide dared to wait upon his master. Carefully balancing the ewer of warm water, he carried it upstairs, glad that within the confines of the master's house, he could shed his heavy black robes. He moved much more quietly and quickly in his simple tunic and breeches.

Easing open the door to the master's bedchamber, Simon picked his way cautiously inside the darkened room. He set down the ewer upon the washstand and then cracked the curtains open, allowing a small ray of afternoon light to penetrate the chamber.

Simon gazed anxiously at the figure shivering on the massive four-poster bed. Monsieur Le Vis had fallen into one of his wild and unpredictable humors ever since their expulsion from Faire Isle. The Comte de Renard's men had been ruthless, driving their brotherhood all the way out of Brittany. Master Le Vis had been grim and silent throughout the entire ordeal, saying nothing even after their return to the house.

He had sealed himself up in his room, refusing to eat or drink, the chamber deathly silent except for the dull thuds and the occasional outcry of pain.

Tiptoeing toward the bed, Simon called softly, "Master?"

Lying on his stomach, his head twisted to one side on the pillow, Le Vis stared at Simon through a matted tangle of hair, his drooping eye glazed over.

But what truly caused Simon to shudder was the sight of the master's back, that pale expanse of flesh criss-crossed with angry red weals.

"Oh, master, what have you done to yourself?" Simon murmured. When the wild mood came upon him, he had known Master Le Vis to attempt to purge himself, but never to this brutal extent.

Simon made haste to fetch the basin closer. Dipping a cloth in the water, he prepared to minister to the master's wounds. But Le Vis thrust Simon's hands away.

"No, boy."

"But, master, you must allow me to help—"

"The only way you can help me is to, to hand me my—"

His features contorted painfully as he bent, groping for the scourge he had dropped upon the floor.

"No, master!" Simon cried. Le Vis's hands closed around the thick handle of the whip, while Simon fought desperately to wrench it away from him.

"Let go, boy. You . . . don't understand. Must continue . . . must purge out the poison."

Simon struggled until he succeeded in pulling the whip away. Ordinarily he could not have prevailed against a man the size and strength of the master, but Le Vis was greatly weakened by the punishment he had been inflicting upon himself.

Simon flung the whip across the room.

"How d-dare you—" Le Vis glared at him.

"You will fall ill and die if you continue in this fashion."

"I am dying already. That witch has poisoned me with her evil kiss." Le Vis pressed trembling fingers to his lips, his features contorting with revulsion.

Simon was at a loss himself to account for what Ariane Cheney had done to his master. But it seemed to him more in the nature of a miracle than anything evil.

"But Monsignor, the lady did save your life—"

"The lady! She is a succubus, using her foul mouth to try to draw out my soul." Le Vis staggered to his feet, a wild light springing into his eyes. But the moment passed. Le Vis sank weakly back down upon the edge of the bed. "That—that witch has put her curse upon me. I—I am doomed."

"No, master. You will be well if you allow me to tend your wounds and then take a little to eat and drink." Simon said. "You cannot hope to fight witches if you do not maintain your strength."

Le Vis released a long shuddering sigh. "You—you are right. M-must stay strong."

He remained docile after that, sucking in his breath and gritting his teeth as Simon ministered to his lacerated back. For his part, Simon was relieved to see the master coming back to himself. Le Vis was always at his most reasonable and calm after his dark mood had passed.

The master claimed these fits came upon him as the result of curses leveled at him by witches conspiring all over France to be his undoing, to prevent the continuance of his holy work. There were times that Simon privately feared the master might simply be a bit mad.

When he had finished tending to Le Vis's self-inflicted wounds, Simon persuaded him to partake of the tray of food he had fetched. After a little wine, some bread, and cheese, the master appeared much better.

He even reached out to tousle Simon's hair and said gruffly, "You are a good lad."

Simon smiled. He was reminded of the man who had so kindly taken him in years ago, giving him far more than food and a roof over his head. Given him the sort of education no mere peasant lad could have even dreamed of possessing. Reading, writing, and ciphering.

Simon often thought that Master Le Vis would have made the most clever and patient of tutors if he were not so obsessed— that is, possessed of a divine mission to destroy witches.

The master's expression turned morose as he sipped his wine. "By all the blessed saints, Simon, lad. What a debacle. To have waited so long to have my chance to destroy the evil women of Faire Isle and to have failed so dismally."

Simon squirmed in his seat, casting down his eyes. The better to conceal his guilty secret, for he was shamefully relieved they had failed, relieved especially that the little girl, Miri, had escaped.

Part of Simon knew that she had not been doing anything wrong. The Lady Ariane frightened him with her strange compelling eyes, her even stranger gift for restoring the dead to life. And the demon man upon his devil horse was a figure of complete terror. But Miri . . . the girl was fully as innocent and sweet as his own sister had been.

Simon shot a nervous sidelong glance at his master. "Monsignor, is it not possible that we might have been wrong about all the women on Faire Isle being evil?"

Le Vis's mouth twisted in a frown. Ordinarily such a comment would have earned Simon a sharp rebuke. But the master must have been mellowed enough with wine and exhaustion that he only chided, "Ah, Simon. You are still such an ignorant lad. I daresay I should not have yet taken you to a place so dangerous as Faire Isle. You were not ready for such a test of your faith. I fear you may have been bewitched by that clever little sorceress with her shining blond tresses and strange silvery eyes."

Simon flushed hotly. "I have not, sir. Miribelle Cheney is—is only a child. In my experience, many women are but simple creatures, easily led—"

"Your experience. All fifteen years of it," Le Vis scoffed. "I was far wiser at your age and you would be too if you had had a mother such as mine. Given to drink and fornication with any man who possessed a sou."

Simon had heard the sad tale of the master's wicked mother many times. But his own mother had been far different, virtuous and hardworking, as gentle and loving as his sister had been. He had seldom dared to contradict the master before, but he could not seem to hold his tongue.

"We were sent to the Faire Isle because we were told that the Cheney women were hiding a dangerous heretic, practicing witchcraft, weaving evil plots against the crown. But surely such schemes require too much cunning for the female mind. The Comte de Renard is the one to blame."

"Don't be absurd, lad. Renard hopes to marry the Lady of Faire Isle. *She* is the one who holds sway over him, but only a man who is evil himself would want to mate with a witch and he shall be punished along with—"

The master was interrupted by a light knock at his bedchamber door. When he uttered a curt command to enter, Brother Jerome appeared, the tall ascetic man looking paler than usual.

"Your pardon, Master Le Vis. But you have a visitor."

Le Vis scowled. "Bid whoever it is to be gone. Did I not say I have no wish to be disturbed?"

"You have little choice, master. It is the queen."

"The—the queen? *Here?*"

"I fear that somehow she has learned of what transpired in Faire Isle. She has come in great secrecy and demands to see you at once. You—you had better make haste."

Le Vis absorbed this in grim silence, then nodded. "Tell Her Majesty I will be down at once."

Le Vis shoved aside the food tray, rising stiffly to his feet. He snapped his fingers, commanding Simon to fetch his clothes. The boy scurried to help the master into his robes.

Surely this was odd behavior for any queen, to come by stealth at sundown to pay a visit to the master of witch-hunters. Simon cast an uncertain look up at the master, his mind bursting with questions. But one look at the dark expression settling into Le Vis's eyes warned Simon that this was one of those times he would do far better to hold his tongue and use his eyes and ears instead.

☙ ☙ ☙

SIMON TRAILED QUIETLY AFTER HIS MASTER, HIS OWN DARK ROBES brushing against the wooden floor. The private parlor of Vachel Le Vis was an austere chamber, unsoftened by carpets or hanging tapestries. The walls were adorned instead with paintings inspired by the Bible, grim reminders of the perfidy of women, Eve coaxing Adam to bite into the forbidden fruit, Salome holding up the head of John the Baptist, a hapless Samson being shorn by the treacherous Delilah.

The paintings were barely visible as the gloom of evening settled over the parlor. Only a few candles had been lit, but the master's unexpected guest seemed to prefer it that way. A woman of medium stature and robust frame, she was garbed entirely in black from the hem of her gown to the cloak falling from her shoulders. The only thing that relieved the darkness of her attire was the gold, ruby-encrusted cross that glittered around her neck.

Despite the veil that hid her face, there was little doubt of her identity. Queen Catherine had a regal carriage that was as hard to disguise as the imperious way she held out her hand to Monsieur Le Vis.

Simon had never seen the master accord respect or courtesy to any woman before. But Le Vis forced himself stiffly to his knees before the queen, paying homage to her outstretched hand.

"Majesty . . . this is an unexpected honor."

"Is it?" a dry voice inquired from behind the veil. "I wonder . . ."

She commanded Le Vis to rise. As the master struggled to his feet, Simon shuffled his feet awkwardly, wondering if he too would be expected to make some obeisance.

But as so often happened when he trailed in the master's wake, his silent presence went unremarked. He shrank back even farther against the wall, but he could not help gawking as Her Majesty lifted her veil. It was not often that a simple peasant lad ever got the chance to lay eyes on a queen.

He held his breath, not quite knowing what to expect. The form of Catherine de Medici was as plump as any good matron of the city. But there was no softness in the face revealed by the flickering candlelight, her features as cold and white as alabaster. This was as nothing compared to her piercing eyes.

Simon could not repress a shiver as the queen frowned at his master. "I was astonished, Master Le Vis, to hear of your return. And yet you sent no word to me regarding the outcome of your expedition."

"I—I am only just returned, Majesty. I planned to wait upon you tomorrow."

"That is no longer wise. There are prying eyes at the palace who would interfere with our work."

"Spies in your own household?" Le Vis looked much shocked.

"That can hardly surprise you, monsieur. Were you not the one who warned me that there are witches abroad everywhere these days, turning up in the most unexpected places?"

Simon thought that an odd half-smile played about her lips as she said this, but in the semidarkness it was difficult to tell. She continued, "With such evil abroad, all the more reason that I was bitterly disappointed to learn of the failure of your mission. Tell me what happened."

Le Vis bristled. The master was not accustomed to accepting commands from any women, even a queen. But he complied, relating the tale, grudgingly at first, then waxing ever more indignant as he described the defiance of Ariane Cheney and the interference of the Comte de Renard.

"Renard?" the queen interrupted. "How strange. The Deauvilles have ever been noted for casting their lot on the side of power. No Deauville would ever seek to defy the crown, unless of course he perceived some advantage in it for himself."

"The advantage this Justice Deauville seeks is union with a witch. He is that Cheney woman's lover."

"Then it was foolish of you, was it not? To allow Mistress Cheney to send to the comte for help."

The master flushed, looking much stung. "I allowed nothing. No messenger was permitted to leave the island. That Cheney witch conjured up her lover with witchcraft, summoning him by some unnatural means. I know not how."

"I do," Simon blurted out, then was immediately sorry when two heads swiveled in his direction, the master clearly furious at his impertinence, the queen, cool and assessing.

"And who might this be?" she asked.

"No one. Just young Simon Aristide, a novice of my order."

The master glowered and was about to dismiss him when the queen intervened.

"Come here, Master Aristide," she said, beckoning.

She spoke to him in a kind manner that strangely made him feel the more afraid. He moved haltingly toward her until he stood, head bowed, before the Dowager Queen of all France.

"Now, monsieur, what did you have to say?"

"The boy knows nothing," Le Vis growled.

"Silence. Allow the lad to speak."

The queen's icy command caused the master to subside with an angry hiss. She crooked her fingers beneath Simon's chin, forcing him to look up at her. "Don't be afraid. I understand boys. I have many sons of my own."

And devour them regularly for breakfast. Simon did not know why such an irreverent thought should have popped into his head. He found himself reluctant to tell her anything, but a strange thing happened. The longer he looked into the piercing depths of her eyes, the more he felt compelled to speak.

"Well, I—I—. It is probably nothing but when we were in the church, I noticed Mistress Cheney fidgeting with a ring dangling on a chain about her neck. Then later, by the pond, I saw the ring again. On her finger and—and she was twisting it and muttering.

"And when Monsieur le Comte pulled me from the pond, he was also wearing a ring and it matched Mistress Cheney's."

"So they were wearing betrothal rings," Le Vis said impatiently. "There is nothing remarkable in that."

"These were strange betrothal rings. Of plain metal with curious markings."

The queen said nothing, but her eyes narrowed. She stalked over to Master Le Vis's desk and snatched up a quill, dipping it in ink. While Simon and Le Vis watched, mystified, she scratched out something on a piece of parchment.

Blowing the paper dry, she carried it over to Simon. "Were the markings like these, Master Aristide?"

Simon squinted down at the odd symbols. "I cannot say for certain, but yes, I believe very like."

The queen slowly crumpled the parchment, murmuring, *"Le cercle d'amour.* Rings of great and ancient power."

"And doubtless of great evil," Le Vis said.

"Oh, no doubt," the queen agreed placidly.

Then how did she know of such things? Simon thought. There was something in her intent gaze that reminded him of Ariane Cheney and he wondered if the queen likewise possessed the ability to steal a person's thoughts. But surely that was impossible because that would also make the queen a—a—

She smiled and flicked the tip of one fingernail lightly against his cheek. "You are a clever boy, Master Aristide, with sharp, observant eyes. You will likely go far in this world—if you learn to be more circumspect."

The Queen Mother of France had just paid him a great compliment. Simon thought he should have flushed with pleasure. But her wintery smile seemed to splinter inside him like falling icicles striking the pavement. He shuddered and was excessively glad when Master Le Vis thrust him aside and he could retreat to his corner.

"If Your Grace will but give me a small command of soldiers," Le Vis said. "I will return to Brittany and settle the score with this demon comte. Then no ring will avail Mistress Cheney. I will be able to continue my trials for witchcraft—"

"Your witch trials do not interest me, Le Vis."

"But—but—" Le Vis frowned at her, uncertain. "When you first summoned me to the palace, you said that you had been directed by God to help me in my holy crusade against witches."

"I am afraid God will have to wait," she said drily.

Le Vis let out a sharp gasp, shocked by the queen's blasphemy, as was Simon himself. A flicker of irritation seemed to cross the queen's face, but was quickly smoothed over.

"Do not misunderstand me, monsieur. I, too, want to rid France of witches. But it is far more important for the security of my realm that I rid myself of other heretics first. I did not dispatch you to Faire Isle to make a great public spectacle by burning witches. I only wanted you to frighten Mistress Cheney into surrendering Captain Remy. I must have that man's head and soon before he succeeds in finding some way to disrupt the marriage of my daughter to the king of Navarre."

"That is something I do not entirely understand," Le Vis said, pursing his lips sourly. "Why a great Catholic queen such as yourself is so eager to wed our princess to a heretic."

"I have my reasons. Matters of state that do not concern you. Your only province is to destroy Remy and get me those gloves."

"That is something that also confuses me. What is so important about those gloves?"

"Because they are my gloves, you fool. Only think what those witches on Faire Isle could do with an article of my clothing in their possession. What dark spells they would weave against me. Do you wish to be responsible for my death, Le Vis?"

"No, most certainly not, Your Grace, but—"

"Then do as I tell you. Return to Faire Isle, but use a little more good sense and stealth this time. Go under cover of darkness and raid the house at Belle Haven—"

Le Vis bridled with indignation. "I pursue my justice in the open where all heretics and witches may see, tremble, and be afraid."

The queen sneered. "Do not be such a fool, Le Vis. If you wish to serve me, you will do as I instruct."

The master puffed out his chest. "I serve no woman, Your Grace. Only God."

"God may reward you in heaven, but I have the ability to do so here and now."

"I have no interest in amassing riches."

"I am not talking wealth, Le Vis, but treasure of a different sort. Power." When she stalked toward him, the master attempted to turn sullenly away. "Look at me, Le Vis."

He did so reluctantly, his gaze locking on hers.

"Get me Captain Remy and those gloves. Succeed and I will reward you beyond your wildest imaginings. I will make you my Grand Inquisitor with authority over every other court in the land. Your name will be set down in the annals of history. You will have unbridled power to rid France of every last heretic and witch."

"Every last witch," Le Vis repeated.

Simon had to fight a strong urge to rush at the master, break that strange unblinking contact of his eyes with the queen's. But the queen herself had already done so.

Lowering her veil, she said, "Return to Faire Isle at once and do not fail me this time. I seldom accord second chances."

"Yes, Your Majesty," the master said, in an unnerving monotone.

The queen took her leave. As she rustled past Simon, he shrank back. He should have leapt forward, bowing to open the door for the queen, but he seemed unable to move until after she had gone. He hastened anxiously over to his master.

Le Vis still looked dazed.

"Master?"

When Le Vis did not respond, Simon shook his arm. "Master Le Vis!"

The master blinked, gazing in some surprise at Simon and then around the empty room. "The queen?"

"She is gone, master. And I thank God for it," Simon could not resist adding fervently.

The master only gave him a bemused smile. "Did you hear what she said, young Simon? I am to be a great man, the Grand Inquisitor of all France."

"Y-yes, master. But I am not sure you should put such faith in the queen's promises."

"What do you mean?"

"Well I—I—" Simon squirmed beneath his master's heavy frown. "There is something so strange about the queen. Her eyes, the unusual things she knows about rings and such. I was wondering if she might not possibly be a witch herself."

Le Vis looked thunderstruck. "Are you mad, boy?"

"I am not the only one who wonders," Simon said defensively. "I have heard rumors in the street. Whispers. There are some who call her the Dark Queen and Sorceress."

"Scurrilous lies. And foolish ones as well about a woman who is a great Catholic monarch and the niece of a Pope. Good lord, boy," Le Vis snarled. "Do you think I would not know a witch if I met one?"

"Yes, m-master. I mean no, master."

"Then never let me hear you speak of such treasonous nonsense again."

"No, master." Simon ducked his head to conceal the stubborn set of his lips. Master Le Vis had accused him earlier of being charmed by little Miri Cheney, but Simon feared it was the master who was bewitched. Befuddled by Catherine de Medici's cold, compelling eyes, cozened by her honeyed promises.

※ ※ ※

THE QUEEN SETTLED BACK AGAINST THE CUSHIONS IN HER CARRIAGE, delicately pressing a handkerchief to her nose as though the witch-hunter's house had left a foul stench in her nostrils. A house that she knew had been purchased with blood money.

Accusers were entitled to a share of the condemned's estate, a strong inducement for good citizens to level charges of witchcraft against neighbors and Le Vis had profited more than most.

Le Vis, however, had been telling the truth when he had said that accumulating riches was not his prime goal. Wealth only enabled him to pursue his crusade against witchcraft, an obsession compounded out of his mad notions of religion, hatred for women, and lust for power. Fortunately, the minds of such fanatics were always easy to cloud.

Now the boy, Simon Aristide, was another matter. He viewed the world with that simple clarity often accorded the young and innocent. Catherine had been partly amused by the boy's sharp-eyed perception and vaguely disquieted as well. She had been able to read his mind, his entire pathetic history, how he had lost everything he'd cherished at the tender age of eleven, how his entire village had been destroyed by the malevolent act of some old crone.

The boy certainly had reason enough to hate witches, to want to destroy them. Looking into Simon's dark eyes, Catherine had been beset by a strange premonition that if Le Vis's pup ever had a chance to become full-grown, he might pose a threat, even to her. Some instinct urged her to have the boy destroyed now.

But she had greater things to worry about than a mere boy. Such as what use the fugitive Captain Remy and Ariane Cheney might be preparing to make of those gloves. Resting her head against the squabs of the swaying carriage, Catherine thanked God, or perhaps she should say Marie Claire, for sending Louise Lavalle to spy upon her. The courtesan's smug expression and the secretive gleam beneath her thick lashes had alerted Catherine to Le Vis's failure. Louise was good at concealing her thoughts, but Catherine was growing increasingly better at piercing the girl's mind.

Although . . . there were times that she feared Louise, fully aware of Catherine's suspicions, was playing games with her. Allowing Catherine to read her eyes, just enough to glimpse snippets of thoughts, both tantalizing and frustrating her.

She would deal with Louise soon enough. Her main concern was the Lady of Faire Isle, putting a stop to Ariane Cheney's interference with her plans. At least she had gleaned one tidbit from that fool Le Vis and his sharp-eyed boy.

So little Ariane Cheney had taken for herself a lover, this Comte de Renard. Ariane must be indeed besotted with the man to have bound herself to him using the *cercle d'amour*. An interesting piece of information and it was always good to know the weaknesses of one's enemies.

Catherine closed her eyes, seized by a small twinge of compunction. She was fully aware that despatching Le Vis back to Faire Isle was like setting loose a mad dog. Humiliated by his first failure, he would do far more than raid the house at Belle Haven to search for Captain Remy.

Le Vis would raze the place, destroying all who dwelt within, all of her dear friend Evangeline's pretty daughters.

Catherine sighed and murmured, "Forgive me, Evangeline. You know that *I* never wanted it to come to this. Your foolish girl has left me no choice."

ψ ψ ψ

ELSEWHERE IN PARIS, THE MASTER WITCH-HUNTER WAS NOT THE only one receiving an unexpected visitor that evening. Madame Hermoine Pechard cracked open her kitchen door and then hastily dragged the hooded woman waiting on her stoop inside.

It was not unusual for the tall, spare woman to receive guests at her back door. Her husband, Emile, was a distinguished doctor and lecturer at the University of Paris. But all the students knew if one suffered from any serious ailment, it was far better to consult Madame Pechard.

Madame's current visitor did not appear to be suffering the effects of ill health. As Louise Lavalle flung back her hood, her freckled cheeks were flushed with excitement, her blue eyes sparkling with a sense of adventure.

Madame peered out in the darkened yard before quickly closing the door. Fortunately she had already taken the precaution of dismissing her servants to their beds. As she threw the latch, she scolded the girl, "I vow, Mademoiselle Lavalle. You can be so infernally reckless. You should have waited until later at night. What if you had been followed from the palace?"

"Don't fret, my dear Hermoine. The Dark Queen's eyes were trained elsewhere tonight. And I needed to borrow one of your little friends to get word to Marie Claire."

Louise nodded toward the cage of cooing pigeons tucked in the corner.

"I hope you mean to write to tell her that you are leaving the court as she warned you to do."

"Why? When I am doing so well?" Louise asked with a serene smile. Plunking down an exquisite muff on the kitchen table, she produced a small strip of parchment from the fur-lined depths. "Have you pen and ink? It was difficult to complete my message. Even with Catherine preoccupied, there are always some of her creatures lurking about."

Madame Pechard frowned, but moved to fetch the desired articles. Louise settled at the table, wielding the quill with deft, clever fingers. She began to compose an encrypted message with amazing tiny strokes set in a meticulous hand.

Madame watched her with a disgruntled frown. She disapproved of Louise's morals and way of life. She disapproved of her pert manners and recklessness. And most of all Madame Pechard disapproved of this dangerous enterprise. When she had first started using her birds to communicate with Marie Claire, it had merely been for the pleasure of staying in touch with another wise woman of great learning. Madame had never bargained for being drawn into intrigues involving the Dark Queen.

While Louise finished her note, Madame paced nervously. "You and Marie Claire were ill-advised to have attempted this spying on Catherine, even to help the Lady of Faire Isle. You may fancy yourself very clever, Mademoiselle Lavalle, but the Dark Queen will find you out."

"I know that. Actually, I have been permitting her to read my eyes."

"You what!" Madame Pechard paused in her pacing to slam her palms down on the table, staring down at the girl.

"Take care, Hermoine. You nearly overset the ink," Louise said coolly.

"It is *Madame Pechard* to you, Mistress Sauce. Now tell me. What have you done?"

Louise leaned back in her seat, looking smug. "Just played a little cat and mouse with our dear Catherine. I let her read my eyes enough to realize the dismal failure of her witch-hunters. You should have seen her face."

Louise chortled. "The Dark Queen actually showed some honest emotion for a change. I vow she went positively pale."

Madame Pechard felt herself going a trifle pale. "Are you quite mad, girl? Why did you do that?"

"Strategy, my good Hermoine. Alarmed people often make mistakes because they become less cautious."

"Yes and they also wax far more dangerous."

"Don't be such an old hen. I am having an amusing time with the Dark Queen, feeding her bits of information, some true, some false. I truly was getting bored with seducing all the men at court. This is far more stimulating than taking a new lover."

As Louise serenely rolled up the message to a size capable of being attached to the band on the pigeon's leg, Madame Pechard gripped her hands together, saying tersely, "You are going to be the undoing of us all."

Although Louise glanced up at her with mischievous eyes, her smile was genuinely apologetic as she said, "I am sorry if I alarm you, but one gains nothing by not taking a few chances. We grow closer than ever to the date when the king of Navarre is to arrive in Paris."

Louise turned suddenly somber, an expression of rare seriousness darkening her eyes. "I am not as good at reading thoughts as the Dark Queen, but I can tell you one thing. I don't know what that evil woman is planning, but I would wager my finest jewels that it is not merely a wedding."

Chapter Seventeen

A SENSE OF PEACE SLOWLY RETURNED TO FAIRE ISLE, THE ISland basking in a succession of golden summer days. One could almost imagine that the island had never been threatened by witch-hunters or the intrigues of a Dark Queen.

Almost . . . Ariane thought, as she retired to the privacy of her bedchamber late one afternoon. Safe from any curious eyes, she unfolded the note from Marie Claire that Charbonne had just delivered, detailing the recent tidings from Paris.

> *Despite all risks, Louise remains stubbornly ensconced in the palace to keep an eye on the queen. All appears quiet at the moment, Catherine spending a great deal of time in her private closet, but Louise doubts that the woman is devoting that much time to her prayers. She is convinced that Catherine is brewing up some mischief and that she has a hidden workshop somewhere. Louise*

is determined to find it although she fears Catherine has
grown suspicious of her. But she hopes to use that to our
advantage, by allowing the queen to read her thoughts
and using false information to direct Catherine away
from Faire Isle . . .

"Oh, that foolish, reckless girl," Ariane muttered. Louise was playing a dangerous game and Ariane needed to find a way to bring an end to all this madness before the young courtesan or anyone else met the same fate as the unfortunate queen of Navarre.

Ariane had been laboring down in the dungeon until her eyes were crossed and still she was no closer to solving the mystery of those gloves, obtaining the proof that would prevent the Dark Queen from ever harming anyone again. She simply had no idea what else she could do.

Rubbing her neck, Ariane paced to the window, staring out at the fading day. The sun was setting with gentle golden fingers, preparing to draw the mantle of night over Belle Haven, the rustling gardens, the silvery surface of the pond, the sturdy frame of the nearby stables. Usually the sight of all the snug comforts of her home comforted Ariane, but lately all she seemed able to see was everything that she had been neglecting.

Her herb garden badly wanted weeding and the trees in the orchard were fairly bending under the weight of ripening fruit. She needed to organize her household and see the bounty gathered before the apples rotted and they lost the entire crop.

There were still Papa's debts to be considered and she had scarcely found time to even look at her account books. The island folk, made wary by the witch-hunters, were recovering enough to creep back to her, imploring aid with their ailments, and Ariane's store of remedies was growing woefully thin. She needed to be distilling medicines, not devoting herself to the study of poisons.

And then of course, there was Renard.

Ariane rested her head against the window frame. He was never far away, from her thoughts or from Belle Haven. He had elected to remain on the island, lodging at the inn, his men continuing to maintain guard over the causeway from the mainland.

She caught glimpses of Renard himself from time to time, riding through town or at the edge of the woods. A powerful guardian on horseback, keeping her safe whether she wanted him to do so or not.

She had no desire to be any further in the man's debt and for her own peace of mind, she wished him back at his own château. But she was not about to seek him out to tell him so. She preferred to keep her distance lest he read her eyes and see the longing that had beset her of late, the inexplicable urge to use his ring again.

She touched the front of her gown, all too aware of Renard's ring attached to the chain beneath her bodice. Perhaps she should have gotten rid of the ring, as Gabrielle demanded she do, especially now that she knew how dangerously powerful the talisman could be. But she didn't seem able to do that.

Tugging at her neckline, she pulled forth the chain and dangled the ring before her eyes, marveling that such a simple metal band could be the source of such great temptation. Because she had been tempted, more than once, to slip the ring on her finger and send for Renard, even though she was threatened by nothing more than the prospect of another sleepless night in an empty bed. Tormented by that heated fantasy they had shared when their rings had touched, wondering what it would have been like if their lovemaking had been real.

Ariane felt deeply ashamed of her weakness. And yet she knew that the desire for a man was a natural thing, a primal force as old as the earth itself. The hunger to reach out in the darkness and be sheltered in the strength of a lover's arms, to be held and caressed, to revel in his passion and tenderness.

These were things most women dreamed of, but as the Lady of Faire Isle, Ariane needed to be strong in herself, dependent upon no man. Besides, she reminded herself sadly, passion without love was an empty thing. That was exactly what had caused her poor sister Gabrielle to end up on her back in a barn, losing her most precious gift to a man completely unworthy of her.

There could be no possibility of a real love flourishing between Ariane and Renard despite all his quaint old grandmother's so-called visions of destiny. Whatever heart he might have possessed Renard had given long ago, to a buxom shepherd lass named Martine. As for her own heart, Ariane had dedicated it to the people of this island and her sisters, to keeping them happy, healthy, and safe.

Ariane stole one last wistful glance at the ring, before she forced herself to put it away.

At least one good thing had come from Renard maintaining his stubborn vigil on the island. She believed that his presence had likely deterred the return of Le Vis, buying time for Remy to heal.

The captain would be well enough to leave Faire Isle soon and that would be a good thing for all their sakes. With the danger at bay, Ariane had moved him up from the dungeon to her father's bedchamber and Gabrielle had been spending far too much time in the soldier's company, reading to him, playing her lute, fetching him tidbits to tempt his appetite.

Gabrielle had rarely ever had patience for entertaining an invalid. Perhaps she was feeling a trifle guilty over the havoc she had wrought by taking Remy's sword. Ariane was certain her sister did not mean to be cruel, but the girl could be quite heedless at times. Gabrielle certainly did not possess the ability to read eyes or she would have seen what Ariane had realized long ago.

That the solemn young captain was falling desperately in love with her.

※ ※ ※

GABRIELLE TUGGED AT REMY'S HAND, STEALING A GLANCE BACK toward Belle Haven. The gray stone house with its ivy-covered walls basked peacefully in the afternoon sun, not a soul stirring. But Ariane's face could appear at one of the windows at any moment.

"Hurry!" Gabrielle was tempted to break into a run, her bare feet flattening the grass as they crossed the last stretch of the open field leading to the line of trees. But Remy resisted. Digging in his boots, he forced her to come to a halt.

Gabrielle pulled more insistently at his hand, but she might as well have been trying to move a pillar of stone. Remy shook his head, despite the slight smile that tugged at his lips.

"Gabrielle, we should not be doing this," he said. "You said we would take a brief turn about the garden, not come this far. Ariane gave me permission to get up, but she requested I remain in the house. Or at least go no farther than the garden."

"Gave *you* permission? Since when did Ariane become your commanding officer? You don't have to listen to what she says." Gabrielle added with an impish smile, "*I* certainly never do."

"Perhaps you should," Remy said. "Ariane is exceedingly wise. If Catherine's soldiers or that infernal Le Vis should return and find me wandering out here, you will pay the cost as well. I have already put you and your sisters in enough danger."

"Ariane's great oaf of a suitor drove Le Vis and his witch-hunters away. And if they do return, I'll protect you."

That provoked a rare laugh from Remy. Gabrielle moved closer, peeking up at him through the thickness of her lashes.

"Please, Remy. Come with me," she coaxed. "You have not seen my special place and I want to show it to you."

"All right." He sighed. "But just for a little while."

She led him toward the forest that ringed Belle Haven. Clad

only in his white shirt, brown venetians, and high leather boots, he still looked every inch the soldier, marching with an upright bearing.

Gabrielle could not help admiring the lean, masculine grace of his figure. Remy was not excessively tall, a brawny brute of a man like Ariane's suitor, the Comte de Renard. The captain was far more lithe and compact and Gabrielle imagined he'd be very quick on his feet when he was at his full strength.

As they trudged farther into the woods, Gabrielle thought she could feel renewed vitality returning to Remy's hand. He tipped back his head, breathing deeply of the loamy ground and crisp scent of the trees, his eyes aglow with appreciation.

Ancient trees strained skyward like a tribe of elderly sentinels keeping watch over the island. Moss and vines crept up the trunks of mighty oaks, elms, and sycamore. Here and there one could spot the white bark of a birch dancing in the breeze like some slender dryad.

The forest floor was thick with underbrush and bracken so dense, it was difficult for anyone to walk there except for Miri. Gabrielle's little sister seemed able to skitter through the most tangled thicket as adroitly as any rabbit or fox.

Gabrielle took care to keep Remy to the path, not only for his sake but her own as well. She winced when her bare foot cracked down on a sharp twig, her soles not as toughened as they had been during the days of her youth. She'd always hated the bother of shoes and stockings, just one more thing to put on and delay her when an entire world waited, so many glorious sights and scenes to capture on her canvas while the light held good.

As she led Remy round a curve in the path, Gabrielle glanced down and caught a flash of her bare toes, noticing how dirty they were.

She reflected ruefully how hard she'd worked this past year to get rid of her calluses, applying lotion to make her feet as dainty, white, and smooth as the rest of her body. As hard as she had worked to tweeze her eyebrows, manicure her nails, apply rinses to bring out the golden sheen in her hair. Looking in the mirror, she'd practiced arranging that hair into more sophisticated styles, grooming herself for the elegant and alluring enchantress she meant to become, a woman of great wealth and power, a *courtesan.*

Nicolas Remy's intrusion into her life had curtailed these activities, though Gabrielle scarcely knew why. She felt perfectly comfortable wearing her oldest and most comfortable gown around Remy, her hair cascading untamed down her back, her shoes abandoned beneath her bed.

The path widened into the clearing where a stream cut the forest in two. The brook meandered slowly, breaking over rocks with a sparkling sound that had made Gabrielle, in more romantic days, think of some silvery-haired nymph singing paeans to her lover, the dark, wild spirit of the forest.

This place had been enchanted to her once. During her childhood, she'd often come to this stream to play with her little sister, Miri. As she grew older, the clearing had become her retreat, a solitary refuge in which to dream, to bring her easel and paints.

But when the magic had faded from her hands, it had faded from the forest as well. She seldom came here anymore, the place just one more melancholy reminder of all that she had lost. Yet with Remy taking such delight in the natural beauty that surrounded them, Gabrielle felt a stirring of her own pleasure return. She rushed ahead to the edge of the bank, dipping her toe in the stream, shivering as the icy water lapped against her foot. But it felt good on such a warm day.

She stooped, cupping her hand to take a drink, the water so cool and soothing as it slid down her throat. "Captain Remy, you must come here and have a drink. I vow you will never taste anything so . . ."

Her voice trailed off as she glanced back at him and realized he was moving much more stiffly and slowly than before. He had one hand pressed over the region of his wound, but he dropped his arm immediately back to his side when he saw her looking.

"What is the matter? Are you all right?" she asked.

"Y-yes, I'm fine." Remy appeared as exhausted as the ancient Greek who had collapsed after running the marathon, sweat dampening the dark gold strands of hair clinging to his brow.

"You don't look fine." Gabrielle hastened back to him, alarmed when Remy swayed a little on his feet. "What is it? You haven't torn open your wound."

"No, it's nothing. I—" He swore softly under his breath, something that Remy rarely did in the presence of a woman.

He continued in a voice laced with self-disgust. "I suddenly feel as weak as someone's ancient grandmother."

Gabrielle bit down on her lip, berating herself that she had not noticed sooner that something was wrong. But Remy had made no complaint. Indeed, he'd hardly spoken a word during their entire walk, allowing her to drift off with her own thoughts, something that did not surprise her.

She regarded him with exasperation, wanting to box his ears for being so stoic, so stupid. But he wasn't the stupid one, she reflected guiltily. She was.

"This is my fault," Gabrielle said, offering him the support of her arm. "I should never have brought you out so far."

"Far!" Remy grunted out a pained laugh. "Gabrielle, I am a soldier, used to marching. Normally I could tramp the entire width of this island without pausing for breath."

"Here, lean on me," she urged. "I'll help you get back to the house."

But Remy pulled away from her. "No, Gabrielle," he panted. "It is all right. I just need to sit, rest for a moment."

She frowned, starting to insist when Remy gazed at her, despite how drained he was, a wistful expression springing to his eyes. "It is so good being out here. I was going a little mad cooped up in the house. I feel like I can breathe again."

Then why did he look as though he might stop doing so at any moment? But she guided him over to the bank. Bracing against the trunk of an aging sycamore whose gnarled roots twisted down toward the brook, Remy slowly lowered himself to the ground, the process clearly an arduous one.

His teeth were clenched in a way that did not ease until he was seated. Then he leaned back against the tree with a grateful sigh. "Ah. That's better."

Gabrielle regarded him helplessly, cursing herself for not thinking to bring a flask of the medicine along. Ariane certainly would have remembered. Scrambling to the edge of the stream, Gabrielle groped in the pocket tied about her waist and dragged out a handkerchief. Wetting the linen cloth, she wrung it out, then hastened back to Remy.

Kneeling close beside him, she sponged his forehead and cheeks, growing a little alarmed when his eyes fluttered closed. But then she realized he was only savoring the feel of the cool cloth against his skin.

To her relief, color seeped back into his face. She brushed the damp strands of hair back from his eyes. When Gabrielle had first seen Remy half-dead, hidden away in the dungeon room beneath Belle Haven, she had thought the captain's hair a kind of dull, lanky brown. But that had been before they had bathed and cleaned him up.

Hints of sunlight dappled through the trees, playing across Remy's face, and Gabrielle realized his hair was actually a mixture of blond and more shades of brown than she could possibly have imagined. She was unable to resist sifting her fingers through it, marveling at the surprisingly silky texture, at the way the strands shifted color in the light, now a rich walnut, the next burnished gold.

If she had ever been going to paint Remy's portrait, she wondered if she would have ever found enough hues in her palette to capture the remarkable blend of sun and shadow that was in Remy's hair.

His beard was decidedly lighter, a rough sugaring of hair that coarsened his jaw. The fringe of his mustache made a marvelous contrast to his mouth, emphasizing the sensitive curve of his lips. But Gabrielle had always preferred clean-shaven men. Remy's face appeared carved on such strong lean lines, it seemed a pity to—

The captain's eyes fluttered open, regarding her with a look of such surprise that Gabrielle froze, suddenly aware of what she was doing. Tipping Remy's face to one side as though she was preparing him for a sitting, stroking his beard, exploring the angle of his jaw. Pressing herself so close, her breath mingled with his, one of her breasts flattened against the hard muscle of his shoulder.

The surprise in Remy's eyes flared to a look of such desire, it stirred answering warmth in Gabrielle. She'd fancied herself numb to all such heat and she wrenched back in a panic, wondering what the devil had gotten into her.

Remy's eyes slid away from hers, looking self-conscious. It was that more than anything that helped Gabrielle recover herself.

"Are you feeling any better, Captain?" she asked in what she hoped was a cool, collected voice.

"Y-yes, thank you, mademoiselle," Remy replied in an equally formal tone. "You clearly have a healing touch."

Gabrielle shrugged. "That's Ariane. Not me."

When she saw Remy open his mouth to gallantly argue the matter, she rushed on, "If you are feeling recovered, no doubt it is owing more to . . . to these woods. My little sister insists there is a very old magic here."

"Yes, Miri told me that." Although Remy winced a little, he managed to sit up straighter. Gabrielle scooted back to the bank, draping her handkerchief over a rock to dry in the sun. She curled up, arranging the folds of her gown demurely over her feet. Hugging her knees to her chest, she stared out over the brook.

Behind her, she sensed Remy moving away from his resting place beneath the tree. He inched along the bank until he was seated beside her. Gabrielle involuntarily tensed until she saw that he took great care to keep a decent space between them. She relaxed in spite of herself, stretching out her legs, crooking her toes so that the reeds at the edge of the stream barely tickled her feet.

Gabrielle half-closed her eyes, marveling a little. She was usually so restless, never able to sit still except for those long-ago days when she had been so completely lost in working at some painting or sculpture. But it was impossible not to feel at ease in Remy's presence. There was something so strong and steady about him, like one of those sturdy oaks that guarded the forest, promising shelter from the most blistering sun or heaviest rainfall.

She saw no sign of that soul weariness in Remy's eyes that Miri spoke of. He looked remarkably at peace as he idly plucked a wildflower and tossed it in the stream. As they both watched the white petals carried away in the lazy current, Remy murmured, "It is so beautiful here, so peaceful. I feel as though I would be content to remain on this island forever."

"Would you? Most of the time I long to escape from here."

Remy twisted to regard her with grave surprise. "Would you, Gabrielle? But where would you go?"

Once the answer to that would have been so easy. To Italy, to improve her art by studying some of the masterpieces she had heard were being created there. It was said that a man from Florence, one Michelangelo, had covered the Sistine Chapel with paintings beautiful enough to make the angels weep with envy of his genius.

It hardly mattered anyway. Her hunger to become a great artist had always been an impossible ambition, even for a wise woman from Faire Isle. It was merely a dream that had drifted away from Gabrielle like that fragile flower disappearing downstream.

"Oh, I would like to head off to Paris, to make my fortune," she said, answering Remy's question at last with an airy laugh.

She was immediately sorry she had mentioned Paris when she saw Remy's eyes darken grimly. That was where Remy had been when he had been forced to flee the Dark Queen. Gabrielle had no idea exactly what Remy had done to draw Catherine's wrath down upon him. She suspected it might have something to do with the death of Remy's own queen, Jeanne of Navarre.

Whatever had occurred in Paris, Remy refused to tell her, no matter how Gabrielle coaxed. She was better off out of it, he insisted, a response that irritated Gabrielle.

But since she had no wish to disturb the harmony of their afternoon together, Gabrielle amended her answer to one more vague. "I suppose I simply want to see more of the world than Faire Isle."

"The world outside this island is often not a very pleasant place," Remy said gravely.

"Mine will be," Gabrielle insisted, shaking her sun-warmed hair back from her face. "Full of beautiful palaces, feasts and masques, grand ballrooms with dancing until dawn."

"And many ardent suitors, no doubt." Remy gave her a sad smile. "Likely you will not even miss—"

He hesitated, and Gabrielle's heart stopped.

"Er—miss Faire Isle that much," he finished awkwardly and Gabrielle found she could breathe again.

She had been so afraid he was going to say, *you will not miss me.* So far Remy had confined himself to the occasional admiring glance, and she fervently prayed he'd never go any further. Then she would have to reject him and any comfort between them would be destroyed forever. And she quite liked this ease she felt most of the time with Remy. She'd never been friends with a man before.

Remy absorbed himself in plucking another flower. He was about to toss it into the stream when he stopped, looking almost comically stricken. "Oh, Lord, I forgot. I am not supposed to be doing this. Miri warned me that if I ever came into these woods, there are fairies here. I'd be safe only as long as I did no harm to the forest."

"Yes, that sounds exactly like something that Miri would say."

"She also informed me that a unicorn grazes in these woods, but being only a lowly man I should not expect to see him," Remy added.

"Oh, as if she ever has either," Gabrielle said scornfully. "Although I swear Miri has been hunting for one ever since she was old enough to walk."

Remy cast an odd sidelong glance at her. "But you must have seen the unicorn."

Gabrielle laughed. "Whatever would make you think that?"

"The painting that you did for Miri."

Gabrielle's smile faded. Miri had shown *that* to Remy. The little fool. She was going to wring her sister's neck.

"That painting was mere nonsense to amuse Miri," she said. "If I'd had my way, I would have broken it up and used the canvas and frame for kindling."

"That would be a great shame, for I have never seen any painting more remarkable in my life." Remy floundered, clearly not a man accustomed to putting his feelings into words. Though he looked a little embarrassed, he stubbornly soldiered on. "I felt that if I reached out my hand, I could actually touch that unicorn's mane and it would feel like silk. His breath would be warm against my fingers. Your painting was—was like—"

Gabrielle averted her face, hoping Remy would not ask the dreaded question, but he did.

"Why didn't you ever finish it?"

That painting had been the last one she'd ever worked on before Danton had come to invade the peace of her island. The day after he'd ridden away, she'd arisen from her bed, somehow hoping if she ignored the bruises and soreness of her body, her life would go on just as before.

She dragged her easel, palette, and the canvas out to the bank of the stream as she so often did. But as the hours passed, she found herself staring at the painting. As the day waned and the shadows lengthened, her despair did too.

Every time she lifted her brush to the unfinished portion of the canvas where the unicorn still awaited legs so he could gallop like the wind, her fingers trembled and she could not make so much as a single stroke.

The silvery unicorn seemed to regard her with such sad, reproachful eyes. *"I am sorry, milady. But only a maiden who remains pure and true can ever hope to capture me. Your magic is lost."*

But that was a grief that was behind her now. She had other dreams, other ambitions, Gabrielle reminded herself. Turning back to Remy, she even managed a brittle smile.

"Why didn't I finish the painting? Goodness! I—I have more important things to do. Besides, that picture only encourages Miri in her childishness. You might not know it, but my sister is nearly thirteen. But if she had her way, she and I would still be out here romping in the woods, playing knights and dragons."

Gabrielle didn't know if Remy entirely accepted her explanation about the picture, but he was too much the gentleman to press her further. He flinched, shifting one hip as though seeking a more comfortable position.

"Knights and dragons?" he repeated. "What on earth is that?"

Gabrielle regarded him incredulously. "You know, the knight rescuing the fair damsel from the fire-breathing dragon. You must have played something similar as a boy."

"No, I cannot say that I did."

"Well, what *did* you play?"

"Nothing that I recall. By the time I was six, I was already learning to drill with my father's regiment, banging the drum as we marched into battle."

Gabrielle's eyes widened in shock. "I am astonished your maman would allow such a thing," she said.

"My mother had little say in the matter. She died before I was three. I scarcely remember her except as a gentle touch in the dark when she was tucking the blankets around me at night."

Remy spoke calmly, his voice matter-of-fact, but there was a wistfulness in his eyes that tugged at Gabrielle's heart. She had lost her own mother but two years ago. She'd been sixteen and that had been hard enough. But to be motherless from the age of three . . .

Strands of Remy's gold-tipped hair straggled across his forehead again and she reached out to brush them back, only to check the movement, burying her hand in her lap.

Clearing her throat, Gabrielle sought to bring the conversation back to a lighter note. "Well, Miri and I often played at knights and dragons, right here on this very spot."

"And no doubt you were the damsel in distress, all fair and golden," Remy murmured, his eyes resting admiringly on the hair cascading down her back.

Gabrielle shook out her tangled mane with a proud sniff. "That shows all you know of me, monsieur. I was ever the knight, brave and bold. Miri was the princess."

"And Ariane was . . . was the dragon?" Remy asked dubiously.

Gabrielle choked with laughter at the idea of such a thing. When she'd recovered, she said, "I admit Ariane seems very suited to the role. But no, she never played with us at all. She was too busy learning healing from Maman, preparing herself to become the next Lady of Faire Isle."

Gabrielle's mouth curled with mischief. "So you never played at knights and dragons? No wonder you are so solemn and serious. I think I should make you play with me right now."

"Oh no!" Remy said, shaking his head, looking as horrified by the suggestion as Gabrielle had known he would.

"I am sorry." She gave a mock sigh. "How thoughtless of me. I forgot how weak you are feeling."

"I am not feeling weak," he protested. "It was only a brief spell of—of—I am quite recovered, thank you."

"Good. Then there is no obstacle to our game." Gabrielle scrambled to her feet and caught hold of his hand to help him up. "Come on."

"Gabrielle," Remy groaned. "I am not good at games. Especially ones requiring any imagination."

"It's not that difficult. I'll teach you."

When he continued to resist, Gabrielle cast him her most melting look. "Oh, please. It will be so much fun."

Remy rolled his eyes up as though appealing to the heavens for help, clearly torn between his desire to please her and a masculine dread of making an ass of himself.

But Nicolas Remy needed someone to ease that grave look from his eyes, to make him laugh, to forget for a time whatever heavy burden of danger he'd carried away with him from Paris.

Gabrielle gave him no peace until she got him on his feet. Remy rose slowly, dusting himself off with a long-suffering sigh.

"Very well, milady. But let me make one thing perfectly clear. There is no way I am going to be the damsel in distress."

"Oh, all right. If you insist, I will allow you to be the knight."

Remy's teeth flashed in a broad grin, and Gabrielle was surprised to feel her heart skip a beat. When the man allowed himself to relax, he had a devastating smile, a sweetness of expression at odds with his stern masculinity, made all the more endearing by a slightly crooked lower tooth.

Gabrielle gave herself a brisk shake, remembering that she was too wise to go all weak in the knees over a man's smile. Turning from Remy, she said, "The first thing we have to do, my bold chevalier, is find you a sword."

"I believe I had one," Remy said sternly. "Until you stole it."

Gabrielle still felt guilty about that, but she tossed her head and proclaimed, "I didn't steal your sword. I only borrowed it."

"Then why haven't you given it back to me?"

Gabrielle didn't have as ready an answer for that. Perhaps because she feared when he had his sword back, Remy would leave Faire Isle and do something rash and reckless. Like get himself killed.

"When it is time for you to be gone from here, I will give you your sword. Not a moment before," Gabrielle informed him. "In the meantime, you will make do with this."

She located a stout branch laying upon the bank, the dark wood gnarled and dry, one end arched in a crooked curve. Gabrielle presented it to Remy with a dramatic flourish.

"Here is your trusty blade, Sir Knight."

Remy held up the branch for inspection. "Er—my trusty blade appears a trifle bent, milady."

"Oh, unfortunately that happened when you fought the ogre."

"Did I win?"

"Of course," Gabrielle said with a haughty lift of her chin. "Would I tolerate a knight for my champion who lost his battles?"

"I don't suppose you would," Remy replied. "So. Where exactly is this dragon you want me to slay for you?"

"You are standing on his tail."

"What?" Remy glanced down in confusion at the tree root curled beneath his boot.

"Oh, beware, Sir Nicolas," Gabrielle screeched with high dramatic effect. "The dragon is right behind you, raising his razor-sharp claws."

Remy spun around, glancing back at the spreading branches he had so recently rested under. "Ah, forgive me, milady. But all I see is an ancient tree."

"Alas," Gabrielle cried. "I have a near-sighted knight." She cowered behind Remy, resting her hands on his shoulders, pretending to shiver.

"That is Old Sycamore, the most ferocious maiden-devouring beast to inhabit these woods." Gabrielle peeked from around Remy's broad back. "It is a miracle his fiery breath has not reduced us both to ashes by now."

Remy cleared his throat, trying desperately to get into the spirit of the game. "Um . . . fear not milady. I will save you from—from yon dragon. Er—over yonder."

Clutching his branch, Remy stalked forward and Gabrielle bit down hard on her lip to keep from smiling, reflecting that never had any knight looked more adorably sheepish than Remy did at this moment.

But he squared his shoulders as he lifted the branch, as though he truly was wielding a sword, instinctively adopting the stance he must have assumed in countless battles. Legs braced, his entire body tensed and at the ready. Gabrielle could not help noting that he shifted most of his weight to the side away from his wound, compensating as he would do if he charged away from Faire Isle to fight the Dark Queen's soldiers.

She had done quite right to keep Remy's sword hidden from him, Gabrielle reflected grimly.

Remy stared up at the towering sycamore, lips slightly parted as though he thought he ought to say something. But apparently not even for Gabrielle could he bring himself to hurl threats at a tree.

He swung back the branch instead, preparing to deliver a mighty blow to the trunk, when Gabrielle rushed forward.

"Wait. What are you doing?"

He glanced down at her, his rich brown eyes a mixture of embarrassment and doubt. "Dealing with the dragon?"

"Not like that."

Gabrielle could not help grinning. "You forget who I used to play this game with. *Miri.* She would never be able to endure anyone slaying our poor dear old dragon."

Remy lowered the branch, looking pardonably exasperated. "Then exactly how I am supposed to save you from the beast?"

Gabrielle fluttered her lashes with a mischievously demure smile. "You have to sing him to sleep."

Remy stared at her, his expression completely aghast. He shook his head with the vehemence of a man finally pushed to his limit. "No, Gabrielle. *No!* Absolutely not."

Casting the branch aside, he looked fully prepared to bolt back to the safety of Belle Haven, his wound be damned. But Gabrielle clung to his arm.

"What! Will you abandon me to the dragon's clutches?"

Remy cast her a disgruntled look. "Frankly, milady, yes. The idea begins to have a certain appeal."

"Sir Nicolas!" Gabrielle said reproachfully, peering up at him with wide, beseeching eyes.

"Gabrielle." Remy groaned, a man clearly pleading for mercy.

But Gabrielle had none. "Sing," she commanded. "Or you will never see your fair damsel again."

Remy glanced about him like a man looking desperately for some avenue of escape and finding none. Remy shifted back to the tree. His chest heaving with the deepest sigh yet, he cleared his throat and began to sing. If Remy did what she had demanded at all, Gabrielle had anticipated that he would produce a martial air, some soldier's marching song.

Instead he crooned out the words of a lullaby, his voice low and gruff, a little off-key and hesitant as though he struggled to remember words he'd heard far too long ago in his cradle.

But the tune and words were both painfully familiar to Gabrielle. Her maman had often sung her to sleep with them. Evangeline Cheney, the incomparable Lady of Faire Isle, regarded as almost a patron saint to the people of this island.

She had often seemed just as beautiful and distant to Gabrielle, more Ariane and Miri's mother than hers. Ariane as the eldest daughter and her successor had been closest to Evangeline, Miri, the much loved and protected babe. Gabrielle had frequently felt lost and forgotten, somewhere in between, except for certain nights in her childhood when she had stubbornly remained awake while her more obedient sisters drifted off.

"Ah, my restless little Gabrielle," Maman would scold gently. *"Whatever am I to do with you?"* Her answer to that question would always be to rock Gabrielle in her arms and sing that lullaby, lulling her into a state of peace Gabrielle had seldom known since.

How odd now to find a trace of that old magic in the rough-timbered voice of a soldier. Her eyes burned with tears she seldom allowed herself to shed.

Remy's voice stumbled to silence. "I am sorry. I don't remember any more."

Gabrielle blinked hard, fighting to recover her composure. "That is quite all right, Sir Nicolas. You—you did well. The dragon is asleep. The damsel is saved."

"Good." Remy took a step toward her. "So does this game include a part where the fair damsel rewards her bold knight with a kiss?"

He tried to make the question sound like a jest, but his deep brown eyes were far too serious for Gabrielle's comfort. She moved away from him, sweeping her skirts in a grand manner. "A kiss? Fie upon you, Sir Nicolas. It is clear you understand nothing of damsels. We are a cold and cruel lot, requiring our champions to worship us from a distance. The most we ever allow is our knight to kneel at out feet and swear eternal devotion and service."

She spoke with forced playfulness, never expecting Remy to comply with her request. But to her consternation, he stepped in front of her and began to slowly lower himself.

"Oh, Remy, I was only jesting—" she began, but Remy went down on one knee, the effort obviously costing him some pain, for he flinched.

"Remy, stop," she said. "The game is over. Do get up."

"Nay, milady. You suggested this. Now we will see it through."

"Don't be an idiot. Stand up before you hurt yourself." She tugged at his sleeve, trying to force him back up. But he captured her hand, imprisoning her fingers in the warm strength of his own.

Gabrielle attempted to tug herself free, but when Remy tilted his head to look up at her, she stopped, held spellbound. The sun turned his hair to burnished gold, accenting every line worn by pain and hardship on his beard-roughened features. But his eyes seemed to shine with a light of their own.

"Milady, my sword is ever at your service," he said, gathering her hand close to the region of his heart. "I vow by my life's blood to serve and protect you forever."

Gabrielle found herself curiously unable to speak. It was as though the embodiment of every maiden's dream had sprung to life at her feet. The battered knight after much toil and care, fighting his way to his lady's side, to sweep her off on his charger and into the shelter of his arms.

A man of complete honor, integrity, and courage, traits that she had once mistakenly supposed belonged to the Chevalier Eti-enne Danton. But Danton had only borne the title. He'd been no more a knight than Gabrielle was any longer a maiden.

Only Nicolas Remy was real and true. Unfortunately, he'd arrived on her island much too late.

Gabrielle wrenched herself free and stalked away to the edge of the bank, wrapping her arms tightly around herself, disturbed to discover she was trembling.

When he looked at her, all he saw was the smooth complex-ion, the golden hair, the blue eyes. He didn't see all the dark flaws, the ugly stains on her soul. How quick he'd be to turn away if he knew the real Gabrielle.

She stiffened when she heard Remy's footfall, sensed him standing close behind her.

"Gabrielle?" His deep voice sounded sad and bewildered. "Did I do something wrong? I am sorry. I told you I was no good at playacting."

Gabrielle swallowed past the lump in her throat. "On the contrary." She attempted to laugh. "You do it far too well. You almost sounded as though you meant those words."

"I did," he rasped.

Remy rested his hands gently on her shoulders and a tremor coursed through Gabrielle. Her heart beat as hard as though she suddenly found herself teetering on the brink of a terrifying precipice.

All she had to do was turn around and she knew that Remy would draw her safe back into his arms and kiss her. One small step on her part and she might change both of their destinies for-ever.

The entire forest around them appeared to have gone quiet and still, except for the relentless rush of the stream, the distant call of a curlew, seeming to ring out with a melancholy cry. *Too late.*

Gabrielle stared across the sun-sparkled waters and shrugged Remy's hands from her shoulders.

"I think it is time we returned to the house," she said numbly.

ʞ ʞ ʞ

NIGHT SETTLED OVER BELLE HAVEN, STARS PIERCING THE CLOUD-less sky, a half-moon shedding its solemn light over the ivy-covered manor. The rest of the household had long since retired when Remy stole out of the house and into the garden. He was unable to sleep, but it was no longer any ache from his wound keeping him awake. It was the bitter consciousness of the mistake he'd made this afternoon by revealing his heart to Gabrielle Cheney.

He had no right to be declaring his love to any lady in his present grim circumstances. Even before he'd become a fugitive, it was not as though he had much of a future to offer a woman, especially one as dazzlingly beautiful as Gabrielle, who wove girlish dreams of glittering balls, masques, handsome suitors by the score. Remy had neither wealth nor a title to recommend him. Little charm or wit either, his only talent, his skill with a sword.

Small wonder Gabrielle had shrunk from him. Oh, she'd continued to be kind to him after their return to the house, but she was quiet and withdrawn during the supper he'd shared with the family. And after the meal, when he had gone back to his room, he had found *this* awaiting him.

Remy clapped his hand to the weapon strapped to his side and slowly unsheathed it. His sword. No action could have made her feelings plainer.

Clearly he had so discomfited her with his clumsy avowals of devotion, she thought it would be better if he left Faire Isle. And she was right.

Ignoring the twinges from his wound, Remy practiced several feints with his sword, parrying against an imaginary enemy. If he ever hoped to regain his strength, he needed to force his body back into the rigid discipline he had maintained all his life. His muscles ached from disuse, but it felt good to force them to stretch and respond at his command.

On Faire Isle, he felt far removed from the real world. Perhaps even now his young king was setting out for the wedding in Paris, unaware of the lurking danger.

Remy cursed himself. He had already failed his queen. He should have returned to protect her son, the only heir and hope of Navarre, if he had had to crawl on his hands and knees to get there. He was deeply ashamed of lingering here when it was his duty to be elsewhere, even more so when his weakness in remaining stemmed from more than his wound.

He had fallen under the spell of the serenity of this quiet place. He had never quite known what a home could be before coming to Belle Haven. He'd spent most of his youth trailing after his soldier father, learning his trade, his only home a tent or garrison or being quartered as an unwanted stranger in some conquered foe's dwelling.

He'd never before experienced all the domesticity and warmth of sharing a roof with so . . . so many women. He had allowed himself to be beguiled by Ariane Cheney mothering and nursing him, by shy little Miri bringing her injured fox to show him, to reassure him that he should not worry, if the fox could get well, then Remy could too.

Even as he smiled at the memory, Remy knew it was not thoughts of Ariane or Miri that made it so hard for him to think of leaving Faire Isle.

It was her . . . Gabrielle. A beautiful enchantress so far out of his reach, she might as well have been some distant star.

He should have mastered this infatuation he felt for her, and maybe he could have done so, if it had been merely her beauty that had dazzled him. But Gabrielle had let him see beyond that cool sophisticated façade she tried so hard to maintain, afforded him glimpses of her kindness, her gentleness, that playful streak so different from his own solemn nature.

There were times that Gabrielle seemed quite young to him. And then at other times, she seemed far older and more worldly-wise than he. Was that the way of a sorceress or merely a woman, mysterious and unpredictable creatures that they were?

She could be lively and laughing at times, sweetly teasing him. Or quiet and thoughtful, her eyes haunted by some inexplicable sadness that plucked at his heart. Or she could be so distant, it was as though she had entirely forgotten his existence, which is likely what she would do once he had gone.

He needed to put her out of his mind and heart as well. But even as he made this resolve, he felt his pulse quicken at the sound of a footfall, the light rustle of the bushes. He sheathed his sword, eagerly awaiting the woman he spied coming down the garden path, carrying a lantern.

But it was only Ariane. He swallowed his disappointment. No doubt she had checked in on him as she often did at night and become alarmed at finding him missing from his bed.

Remy was aware that Ariane frequently labored far into the night after everyone else was long abed, tending to the many tasks of running her household or seeing to the ailments of the island folk. She was still wearing her work-worn gown, soft brown tendrils escaping from her chignon to straggle about her pale face.

She held up the lantern as she approached. "Ah, Captain Remy, I hoped I would find you here. You should be in bed, monsieur."

"So should you, mistress," he retorted. "Do you never sleep?"

"Sometimes it feels that way," Ariane murmured. "But I am glad you are still awake. I need to talk to you, but I fear you have been enough on your feet for one day. Please do sit down."

But Remy shook his head. "If I cannot exert myself to stand

and pay respect to a lady, I can hardly be considered fit to ride a horse, can I? Unless the Lady of Faire Isle hopes to keep me her prisoner forever?"

"No, I have no intention of doing that," she replied with a sad smile. "You must go."

If only Gabrielle had sounded quite that regretful, Remy thought with a pang. Ariane's gaze fixed on his and Remy was certain she had guessed the hopeless nature of his love for her sister. He believed those solemn eyes of Ariane missed little, but she was far too wise to comment on her perceptions, and for that Remy was extremely grateful.

He took the lantern from her and forced her to sit, which she did reluctantly. The Lady of Faire Isle never appeared comfortable allowing anyone else to take care of her, but the poor woman looked more drained than he was.

Ariane folded her hands in her lap with a tired sigh. "I have received word from Paris. We have placed a woman in the palace to spy upon Catherine. One of our own . . . another daughter of the earth."

Remy wondered if he himself would have had the iron nerve to play such a dangerous game with the Dark Queen. "The courage of you ladies astonishes me."

"I don't know if it is courage or recklessness. But Louise has discovered this much. Your worst fears are true. Louise is convinced that Catherine has no intention of ever seeing your king wed to her daughter. She has something else far different in mind for Henry of Navarre. Very likely a funeral."

Remy's mouth set in a grim line. "Then I must leave immediately."

"Yes, you must return to Navarre as soon as possible. Stop your king from going to Paris."

"That will not be easy. He is surrounded by high-ranking ministers far too eager for this so-called marriage and truce. The word of an army captain ranting about witchcraft will not count for much without proof, unless you have succeeded with the gloves?"

One look at Ariane's downcast face swiftly put an end to that hope. "I have studied and studied those gloves to no avail. And even if I can figure out what poison Catherine used, I am not sure how we would demonstrate my knowledge. Who will understand the kind of scientific proof I would offer?"

Unfortunately, Remy quite agreed with her. He knew he would never be able to understand the Lady of Faire Isle's mysterious "science" himself and he doubted his countrymen would be any wiser.

Using the gloves to defeat Catherine had always been a forlorn hope and yet Remy could not help feeling bitterly disappointed.

"The de Medici witch is going to get away with it, isn't she? Murdering my queen."

"I fear so."

Remy paced away from Ariane, muttering a low oath and striking his palm against the bark of a tree.

"My mother always said that evil carries its own punishment," Ariane went on hesitantly. "That eventually Catherine will be consumed by her own darkness."

"When? After a lifetime of wreaking havoc on innocent people, when she is resting comfortably in her grave? I was hoping for retribution a little sooner."

"So was I. I am so sorry, Remy. I wish I were the mighty sorceress that you believed me to be when you sought me out. Then I might have actually done you some good."

At the sight of Ariane's bowed shoulders and weary, defeated expression, his own anger faded. He returned to rest one hand gently on her shoulder.

"You have done me much good, lady. I would be dead if not for you."

She only shook her head sadly. "Any wise woman could have

healed you. You came to me expecting so much more and all you did was endanger your life further. Wasting your time, journeying all the way to Faire Isle for—for nothing."

"No, not for nothing." Remy gave her shoulder a bracing squeeze. "I have learned a great deal from you."

"And just what would that be?"

"Well, for one thing how to tell the difference between a witch and a wise woman. That all daughters of the earth are not as evil as the Dark Queen."

His words coaxed a reluctant smile from Ariane. She rallied, rising to her feet.

"Fretting over my failure with the gloves will do neither of us any good," she said. "I need to turn my attention to more practical matters. Such as securing you a good mount for your journey. Unfortunately, most of the ponies here on the island are of the sturdy, plodding variety. The only one possessing horses of any swiftness is—is the Comte de Renard."

Ariane sighed. "And I would as soon keep my distance from him."

Remy regarded her curiously. "Are all you ladies of Faire Isle so determined to drive away your admirers? You seem to be a singularly independent and solitary breed of female."

"Many of us are," Ariane conceded with a wry smile. "Perhaps that is why they call us wise women."

☽ ☽ ☽

BUT ARIANE DID NOT FEEL ESPECIALLY WISE AS SHE STOOD BY HER bedchamber window. All she felt was small and alone with the night pressing down on her. Yielding at last to the temptation, she slipped Renard's ring back on her finger and called to him.

"Renard, come to me. I need you."

She was answered by a powerful wind tearing past her casement. And then within moments, Renard was there, silhouetted in her bedchamber doorway, a man of such rugged flesh and sinew, he seemed fashioned from the very bones of the earth.

His green eyes glinted with triumph beneath his hooded lids as he murmured, "Ma chère . . ." and held out his arms to her.

Ariane rushed toward him and he caught her hard against the welcoming warmth of his strong body. Whispering heated kisses across her face, he swept her off her feet, carrying her over to the bed.

Renard pressed her down into the mattress, his large frame looming over her, his mouth claiming her in a fiery mating of lips, tongues, and breath. Ariane moaned softly, burying her fingers in the thickness of his golden-brown hair. Her heart hammered in rhythm with his as he slowly began to ease her nightgown down her shoulder.

But to her consternation, Gabrielle suddenly burst into the bedchamber.

"No!" She launched herself fiercely at Renard.

"Gabrielle, what—what are you doing?" Ariane tried to protest but her sister gave her a savage shake.

"What are *you* doing? Do you want to lose your magic the way I did?"

"Let me go." Ariane struggled to push Gabrielle away, but her sister only shook her harder.

"Ariane? Ariane! Wake up."

Ariane groaned and surrendered her dream, her eyes fluttering open. Shoving her sister's hand away, she struggled to a sitting position, saying grumpily, "Good Lord, Gabrielle. Can you not even let me enjoy my dreams in peace?"

But as Ariane came more fully awake, she realized it was not Gabrielle bending over her, but Miri. Her little sister looked like a phantom in her nightgown, pale and trembling so badly, the candle she held was in danger of setting the bedcurtains afire.

Ariane took the candlestick from her gently and set it down on her night table. She feared that Miri was having one of her sleepwalking episodes, but her sister had never been known before to pause to light a candle when she was in such a trance.

And although her eyes were wide, dilated with fear, the girl looked very much awake.

"What is it, dearest? Have you had another of your nightmares?"

Miri stared at Ariane, forcing one word past her white lips. "N-necromancer—"

Ariane started as the cat itself leapt upon the bed, a sleek shadow with ghost-white paws and gleaming amber eyes. Necromancer emitted a growl from low in his throat, the sound so strange and eerie, it caused the nape of Ariane's neck to prickle.

Ariane shrank back, wrapping one arm protectively around her sister. "Good heavens, Miri! What on earth is the matter with him?"

Necromancer slunk forward, his eyes glinting as fiercely as a jungle cat. He pawed urgently at Ariane's hand, nearly scratching her in the process.

"He is trying to tell you that he was out hunting tonight. In the woods." Miri shuddered. "And he—he's seen them."

"Seen who, dearest?"

"Oh, Ariane! The *witch-hunters* have come back."

Chapter Eighteen

ARIANE TORE THROUGH THE HOUSE, LIGHTING CANDLES and rousing her servants. She all but had to drag Gabrielle from her pillow.

"I can't believe you are rousting me from my bed in the middle of the night on the word of a cat," she complained.

Ariane could hardly believe she was doing it herself, but she had seen too much of Miri's uncanny ability to communicate with animals to doubt they were all in danger.

Flinging a shawl over Gabrielle's shoulders, Ariane propelled her grumbling sister from her bedchamber and down the stairs, Necromancer bolting ahead while Miri trailed behind. The rest of the household was already gathered in the great hall, fear and confusion evident in the faces set beneath nightcaps that had gone askew.

The young page Leon had returned from fetching old Fourche from the stables, the boy's face ashen beneath his mop of carrot-colored hair. "Milady, you were right. There is someone out there. M-master Fourche and I saw them."

"Witch-hunters. An army of them, mistress," Fourche quavered. "Creeping out of the woods like a pack of wolves. Sh-shall I fetch my pitchfork and—"

"No. We must remain calm," Ariane said, although she felt her own heart start to race. Leon and Fourche's report only added to the sense of mounting panic, the old cook Agnes moaning and clutching her heart while the little housemaid Bette started to cry. Gabrielle wrapped her arm around Miri's trembling shoulders as Necromancer emitted a sharp hiss that sliced through Ariane's taut nerves.

The only one who appeared calm was Remy as he descended into the hall. He alone had taken the time to dress and arm himself with the swiftness of a man no doubt accustomed to being roused to face danger at a moment's notice.

"Mistress Cheney. What is amiss?" he asked sharply.

"The witch-hunters, Captain. They have returned."

Remy strode toward the front window with Ariane hard after him. Together they stared past the diamond-paned window into a night that seemed at first still and undisturbed. Then Ariane caught the first flicker of light, the bobbing of a lantern illuminating movement in the stableyard, dark-robed figures melting like shadows from the woodland beyond. Not hundreds of witch-hunters, but certainly far too many.

Ariane slammed the shutters closed. She exchanged a grim look with Remy and could tell that like herself, the captain fully appreciated the gravity of their situation. Belle Haven had not been designed as a fortress. The barred doors and windows would not hold off any attack for long and they had no weapons.

The wise women of Belle Haven had always refused to have their walls adorned with swords, daggers, and other symbols of male aggression, so foreign and disruptive to the peace and harmony of the island. They had never had need of such armaments before, but now Ariane thought she would have welcomed the sight of a few stout battle-axes displayed among the tapestries.

But such weapons would be of little use, she reflected. Who would wield them, an old man, a boy, a handful of untrained women, and a soldier, barely healed from his last wound?

Remy's strong hand closed over Ariane's. "Mistress Cheney, you must let me go out and surrender—"

"No!"

"But we both know it is me that the Dark Queen has sent Le Vis after. And those accursed gloves."

"And you think Le Vis will leave the rest of us in peace? The man is a witch-hunter and I doubt he sneaks here under cover of darkness to negotiate or hold any more tribunals. Once he has you and the gloves, he will simply murder us all."

"Then you must flee through the woods to safety while I do my best to hold off Le Vis and his men."

Ariane shook her head. "It is far too late for that. There is only one thing to be done. We must summon help."

"Help from where, mademoiselle? Do you mean this Comte de Renard?"

"Yes. I fear I may have already delayed too long. I should have sent for him as soon as the cat warned me—"

"What?" Remy cast her a look as though he'd begun to doubt her sanity.

The poor man only appeared further mystified as Ariane tugged on the chain, pulling Renard's ring from beneath her gown.

At that moment, Gabrielle joined them. As soon as she saw what Ariane was about to do, she shrieked.

Gabrielle made a frantic lunge at Ariane. But Ariane dodged away from her sister, yanking the metal band from the chain. She jammed Renard's ring back upon her finger while Gabrielle swore and Remy looked as though they had both run mad.

Ariane pressed the ring over the region of her heart. Suppressing her fear, she fought to concentrate, send her thoughts winging to Renard through the night.

Renard. Please come to me. I need you. The witch-hunters have returned.

❧ ❧ ❧

SIMON CROUCHED BESIDE THE STABLES, A SHADOW AMONG OTHER shadows, concealing the pale oval of his face beneath his hood. Even Master Le Vis had abandoned his bloodred robes for one of black, the better to blend with the night.

Belle Haven stood in the distance, moonlight shimmering over the ivy-covered manor. Simon watched tensely as Brother Finial slunk toward the gardens, sent to subdue any manservant guarding the house. There was an air of eerie abandonment about Belle Haven. Not a soul stirring, nothing to disturb the quiet of night beyond the rustle of wind through the trees. Not even the bark of a dog.

Simon had hoped that Miri, with her love of animals, might own some large fierce mastiff to rouse the household and force Monsieur Le Vis to abandon this raid. A wish disloyal to his master, but Simon felt sick at heart to be here, preparing to break into Miri's home like some common thief.

He could tell Brother Jerome felt the same. The lantern that Jerome carried cast somber shadows over his lean, ascetic face. He inched his way over to Monsignor Le Vis and from their low, urgent tones, Simon could tell they were arguing. He craned his neck, anxiously straining to hear.

"Le Vis, we are supposed to be witch-hunters, not assassins. There is no righteousness in this and it is reckless besides. It is a miracle we were not already dashed on the rocks landing in that treacherous cove."

"That only proves that God is on our side," Le Vis whispered back.

"Or preserving us for a more terrible judgment. Have you forgotten the Comte de Renard?"

"We have eluded him so far. He is merely an ignorant man, the tool of witches. I don't share your supernatural dread of him."

"You should. At least leave the boy out of this." Jerome gestured toward Simon. "Send young Aristide back to wait with the boats. He has no stomach for this kind of work."

"Then he must learn," Le Vis growled. "Now get back to your place and be silent."

Jerome vented a sound full of disgust and frustration, but he scrambled back to crouch beside Simon. Simon attempted to reassure Jerome as much as himself.

"We are only here to capture the heretic, Captain Remy, not—not kill anyone. The master would never harm anyone without benefit of trial. He has promised and he—he would never lie to me."

Jerome merely gave Simon a sad look, but before he could reply, Brother Finial darted back across the yard. His broad face was flushed with triumph. "There is no sign of anyone near the house, Monsieur Le Vis. Maurice and Gaston have checked the barn and stables. All empty. The entire place might well be deserted."

"Perhaps they knew we were coming and all fled," Simon suggested hopefully.

"Nonsense." Finial sneered. "More like the stupid wenches are all asleep in their beds."

"Then we will give them an awakening they'll not soon forget," Le Vis said. "Surround the house. Find a way to break in. Move quickly and block all exits. I want no escapes or interference this time."

Finial and the others hastened to obey. But the master detained Jerome long enough to use his lantern to light a torch. Simon shivered. He had seen his master in dark moods, but this feverish glaze in his eyes was somehow far worse. He had been this way ever since the queen's visit, as though that woman had somehow bewitched him with her painted visions of power and glory.

Commanding Jerome and Simon to follow, Le Vis led the way across the yard, brandishing his torch, no longer making any effort at stealth. Anyone in the house could have seen his approach through the windows and yet all remained silent. Simon's heart hammered in his chest.

Somehow this seemed all too easy. Was it truly possible to take a sorceress this much unaware?

Simon thought again of Ariane Cheney's peculiar ring and wondered if she might even now be conjuring the demon Renard to appear astride his devil horse, snorting fire. Simon shuddered, remembering all too well the terrible threats the evil Comte had made against his master if he ever caught Le Vis returning to Faire Isle.

※ ※ ※

THE WITCH-HUNTERS HAD BREACHED THE HOUSE. EVEN DOWN IN the fastness of the dungeon, muffled sounds carried from above, the shattering of a window, followed by the heavy tramp of feet.

Ariane twisted the ring on her finger and tried to remain calm and tell herself that Renard would come soon. He would be here. He had not failed her before. But something felt disturbingly different about her use of the ring this time. It was as though she had sensed her own silent cry penetrating the night, but she had felt no answer. No warm whisper of Renard's reassurance.

One lone candle on her worktable broke the suffocating darkness of the dungeon, but the small flame was enough for her to see the fear and tension in the faces surrounding her.

The trap door was too well hidden. One had to know where

to find the hidden spring to shift the heavy settle in the kitchen and the bench appeared permanently fixed to the wall. They would all be safe until help arrived as long as Ariane could keep everyone contained below stairs.

But that task was proving more difficult as the tense seconds crawled by and the sounds coming from above grew ever more ominous. Ariane scarcely knew who was worse, Remy poised at the foot of the stairs, clenching the hilt of his sword, looking like a penned-up warhorse, being reined back from battle. Or Miri clutching Necromancer in her arms, fretting over the safety of her other animals.

"I shouldn't have left Butternut out in the stables," she whispered. "Or my rabbits. Ariane, you must let me try to go and get them."

"The witch-hunters are not after that fat old pony or your bunnies, Miribelle," Gabrielle assured her.

A particularly loud crash from above caused them all to start. Gabrielle stomped over to Ariane to demand through clenched teeth. "Do you truly expect us just to stay tamely down here while those villains tear our house apart?"

Remy was hard behind her, urging, "Please Mistress Cheney, you must at least allow me to go up and put a stop—"

"No! No one is going to risk dying for a few sticks of furniture," Ariane shot back fiercely, although she was finding it equally as hard to do nothing. Bad enough to have witch-hunters invade the island, but Belle Haven, her very home. The sense of violation almost made her feel sick.

But she clutched her hand bearing the ring and repeated almost like a mantra, "Renard is coming. He will be here soon."

"And what if he isn't?" Gabrielle asked. "What if the comte does not prevail this time? The witch-hunters managed to get past his patrol. What if Le Vis already dealt with Renard? What if he's dead?"

Ariane felt herself pale at Gabrielle's words. That dire possibility had never occurred to her, although perhaps it should have. She remembered the malevolence of Le Vis, the raw hatred in his eyes when Renard had driven him from the island. What if the master witch-hunter had managed to take Renard unaware? Or worse still, what if by calling out to him, Ariane had led him straight to his death?

Her fingers trembled as she pressed her ring-bearing hand over her heart.

"Renard, please answer me. Where are you?"

The silence that greeted her was so terrible, she felt the blood drumming in her ears. She attempted to call out to Renard again, but Remy's grim voice broke her concentration.

"Forgive me, Mistress Cheney. But if Le Vis doesn't find me, he may simply set your house afire and we will all be trapped down here. And even if the comte does come, I can cower here no longer while another man fights my battles."

"No, Remy, stop!" Ariane cried, but Remy had already started up the steps. Ariane's heart lurched with fear. Not only was the rash young captain going to get himself killed, he would betray the location of secrets the wise women of Belle Haven had kept hidden from outsiders for centuries.

Ariane started after him, but she had a brief tussle with Gabrielle at the foot of the stairs, her sister likewise determined to go after Remy.

Ariane finally managed to thrust Gabrielle out of the way. "Stay here," she commanded sharply. "And look after Miri."

Then she plunged up the darkness of the winding stone stair, but her heart sank as she realized she was too late.

꞊ ꞊ ꞊

"RENARD, ANSWER ME. WHERE ARE YOU?"

Ariane's urgent call whispered through Renard's mind, but he could not spare a moment to pause and summon enough thought to answer. His head was filled with but one grim purpose, to reach Belle Haven before it was too late.

He urged Hercules on faster, the horse racing at a blurring speed, Renard thundering into the courtyard ahead of his men. His heart twisted with dread as he reined in sharply, spotting the yawning door, the shattered window.

The bastards were already in the house.

Barely waiting for Hercules to come to a halt, Renard leapt from the animal's back, tossing the reins to one of his squires. Drawing his sword, his heart pounding as hard as his boots, he ran to the house.

Reaching the front door, he caught the flicker of light in the great hall. For a horrified moment, Renard feared Le Vis had set the house afire. But it was only the flare of torchlight as the witch-hunters overturned furniture, smashed the contents of the aumbry, deliberately carving a path of destruction as they ransacked the house.

Renard would do Ariane and her sisters no good by blindly rushing in. He approached stealthily, sword at the ready, hovering on the threshold, assessing the situation.

Three witch-hunters were in the great hall, the rest crashing about upstairs. Someone called out from above. "There is no sign of anyone, master."

Renard heard Le Vis's vexed oath. "They have to be here, hiding somewhere."

Renard tried to pick out the form of the master witch-hunter. They all looked alike in their cursed black robes. Then Le Vis turned, his torch spilling a fiery glow over his ugly, twisted features. "If we can't find them, we will burn them out."

"Le Vis!" Renard stepped out into the open. For a moment, all the witch-hunters froze. Renard was dimly aware of the young boy Simon letting out a terrified cry. Le Vis glared at Renard.

"You!" Le Vis's voice trembled with loathing. But he retreated as the rest of Renard's retainers poured into the room.

"Upstairs. Go after the rest of them." Renard issued the terse command to his men. "I'll take care of Le Vis."

As Renard advanced, Le Vis shrank away from him, baring his teeth with the desperation of a cornered animal. Even at such a distance, Renard was able to read the thought chasing through his mad glazed eyes.

"Damn you, Le Vis, no—" Renard roared, but in a whirl of black robes, Le Vis rushed toward the wall, setting his torch to the nearest tapestry.

Renard lunged forward, only to have his way barred by one of the other witch-hunters. A burly man with a round face, wielding a sword. Renard furiously beat his weapon aside. When he disarmed the man, the witch-hunter gave a cowardly whimper and fled.

Flames licked up the side of the tapestry and Le Vis darted toward another. But Renard was upon him. He cut the torch from his hand. Le Vis shrieked, clutching his bloodied fingers. He fell to his knees, still groping for his fallen torch.

With an enraged snarl, Renard raised his sword just as someone hurtled past him. He caught a flash of a terrified young face and barely managed to check his deadly blow as Simon flung himself forward to shield his master.

Renard felt himself seized from behind, a black-robed arm crushing against his neck. Renard grunted and fought, flinging his assailant off him. He swung about, recovering just in time as the witch-hunter charged him again.

The man rushed forward, impaling himself on Renard's sword. Renard wrenched his weapon free as the witch-hunter sagged to the floor. Flames now threatened to engulf the tapestry. The entire house had erupted into a hellish chaos, witch-hunters pounding down the stairs, hotly pursued by his men. Renard coughed, struggling to clear his eyes, find Le Vis. There was no sign of him or the boy. But someone else loomed before Renard, his grim face shadowed with a dark beard. Renard's mind dimly registered the fact that he was not wearing black robes like the rest of those devils.

But he was brandishing a sword and that was all Renard needed to see . . .

☙ ☙ ☙

ARIANE STRUGGLED THROUGH THE TRAP DOOR TO FIND THE KITCHEN dark and deserted. But sounds of some desperate battle being waged carried to her to the great hall. She snatched up a poker from the kitchen hearth.

Peering past the screen that separated the kitchen from the great hall, she froze, stifling a cry of alarm. One of the magnificent tapestries crackled with fire, the flames throwing a dancing light over the macabre scene before her. Her home resembled a battlefield, one witch-hunter stretched across the stairs, another tossed like a broken doll over an upended table, still another diving through a broken window to escape. Ariane nearly tripped over another hooded dark figure, sprawled in a pool of blood.

She shrank back involuntarily as two men rushed past her, but to her relief she caught a glimpse of familiar gold-and-black livery. Renard's men. They rushed toward the fire, coughing and choking as they wrenched the blazing tapestry from the wall.

But in the midst of all the confusion, men still fought on. Through the haze of smoke, Ariane could make out the form of two silhouettes locked in a deadly combat, steel clanging against steel. Her breath squeezed from her lungs in a rush as she realized that one of them was Remy and the other . . .

Renard!

Remy's sword crashed down, snapping Renard's blade in half. Renard flung his useless sword aside, tackling Remy. He drove the captain back, trapping his sword hand, slamming it repeatedly against the wall until Remy was forced to drop his weapon. Renard's other huge hand closed about Remy's throat.

"No, Renard. Stop!" Ariane cried, rushing toward the two men. Dropping her poker, she used both hands in a desperate effort to loosen Renard's ferocious grip.

"Please, Renard. Let him go. He—he is a friend."

Renard seemed far too caught up in the heat of battle to pay her any heed. Then his eyes flickered toward her, recognition setting in. He released Remy so abruptly that the captain sagged to the floor, gasping for air and clutching his throat. Ariane hovered anxiously over him.

"Remy? Are you all right?"

"Remy?" Ariane heard Renard echo in a strange voice, but before she could offer any explanations Gabrielle burst upon them. Thrusting Ariane aside, she sank to her knees beside the captain, pressing her hand to his chest.

"Remy? Are you hurt? My God, Ariane! What has your ogre done to him?"

"N-nothing," Remy gasped in a voice laced with self-disgust. "Merely dis-disarmed and knocked the wind from me."

"Choked is more likely," Gabrielle said. As she struggled to loosen the neckline of his shirt, she cast a blistering look up at Renard.

But the comte was quite oblivious. He retrieved the captain's fallen sword, examining the weapon closely. "Well, well. The owner of the mysterious sword. Are you not going to introduce us, ma chère?"

Ariane gaped at him, trying to gather her disordered wits. Her great hall was a shambles of broken furniture, shattered glass, and fallen men. The burning tapestry was nearly out but still smoldering. And Renard . . . who minutes ago she had almost given up for dead, stood before her, large and solid and—and very much alive. And calmly drawling out a request for introductions. Ariane hardly knew what she wanted to do most, fling her arms around the man or hit him.

"Where have you been? Why didn't you answer me?" Her voice came out astonishingly shrill, close to the edge of hysteria.

Renard frowned. "Your pardon, milady. I was a little preoccupied trying to rid you of your uninvited guests."

"You could have spared a moment to let me know you were all right. I thought something had happened to you. I even thought you might be d-dead, you great, s-stupid—."

Ariane gulped, struggling to compose herself, winking back furious tears. Renard closed the distance between them, wrapping his arm around her waist. "Ah, chérie, I am sorry if I worried you. Please don't cry. Not over me."

"I—I am not crying over you. It's the s-smoke from the tapestry." Ariane held herself rigid as he drew her closer, but she found herself too weak to resist the lure of his powerful shoulder. She rested her cheek against him and closed her eyes, lost to everything but the comfort of Renard's strong embrace.

Renard brushed his lips across her brow. "Forgive me, ma chère. I nearly failed you tonight. I don't know how those bastards managed to slip past my patrols, but I promise you. You are all safe now."

"Ariane? G-gabrielle?" Ariane heard a small voice calling out.

Miri! Ariane's eyes flew open. She did not want her little sister stumbling into this grim scene, but she was too late.

Miri emerged cautiously from behind the screen that blocked off the kitchens, still clutching Necromancer in her arms. She surveyed the hall with wide eyes, her stricken gaze coming to rest upon the fallen witch-hunter nearest her, the dark cowl still pulled over his face.

Miri dropped the cat with an agonized cry. "S-simon?"

She stumbled toward the body, her face as white as her nightgown. But if it was the boy hidden beneath that cowl, Ariane did not want her little sister to be the one to discover the fact. Wrenching free of Renard, she darted across the room just as Miri was bending down.

Ariane gently pushed her aside. She hunkered down beside the inert witch-hunter. There was no sign of life, the black robes soaked in blood and Ariane hesitated to draw back the hood herself, fearful of what she might uncover.

Bracing herself, Ariane peeled back the cowl and then joined in Miri's tremulous breath of relief.

It was not Simon, but a man Ariane only remembered vaguely as being part of Le Vis's unholy band. But she had no idea who he was or more accurately who he had been. He stared up at her with empty eyes. Whatever ignorance, whatever delusions had prompted this man to join in the persecution of innocent women, what waste he had made of his life was over now, all stripped clean by the hand of death. Ariane could not help but feel a stirring of pity as she brushed her fingers down his face, closing the witch-hunter's eyes.

She glanced up to find Renard towering over her. His own eyes were completely dispassionate as he gazed down at the dead man, but his voice was gentle as he said, "Come away, chérie. There is nothing that even you can do for this fellow."

He held out his hand to Ariane and wrapped his other arm around Miri, turning the girl's eyes away from the terrible sight.

∗ ∗ ∗

THE FIRST GRAY TRACE OF DAWN LIT THE SKY OVER BELLE HAVEN and no one had yet slept. The servants, from old Agnes to young Leon, were anxious to begin setting the house back to rights, but Ariane insisted that that could wait. She assembled her wearied household in the kitchen for a warm breakfast, then she herself slipped back into the great hall to assess the damage.

She had not yet had the courage to go above stairs and see

what havoc Le Vis's brutes might have wrought there. The main hall was bad enough, the wood floor stained with blood, one wall scorched from the fire, a stale smell of smoke still hanging in the air despite the fact that windows had been flung open. Chairs and tables were broken, crystal and plates smashed.

Ariane picked her way through the shattered glass to where Maman's chair lay knocked over. Ariane placed it back into position before the hearth. The simple gesture afforded her some small comfort and she needed it as her gaze rested on the blackened remains of the once-magnificent tapestry.

It seemed a sad irony that Le Vis had chosen to begin his assault with this particular one, the weaving of Great-aunt Eugenie serenely at work with her quill and parchment, the same one Renard had admired so long ago.

Ariane reached down to fold back one corner, but no trace of the subject of the great tapestry was left discernible. She mourned quietly, thinking of the countless hours of labor that had gone into it, each thread so lovingly and patiently woven by feminine hands. All destroyed in mere moments by one madman.

There had not been such violence done at Belle Haven since the days the island had been the site of a Roman fortress, long before the wise women had claimed this peaceful place to be their own.

Ariane's shoulders slumped, briefly overwhelmed once more by a sense of her own failure to preserve, protect. She drew back from the tapestry, wiping the soot from her fingers, giving herself a brisk mental shake as well.

It was only a house, after all. The remains of the tapestry could be cleared away, the bloodstains scoured. The important thing was that the attack had proved no worse. None of her own people had been harmed and any injury to Renard's men had been but slight.

The witch-hunters had not fared as well. Ariane had counted five among the slain that Renard's men had carted away, but neither Le Vis nor the boy were among them. Renard and his cousin Toussaint were even now out riding the woods, attempting to track the escaped witch-hunters down.

She could not help hoping that Le Vis and the others would escape, leave Faire Isle and never return. She wanted no more bloodshed. But even in the unlikelihood that Le Vis would simply give up and leave them all alone, Ariane knew there was one who would not . . . the Dark Queen.

Ariane stole out of the house, seeking the relative peace of her garden. The early morning light flooded softly over the beds of her herbs, beads of dew clinging to velvety rose petals. And somewhere from one of the trees in the orchard, a lark was twittering with the promise of a new day.

Ariane knew that there were some bitter folk, perhaps her own sister Gabrielle amongst them, who would insist nature was cruel. But as Ariane lifted her face to catch the soft breeze, she believed as her mother had taught her, that nature was a comforter, a gentle healer, and that was what a daughter of the earth was also meant to be.

She wondered how Catherine had become so twisted, using the arts and knowledge that had been passed down to all wise women for such dark purposes. Of course, the queen was not the first to do so. There had been the legendary Melusine, rumored to have vented her malevolence against entire villages, spreading poison and plague.

Catherine had not yet practiced her evil on such a wide scale, but Ariane had a grim feeling the woman was drawing ever closer to it.

At least it would take awhile before the Dark Queen learned of her witch-hunter's second failure. But it was more important than ever to get Remy safely away from here, especially now that Renard knew of his presence.

Observing Remy himself slipping into the stables, Ariane

headed in that direction. The stables appeared blessedly normal in the early light, the morning breeze carrying to her the comforting and familiar scents of hay, leather, and horse. The bunnies that Miri had so worried over were nestled asleep in their bed of straw and Butternut chomped placidly on his oats.

She was surprised to see Remy in another of the stalls, watering a sleek brown mare. Like everyone else at Belle Haven, the captain's face showed the strains of the night before, but he managed a wan smile at Ariane's approach.

"Good morrow, Mistress Cheney."

"Yes, it is, isn't it?" Ariane leaned into the stall to stroke the muzzle of the horse. "Where did this come from?"

"A gift to me, apparently. Courtesy of the Comte de Renard."

"Renard? Has he returned, then?"

"No, he is still out pursuing Le Vis as far as I know. But he took the time to dispatch one of his men back with this fine animal for me." Remy patted the mare's glossy neck.

Ariane took in this information. "Then . . . even knowing you are a fugitive from the crown, the comte intends to help you?"

"Yes, he seems most eager to send me on my way. In fact, he strongly urges that I leave at once."

"But you can't. You have had so little sleep. You must at least take one more day to rest—"

Remy cut her off with a sad shake of his head. "No, Mistress Ariane. I have already endangered your family enough and last night was but final proof of how bold and desperate the Dark Queen has grown to stop me. She must be planning some dread fate for my king indeed. I must reach Henry and prevent him falling into her trap."

Ariane wanted to argue with him, but she feared he was right. Remy could not afford a moment's more delay.

Leaving him, she hurried back to the house, long enough to

prepare a pouch of supplies. By the time she returned to the stables, Remy already had the mare saddled and led out into the yard.

Ariane shifted the pouch from her shoulder and handed it to him.

"What is this?" he asked in surprise.

"Just a few things I put together for your journey. Some food, some wine, and the small flask contains the rest of the medicine I have been giving you."

When Remy pulled a face, she added sternly, "You will continue to take it, monsieur, until it is all gone."

"Yes, mistress. I would scarcely dare to defy the Lady of Faire Isle," he promised with one of his grave smiles.

Ariane watched him sling the pouch across his saddle with a heavy heart. She had grown fond of the somber young captain and was afraid for him. The mist-laden road through her own woods seemed perilous enough. Who knew what danger he would face once he had left the relative safety of Faire Isle?

"You will take care, Captain," she said anxiously. "The Dark Queen may have sent others after you besides Le Vis. Her royal guard could be out there waiting."

"I will watch my back, mistress. Although . . ." Remy gave one of his rare laughs. "I confess I might almost welcome a clash with something as normal as another soldier after dealing with witch-hunters, cats that give warnings, and magic rings. Your Renard appears to be far more comfortable with such strange doings than I."

"He is not my Renard," Ariane said, annoyed to feel a faint blush tinge her cheeks.

Remy cast her a dubious look, but said nothing. He started to vault into the saddle when he stopped, turning gravely back to her. "There is one thing we have not decided, Mistress Cheney. What is to be done with the gloves?"

Ariane reflected for a long moment. "With your permission, I will keep them."

"That hardly seems wise, mademoiselle."

"Indeed it will be for the best, Captain. Only think. If you were to be captured and did not have the gloves in your possession, there might still be a way we could barter with the Dark Queen for your life."

"Or place yourselves in still more danger."

"I believe we will be safe enough once you are gone. I intend to send a message to Mademoiselle Lavalle in Paris. She appears to be a daring and resourceful woman. I am hoping she might be able to mislead Catherine into thinking you have fled with the gloves to England. It may buy you a little more time."

Remy looked clearly unhappy with these plans, but he appeared to realize there was little he could do to alter Ariane's determination.

"You have all been far too good to me," he said huskily, grasping Ariane's hand. "And courageous. No matter where I go or what becomes of me, for the rest of my life, I will always remember the ladies of Faire Isle."

Even as he carried Ariane's hand to his lips, she could tell that there was one lady uppermost in his mind. His gaze strayed hopefully toward the house, but it was obvious there was little chance of Gabrielle emerging to bid him farewell.

Remy's eyes filled with such sad resignation that Ariane could not restrain the impulse to give him a hug and kiss his cheek.

"Take care, Remy and—and Godspeed."

Remy nodded. "Once I have reached the side of my king and believe all is well, I will try to get word to you."

He swung into the saddle. Ariane stepped back as he urged the gelding forward. She lifted her hand to wave, but Remy galloped from the stableyard without looking back.

꙳ ꙳ ꙳

THE MORNING WAS WELL ADVANCED WHEN RENARD FINALLY RE-
turned to Belle Haven. By the time Ariane emerged from the
house, she saw only Fourche leading Hercules into the stables.

She found Renard himself at the well near the kitchen door.
He had stripped down to his shirtsleeves and was preparing to
wash off some of the dust of the road. Hauling up the bucket, he
splashed water over his face, looking hot and tired.

But his grim expression lightened when he saw Ariane approach offering him a towel. He murmured his thanks, slicking
back the damp ends of his hair. He rubbed the coarse linen vigorously over his face and the strong cords of his neck.

Except for the faint shadows beneath his eyes and the hint of
stubble on his chin, Renard scarcely looked the worse for having
spent his night fighting and pursuing witch-hunters. Ariane en-
vied him his astonishing fortitude. Small wonder she tended to
think of Renard as invincible. He was like a man forged from iron.

Scooping up a handful of the water, he drank deeply and
sighed, "Ah, that is better."

"How fared your search?" Ariane asked anxiously.

"Ill. We managed to take care of three more of the devils, but
two still elude us. That boy, and worst of all, Le Vis."

Renard flung down the towel. "He has escaped me twice
now, saved once by you and then by that foolish lad of his. What
is it about that black-hearted miscreant that inspires such regard
for his welfare?"

Renard dragged his hand back through his hair in a frustrated gesture and it was then that Ariane noticed the blood stain
on his sleeve.

"Renard! Are you hurt?" she cried, catching hold of his arm,
starting gently to ease back the sleeve.

Renard regarded the stain with indifference. "No, the blood
isn't mine."

"O-oh." Ariane immediately recoiled, the import of his previous words striking home.

"We managed to take care of three more of the devils."

"So how many of Le Vis's men were—were—"

"Killed? Some six or seven altogether, I suppose."

Ariane suppressed a shudder. She said nothing, but as usual Renard was able to read her eyes all too clearly.

He swore. "God's teeth, Ariane. Those witch-hunters came here to murder you all in your beds, burn the house down around your ears. What did you expect me to do? Disarm them, tenderly escort them off the island, and ask them not to come back? I tried that once, as you may recall. It obviously did not work.

"My men and I destroyed no one who was not trying to do the same by us." Renard rolled his arm to display the stain on his sleeve. "This blood is from a fellow who attempted to ambush me in the woods, seeking to unseat me by coming with a dagger at my horse. I would never strike down any man in cold blood."

"I—I know that," Ariane replied in a small voice. "The measures you took were necessary, but I still cannot rejoice in them. There has never been bloodshed before at Belle Haven."

Some of the impatience melted from Renard's face. "I would have given anything to have kept this danger and violence from your door. I should have been more vigilant."

Ariane shook her head. "This was more my fault than yours. I am the one responsible for the safety of my sisters. I am not unaccustomed to the sight of death, but Miri, she was quite devastated. I should have taken more care to keep her below stairs last night, never allowed her to see such grim sights. She—she suffers enough from strange nightmares."

"How is the child this morning?" Renard asked.

"Well enough, all things considering. I made her a tisane and tucked her back in bed with her cat. She drifted off to sleep, but she was very much worried about that boy, Simon."

"My cousin Toussaint has gathered up a fresh patrol and is still out searching. We will get the boy."

"That is what Miri is afraid of."

"That boy is not exactly an innocent, Ariane. He serves Le Vis."

"Miri thinks that Simon is just confused and so you or I might be if we were apprenticed to a witch-hunter. Perhaps even raised by one."

"A man breeds a dog, teaches it to be savage and attack. It might not be the dog's fault, but the animal is still dangerous."

"A boy is not the same as a dog, my lord."

"No, because the dog can sometimes be gentled and re-trained. As for that boy, there is no telling to what lengths he might go to defend his master when we close in on Le Vis. I will do my best to spare the lad, but I can make no promises."

Ariane nodded, forced to be content with that. "Will it please you to come into the house, my lord? Agnes has a hot stew waiting, fresh bread, and wine. For your men as well."

She started to lead the way back to the house, but Renard stopped her. "The food can wait. Come talk to me a moment, lady."

He sank down on the grass, propping his back against the trunk of a stout oak with a wearied sigh. He smiled, reaching his hand up to her in invitation. Ariane hesitated, fretting her lip.

Last night when she had been recovering from her fear for Renard's life, it had been the easiest thing in the world to melt into his arms. Daylight brought the return of reason and memo-ries of the awkward way they had parted the eve of the supper.

She was especially wary of that outstretched hand with the ring glinting on his finger, remembering the heated sparks that had flown between them when her own ring had touched against it.

She settled herself on the grass a safe distance away. She folded her hands in her lap, taking great care to keep her ring safely buried in the folds of her skirt. If Renard noticed her extreme caution, he made no remark.

Resting his head against the trunk of the tree, he regarded her through narrowed eyes. "So, where is your gallant friend, the captain?"

"Remy has already left, as I gather you ordered him to do," Ariane said tartly. She softened her tone. "Thank you, my lord. For helping him, for giving him that horse."

"The pleasure was all mine, chérie, I do assure you. I would have gotten rid of—that is, helped the captain much sooner if I had known of his existence."

"I only hope that he will be all right."

"I am sure he will be fine." Renard shrugged. "He wields his sword well enough for a Huguenot and any man able to escape from Paris under the very nose of the Dark Queen obviously has some wits about him."

"So Remy told you everything? All about who he is, why he had to flee?"

"Not directly. The rash young fool's eyes are even easier to read than yours, ma chère. You should have told me from the beginning what has been going on, Ariane."

Although she had not the least reason to feel guilty, she rushed to explain, "I *would* have told you about Captain Remy, but I was not certain how you would feel—"

"About my betrothed hiding a handsome young officer in her cellar?"

"I am not your betrothed, my lord, and I meant how you would feel about aiding a fugitive from the crown. The old comte certainly would never have lent his support to a Huguenot rebel."

"I seem to spend a great deal of energy convincing people that I am not like my late grandfather. But I would have thought by now that I would no longer have to do so with you, milady."

So Renard was not invulnerable after all. He could be hurt,

and Ariane realized that she had managed to do so. She reached toward him, only to check the impulsive gesture.

"I am sorry, Renard. I don't believe you are like your grandfather, but I felt I had to be extremely cautious with Remy's life at stake and we have never precisely discussed your views on politics or religion."

"They are very simple, ma chère. I tend to my own affairs and expect other men to do the same."

"Then that is all the more reason I appreciate you taking the trouble to help Remy."

Renard frowned. "You seem to have developed a remarkable fondness for that young man on such short acquaintance. Pray forgive me if I wax a trifle jealous."

"But that is quite absurd. Even if I were your—your betrothed, there would be no need for you to be. I regard Remy as nothing more than a friend and as for him, he would scarcely know I existed when set next to my sister, Gabrielle."

"Then the man's judgment is extremely wanting." Renard's frown faded, and Ariane felt herself blush a little.

It was foolish to feel so gratified by Renard's words or the warm light that sprang to his eyes, but she could not seem to help herself. He reached out to capture her hand. Since the hand that did so was not the one bearing his ring, it seemed safe to allow him the liberty.

That is until Renard carried her hand to his lips and not at all in Remy's polite manner. His mouth lingered, kissing each fingertip in a way that caused her to tremble.

"I—I also have to thank you on behalf of my family, and myself," Ariane said primly, struggling to ignore the sensations he was arousing. "Once more we all owe our lives to you."

"You owe me nothing, ma chère. Our bargain of the ring . . . you summon me and I fly to your side, remember?"

"But you can't fly, Renard. That is one thing that has been puzzling me. I called to you not long before the witch-hunters broke into the house. And still you managed to arrive in time to prevent Le Vis from burning down Belle Haven. How did you get here so quickly?"

Renard turned her hand over, pressing a light kiss in the center of her palm, sending a warm shiver through her. "I was already out and about, patrolling the harbor."

"Even so, the harbor is several miles from Belle Haven."

"Hercules is a fast horse."

Ariane studied Renard, his hooded eyes taking great care to make no contact with hers and she was struck by a sudden realization, something that should have occurred to her much sooner.

"You must have been alerted that Le Vis had landed and was marching on Belle Haven. I never even needed to use the ring to summon you."

"Of course you did." Renard pressed his lips to her wrist. But Ariane wrenched her hand free, refusing to be further distracted.

"No, I didn't. You were already on the way to save us before I even slipped your ring on my finger. Were you not?"

"Don't be ridiculous, chérie. How could I?"

"And what is more," Ariane continued inexorably. "I doubt I really needed to use the ring the first time either. If you had known Miri was in danger, you would have come anyway."

"Ah, but I didn't know—"

"But if you *had,* you would have galloped to the rescue, ring or no ring."

"I hardly see how any of this matters."

But it did matter very much. In fact, Ariane felt strangely as though a large weight had been lifted from her heart.

"You, my ruthless Comte de Renard, are a great fraud," she said softly. "Always pretending to be so hard and pragmatic when underneath it all, I think you are as rash and gallant a fool as Captain Remy."

Renard folded his arms stubbornly across his chest. "What I might or might not have done on my own is of no significance. You still used my ring. Twice."

"I can count, my lord," Ariane said with a wry smile. "However, I will not be using it again and not just to avoid becoming your wife. I never fully considered the danger to you until last night. I might have drawn you straight to your death."

Renard flung up his hands. "Mon Dieu. Now in addition to her other burdens, the Lady of Faire Isle has decided she must seek to protect a great oaf like me."

"But I had no right to put you at risk."

"You have every right. I gave it to you when I gave you the ring."

"Nonetheless, as soon as Le Vis is captured, I think you need to return to the mainland—"

"Think again, chérie," Renard retorted. "You have a far greater enemy than that witch-hunter and until this threat from the Dark Queen is over, I am going nowhere."

"But you cannot mean to stay here indefinitely, lodging at an inn—"

"I don't intend to. I am staying right here."

"At Belle Haven?" Ariane stiffened. "That is completely out of the question, milord."

"Twice now, I have allowed danger to come far too close to my intended bride. I don't ever intend to be that careless again. I mean to remain close to your side even if I have to make camp in the woods, set up my tent at your gates."

"But—but you can't—" Ariane had been having difficulty enough resisting the strange temptation to use the ring to summon Renard to her bed. How much harder would it be to resist with the man camped on her doorstep?

But Renard rose as though he considered the matter settled. He sketched her a courtly bow. "Now if you will pardon me, milady, I must go and rejoin the hunt for Le Vis."

As he headed toward the stables, Ariane scrambled to her feet, trailing desperately after him. "But Renard—My lord, I appreciate your offer of protection, but I would not have you stay here neglecting your own affairs, your estates—"

"My estate will be fine," Renard said serenely. "I took your advice and found myself a better steward."

"And—and there is another reason that remaining in Belle Haven is not in your interests."

"How so?"

"Because if you guard me so closely, you cannot hope I will have need to use your ring ever again."

Renard paused in his lengthy strides to cup her chin, his eyes warm and intent upon her face. "Ah, but I don't want you in peril, chérie. I hope you will find a far different reason to summon me in the night."

That was exactly what she feared. As usual, she was certain Renard read her thoughts all too clearly. He smiled and pressed a soft, lingering kiss to her lips before continuing to the stables.

Ariane watched him go with a sigh, uncertain what troubled her more. The fact that there was nothing she could do to shake Renard's steely resolve or the realization that she very much wanted him to stay.

Her dismay deepened when she turned to see Gabrielle coming through the gardens. Her sister had been angry and distressed enough when Ariane had merely asked Renard to dine. She could not imagine what Gabrielle was going to say when she learned that the comte meant to install himself at Belle Haven.

Gabrielle was already frowning as she marched up to Ariane. "Well? Is he gone?"

"Renard? Ah, er, yes he just went into the stables, but—"

"Not your ogre!" Gabrielle flushed. "I—I mean Captain Remy."

"Yes, he left early this morning."

"Oh." Gabrielle's thick lashes swept down, veiling her expression. "Well, it's a good thing the man is gone when we have witch-hunters tearing the house apart looking for him. Only now I don't suppose I will ever know what this was all about, what kind of trouble Remy was in."

"I am sorry, Gabrielle. I only thought it best that—"

"Oh, never mind." Gabrielle swept her apologies aside with an irritated gesture. "I really don't care to know anymore. With Remy gone, that is an end to the matter."

She stared at the empty road leading away from Belle Haven and, to Ariane's surprise, Gabrielle's fierce expression crumpled, rare tears springing to her eyes.

"The fool thought he was in love with me," she whispered.

"I know, dearest," Ariane replied.

She turned back to Ariane with a woebegone look. "I— I truly didn't ever want to hurt him. But I couldn't love him, Airy. I don't have a heart to give to—to anyone."

No, Ariane thought sadly. The problem was that Gabrielle had far too much heart, proud, passionate, and still recovering from wounds far beyond Ariane's ability to heal.

Instead, she merely held her arms out to her sister and after a brief hesitation, Gabrielle came to her. Nestling her head on Ariane's shoulder, she shed a few quiet tears.

"Never mind, dearest." Ariane stroked her younger sister's golden hair. "Everything will be all right . . ."

Ariane faltered, wincing over the inadequacy of her words. "I know that you—that all of us have been through some—some grim times of late, but I am sure that all will be well again, just the way things used to be."

Gabrielle lifted her head from Ariane's shoulder to smile bitterly. "With Maman dead and Papa gone missing. Everything was really not all that wonderful, was it, Ariane?"

"No," Ariane said sadly. "I suppose it wasn't."

Gabrielle dashed her hand across her eyes, wiping away the last vestige of her tears. "Sometimes I envy Papa sailing away like he did. I'd rather like to run off myself. Perhaps I should have gone with Remy."

Ariane cast Gabrielle a sharp look. "Gabrielle, are you certain you did not fall in love with Remy?"

"With the Scourge? Hardly. But since you don't approve of us going to Paris, perhaps I might obtain a glimpse of the court in Navarre and . . . its king."

Ariane tensed. "Gabrielle—"

"Oh, don't look so alarmed. I am only jesting. I daresay Henry of Navarre would be as somber as Remy. No doubt those Huguenots prefer their women submissive and virtuous, which I certainly am not. I suppose I must be content to remain where I am."

For now.

Ariane read the unspoken thought clearly in Gabrielle's eyes. The girl's brief moment of vulnerability was over and Ariane could almost feel Gabrielle distancing herself again. Her heart tightened with the knowledge that she was not going to be able to check her sister's unhappy ambitions forever.

Chapter Nineteen

*M*IRI CROUCHED LOW BEHIND THE TREES AS THE PATROL GAL-
loped by, single file down the narrow path through the woods.
None of the riders spared a glance in her direction. After a futile week of attempting to track down the remainder of the
witch-hunters, the comte's men were no longer being so vigilant.
Most of them, including Renard's cousin, Toussaint, had all but
given up.

She crept from her hiding place, shaking the leaves from
her skirts, then tore off running, dodging nimbly through the
trees. Unhampered by the haversack fastened to her back, she
did not slow her pace until the woodland thinned, the terrain
growing more barren and rough. It ended abruptly in a rugged
stretch of coast, the channel water slapping against the jagged
rocks.

Miri picked her way more carefully as she climbed up the

cropping of rock that jutted out over the secluded cove. Halfway up the ledge, bracken concealed the narrow entrance to the cave where Miri had frequently come to grieve in solitude for her mother and pray for the return of Papa. Her own secret place that she had never shared with anyone . . . until now.

Miri placed her fingers in her mouth and imitated the cry of a curlew. She waited anxiously until she heard a shrill reply. As she drew closer, the brush at the mouth of the cave rustled and a lithe figure emerged.

Clad in a simple linen tunic and trousers, he appeared little different from any of the other fisherman's sons or peasant boys on the island. Simon's dark curls tumbled over his milky brow, his hair swept by the breeze coming in off the sea.

Her heart did a little lift to see him safe and undiscovered for another day. Since word of the attack had spread, most of the people on the island would willingly have seen Simon dangling from the end of a rope.

Miri only wished she could find the words to make them all understand that Simon was different. Separated from his dread master, his hideous black robes discarded, he was neither witch-hunter nor devil. He was only . . . Simon.

As she clambered up the last few rocks, he reached his hand down to help her the rest of the way and Miri was grateful. Her skirts were something of a nuisance, but she knew that Simon did not approve of a girl going about in boy's clothing. Besides, he was now wearing most of what masculine apparel she owned.

His lean strong fingers closed about her wrist, hauling her up beside him.

"Ah, mademoiselle. I was beginning to fear you had abandoned me."

"That I never would," she assured him.

Simon flashed her one of those smiles that caused her insides to melt. She was glad when the sea breeze tangled her hair across her face, concealing her faint blush. She divested herself of the haversack and Simon pounced upon the contents eagerly.

He laughed a little when he saw all that Miri had brought, bread, fruit, cheese, half a roasted chicken, some cake.

"You are not feeding an army, mademoiselle."

"But I don't want you to starve," Miri protested.

"There appears to be little danger of that," Simon said. He perched on the ledge of the cliff as he began his meal, dangling his feet over the side.

He devoured a leg of chicken, some of the bread and cheese from the pack, pausing to take sips from the small flask of cherry cordial. Miri was content to watch him, marveling that she should find a mere boy of such interest. Everything about Simon fascinated her. Gabrielle had told her that witch-hunters were distorted, that their man parts were all puny and shriveled. That was why they hated women so. But Miri could not believe that any such thing was wrong with Simon.

He took a deep swallow from the flask, beads of moisture clinging to his lips. He wiped his mouth clean with the back of his hand. His lips looked so smooth and firm and a strange quiver went through her.

When Simon noticed her intent regard, he smiled a little. Miri had a feeling that just like Gabrielle, Simon was not unaware of the powerful impact of his own beauty. She blushed.

"So have you had enough to eat?" she asked.

"More than enough. I will save the rest of your bounty for later. You have done far better by me than the poor supper that I once provided for you. Our fortunes appear to have quite reversed."

"But you are not a prisoner like I was, Simon."

"Am I not? I see no way of escaping from this island and I doubt if I can keep hiding forever, even with your help."

Miri fretted her lower lip. "I have been giving some thought to that. I believe we should approach my sister, Ariane—"

"No!"

"But Ariane is a great deal like my Maman. She is very wise and—and forgiving."

"She is also in thrall to the demon, Renard."

"Renard is not a demon—"

"Oh, is he not? You did not see what he did to the rest of my order."

"Yes, I did," Miri whispered. Her mind was still haunted by the images of that dreadful night. The violence of men was something that horrified and confused Miri, this strange ability to hate and maim, spill blood over what often seemed the most senseless of reasons. For gold or possessions, or . . . or because one didn't like the way another man looked or prayed. Or even worse, sometimes merely for sport.

"If you saw the comte's handiwork, I don't know how you can defend him," Simon went on thickly. "Brother Jerome was a kind and righteous man. He was only trying to help me save my master when Renard pierced him clean through."

"But your master was setting our house on fire," Miri said in a small voice.

"That was an accident. Master Le Vis was attempting to get away and he brushed his torch against the tapestry. We didn't come to your house to hurt anyone, Miri. We were only searching for Captain Remy, a heretic and dangerous rebel."

Did Simon truly believe that? Miri wondered. She saw from his expression that he was trying hard to do so, but his eyes were filled with a certain amount of shame and confusion.

"I know that you think my master an evil man and perhaps sometimes in his zeal for—for justice, he does make mistakes. But if you only realized how good he has been to me."

"But he abandoned you. You said that he got away in the boat and just left you here."

Simon's lashes swept down, momentarily concealing his dark, expressive eyes. "We got separated during the flight. Master Le Vis probably believed that I was dead like all the others."

Miri touched his hand timidly. "Then this could be your chance to begin a new life, Simon. Become something else besides a witch-hunter. Please let me go to Ariane and the comte and intercede for you."

Before Simon could protest, she rushed on. "I thought the comte a very bad man when I first met him, but truly he is not. He sometimes can be too overbearing with Hercules, but we have been working on that these past few days. Renard is getting much better at charming horses."

"Mon Dieu, Miri! You should not allow that demon man to teach you any of his evil magic."

"*I* have been teaching *him*," Miri said indignantly. "And not all magic is evil."

Simon pursed his lips. "Master Le Vis frequently read me the Bible, and the Good Book warns against any sort of necromancy. Thou shalt not suffer a witch to live."

"Well, my father used to read *me* the Bible and it also says that the great King Saul consulted the augury of a wise woman."

Simon regarded her in astonishment. "*You* are familiar with the Bible?"

"I am a daughter of the earth, not some ignorant savage. We believe in God. We also believe in the spirit of the great mother earth. My maman taught me that religion does not have to be so narrow."

Simon only shook his head and patted her cheek. "Ah, Miri, there is so much you don't understand."

Miri liked the feel of his hand, but she resented his patronizing tone. "I understand far more than you do, Simon Aristide. Even if you are three years older than me."

"*Three* years, is it? I thought you told me you were fourteen."

Miri, mortified to be caught out in her lie, folded her arms across her chest, turning away from him. When Simon cupped her chin, trying to get her to look at him, she angrily tossed her head.

But he persisted. "Miri, please don't be mad at me. I hate it when we quarrel."

She hated it too, but sometimes the gulf between her view of the world and Simon's seemed too wide to ever be breached. But she was not proof against his coaxing dark eyes or the gentle way that his fingers curled around hers. His hand was so warm.

"There may be something in what you say," he began hesitantly. "I might consider abandoning my profession and going to Ariane for help, but one thing worries me. Your sister might use her ring to send for Renard to cut me down before I have a chance to say a word."

"You know about the rings?" Miri asked in astonishment.

"I noticed that they both wear identical metal bands with strange markings. That is how Ariane is able to conjure up the demon man so quickly, is it not?"

"I wouldn't call it *conjuring*," Miri objected. "But yes, the rings are magic. Ariane can use hers to summon the comte anytime she is in trouble. But she can only do so three times and then she will have to marry him. And she has already used the ring twice."

"And this makes you unhappy?" Simon asked softly.

Miri sighed. "I—I don't dislike Renard, but if Ariane married him, she would have to go live in his château on the mainland and perhaps I would, too. I love Faire Isle. This is my home and I don't want to leave."

Simon squeezed her hand. "Do Ariane and the comte always wear their rings?"

"I am not sure about the comte, but Ariane takes hers off sometimes."

"And what does she do with it?"

"I don't know." Miri squirmed, Simon's interest in the rings, his questions beginning to make her feel strangely uneasy. "Why do you ask?"

Simon shrugged. "Only because I would be much more easy about surrendering to your sister if she wasn't wearing that evil ring."

"But I don't think there is any need for you to worry. If I speak to Ariane first—"

"No!" Simon said sharply, then forced a smile to his lips. "I prefer to speak for myself, but I must be sure Ariane won't summon Renard to slay me."

"She wouldn't—"

"She already did once. Miri, I am sure your sister is a good woman. But I only want to be safe."

"I want that too."

"Then help me."

"What do you want me to do?"

"Just notice when Ariane removes the ring, find out where she keeps it and come and tell me. I'll know then that it would be safe to approach her. And if she is as wise and compassionate as you say—"

"She is!"

"Then I will renounce my profession and stay here on Faire Isle forever."

Miri turned Simon's request over in her mind and could not quite see the harm in it, but she still felt deeply troubled.

Simon squeezed her hand. "You do want me to be able to stay with you, don't you?"

"Oh, yes." Miri could scarcely remember wanting anything more. She had often felt so miserable and lonely since Papa had left and Maman had died. The advent of Simon into her life had somehow changed all that.

He leaned forward and her heart missed a beat when she realized what he intended to do. She shyly tipped up her face, closing her eyes. Simon touched his mouth to hers, so lightly, but the kiss seemed to blossom inside her, sweet and warm.

Miri drew back immediately, blushing hotly and pressing her hand to her lips. She scrambled away from Simon muttering, "I had better get back before I am missed."

Simon rose as well, asking anxiously, "But you will come back again soon?"

Miri nodded, too bashful to meet his eyes. But after a brief hesitation, she planted a kiss on his cheek, then darted away, quite overcome by her own daring.

Simon stood and watched until she reached the edge of the woodland. She paused at last to glance back with a bashful wave. Simon smiled and waved back. But as Miri disappeared from view, he lowered his hand, his smile fading.

He was certain that he had just given Miri Cheney her first kiss. A moment that should have been quite special and full of wonder . . . for him as well. Instead he felt like Judas.

"Is she gone?" a cold voice demanded.

"Yes, master." Simon turned as Le Vis stole up behind him. These days he would have been hard-pressed to convince anyone that his master was not evil or mad. His robes were torn and stained, his face haggard, his eyes so raw from lack of sleep, they were almost like two burning coals set into the sockets of a skull.

"Well, does the girl trust you? Will she do as you asked?"

"I believe so," Simon said miserably.

"Good."

Although he knew it to be futile, Simon made one more attempt to persuade his master to the course he had been urging for days.

"Please, master. Would it not be best if we simply uncovered the boat and left Faire Isle?"

Le Vis gave him a dark look that caused Simon to shrink back. "Would you have us leave with our work undone?"

"But Miri told me that Captain Remy is gone and no doubt the gloves as well."

"Remy? Bah! That heretic is of no importance when set beside that—that—" Le Vis spluttered, all but frothing at the mouth in his pent-up fury. "That son of Satan. *Renard.*"

"But we are no match for him, master. There are only two of us left and—"

"Yes, because he slaughtered the rest of our order, or have you forgotten that? Or what he did to me?"

Le Vis thrust his hand wrapped in bloodstained bandages up close to Simon's face. Simon flinched. He had done his best to tend to the master's wounds and although the demon man had not severed any of Monsieur Le Vis's fingers, Simon doubted that his hand would ever heal properly to be of use again.

And yet Simon could not help reflecting that none of these disastrous events need have occurred if they had not attempted to attack Belle Haven in the middle of the night like a parcel of brigands.

He feared that some of his rebellious thoughts must have shown in his face because the master loomed over him scowling, his good hand gripping Simon's shoulder so tight, he nearly cried out.

"It was you who warned me about Renard and those cursed rings," he growled. "I should have listened to you. Now you must heed me and prepare to avenge the blood of our brothers. We must destroy the demon comte and his entire coven of witches."

"But not Miri." Simon tipped up his chin in defiance. "She is not like the rest of them. I hate telling her all these lies, deceiving her."

Le Vis sighed, easing his grip on Simon. "Of course you do, because you are a good honest lad. But sometimes one must employ the tools of the devil in order to defeat him."

"Miri is not the devil."

"No, but she is being led astray and you can save her from the curse of witchcraft, as you were never able to do with your sister or the rest of your family. Or will you simply turn tail and run, abandon your little friend to the powers of darkness?"

"No," Simon whispered.

"Then you know what you have to do."

❦ ❦ ❦

DARK MAGIC WAS EASIER TO SUCCUMB TO THE SECOND TIME. OR SO Evangeline Cheney had always warned her daughters, but it was an admonition Ariane chose to ignore as she descended into the hidden workshop.

She fetched down the ancient books of forbidden spells and laid out the copper basin and black candles. She had only the merest qualm as she remembered promising her mother she would never resort to practicing this kind of necromancy again. But if anything she was far more desperate than she had been the first time she had summoned Evangeline's spirit.

Ariane bustled about the workshop with an almost feverish determination, lighting the black candles and setting the incense to burning. As the heavy fragrance filled the chamber, she prepared the potion and downed the bitter-tasting brew in one gulp.

The powerful mixture burned through her veins as the incense clouded her mind, spiraling her deeper into the trance that would enable her to part the veil between two worlds, that of the living and that of the dead.

"Maman . . . please, appear to me. I need your help."

She bent over the copper basin and peered into the water, doing her best to bring her mother's image into focus. When Evangeline's face appeared at last, her features were a little more blurred than the other time Ariane had performed this dark spell.

But there was no mistaking the sad reproach in her mother's voice.

"Oh, Ariane, you promised . . ."

"I—I am sorry, Maman. But I could not help myself. I needed to talk to you, even more desperately than before. Everything seems to be getting worse and—and I missed you so."

Ariane paused to catch her breath, her voice breaking a little as she continued, "I just needed to see you one more time. I don't even understand why this is so wrong."

"Conjuring someone back from the dead?" Evangeline's voice echoed with her disbelief. *"Oh, my dear one. My time in your world is over. You must stop grieving for me and get on with your life. And do you remember nothing that I taught you of the dangers of dark magic? This necromancy could go so easily awry. You could open up a portal into hell and let loose something truly evil."*

"More evil than the Dark Queen?"

Evangeline's voice waxed sharper. *"Catherine has been troubling you again?"*

"Yes, she has sent witch-hunters after us, twice now. The last time, they even attacked Belle Haven."

"Witch-hunters?" Evangeline murmured. *"Is Catherine truly that much lost to the darkness?"*

"She is plotting something terrible against the Huguenot king and she has come to regard me as a threat to her plans." Ariane choked on a bitter laugh. "The sad truth is that I am as afraid of the Dark Queen as the most ignorant peasant wench. I should have found some way to solve the mystery of those gloves and bring her to justice. Perhaps I should have even accompanied Captain Remy on his quest to—"

"No, Ariane. You cannot hope to challenge Catherine alone. Your province is here, protecting your sisters."

"I have not exactly been doing so well at that," Ariane said glumly. "Miri was completely devastated by the bloodshed here at Belle Haven. She has been behaving strangely of late, so quiet and—and tense."

"Miri will recover. Your little sister is far tougher than you might imagine. And what of our Gabrielle?"

Ariane grimaced. "I had hoped we were drawing close again, but now Gabrielle is angry with me because—well, she accuses me of having allowed a man to invade Belle Haven."

"The witch-hunters? She can hardly blame you—"

"No, not a witch-hunter. The man who saved us from the attack. The Comte de Renard. He has now set up camp in our woods."

Evangeline Cheney's image in the water grew clearer. Ariane could now easily detect the disapproval in her mother's eyes.

"This man saved you all and yet you oblige him to sleep in a tent? My dear child, this is not the hospitality of the lady of Belle Haven. Why did you not offer him a bed?"

"Because I am afraid he might end up in mine," Ariane blurted out. An embarrassing admission to make to one's mother, but she had always been able to tell Evangeline anything.

Her mother's image shimmered, that beautiful careworn face seeming so alive, so real, Ariane nearly sobbed. She swallowed past the aching knot in her throat.

"Oh, Maman, I fear it is Renard who troubles me beyond anything. He is the son of a daughter of the earth and that strange ring he gave me is full of a most powerful magic and you always told me such charms could not be real."

Evangeline offered a sad smile. *"Eventually you must come to the realization all children face. That even one's maman is not all-knowing and beyond making mistakes."*

Ariane could never think of Evangeline as less than perfect. "Well, Renard's ring certainly does work." She held up her hand so the light glinted off the strange metal band encircling her finger.

"All I have to do is clasp the ring to my heart and reach out to him with my mind and he comes. I have already done so twice. Once more and I must marry him. I am desperately afraid that I will use the ring again and for no other reason than I find myself wanting him. Sometimes late at night, the longing to be in his arms is so strong, I can scarcely bear it."

"Is that such a terrible thing, then? To want a man?" Evangeline asked quietly.

"That is how Gabrielle lost her magic, trusting the wrong man. I am afraid Renard may succeed in overcoming my reason. There are times when he seems so guarded, so hard-edged and cynical. But other times—" Ariane trailed off. The harsh contours of his face, his massive size, could be so alarming and yet she had seen him be more gentle than any other man she had ever known.

"What I am most afraid of, Maman . . . ," Ariane said in a low voice. "Even more than Renard seducing me to his bed, is that he may succeed in touching my heart. I never thought I could be so weak."

"You see love as a weakness, my daughter?"

"Yes, because it is . . . isn't it? I don't want to become that dependent upon any man's love the way you—" Horrified, Ariane checked what she had been about to say. But her mother understood her all too well.

"The way that I was with your father."

"Yes!" Ariane could not keep the bitterness from her voice. "You gave him all the devotion of your heart only to have him betray you."

"It pains me to hear such anger when you speak of your father, child."

"Do you never feel anger at him?" Ariane asked.

Evangeline smiled sadly. *"Whatever hurt and anger I felt passed a long time ago. I understood my poor sweet Louis."*

"You understood why Papa would betray you with another

woman, then abandon you when you were dying?" Ariane demanded.

"Your father is a man of great courage when it comes to swords, battle, risking his life. What he could not face was watching me grow ill and die. It is often thus with even the most valiant of soldiers when facing the loss of the woman they love."

Ariane's lips tightened stubbornly. "If Papa loved you so much, how could he have been seduced by that creature of Catherine's?"

"That was partly my fault. I never cared for life at court. All I wanted was the peace of my island, my girls. I knew that that was not enough excitement for your Papa. I should have spent more time in Paris with him, kept watch. Louis was never as strong as I, something that I always realized and accepted. It did nothing to diminish my love for him and that is why I was able to forgive him.

"You need to forgive your father his weakness too, child. And not allow it to cast a shadow over your own pursuit of love."

"I fear I could never be as wise and understanding as you, Maman," Ariane murmured.

"We are different in many ways, child. The sort of union that I had with your father would never do for you. You must find a man who is your equal in strength."

"You mean . . . Renard?" Ariane frowned. "His grand-mère was this old wise woman, a peasant from the mountains. She claims to have had visions of Renard and me, that we would one day be together. But you always taught me not to set store by such things."

"And yet I always had a great respect for those old women from the hills. Their learning does not come from books but from a wisdom as deep as the bones of the earth."

"Then you think old Lucy was right and I am fated to be with Renard?"

Evangeline gave a gentle laugh. *"Alas my dear, I cannot tell you that. The only wise woman who can chart your destiny is you. But I will give you one piece of advice."*

"Please do, Maman," Ariane said eagerly.

"Remove the ring from your finger and lock it away where you will no longer be tempted to use it. Whatever conclusion you reach about Renard, you should not be influenced by either the magic of a ring or an old prophecy. Only your heart should decide."

Ariane saw the wisdom of her mother's counsel. But before she could promise to heed her mother's words, the water rippled. Her all-too-brief time with her mother was once more at an end. She could only watch sadly as the water in the bowl clouded, Evangeline Cheney's face vanishing in the mist.

Ariane raised one hand in a desperate attempt to reach out to her mother, but her arm dropped back to her side, feeling as heavy as her eyes. She swayed a little, then slumped forward. As she pillowed her head against the hard table, the potion did its final work and she fell into a deep sleep.

Even hours later she remained oblivious to the footfall on the stairs, the shadow of the man that towered over her.

"Ariane?" Renard called softly, tensing when he spied her inert form slumped over the table. He set down his own candle and bent over her, brushing back the silky brown hair from her pale face.

"Ariane!" He gave her a slight shake, alarmed when that failed to rouse her. He pressed two fingers to the column of her throat and was relieved to discover that her pulse beat strong and steady. She was merely lost in the deepest of slumbers and when his gaze roved past her to the articles upon the table, he understood the reason.

The black candles, the copper basin, the incense burner were objects not unfamiliar to him. He had watched old Lucy at her conjuring many times and knew enough of the old ways to guess what Ariane had been doing.

He bent over her, tenderly pressing a kiss to her brow.

"My poor chérie," he murmured, thinking of the burden of worry and fear that must have driven Ariane to such a drastic measure. But he could not be unaware that he was part of Ariane's burden and as for trusting him—Renard sighed. Here he was, creeping about her house, invading her most private sanctum without an invitation.

With the exception of Gabrielle, the entire household at Belle Haven stood in awe of him. Filled with gratitude, they accepted his presence, no one even questioning his movements as he came and went.

At this late hour, everyone else was long abed. But it had not been difficult for Renard to figure out where Ariane was or even how to operate the hidden spring to open the trap door. His lady's eyes had become an open book to him this past week.

Ever since she had come to think of him as . . . as *rash and gallant a fool as Captain Remy,* Ariane had been far more trusting of him.

Renard stroked his fingers lightly down Ariane's cheek with a brooding frown, reflecting that he was nothing like the idealist captain. Nicolas Remy was the sort of man who would ride to a lady's rescue without demanding so much as a kiss in return. Renard knew that he could never be that selfless, especially not with Ariane.

Renard was far too much Lucy's grandson not to be intrigued by all the shadowy contents of this room's shelves, the parchments and ancient texts, power and knowledge beyond any man's wildest dreams.

The book that Ariane had left cracked open on the table presented the greatest of temptations. But it was bad enough that he had entered Ariane's workroom without her permission without doing any further prying while she slept, unaware.

He resisted the lure of the open book, scooping Ariane up into his arms. She stirred a little, then nestled her head against his shoulder with a sleepy sigh that provoked a tender smile from Renard.

He carried her upstairs to her room, then tried to lower her gently to her bed as though she were the most fragile of treasures, easily broken by a clumsy touch.

As Ariane's head plunked against the pillow, her eyes fluttered open. "Renard?" she murmured sleepily.

"Er, ah, yes." Renard tried to think of some plausible excuse for his presence, but he was given no further opportunity.

To his astonishment, Ariane wound her arms around his neck. Pulling him down to her, she fastened her mouth to his. Renard's eyes flew wide. For a woman who had known nothing about kissing when he had first met her, Ariane's education had taken a mighty leap.

Her lips parted with a soft sigh, her tongue flickering against his mouth, luring him into a heated mating. He resisted for but a moment, then with a low groan, hungrily returned her kiss, all but in danger of forgetting he was dealing with a woman still lost in the throes of a potion-induced haze.

Ariane had no idea what she was doing, would likely forget he had even been in her room come morning . . . as long as he did not allow matters to progress any further. But her lips devoured his with such sweet seduction, sending fire straight to his loins.

It took all the will he possessed to wrench away. Disentangling from her arms, he retreated into the shadows. Ariane groped for him, then with a whimper of disappointment, she subsided, cuddling up to her pillow.

Renard expelled a deep breath as she settled back into a deep slumber, but with a soft languorous smile that continued to wreak havoc with his aroused senses. He wondered if he should attempt to undress her, but he feared that would put his forbearance to far too great a test.

Perhaps there was hope after all that the Lady of Faire Isle might make some sort of hero out of him, but he was never going to be a saint. Gingerly he pulled the covers over Ariane, then beat a hasty retreat.

"Sleep well, my lov—" he began. Startled, Renard caught himself just in time and quickly amended. "My lady."

With a last longing glance, he tiptoed from the room.

≮ ≮ ≮

LIGHTS BLAZED BEHIND THE WINDOWS OF THE LOUVRE, THE SOUNDS of music and revelry drifting out over the Seine far into the night. The king of Navarre had but lately arrived in Paris and it was only natural there should be some sort of welcome preceding the wedding that would take place soon.

But tension filled the halls of the palace as much as gaiety and laughter. The members of Navarre's Huguenot entourage received the insincere smiles of the Parisian courtiers with scowls of deep suspicion. The Princess Margot regarded her prospective bridegroom with ill-concealed dislike, while Henry of Navarre's eyes already roved toward some of the lovely ladies-in-waiting. King Charles was in one of his highly nervous states that often precluded a bout of madness and the Queen Mother mounted a diligent guard over her son's uncertain temper.

One of the few people who had actually enjoyed the fete had been obliged to retire early. But Louise Lavalle doubted she would ever get a chance like this again with the rest of the court so preoccupied and Catherine as well.

Shielding her candle from the draft, Louise stole undetected toward the queen's private closet. Louise was feeling more than usually pleased with herself. She was fully aware of having been one of the loveliest and most seductive women present at tonight's celebration. Even the king of Navarre had noticed her.

But far better than that, after days of playing out this chess of the mind with Catherine, Louise was conscious of winning. She had sacrificed a few pawns of false information, convincing Catherine that Captain Remy and the gloves were fled to England. She had overheard the Dark Queen only that afternoon dispatching a small band of her private guard to cross the Channel, to continue the search for the captain. Louise had been obliged to stuff her handkerchief in her mouth to stifle her laughter.

Hours later, she was still smiling to herself because she had achieved an even greater coup. Finally she had managed to break past Catherine's guard and read the eyes of the Dark Queen. With one final furtive look over her shoulder, she slipped inside Catherine's private closet. Her lip curled slightly at the sight of the altar.

Trust Catherine to hide her witchcraft behind a semblance of piety and prayer. She began to run her hands over the altar cloth, feeling behind the crucifix for some sort of lever that must trip the hidden door. As the moments ticked by, she was aware that she was taking too long.

But the realization only heightened her sense of excitement, of danger, causing her pulse to race faster. All this intrigue was better than seeking out a new lover. Well, almost, Louise amended, recalling the spark in Henry of Navarre's eyes.

It was rumored that Navarre was a lusty young man and Louise thought she might not mind a toss between the sheets with him. She had never bedded a king. But first she supposed she had best see about preserving his life.

When she at last shifted the candlestick that triggered the spring, Louise grinned in triumph. She stepped back as the altar swung out, revealing the dark, mysterious room beyond.

"Oh, Catherine, I do believe this is *check*," Louise chortled. "The queen is in grave danger and you have no more pawns left to save you."

Snatching up a candle, she squeezed into the narrow chamber, her heart pumping hard with suppressed excitement. The light flickered over shelves crammed with ancient texts, dusty vials, and bottles.

Her latest project was still set up on a small wooden table and Louise moved in for a closer look. A mortar and pestle lay discarded near a small brazier filled with cold ash. Nearby was a rack filled with vials containing some cloud-colored liquid, which Louise could not begin to identify. Some sort of vile poison, she made no doubt.

Catherine had also left out a scroll of some old parchment, obviously the detailed recipe for whatever hellish brew she was concocting. Louise was not good at translating some of the more ancient languages and was relieved to see that the parchment was transcribed in French.

Holding the scroll closer to the candlelight, she perused it eagerly. But the more she read, the more her stomach clutched with dread.

She dropped the parchment as though she had been handling a snake. She had been ready enough to believe that Catherine was plotting the death of Henry of Navarre. But that she might be contemplating a crime worse than that . . .

"A—a *miasma*. She is conjuring up a miasma," Louise whispered hoarsely. "I must get word to Faire Isle."

Louise whirled about to flee the room, only to nearly collide with the dark figure who had been watching her from the doorway. She staggered back with a frightened cry, but Catherine appeared completely unperturbed.

She was even smiling a little as she said, "Checkmate, my dear Louise."

Chapter Twenty

THE DAY PROMISED TO BE A HOT ONE, THE JULY SUN BLAZING overhead, the air warm and stifling by mid-morning. As Ariane trudged from the house in search of Renard, her gown already felt damp and clinging, but she was determined to speak to the comte before he rode out again to resume the search for Le Vis.

When she had awakened, her mother's gentle reproof echoed clearly through her mind.

"This man saved you all and yet you oblige him to sleep in a tent? My dear child, this is not the hospitality of the lady of Belle Haven."

As usual, her mother was right. Ariane headed toward the woods that fringed Belle Haven and felt some relief from the heat as the cool canopy of leaves closed over her head. She breathed in the crisp scents of the forest.

Renard had not done as he'd threatened and set up his tent at her very gates. He had elected instead to camp near the brook that cut across the Belle Haven estate. As Ariane approached the site, she hastened her steps, fearing that she might be too late.

But someone was definitely still at the camp. She could hear the dull thud of an ax splintering wood. As she parted branches and peered into the clearing, she saw Hercules tethered in the shade not far from a tent of impressive proportions, the canvas fashioned of bright blue and cream stripes. It looked like something a knight might have erected near a tournament field, a place to relax between bouts at the lists.

But there was more of the brawny woodsman than knight about the man wielding his ax nearby. Sunlight picked out the gold in Renard's light brown hair and glistened off the sweat-slick skin of his forearms. Clad only in his trunk hose and loose-fitting linen shirt, his sleeves were shoved up to the elbows. His bare feet braced a little apart, he swung the ax in a seemingly effortless rhythm, splitting the thick log into firewood.

Despite the fact that his hair was already damp with sweat, his mouth was taut with a certain satisfaction in his work. Renard seemed to take a great deal of pleasure in such simple tasks, perhaps because the pursuit of Le Vis was proving futile and Renard did not have enough to fill his time.

Ariane's horrified servants had reported to her only that morning that these past few days while she had been occupied delivering a baby and treating an outbreak of ague among a local family, Renard had been busy. Harvesting her apple crop, mending shutters broken in the raid, even helping to muck out the stables.

"I—I tried to stop him, mistress," Fourche had quavered. " 'Tis no fit work for a gentleman, especially a comte."

Gabrielle had remarked that the longer Renard remained on Faire Isle, the more primitive and peasant-like he became. But Ariane thought it was as though in some odd way, Renard was becoming more and more himself.

Ariane felt as though she caught a glimpse of the lad Renard had once been when he had roamed free in his mountains, open-hearted, uncomplicated, full of a zest and enthusiasm for life.

Renard was so absorbed in his wood-chopping he did not even notice when Ariane entered the clearing. Hercules was the first to become aware of her presence. The great beast stiffened, arching its neck and pricking up its ears. The stallion emitted a shrill whinny, sounding as though Hercules called out a warning to Renard.

Renard paused in mid-swing, gripping the ax. He tensed, nostrils flaring, scenting the wind like a wild stallion himself. But he relaxed, his face lighting up when he saw Ariane. Lowering his ax, he embedded it in the log and strode over to quiet the restive horse.

Patting Hercules's neck, Renard said, "Easy, boy. Where are your eyes? It is no witch-hunter stealing upon us, but our lady."

To Ariane's surprise, Hercules whickered, nuzzling his nose against Renard. Renard pretended to lean confidingly toward the horse. "What is that you say? You were only alarmed because you heard tales these woods are haunted. And now you realize there are fairies that wander here."

As Ariane came across the clearing, she was both amused and astonished by the camaraderie between Renard and his skittish horse. Hercules was actually nipping playfully at Renard's ear.

"You and Monsieur Hercules seemed to have reached an understanding," she remarked. "Has my little sister been teaching you how to speak horse?"

"She has been trying." Renard said with a slight smile. "Perhaps it is more that I have begun to remember some of the old ways I learned as a boy before I became so impatient with the world."

A trickle of sweat cascaded down his brow and he mopped it away with his arm, casting Ariane an apologetic look. "Your pardon, milady, for the er—informality of my appearance. Hercules and I were not expecting company. Allow me to try and render myself a trifle more presentable."

Ariane started to assure him that that was not necessary, but Renard was already striding toward the bank of the stream. She trailed after him, asking, "You are quite alone here today? Where are all of your men?"

"I sent Toussaint and the others over to the mainland, to see if Le Vis might have been spotted crossing over, but I am beginning to fear it is a hopeless pursuit." Renard hesitated, then said. "I have not had the chance to tell you, but yesterday we found the remains of a dinghy washed up in one of the isolated coves. It looks as though Le Vis and the boy attempted to make their escape only to capsize.

"Very likely they were drowned or crushed against the rocks, although as yet we have found no bodies."

Ariane could not pretend to grieve for Le Vis, but the boy . . . An image flashed through her mind of Simon's confused and tormented face the day Miri had been condemned to suffer the ordeal by water.

"This will be very hard to tell Miri. She seems to have developed a certain liking for young Simon."

"A witch-hunter who tried to burn her house down?"

When Ariane started to come to Simon's defense, Renard cut her off with a weary gesture. "Peace, milady. It is far too hot for us to renew our dispute over that young villain. If his death will grieve Miri, I am sorry for it. But there is no need to distress the child until we are sure."

Renard knelt down on the edge of the grassy embankment, leaning forward to splash the silvery water over his face. When he cupped his hand to take a drink, Ariane's attention was drawn to the full curve of his mouth.

She touched her hand to her own lips, assailed by the recollection of a kiss, heated and passionate. Ariane frowned. She had no idea how or when she had stumbled upstairs to her room last night. But she had this memory of being swept up in Renard's arms, tenderly carried to her bed and sharing the most delicious kiss, feeling quite bereft when Renard had faded into the shadows. The recollection was suddenly so vivid that she was almost tempted to ask Renard—

Renard straightened from the bank, slicking back the damp ends of his hair. As he did so, Ariane caught the glint of his ring on his finger. She buried her hands in the folds of her skirt, guiltily covering the empty spot on her own finger.

Mindful of her mother's council, she had removed the ring and locked it safely away in the chest at the foot of her bed. She dreaded the moment when Renard noticed the ring's absence and realized she had broken their pact. Perhaps he would demand his forfeit at once, taking all decision out of her hands.

But if he had observed the ring missing from her finger, he made no remark upon it. Perhaps he thought she had simply fastened the band back on the chain around her neck.

Far from looking vexed, he regarded her with a particularly gentle smile as he demanded, "And so to what do I owe the honor of this visit from the Lady of Faire Isle?"

"An attack of conscience, I fear."

Renard's heavy brows arched in surprise and she folded her hands primly before her. She had rehearsed her speech on the way here. It had been both dignified and gracious, but she seemed to have forgotten every word of it.

She heard herself stammering instead, "I—I have been thinking. You have been most good to us . . . risking your life, fighting witch-hunters and—and cleaning the stables—"

"That wasn't particularly dangerous, chérie. Unlike Hercules, Miri's pony does not tend to bite, although her rabbits did glare at me."

She rushed on, "What I am trying to say is that you have been very generous and I . . . I have not. You remained here to protect us and much to my shame, I allowed you to be banished to the woods."

"That is no fault of yours. You forget that I was the one who insisted on staying. You did not want me here."

"Nonetheless, after all you have done for my family, the least that I can do is take you to bed—" Ariane blushed and hastily amended, "I mean offer you a bed . . . in—in my father's old room . . . in—in the house."

She trailed off weakly, annoyed when Renard grinned.

"Damn it, Renard. You understand perfectly well what I am trying to say. You saved our lives and it is not right that you should be left to sleep curled in a wretched blanket on the cold, hard ground."

Renard threw back his head and laughed. "Come with me," he said.

She stiffened in some apprehension when she realized that Renard was tugging her toward his tent. But when he opened the flap and motioned her to look, she took a timid peek inside.

Her eyes widened. An exquisite Turkish carpet formed the floor of the tent and a wooden cot set off to one side was draped with pillows and furs. There was even a small linen-covered table bearing a decanter of wine and bowl of fruit.

"This is all Toussaint's notion, you understand, not mine. Like your good Fourche, my kinsman has certain notions about upholding the dignity of a comte. Sometimes I think he confuses me with the king.

"Myself, I would be better pleased with a mere blanket. I often slept that way as a lad, out in the open, drifting off as I counted the stars."

"You would not see many stars here. Not with all the trees."

"Ah, but the trees can be as pleasant a roof as the sky. The wind sighing through the leaves, every so often parting the branches enough to allow the lady moon to smile down on me.

Your woods are a very beautiful place, ma chère. There is a quiet and gentle spirit that roves here beside the stream."

"I know. Gabrielle and Miri often used to come here to play when they were younger."

Renard smiled at her quizzically. "Only Gabrielle and Miri? Never Ariane?"

"I was too busy even then trying to learn all I could of my mother's craft. But yes, I did come here sometimes with my father those rare times he could be coaxed away from Paris."

Ariane explained, "My father took pains to teach his daughters things most men would find extremely odd. Perhaps it was because he had no sons. He was actually the one who taught Miri to ride so well and he acquainted Gabrielle with the use of a sword."

"And you?"

"Oh, he gave me an accomplishment that was even more scandalous and unladylike. He taught me to swim."

"Scandalous indeed," Renard said lightly.

"I suppose it was because I was always trailing after my mother into the stream to gather up moss for our healing potions. Papa was afraid I might slip and drown if I did not learn to swim properly."

It was a memory of her father she had all but forgotten. Her gaze traveled toward the brook and she was surprised to feel a tug on her heart.

"Your father has been gone on his voyage a long time," Renard said quietly. "You must miss him a great deal."

"Yes, I—" Ariane began, then checked herself, astonished by what she had nearly admitted. She had been far too angry with her father to ever allow herself to miss him before.

She wandered to the edge of the bank, the stream meandering past in a lazy curve. The waters seemed to sparkle with the image of a handsome golden-haired man with a ready smile, whose eyes crinkled when he laughed, and he had tended to laugh a great deal.

His strong hands supported a little girl with a mass of brown hair, her thin body beneath her linen shift already too lanky with legs and arms she did not quite know how to manage. As he eased her into a floating position, she held herself rigid, her eyes dark with fear.

"Don't be afraid, Ariane," her father's voice echoed in her ear. *"You are like your maman, a most capable lady. You can learn to do this. Just relax and close your eyes. Trust me. I won't let you sink."*

And so she had done so. Closed her eyes and trusted him because he was her father, tall, bold, and quite magnificent, never afraid of anything. Except for watching her mother die.

Ariane's eyes blurred with unexpected tears. She became aware that Renard was standing close beside her. She felt the warm touch of his hand against her cheek.

"I am sorry, ma chère. I did not mean to make you sad."

Embarrassed, Ariane swiped at her eyes. "I just realized that I do miss my father and I don't expect to ever see him again."

"And yet I have known many men presumed lost, gone far longer than your father, only to return safely one day."

Ariane composed herself with a tiny sniff. Forcing a smile, she turned away from the stream. "Well, I should be getting back to the house. If—if you would like to return with me—"

She left the thought unfinished, expecting somehow that Renard would eagerly accept her offer. She was therefore surprised when he declined with a thoughtful shake of his head.

"No, for the time being, I think it best I remain just where I am. Your sister Gabrielle is already annoyed enough."

"Oh, you need not worry about Gabrielle. I will not permit her to plague you."

"I am more worried about her plaguing you, ma chère. You

have more than enough to distress you, and I would do nothing to add to your tension." He chucked her lightly under the chin and smiled. "Besides, all this talk of swimming makes me quite long for a dip myself."

He stepped away to the edge of the bank and began tugging his sweat-dampened shirt off over his head.

And the man claimed he didn't want to add to her tension, she thought in dismay, her eyes taking in the broad expanse of his shoulders tapering down to a hard flat stomach and narrow waist. His powerful chest glistened with perspiration and a dusting of fine golden hair.

It wasn't as though she had never seen a half-naked man before or even one completely nude. She had often had to set maidenly modesty aside when treating the sick or wounded and had done so in the most matter-of-fact manner.

But there was nothing sickly about Renard. Smooth skin stretched over the taut muscle of a physique that radiated masculine vitality.

Ariane found herself moistening her lips. Of course, there was not the least reason in the world that she needed to stand there, ogling him. But she could not seem to wrench her eyes away, even when Renard became aware of her stare.

He dropped his hands to his waistband and for one horrified and fascinated moment, she thought he meant to shuck off his breeches as well. But he gave her a mischievous smile.

"Don't worry, ma chère. I may have all the modesty of the crudest peasant, but I will spare yours. Especially if you consent to join me."

"W-what?" she breathed.

He held one hand out to her, the gesture part command, part invitation. "Join me. Come for a swim."

She hastily backed away. "Oh, no, I haven't swum in that brook since I was a girl of Miri's age."

"It is not a skill that you forget. It will all come back to you."

"No, I could not possibly."

"Why not?" he demanded. "It is the very devil of a day and you look so hot and tired."

He caressed her face, skating the pad of his thumb over the hollows beneath her eyes. "You always look so tired, ma chère."

Ariane trembled, wondering how a touch that was so gentle could be so rife with temptation and . . . and seduction. She sighed, stepping away, firmly shaking her head.

"No, milord. I can't. I have a great deal to do and the day has already half gotten away from me."

"Then let the rest of it go as well," he coaxed. "I am sure all your endless tasks will still be there tomorrow."

"But I am hoping there might be a message from Marie Claire. It has been awhile since we have had a report from Louise about the Dark Queen—"

"If there is such a message, it can wait. Neither this island nor the world will come to disaster if the Lady of Faire Isle plays truant for a bit."

Renard regarded her through narrowed eyes, then nodded his head sagely. "Ah, I see what the problem really is."

"What?"

"You exaggerated your ability to swim and now you are ashamed to admit it. Do not distress yourself, chérie. It was a most strange thing for your father to have attempted to teach a daughter. No one could have expected you to have learned as well as a boy."

"I will have you know that I mastered the skill quite well."

"Of course you did," Renard said in a soothing tone that raised her hackles. "And in any case, *I* will be there. I won't let you drown."

"You? You—you great oaf," Ariane cried. "I could swim rings around you."

"Then prove it."

Renard was deliberately goading her, his eyes twinkling with all the wickedness of a boy daring her to mischief. The sort of mischief she had always resisted, even as a very tiny girl. She had ever been the solemn and serious one, aware of her responsibilities, first as the eldest daughter of the house and then as Lady of Faire Isle. Never once had she strayed from the virtuous path of duty to pursue the mildest sort of pleasure or adventure. Suddenly it struck her that there was something rather sad about that.

Renard closed the distance between them, his large hands spanning her waist. "Of course, I could just simply toss you in."

"No!" Ariane tensed in alarm, but Renard's hands immediately gentled.

"I was only teasing you, chérie. I would never do a thing like that. I have no desire to force you into something you truly do not want."

His gaze locked with hers and Ariane realized he was referring to far more than swimming. Did Renard really mean that? He'd been so determined to have her for his wife at all costs. He released her with a regretful smile.

"Ah, well, it seems a great pity to waste such a summer's day. If you change your mind, you know where to find me."

He stepped to the edge of the bank and leaped into the brook with a mighty splash. The water sprayed all the way back to Ariane, showering her like a light rain.

One drop trickled down her face and she tasted it, pure and cool on her tongue. Her gown felt more sticky than ever and she tugged on the neckline as she watched Renard surface midstream.

He came up out of the water, shaking back his wet hair like a giant mastiff. Then he launched himself on his back, stroking through the water with an easy abandon that Ariane found herself envying, perhaps because she had never known anything like it.

She hesitated but a moment longer. Before she could pause to question the rashness of her actions, she sank down upon a stump and began to tug off her shoes. Stripping down to her shift, she poised on the bank of the stream, self-consciously wrapping her arms across her bosom.

She dipped one toe in the water and recoiled immediately. Lord, she had forgotten how cold the brook could be, even in the heat of summer. She must be quite mad to have ever allowed Renard to goad her into this. She was suddenly very much aware of the hushed seclusion of the glade, of the man waiting for her in the stream below.

Renard was a glistening Goliath, water streaming from his wet hair, trickles cascading down the hard muscles of his chest and arms, filling her head with all those fantasies of him she'd been having in her lonely bed, the urge to use his ring to call him to her side. It was no longer night and she wasn't wearing the ring. But the temptation was still there.

Renard smiled up at her. "Come, chérie. It is better not to think so much. Take the plunge and just get it over with."

His eyes were warm and open and he held out his arms to her, a reassuring smile on his lips.

"Find the man who is your equal in strength, Ariane." Her mother's voice echoed. *"Let your heart decide."*

Hesitating only a moment, Ariane drew in a deep breath and jumped down into Renard's strong arms.

❦ ❦ ❦

GABRIELLE SAT IN THE SHADE OF THE OAK TREE THAT OVERLOOKED the garden, too absorbed in her work to pay much heed to the heat of the day. She balanced the makeshift desk on her knee to steady the sheet of parchment as she sketched, wielding the stick of charcoal with deft strokes.

Beneath her hands, a face slowly began to emerge, strong, lean, the jaw shadowed with a beard, close-cropped hair framing a high forehead. A straight nose, a solemn mouth. All good.

But it was the eyes that were the problem. Try as hard as she might, she could not seem to capture their expression, dark with sorrow, ancient with care, too gentle for the face of a warrior.

Gabrielle erased, shadowed, erased again, but it did no good. The eyes remained flat. They had no soul and without that the rest of the sketch was wooden and lifeless, mere marks on a piece of paper.

Her own eyes burning with tears of angry frustration, Gabrielle scribbled violently over her efforts, then rent the parchment to bits. She cast them to the ground, flinging the charcoal down as well. The little desk followed, landing with a loud thud in Ariane's herb gardens.

Gabrielle buried her face in her hands, completely disgusted with herself for even trying to sketch again. Her magic was no longer in her fingers. It was in her face and she had best remember that. Why waste her time even trying to recapture her old abilities and with, of all subjects, Captain Nicolas Remy?

Perhaps because she could not get the man out of her head, with his wistful smile and the sad longing she could not seem to capture in his eyes. Maybe if she had been able to confine his memory to a piece of paper, she could finally dismiss him from her mind and all her guilt and regret as well.

It was not as though she had asked Remy to fall in love with her. He would get over it fast enough . . . if he lived long enough.

He'd been gone nearly a week. One would have thought he could have managed to send some word to assure them all he was safe. Not that she intended to lose any sleep over it, or at least not any more than she had.

She wouldn't be worrying over Remy at all except for the fact that she was so—so bored and hot and miserable. No doubt she had sunburned her nose and would end up with freckles and a nasty headache as well.

She needed Ariane. Gabrielle flounced into the house in search of her older sister and was irritated when she could not find her. Bette ventured the opinion that the mistress was perhaps off in the woods gathering plants for her potions.

Wasn't that just like Ariane to be out picking weeds when her own family needed her? Gabrielle sighed, pinching the bridge of her nose, realizing she was being cross and unreasonable.

She was grateful her sister was not off somewhere in the company of Renard. Ariane had finally gotten rid of the damned ring. Not tossed to the bottom of the channel as Gabrielle would have liked, but at least locked away in her chest where Ariane would not be so tempted to use it.

But Gabrielle feared it was already too late. There was a softness in Ariane's eyes now whenever she spoke of the comte. Very likely her sister was going to end up marrying the man. If she did, the ogre had best treat Ariane with all the honor and respect she deserved. *Or else he would have her to answer to,* Gabrielle thought fiercely.

As for herself, Gabrielle was more determined than ever to pursue a different course. These recent attacks of the witch-hunters had left her convinced that one of the Cheney women had better end up extremely powerful. So powerful a miscreant like Le Vis would never dare lift a finger against any of them.

Ariane had always been destined to become a wife and mother. Miri . . . Miri would likely end up becoming one of those strange old women who lived contentedly in a cottage with a dozen cats and other sundry creatures. The fate of their family rested in Gabrielle's hands. She needed to begin laying her plans in earnest, but first she needed to rid herself of this dreadful headache. She headed down for the dungeons to seek out the powders to brew herself a tisane.

But she had never been good at the healing arts and to her frustration, she discovered that Ariane had been rearranging things. Organizing, Ariane called it. Her sister never seemed to understand that the best way to find things was to dump them down in the nearest spot and then just remember where you left them.

Her headache growing worse, Gabrielle ended up perspiring and dusty as well as she poked around. She finally reached the topmost shelf, thick with cobwebs.

Moving the footstool, she climbed up and grimaced, poking around through the dust-covered bottles. She found nothing that looked like it could be of use . . . except perhaps a small wooden box. Gabrielle remembered that Ariane had claimed the box held something she had used to cure Remy, but if that was the case why had Ariane been so secretive about it?

There was still some mystery that eluded Gabrielle about the captain. It piqued her the way both Ariane and Remy had treated her like a child needing protection. Gabrielle carried the box down to the table, feeling almost like Pandora. An unfortunate thought. That myth had turned out rather badly. Dismissing the notion, she opened the box and found a small pouch inside. Gabrielle tugged on the drawstrings and shook out the contents with a shiver of expectation.

She was disappointed. The pouch contained nothing but a pair of women's white gloves. Disappointed, she was going to stuff the gloves back into the box when she felt the fineness of the silk cloth. Smoothing them out, she realized that they were of an exquisite workmanship, scented with a delicate perfume.

They had become a little soiled, one fingertip frayed as though someone had scraped at it. But it was nothing that could not be mended. Why should such a treasure be left here, going to waste in some dark corner of the dungeon?

She should not just confiscate them without Ariane's permission, but it would do no harm to try them on. Her headache forgotten, Gabrielle eased the silk gloves on her hands, with a tiny sigh of satisfaction. They were a perfect fit . . .

૪ ૪ ૪

MORNING SLIPPED AWAY INTO AFTERNOON AS ARIANE RACED RE-nard across the stream. She cut through the water with swift strokes, all that her father had taught her coming back to her, arms and legs falling into a smooth rhythm. Renard had long arms and a mighty reach, but she had speed and agility on her side.

As she streaked ahead of him, she suddenly remembered why she had once so loved to swim. This wonderful feeling of being so light and weightless, completely relaxed and free of care, sensations that she experienced so rarely. Taller than her dainty sisters, she had never felt quite as graceful as Gabrielle or Miri. But here in the water, she was lithe and sure of herself. Giving the task her full concentration, she shot across the stream like an arrow released from a bow, easily beating Renard to the other side.

She could stand here, the water hitting her waist-high. She panted, her heart hammering hard, her muscles burning. It was a good kind of ache, far different from her usual sense of exhaustion. Renard fetched up beside her seconds later.

"What took you so long?" Ariane teased.

Renard laughed. "I didn't realize I was chasing some manner of sea-witch.

"But I do appear to have captured you at last," he said with a wicked glint in his eye.

"It can be dangerous to catch a witch. I might decide to turn you into a beast."

"According to your sister, that is what I already am." Renard grinned and braced his arms on either side of Ariane, cornering her against the bank.

They had been doing this ever since she had hit the water,

splashing, ducking, chasing each other. Like a pair of unruly children, except that she had never played with such carefree abandon even as a child. And the hard masculine body that had her corralled against the bank was not that of a boy. There was little more than mere water between her and Renard, her cotton shift, wet and clinging, clearly outlining the curve of her breasts, Renard's breeches riding low on his lean hips.

He reached out to pluck a stray leaf from her hair, his eyes gleaming with a mixture of tenderness and pride in her. "Never again shall I presume to challenge your abilities. You are full of surprises, my lady of Faire Isle."

Something about the caressing way he called her my lady curled itself around Ariane's heart. She sought to steady her breath, but was finding it difficult to do so.

"This reminds me of the day we first met," he said. "You were wading, gathering up your jars full of slime. Do you remember?"

"How could I forget?" she retorted. "You were so hopelessly lost and on your own land too."

"And you found me and led me home just as Lucy always said you would." Renard's expression grew pensive. "It is a strange thing, chérie. But that is how I feel when I am with you . . . as though after so many years of wandering, I am home. I haven't felt that way since the days that I lived in my cottage in the mountains."

"You still miss your old life?"

"Sometimes," he said. "But much as I hate to admit it, I fear there is too much of my Deauville grandfather in me. Part of me enjoys being the Comte de Renard, the power and respect that the position commands. Very likely Lucy was right and I would never have remained content to be a simple shepherd in the hills."

"But what about Martine?" Ariane reminded him hesitantly.

"You would have been married to her and raising a dozen children by now."

"Perhaps . . . and perhaps she simply was not my destiny." Renard's gaze fastened warmly on her, but Ariane lowered her eyes to prevent his reading her confused thoughts.

Being a man's destiny might sound all grand and good, but far better to be his love. Ariane had always considered herself above such romantic wishes, but she now realized that she hungered for love as much as any other woman. And it was Renard's love she wanted. The realization shook her more than her first icy plunge into the stream and she found herself miserably envious of some peasant girl she had never even met.

"I suppose Martine was quite exquisitely beautiful," she said bleakly.

"She was pretty enough," Renard conceded. "She had a fine figure and a merry laugh."

Unlike her solemn self, Ariane reflected, wincing. "Is that what made you desire her so?"

"You know, perhaps it was nothing more than the fact that she wanted me. She never seemed to mind that I was this great oaf or—or about my own less than pretty face." Grimacing, he touched one hand to the bridge of his frequently broken nose.

"I don't mind either," Ariane said quickly. She flushed and added shyly, "In fact, I do not find you all that unhandsome."

Renard laughed. "Mon Dieu, then my ring is indeed having a strange effect on you, except—" He lifted her hand to his mouth, kissing the pale spot on her finger.

"Except that you are no longer wearing it." His voice was soft, but his eyes raked over her and Ariane flinched. Her wet shift had become so transparent, it was obvious now that she was not wearing the ring fastened about her neck either.

"I realize I have broken our agreement, but—"

"But you already used the ring twice and you fear that you will do so again. The prospect of becoming my wife still repulses you that much." Renard did not sound angry or accusing, merely sad.

"Oh, no!" Ariane hastened to reassure him. "It is only that if I ever were to marry you, I don't want it to be because I lost a contest over a ring."

A deep crease appeared between his brows. "Perhaps you are right, chérie, and that is no longer what I want either."

His gruff capitulation caused her heart to go still. She released a tremulous breath, feeling as though some final barrier had crumbled between them.

Slipping his arm around her waist, he eased onto his back, taking her with him, half-supporting her with the length of his frame. They swam together, bodies lapping in a lazy, sensual rhythm that slowly built to a keen awareness of each other. The brush of arms and legs entwining, the bare touch of skin, Ariane could feel the heat emanating between them in stark contrast to the coolness of the water.

She hardly knew at what point all movement stopped. Renard came to a halt midstream, planting his feet. He was able to touch bottom, his chin jutting just above the surface. He wrapped one arm about her waist to keep her from going under as he drew her closer.

Their bodies met beneath the ripples of the water, the curve of her breasts pressing hard against his chest until Ariane could feel the thud of his heart. It was as though the day itself stilled around them, the spirit of the forest holding its breath as Renard's mouth came slowly, ever nearer to claim hers.

Their lips met in a kiss that tasted of clear water and salty skin, the sharp tang of the woods and the warm breath of sunlight, a sweet lingering exploration as though they were embracing each other for the very first time. Ariane's lips parted in a soft sigh, allowing Renard's tongue to invade her with his heat.

She shivered, caressed by the flow of the stream around them and Renard's hands roving over her back, his palms leaving their warm imprint wherever he touched. She tightened her own arms around his neck, kissing him eagerly.

Renard swam them both back to the shallow waters. Scarcely pausing to break the heated contact of their mouths, he swept Ariane high into his arms and carried her up onto the bank.

He laid her gently back onto the grass, her damp hair fanning around her shoulders. Renard poised above her, braced on his strong arms. His face was already suffused dark with passion, but he faltered. "Ariane, are you really sure about this? Do you think—?"

She stopped him by lightly pressing her hand to his mouth. "Renard. I think too much. I want you to make me feel."

Renard breathed a kiss against her fingertips. She could read the hunger in his eyes, but reluctance as well. "When I asked you to stay with me today, my intentions were honorable for once. I only wanted to see you laugh, to make you smile for a little while."

"Then you don't want to make love to me?" She drifted her fingertips over his chest.

"Lord, y-yes." Renard gave a shaky laugh. "But I don't want you to have any regrets after, to feel as if I have stolen your magic. I fear that you are reading things in me that aren't there. There is still much about me that you don't know."

Ariane gazed up at him with a soft smile. "I learned everything I needed to know about you the night of our supper when you finally told me who you were. I have trusted you with my life time and again. I believe I can trust you with my heart as well."

"Ariane—" he began hoarsely, but she silenced him by pulling him down to kiss him. She had never imagined that he would be the one with scruples, she so passionately insistent. It was as though something had broken free inside when she had taken that leap down into the stream and into his arms.

Renard resisted her for but a moment, then with a low groan returned her embrace with an equal hunger, the warm weight of his body pinning her to the earth. She could feel the heat pulsing between them, the hard evidence of his arousal. He kissed her throat, his hand entwining with hers above their heads, his ring pressing against her flesh.

"There is another reason I am glad I am no longer wearing my ring," she whispered. "This time when we make love I don't want it to be all in my head."

"It won't be. Whatever else happens between us, chérie, I promise you that this is going to be very real." Renard's mouth moved down to taste the beads of water at her throat. Her hands braced against his shoulders, she arched her back, stifling a soft sigh of pleasure as his lips sought the curve of her breast. She felt the heat of his mouth through the thin wet sheath of cotton as his tongue caressed her nipple, sending a current of desire racing through her veins.

They scrambled to their feet and undressed each other with a feverish haste, her cotton shift discarded upon the bank, his breeches following suit. Ariane's eyes widened as she studied his naked body, every inch of him carved on a grand scale.

"I am sorry, chérie. I fear I am a bit of an ogre in every respect."

"No, you are quite magnificent," she breathed. "Truly a man of the earth."

He sifted his fingers tenderly through her hair. "And you are the Lady of Faire Isle, all fire and spirit—"

Ariane shook her head. "No, Renard. I am only a woman, just as much of the earth as you are."

She drew him close to her heart, kissing him fiercely, tenderly, and with an ever-growing need. Renard would have carried her into his tent, but Ariane refused. She wanted their first time to be here, their bed of cool grass and sun-warmed earth, their bower the green rustle of trees and patches of blue sky.

She sank to her knees, drawing him down with her, a soft smile of invitation on her lips. As Renard kissed and caressed her, she flung back her head with a deep sigh, a delicious shiver working through her. He buried his face between the valley of her breasts, his mouth working its magic where his hands had lingered before. His tongue flicked over the crest of her nipples, sending a rush of heat through her.

As he laid her onto her back, her heart pounded in time with his, their mouths mating, their hands linked. Trembling with the force of her desire for him, Ariane parted her legs, feeling the velvety tip of his hardened shaft tease against her feminine core. Renard eased himself inside of her as gently as possible but she gasped at the sharp pain as he pierced her maidenhead.

Renard braced himself above her, his green eyes clouding with concern. "I am a clumsy brute. I—I have hurt you."

"N-no, I am all right," she reassured him, brushing her mouth against his. "P-please don't stop."

As she forced herself to relax, miraculously her body seemed to stretch, taking in all of him, filling her with his heat. Slowly, Renard began to move, kissing her tenderly again and again.

With each kiss, he stroked a little deeper, a little faster. Ariane clung to him, her body mirroring his movements until they moved together in a perfect unison. She became aware of nothing but Renard, the thundering rhythm of their mating building to an unbearable crescendo.

Like waves crashing against a shore, they seemed to break as one, and Ariane cried out as intense ripples of pleasure spiraled through her. At the same moment, she felt Renard's massive frame shudder with his own release.

He braced himself on his arms to keep from crushing her beneath his weight as he buried his face alongside her neck. She felt the rise and fall of his breathing, the racing of his heart as it slowed its tempo.

Ariane clasped her arms around him, still savoring the intimate joining of their bodies even as her blood cooled. She felt too awed by what she had just experienced in Renard's arms to even attempt to speak, amazed that she should have feared this consummation for so long, this complete surrendering of herself. As though it might somehow weaken her or diminish her magic.

But never had anything felt so right as giving herself so completely to Renard. Never had she felt so vibrant and strong. And never had she felt so much a daughter of the earth as she did at this moment.

❦ ❦ ❦

THE GREAT HALL AT BELLE HAVEN APPEARED SERENE AND EMPTY, late afternoon sunlight streaming through the windows. There was no one in sight when Miri peeked inside the chamber, all the servants busied at tasks elsewhere.

"Come on," Miri whispered, tugging on Simon's hand. But the boy hung back. She recognized the wary look in his eyes. She had seen that dark expression in the eyes of countless injured wild creatures she had attempted to help, only to have them flee before she could reach them.

"Don't worry," she said. "None of the servants here have ever seen your face. Without your terrible robes, you look like just another fisher lad from here on the island."

"And when someone asks why you are sneaking a fisher lad into your house?"

"I will tell them that I have brought you here to see Ariane." Miri smiled reassuringly. "No one will think anything of it. People come to her all the time to be healed. She is an exceedingly wise woman."

"And her evil ring?"

"I *told* you. She packed it away in her chest only this morning. I saw her myself, so you don't have to worry about her sending for Renard. Don't be afraid," she said, squeezing his hand. "I would never let anyone hurt you."

"Nor I you."

"Then trust me as I do you." Standing on tiptoe, she planted a bashful kiss on his smooth cheek. Her words seemed to offer Simon little comfort. He hung his head, but he did stumble after her as she urged him toward the stairs.

It was the most unfortunate thing in the world that Ariane should be away from home just now, Miri thought. The sooner that Simon could be brought to realize that he had nothing to fear from the Lady of Faire Isle, the better. And as for the comte . . . Miri had no doubt that Ariane would be able to persuade Renard to pardon Simon and help him.

The important thing was to keep Simon from changing his mind, from attempting to flee back to the dark world of his master. Even as she led Simon up the stairs, Miri kept a tight grip on his hand, fearing that at any moment he might slip away.

As they reached the upper landing, Miri said in a low voice, "We will just wait in Ariane's room until she returns. No one will bother you there."

"Miri." Simon came to an abrupt halt, forcing her to pause.

She turned to regard him questioningly. Afternoon shadows spilled across his beautiful face, his dark eyes filled with a strange look of desperation. The set of his mouth was so sad she could scarcely bear it.

"No matter what happens—" he began.

"Nothing bad is going to happen," she said quickly. "Ariane is going to help you. You will be able to stay here on Faire Isle, Simon, and we will be perfect friends forever."

"But if all this does not turn out quite as you believe," he persisted. "I just want you to know that I care for you, Miri. Very deeply."

"I care for you too," she said. Her heart pounded hard as he bent closer, certain that he meant to kiss her again. But all he did was brush his mouth across her cheek. A gentle caress, but disturbing somehow, as though he was about to bid her good-bye.

But she did not have time to dwell on that or to linger on the landing. She needed to keep Simon well out of sight until Ariane returned. She pulled him in the direction of Ariane's chamber, but just as they were about to reach the door, something streaked out of the shadows, startling them both.

A furious hiss rent the air. Simon pulled free of her hand and stumbled back, his face paling with alarm.

"It's all right, Simon. It is only Necromancer."

Simon continued to look wary, as well he might. Back arched, hairs standing on end, the cat appeared as though it had transformed into some wild and feral beast.

Necromancer held Simon at bay, looking fully ready to launch himself at the boy, claws bared. It was necessary for Miri to scoop up the cat before Simon could get by. She held the wriggling creature in her arms, indicating for Simon to precede her into Ariane's chamber.

As he vanished inside, she held Necromancer up at arm's length and scolded. "What has gotten into you?"

The cat rumbled deep in its throat. *Beware, daughter of the earth. You should not bring this boy into your home.*

"But it is Simon. You remember him from the night I rescued you at the circle of stone giants. He was kind to both of us."

He is no longer to be trusted.

"Oh, you are a fine one to speak of that," Miri told the cat crossly. "No matter how often I beg you, you persist in killing the poor field mice in the barn."

The cat's amber eyes blinked up at her. *I am a hunter. It is in my nature. It is his too. You will not change him.*

Necromancer's thoughts filled Miri with dismay. She had ever trusted to the instincts of her four-legged friends, the magical communion she shared with them her only solace since the loss of both her parents. That is until Simon had entered her life, bringing to her magic of a different kind.

She glared at Necromancer and muttered, "What do you know? You are only a cat."

Plunking Necromancer to the floor, Miri followed Simon into Ariane's chamber, slamming the door firmly in the cat's face.

※ ※ ※

IT WAS WARM INSIDE THE TENT AND RENARD PROPPED THE FLAP slightly open to let more air inside. A soft breeze rustled through, stirring the tendrils of chestnut hair that tumbled about the face of his sleeping lady.

Ariane lay curled on his cot, nestled deep in the furs. She slept deeply and soundly as she had no doubt needed to do for these many nights past. Renard was in no hurry to wake her or bring the magic of this interlude to an end.

The first time they had made love had been urgent, a fierce coupling upon the very marrow of the earth. The second time had been more leisurely, a slow exploration of each other's bodies here within the more comfortable confines of his tent.

The third had been nothing short of miraculous. He would not have imagined it possible to couple so completely with any woman, body, mind, and soul.

Now clad in dry clothing, he perched on the edge of the cot, content to observe Ariane sleep, keeping watch over her. He had never felt so tenderly protective of anyone before as he was of this one fiercely independent woman.

With a soft smile, he brushed back the ends of her hair, which were still a little damp, whether from their swim or their other exertions he would have been hard-pressed to say. When the Lady of Faire Isle finally chose to surrender herself to a man, she held nothing back.

Surely after all that had taken place between them in this secluded glade, she would consent to be his bride. He had won her at last, but it was an uneasy victory. Renard frowned as the memory of Ariane's words chased through his head. *"I learned everything I needed to know about you the night of our supper when you finally told me who you were."*

Except that she hadn't. There was still much she did not know about his past and now he wondered how he was ever going to tell her. Coward that he was, he found himself hoping that he would never have to tell her the rest of the tale about his grandmother and the old days.

As though she could somehow sense his troubled thoughts, Ariane stirred restively. She rolled onto her back, her eyes fluttering sleepily open and Renard did his best to smooth the brooding expression from his face.

Ariane blinked, appearing disoriented for a moment, as though uncertain where she was. Then she smiled and reached up to entwine her arms around his neck and he bent down to kiss her, a slow, tender kiss.

"Mmm," Ariane murmured, her body arching in a languorous stretch. "I have had the most wonderful nap."

"I am glad. You needed it."

"But surely it grows late. You should not have let me sleep so long." Even as she reproached him, she urged him to stretch out on the cot beside her.

As he did so, Renard studied her anxiously. "I hope that is your only regret about this afternoon. That you don't feel as though you have lost any of your magic to me."

"My magic is stronger than ever," Ariane said, burrowing her face against his shoulder. "In fact, I feel as though I could go out and cure the ills of the entire world."

Indeed, she could not remember a time when she had felt this content or at peace. Perhaps not since those golden days before her mother had been taken so ill.

As she nestled against Renard, she was aware of tension in

him. She drew back, trying to peer into his eyes. Through all their lovemaking, he had never said that he loved her.

Yet she believed she could read the emotion in his eyes, a feeling for her that ran so deep, perhaps he himself was not fully aware of it. There was also the disturbing shadow of something else.

"What is it?" she asked. "What is wrong?" She smiled, trying to infuse a playful note into her voice. "I hope you are not the one feeling any regrets."

"How could I be?" He pulled her close, brushing a kiss against the top of her head. "When I have done nothing but pursue you since the day we first met."

"Because you were told I am your destiny?"

"Because you are the most remarkable woman I have ever known. Sometimes I even find you a little daunting."

"Me?" Ariane laughed incredulously.

"Yes, you demand so much of a man with those quiet eyes of yours. Honor and strength, truth and courage."

Ariane raised herself up on one elbow to peer lovingly down at him. "And is that so much to ask? You possess all those things."

"I don't think any man can be the kind of paragon you require. You are a woman of amazing strength and such powerful magic. You are like all the legends of this island—"

Ariane cut him off with a rueful shake of her head. "My mother may have been, but not me." She toyed with the lacing of his shirt and mused. "They say that the Faire Isle was once the very center of the world, long ago when time first began. A perfect world where men and women lived in harmony—partners of equal strength working and loving side by side."

"And is that what you have been looking for all these years? The return of that perfect world?"

"No, all I ever wanted was to be able to practice my healing arts and share my learning with the world in peace, without having to be afraid. To be respected, to be called a doctor, not a witch. A foolish ambition for a woman, I know."

"No, it isn't and I wish I could give you all that. But all I can offer you is my respect, Ariane. You have a remarkable gift for healing. If my mother had had someone like you by her side, perhaps she would have survived giving birth to me and I would have had a chance to know her."

"But what about your wise old grandmother? Surely Lucy possessed skills that were the equal of mine."

"Lucy was never that adept at healing. Her skills lay elsewhere. Perhaps if she had paid more heed to brewing medicine than conjuring visions—" For a moment Renard's mouth tightened grimly. Then he shrugged, "Ah, very likely it would have made no difference. There was no way my poor mother could have survived the ordeal of giving birth to a great ox like me. No doubt the mere sight of me was enough to frighten her to death."

Renard tried to jest, but Ariane caught a flash of something painful in his eyes, a guilt too long carried.

She stroked her fingers gently across his brow. "Renard, I have been present at the birth of many babies. Often one life does end as another begins. It is just the sad way of things. I do not think your mother would have wanted you to blame yourself for her death."

"That is what Toussaint always said. He told me that Brianne, my mother, had difficulty even getting with child. When she realized she was dying, she begged Toussaint to tell me that one moment of holding me was worth a lifetime of empty arms."

"All nonsense of course," Renard said gruffly. "Just another of Toussaint's foolish yarns."

"Your cousin is a plain-spoken man who does not exaggerate. I am sure your mother meant every word. The birth of a child is such a gift, a miracle to a woman—"

Ariane trailed off. Actually the prospect of a child was not something she had ever allowed herself to contemplate. Caring for her sisters, Belle Haven, the people of the island required all of her devotion and strength. She had even managed to convince herself that she did not mind so much, but she was suddenly consumed by a deep longing to cradle a child of her own, especially a little girl. With eyes the deep hue of the forest, just like Renard's.

"That can easily be arranged," Renard responded, as though she had spoken aloud. "It would be my greatest joy to see you bearing our child. And my greatest fear. When we are married, I will make sure you have as many daughters as you desire."

"Renard!" Ariane cried, half laughing, half in protest.

"What? You did not just say you wanted a daughter?"

"I didn't say anything at all."

Renard pulled a rueful face when he realized what he had done. "I am sorry, ma chère. I have never been able to read anyone as I do you. It is those quiet eyes of yours. They are like windows to your soul. But I promise to stop peeking in."

"It is all right." Ariane sighed. "It is just that I have kept my own counsel for so long. You will have to allow me time to grow accustomed to sharing so much of myself with you."

Despite his recent promise, Renard peered intently into her eyes. "Then you do intend to do so? Share your life with me? You will marry me, ma chère?"

Ariane only hesitated a moment longer before brushing her lips against his in a tender kiss.

"Yes, Justice. I will marry you."

He pulled her down to him, his mouth moving gently, then more passionately over hers. She felt the desire begin to build between them again when suddenly she became aware of a distant voice calling through the trees.

Renard tensed at the same moment she did, thrusting her

slightly away from him. The voice became more audible, along with the sound of boots trampling over twigs, drawing ever nearer to the camp in the clearing.

"My lord? Justice?"

"Toussaint." Renard shoved to his feet, saying, "I will intercept my cousin, give you time to dress yourself. Toussaint must already suspect you are here or he would not be approaching with all the fanfare of a wild boar. But don't worry. He is discreet."

Ariane nodded, scrambling to dress herself. Her shift was still too damp, but she struggled into her gown, ignoring the way the wool scratched her skin. By the time she emerged from the tent, she found Renard engaged in earnest conversation with Toussaint, the old man busy tethering his horse beside Hercules.

Both men glanced round at Ariane's approach and she could tell at once that something was very wrong. Any sense of embarrassment forgotten, she strode toward them, her heart giving an anxious thud.

"Renard, what is it? What's happened?"

It was Toussaint who started to reply. "Ah, milady, your people have been looking for you everywhere—"

Renard cut him off, placing his hands on Ariane's arms as though he would brace her for some dire tidings.

"Ariane, you need to get back to the house at once. It is Gabrielle. She has fallen very ill."

"What? But I saw her only this morning before I left the house. She was completely well."

"I know." Renard exchanged an uneasy glance with Toussaint. "It scarcely seems possible but somehow Gabrielle has been poisoned."

Chapter Twenty-one

As night fell, a heavy and stifling air enveloped Belle Haven, the magic of the afternoon Ariane had spent in Renard's arms now only a memory. Her entire world felt reduced to the single candle that wavered by her sister's bedside, a feeble glow to hold back the darkness that threatened to descend over all of them.

The terrible spasms that had wracked Gabrielle appeared to have lessened, but that observation gave Ariane little comfort. It was as though her sister's body had simply grown too weak to continue fighting the poison that licked through her veins. Gabrielle was so pale, her once-glorious golden hair lank and damp with sweat, her skin clammy to the touch.

The girl shivered, scarcely possessing the strength to open her eyes. Ariane labored frantically over her, chafing Gabrielle's wrists and arms, piling on more blankets in a vain effort to prevent any more warmth from fleeing her sister's body.

Ariane tried to move with the efficiency she always displayed in a sickroom, but her hands trembled. She fought to conceal that fact and her sense of mounting despair, although there was no longer anyone there to see.

Miri had been so distraught, she had become close to hysterical. The sight of Gabrielle so ill had taken the poor child back to the night their mother had died. Ariane had been grateful when Renard had taken her little sister out of the room.

Only Necromancer remained, curled upon the foot of the bed. The cat regarded Ariane with sad eyes as though trying to tell her something or offer her some comfort. Or perhaps like everyone else at Belle Haven, he was simply waiting for a miracle Ariane was unable to perform.

She had already attempted purging Gabrielle and trying to sweat the poison out. She had even been desperate enough to attempt that ridiculous remedy that doctors on the mainland were so quick to use—bleeding. But nothing had helped.

Gabrielle was slipping away before her very eyes and never had Ariane felt so helpless. She had no magic to fight this evil. Perhaps she should have gone back to the workshop and made one final frantic effort to decipher the mystery of the gloves in hopes of finding an antidote. But Gabrielle had sobbed and pleaded with Ariane not to leave her and Ariane had yielded.

Besides, what good would it have done? Ariane reflected bitterly. If she had not managed to unlock the secret of Catherine's cursed dark magic by now, she could hardly hope to prevail in the next few desperate hours.

Exactly how long did her sister have? Ariane sought to remember what Remy had said about Jeanne of Navarre.

"By the time we returned to the palace, my queen was seized by the most agonizing spasms, as though she'd swallowed an entire cup of hemlock. By the next morning, she was dead."

The next morning . . . Ariane looked at her sister and her

heart was filled with fear. No, it was unthinkable that by this time tomorrow Gabrielle could be— "No, Gabby," Ariane whispered fiercely. "I can't lose you this way. I won't."

Snatching up a linen cloth, she dipped it in the basin of water and gently bathed her sister's fevered brow.

"Please . . . keep on fighting, Gabrielle. You can defeat this dark magic. I know you can. You are so strong."

Truly Gabrielle was much stronger and younger than the queen of Navarre had been, Ariane reassured herself. And perhaps after all this time, the poison in the gloves was no longer as potent.

Ariane's gaze strayed to the gloves discarded on the table, still looking so infuriatingly beautiful and harmless. The bitter thought entered her mind that it had finally been proved beyond all doubt. The gloves were poisoned. Pray God that proof did not send Gabrielle to her grave.

"Airy?"

The rasp of Gabrielle's voice drew Ariane's attention back to her sister. She stirred beneath Ariane's ministrations. Her eyes already seemed far too glazed and aged with her suffering. Her voice was so faint that Ariane had to bend close to hear her.

"Am—am I dying?" she whispered.

"No! You are going to be fine," Ariane insisted. Even weak as she was, Gabrielle was not easily deceived.

"It is the gloves, isn't it? They are poisoned." Gabrielle gave a weak laugh. "I suppose that is what I get for poking among your secrets."

"Oh, no, this is all my doing," Ariane cried. "I should have warned you, showed the gloves to you and Miri both."

"Poor Airy. You have tried so hard to take care of us since Maman died. And all I have done is fight you, given you so much worry and trouble. I—I am so sor—"

Gabrielle's voice faded, her eyes drifting closed. Ariane swallowed thickly. Gabrielle's words of apology were the most painful reproof she had ever received. She sagged down by the bedside, clutching her sister's hand, tears cascading down her cheeks.

"Oh, Gabrielle, I am the one who should be sorry," she wept. Sorry for so many things, for not protecting her sister from Danton that long-ago June, for bringing such danger upon them all by challenging the Dark Queen, and, perhaps worst of all, for not being here today when Gabrielle had needed her.

She thought of her sister writhing in agony, *dying,* and the entire time she had been off in the woods, playing games in the water with Renard, making love to him. It was more than Ariane could bear. She buried her face in the coverlet, giving way to her guilt and grief, her shoulders shaking with muffled sobs.

When Renard returned to the bedchamber and found Ariane weeping over her sister, his heart tightened with the fear that he was too late. But as he rushed over to the bedside, he saw the rise and fall of Gabrielle's chest, heard the rasp of her labored breathing.

"Ariane?" He placed his hands on her shoulders, drawing her away from her sister. "Ma chère, please don't despair. You must compose yourself and help me. We have to get Gabrielle to drink this."

Renard held up the small vial of wine-colored liquid that he had spent the last few hours in Ariane's workshop hastening to distill. Ariane drew in a shuddering breath, struggling to regain command of her voice.

"What—what is that?"

"The antidote."

She wiped the back of her hand across her cheeks, blinking hard to stem the flow of further tears. "Oh, dear God, Renard, I have studied those gloves and there is no remedy—"

Renard squeezed her shoulder. "I am familiar with how this kind of dark magic works. Chérie, you must trust me."

Ariane was torn between doubt and hope. At last, she accepted the vial from him with trembling fingers. Renard moved round the bed to raise Gabrielle up in his arms. She stiffened, giving a low whimper at his touch.

Her lashes flickered and she peered up at him with feverish eyes. "M-monsieur le ogre."

"Mademoiselle." He tightened his hold, fearing she would struggle to get away from him.

"I—I am glad you—you have come before I die. I want to—to tell you I am sorry for insulting you—"

"Hush, ma petite," Renard soothed her. "You will live to insult me for a great many more years. Now please, you must try to drink this."

He nodded to Ariane to hurry. With one final uncertain look at him, she uncorked the vial and held it to Gabrielle's lips. Between the two of them, they got the girl to swallow most of it down. Then Renard lowered her back to the pillows.

He wrapped his arm reassuringly around Ariane's shoulders. "She will be all right, chérie. I promise you."

Ariane leaned wearily against him, her eyes never leaving her sister's face. The antidote did its work swiftly. Gabrielle's breathing grew easier by the moment, the girl's rigid frame relaxing into a deep healing sleep. A hint of color stole into her cheeks.

Ariane peered up at Renard with wide, wondering eyes. She bent over Gabrielle, feeling her sister's brow, then her wrist.

"My God," she said, as though she hardly dared to believe it. "She is warm. Her pulse is steady. It is a miracle."

Ariane turned back to him, her eyes misting with fresh tears, but of joy this time. "Oh, J-justice. Th-thank—"

She hurled herself into his arms with a sob of gladness. Renard held her close, burying his lips in her hair. She was relieved and so grateful to him now, but at some point soon, when Ariane was calmer, she would wonder exactly how he had known about the antidote, why he was so well versed in such dark magic. She would begin to ask questions and Renard hoped she would not despise him for his answers.

※   ※   ※

IT WAS NEARLY MIDNIGHT BY THE TIME ARIANE FELT IT WAS SAFE TO rise from her chair at Gabrielle's bedside. The house was still around her, the servants long since retired. Renard had gone to reassure her anxious household that Gabrielle would recover, thus allowing Ariane to remain at her sister's bedside.

She could not begin to measure her gratitude to the man. In fact, she did not know what she would do without Renard. She was coming to depend upon him so much, it was almost frightening.

Ariane had not been able to keep Miri away any longer and the child had curled up beside Gabrielle on the bed, the two of them now fast asleep. Their arms draped protectively around each other, they looked so young and fragile.

"I will never fail either one of you again," Ariane vowed silently. Drawing the curtains closed, she turned away from the bed.

She returned to her own chamber, where she found candles lit and a late supper of bread, cheese, and wine laid out for her on the table. But a far more welcome sight was the powerful shape of the man silhouetted against her window.

"Justice?" she called softly.

Renard stepped out of the shadows. He scrutinized her face, but said nothing, merely held his arms open wide, as though he understood what she needed more than she did herself.

Ariane stumbled across the room and fell into his embrace. Renard's arms closed around her, warm, strong, and welcoming. With a choked cry, she buried her face against his shoulder. All the fear and tension of these past hours finally overwhelmed her, her limbs shaking so badly, only the strength of Renard's arms held her upright. He swept her off her feet and carried her over to the table, easing her down onto a chair.

Renard poured her a glass of wine, but her hands trembled too hard for her to raise it to her lips. He held the cup for her, urging her to drink. It was one of the potent vintages brewed by the sisters of St. Anne. As Ariane swallowed, she felt the wine's warmth rush through her, reviving her a little.

"Th-thank you." She smiled shyly at Renard. "I am so glad you are still here. I was afraid you might have already gone back to your camp."

"I only waited to make certain that all was well with you before I left."

All was very well with her *now,* Ariane thought as he leaned forward to brush his mouth against hers. Or at least it should have been. His kiss was warm, tender, but over far too quickly. To her surprise, he straightened immediately to his feet.

"You have had an exhausting day, milady." He touched her cheek lightly. "Take a little supper and get some rest. And I should return to my tent."

"Well, yes, but—" Ariane gazed up at him wistfully. Of course she should retire and so should he, but she felt loath to part with him. Her gaze strayed toward her bed and she blushed. She felt guilty for even thinking of her desires at a time like this.

Still she clung to Renard's hand. "I wish you would stay to at least take a cup of wine with me and talk. I have not even had a chance to properly thank you for what you did for Gabrielle."

"There is no need." He deposited a swift kiss on her fingertips. The gesture was a little brusque, as though Renard was anxious to be gone.

Ariane pressed his hand gratefully and then released him. "So once more you came to our rescue. After this I am sure even Gabrielle must call you our gallant ogre."

"She won't be calling me anything more tonight. That medicine I gave her will keep her in a deep sleep until morning, which is exactly what she needs in order to fully heal after such a shock to her system." Although he smiled, Ariane detected a constraint in his manner that made her a trifle unsettled.

"You appeared to understand Gabrielle's condition very well. Where did you learn so much about this kind of poison?" Ariane thought her question natural enough, but she noticed a slight stiffening of Renard's shoulders.

"I don't really recall."

"Don't recall?" Ariane echoed in astonishment. "You are an expert on poisons and you don't remember where you learned?"

"It was just something I picked up on my travels."

"In Italy?"

"I was able to help your sister. Does it really matter where I learned?"

It might not have if Renard had not been acting so strangely. He was behaving like—like—the way he had when she'd first met him, hooding his eyes, guarding his thoughts. But no, surely she was just imagining things. If anyone was at fault here, it was she, cross-examining him when the man was clearly drained.

Ariane rose to her feet and rested her hand on his arm. "I am sorry, Justice. I was just curious, that is all. I could do nothing to save Gabrielle while you were able to do it so easily."

"That is because you have always avoided the study of black magic."

"And you did not?" she asked uneasily. "But from whom could you have possibly learned such things?"

Renard strode away from her to stare out the window into the dark, moonless night. Ariane sensed some great struggle taking place within him and it increased her own anxiety tenfold. At last he turned back to face her.

"From Lucy."

"Lucy? *Your kindly old grandmother?* You said she was a wise woman, a peasant from the mountains, and not particularly skilled in healing."

"She wasn't. Lucy was a little remiss in distilling medicines, but mon Dieu, the old lady certainly knew her poisons," Renard said with a bitter smile. "It wouldn't surprise me if she knew more of the old ways of dark magic than Queen Catherine herself."

Ariane struggled to comprehend what he was telling her. She moistened her lips and faltered, "There was only one daughter of the earth who ever knew as much black magic as Catherine and that—that was—"

Renard raised his lashes, allowing Ariane full access to his eyes and what she read there staggered her, made her feel as though she had just pitched headfirst down a cold dark well.

"*Melusine?* You are telling me your grandmother was Melusine?"

When Renard nodded reluctantly, Ariane blinked, too shocked to credit his words. "*You* are Melusine's *grandson?* No, that—that's impossible. The woman was so evil, even I would not have hesitated to call her a witch."

"Would you? I usually just called her grand-mère."

Ariane waited for him to laugh, preparing to scold him for making such a dreadful jest. Although he smiled, it was the most grim expression she had ever seen, the light never reaching his eyes.

Ariane sank weakly back down onto her chair. It was several moments before she could even find her voice. "My God, Renard. If you had any idea of the stories I have heard about Melusine—"

"I can imagine."

"And will you tell me that they are not true?" she asked desperately.

"I wish I could." Renard shrugged stiffly. "Most of them probably are true, but I am not sure. Even I could never separate my grandmother from her legend. By the time I was born, Lucy had put aside much of the folly of her youth."

"Folly?" Ariane choked. "Melusine blazed a path of havoc and destruction throughout most of Brittany."

His lips thinned. "I am aware of that, but try to understand. You have experienced some of the difficulty and danger of being a wise woman yourself, and you are well born, the daughter of an honored knight.

"Imagine a girl as strong and intelligent as yourself born amidst poverty and ignorance. Lucy's own mother was a simple village midwife. When she was ten, Lucy saw her mother brought up on charges by the lord of the manor because one of the babes she delivered had the misfortune to be born deformed. She would likely have been burned at the stake, but she died from being tortured into a confession of witchcraft first."

Renard stalked over to the table and poured himself a cup of wine. Perhaps he needed fortifying with the potent vintage to be able to talk about his grandmother. Or perhaps he was merely buying a little time, to decide how much he needed to tell her. The suspicion cut Ariane deeply, the more so because she had believed they were finally past all that, Renard's evasiveness, his half-truths.

He took a long draught from his cup before he continued, "After seeing what happened to her mother, Lucy never troubled about learning any more of the healing arts. She devoted herself to dark magic. And let me tell you, if she hadn't, Lucy would have been dead a long time ago, when the witch-hunting tribunals were at their worst throughout France, hundreds of innocent women tortured and slaughtered.

"Lucy made up her mind she would never be caught so tamely. She rallied other women to fight back, their men as well determined to protect their wives and daughters. Simple peasant farmers who had already endured too much injustice in their lives. Overtaxed, overworked, often on the brink of starvation."

"I know," Ariane said in a small voice. "My Great-aunt Eugenie often talked of those days. It was a noble cause at first that swiftly degenerated into a rampaging horde bent on plunder and destruction. And Melusine . . . your grandmother used her dark skills to poison wells, to inflict diseases on livestock, to blight crops, to taint fields so badly that nothing ever grew there again."

"Lucy was fighting a losing battle against powerful forces, including the king and the church," Renard defended. "What else could she do but use what weapons she had?"

"I don't know, but in the end your grandmother's rebellion did more harm than good. It is a great sin for any daughter of the earth to ever seek to poison the land. It—it is like attacking your own mother.

"And my own mother always taught me that wise women were meant to be a force of light in what is often a dark world. To use our knowledge of the old ways for healing, never to bring harm."

"Well, pardon me if my grandmother was not the saint your mother was. Maybe if their situations had been reversed and Evangeline Cheney had been born in a peasant's hut—"

Renard checked himself. "Ariane, I am not condoning the things Lucy did. Only trying to make you understand she wasn't entirely a monster. And God help her, she eventually did pay a terrible price for her sins. But that's all ancient history. Far better you just forget about it."

There was a note of finality in his voice, as though he considered the subject closed. Bending down, he spanned his hands around Ariane's waist, drawing her up from the chair and into his arms.

Ariane stiffened. Her initial shock gave way to searing hurt, a feeling of betrayal. When he tried to kiss her, she ducked her head so that the warmth of his lips merely grazed her temple.

"Why didn't you tell me any of this before?" she asked. "You never told me—not even this afternoon."

"What would you have had me do, Ariane? When I had you

in my arms, whisper tenderly in your ear? Oh, by the way, my grandmother was a wicked old witch."

When Ariane looked up reproachfully, he hastened to add, "All right. Of course I should have said something. But I hate discussing Lucy. I could have willingly gone the rest of my life without ever telling you any of this."

Or at least until their wedding night, Ariane thought, a cold weight settling in the pit of her stomach. When he finally had her safe and secure, unable to escape him. But no, it couldn't be. Not after all they had shared this afternoon. Renard had never said so, but he loved her . . . didn't he? His reason for courting her couldn't possibly have anything to do with his terrible old grandmother.

Renard crushed her closer to him, his mouth descending upon hers in a kiss that was fueled as much by desperation as it was heat and desire. Ariane felt her heart thunder in response, but she could not allow him to beguile her into asking no more questions.

She struggled to break away. Renard's face clouded with such longing and frustration, she feared he might restrain her. He reluctantly let her go, his fingers sliding down her arms.

"Ah, chérie, don't look at me as though I had suddenly become a stranger to you."

Ariane could not help herself. All the doubts she had ever had about Renard came rushing back. She inched farther away until all he retained possession of were her fingers.

"Please, Ariane. Whoever Lucy was, the kind of magic she practiced . . . it has nothing to do with you and me."

"Doesn't it?" she asked. "You once told me your grandmother conjured visions in the fire. That she claimed that one day you would find me—that I was your destiny."

"One of Lucy's better predictions." He pressed a kiss to her fingertips.

Ariane tugged free, putting more distance between them. "You also said your grandmother's predictions tended to be self-serving, things that she wanted to happen. But why would she particularly want me to be your bride?"

"How the devil should I know what went on in Lucy's head?"

But he did know. Ariane was sure of it.

"Do you realize that Melusine once even threatened the people of this island?"

"Did she?" Renard frowned.

"Yes. She had heard that the Lady of Faire Isle possessed a secret store of ancient texts that might contain secrets powerful enough to help her defeat her enemies. When my Great-aunt Eugenie refused to allow the knowledge of Faire Isle to be used for any destructive purposes, Melusine threatened to attack Belle Haven, take the books by force."

Renard looked uncomfortable. "I am sure that was only Lucy blustering. She respected the Lady of Faire Isle too much to do any such thing. Especially when those books wouldn't have done her any good. Lucy couldn't even read present-day French, let alone decipher some ancient language."

Ariane raised her troubled gaze to his face. "And what about you, my lord? I know that you have traveled widely, studied much. Did you ever learn any ancient languages?"

His expression immediately grew more guarded, more wary. "I might have. What of it?"

Ariane drew a deep breath. "I know you must have been in my private workshop. That is the only place you could have brewed the antidote for my sister."

Renard's jaw jutted to a belligerent angle. "Gabrielle was dying. I didn't exactly have time to seek your permission."

"I realize that. But the room is well hidden. How did you even know it existed?"

Renard gave a mirthless laugh. "That workshop of yours is not exactly the best-kept secret around here."

No, it wouldn't be. Not for a man who could read eyes as skillfully as Renard. What else, what darker arts had Melusine taught her grandson?

"What do you think I was after? Your precious books?"

But beneath Renard's display of indignation Ariane detected a flicker of guilt that made her sick at heart. Especially as another realization struck her with painful clarity.

"Today was not the first time you were in my workshop," she said. "The other night I dreamed that you came and carried me up to bed. But it wasn't a dream, was it?"

He shrugged, "No. I came down there looking for you, found you asleep, and took you upstairs."

"And that was all that you did?"

"Yes!" he snapped. He stalked over to the table, started to uncork the bottle only to slam it back down. "Very well, I admit I was tempted to go prowling through your books. Ever since I was a small boy, I had been hearing Lucy's stories about the Lady of Faire Isle, her treasure trove of hidden knowledge. And suddenly there it all was, spread out before me. Ancient books lost behind cobwebs, neglected parchments looking ready to crumble to dust. I doubt you are even aware of all the powerful secrets you have collected down there."

"No, and I don't want to be. I have been far too tempted by the lure of dark magic myself sometimes." Ariane flinched, remembering the forbidden arts she had used to conjure her mother's spirit. "There are some of the old ways better forgotten."

"Sometimes dark magic can have its uses," Renard insisted. "If Lucy hadn't taught me all she knew of poisons, your sister would be dead by now."

"Your antidote would never have been needed if I had been

at home, looking after Gabrielle as I should have been. Instead I was—was—"

Renard's countenance darkened. "Was what, Ariane? Wasting your afternoon making love to me when you had far more important duties awaiting you?"

Ariane would not have put it quite so acidly, but in essence Renard was correct. "Yes," she whispered.

"I wondered how long it would take before you got around to castigating yourself for that," he said bitterly. He bore down upon her, seizing her roughly by the shoulders. "Listen to me, Ariane Cheney and you listen well. *You are not to blame for what happened to Gabrielle. It was not your fault.*"

Although she winced at his bruising grip, she said stubbornly, "I should have been here. I behaved like—like—"

"Like a woman for once with human needs and desires and not like a saint. Not like some god-cursed marble statue erected in the middle of the town square."

Renard's harsh words stung like the lash of a whip. Ariane's cheeks heated, but she arched her neck proudly. "I am the Lady of Faire Isle. I have never been able to make you understand what that means. I have a duty to my sisters and to everyone on this island. To serve and protect."

"And especially from the grandson of Melusine, eh?"

"I never said that."

"You don't have to. Your eyes speak quite clearly." He released her so abruptly, she stumbled back a pace.

Rubbing her bruised shoulders, she said, "I am fully aware of how you have come to our rescue time and again. And I am grateful to you for that, my lord."

Renard let fly such a furious oath, Ariane shrank farther away from him.

"I don't want your damned gratitude," he growled.

"Then exactly what do you want from me?" Ariane cried.

"You read my eyes so well, it feels like you pierce my very heart. But I am not sure if I have ever come close to touching yours. So once again we come back to the question you have never answered. Why do you want to marry me, Renard?"

He shot her a fulminating glance. "If you don't know the answer to that by now, you are never going to."

"So now, you will pretend you have fallen in love with me?"

"No. I told you once before. I would never *pretend* anything like that."

His answer shattered what little hope she had left. But Ariane refused to let him see that. "I am glad you are at least that honest, because it would do you no good. I am not a romantic young fool."

"That is exactly what you are, ma chère," he replied sardonically. "You want a man who will be perfect with no weaknesses, no flaws. A man who never makes mistakes."

"No, all I ever wanted was a man who would be honest and open with me. A man I could trust."

"And apparently you have decided I am not that man." Renard's fierce green eyes probed hers, but Ariane turned away from him, no longer having the energy to continue this quarrel.

She pressed her hands to her temples, which had begun to throb painfully. "I think it would be better if you left now."

She heard the heavy tread of his boot as he stepped toward her and she tensed. Renard stopped abruptly. He refrained from touching her, his fists clenched at his sides.

"Perhaps you are right," he conceded. "We will both behave more sensibly in the morning. I will return to my camp and—"

"No," she said hoarsely. "I—I want you to go home, my lord. Return to your château."

She risked a glance up at him and saw the ominous drawing together of his brows, the hard set of a jaw. She braced herself for a fierce argument.

But the fight suddenly seemed to melt out of Renard as well.

"Very well," he said in brusque accents. "If that is what you want. I will leave Toussaint and my men behind to maintain guard. And if you need me, you know how to reach me. You still have my ring."

Ariane gave an involuntary shudder. She shook her head vigorously. "Do you think I will ever bring myself to touch that ring again? Now that I know it was Melusine who forged it."

At the door, Renard paused to glance back at her. There was more sorrowful resignation on his face than anger. "There was never anything evil in that ring, chérie. Only in the way I tried to used it."

Then he sketched her a stiff bow and was gone.

※ ※ ※

THE CANDLES FLICKERED, THE WAX MELTING OVER THE SILVER HOLD-ers as the tapers guttered low in their sockets. Heedless of darkness about to press in on him, Renard sprawled in his chair, the banquet table in the great hall spread out before him in its solitary splendor.

But the elaborate meal heaped upon the platters went largely untouched as Renard quaffed his wine, quietly getting drunk as he feared he'd done far too many times since he'd left Faire Isle.

How many days ago had that been? He wasn't even sure. He kept hoping that Ariane would send for him. But she hadn't and he'd come to doubt she ever would. He tried to keep his despair at bay by nursing his anger against her. For being so hard, unreasonable, and unforgiving.

But mostly his anger was directed at himself, for being the greatest fool who ever lived to have let such a remarkable woman as Ariane Cheney slip away from him.

Being forced to talk about Lucy, the aspects of her wretched past, had ever made him edgy and defensive. The same reaction he'd always had at any reference to his Deauville grandfather.

One side of his family spawned by a witch, the other side by the devil himself. Lord, what a heritage, Renard thought in disgust as he drained his glass to the dregs. He'd long dreaded telling Ariane the truth about Lucy. But when the issue could no longer be avoided, he should have attempted to remain calm and reasonable instead of waxing so bitter and caustic.

But the way Ariane had looked at him had torn him to shreds. Helpless and frustrated, he had watched the trust he had labored so long to win from her shattered beyond hope of repair.

He could still hear the hurt-filled echoes of her voice.

"So now, you will pretend you have fallen in love with me?"

And his own angry answer . . . *"No. I told you once before. I would never pretend anything like that."*

Because he didn't have to pretend. He *did* love her, would love her until his dying breath, although he didn't know quite when this transformation in him had happened. Perhaps his fall had begun the first moment he'd ever gazed into those quiet eyes of hers.

He loved her courage, her strength, her wisdom. Her compassion, her serenity, her remarkable gifts for healing. He loved the adorable way her mouth quivered when she was trying so hard to remain serious and not laugh at some outrageous remark he'd made. The way she tipped her head to one side when she listened to him, not in that half self-absorbed way most people listened, but so intently, so earnestly. Ariane listened with her whole heart.

He also loved the shy way her eyes glowed just after he kissed her, the rosy flush that spread across her cheeks when she was aroused, those soft little sighs of surrender she breathed when he made love to her. All the more precious because the Lady of Faire Isle did not surrender herself lightly to any man.

Renard groaned, thrusting his glass aside. "You bloody fool," he muttered. Why the devil hadn't he gotten down on his knees and told her all that when he'd had the chance? When he'd first begun his pursuit of her, he had had some idiot notion about acquiring her ancient manuscripts. But he didn't give a damn about those blasted books. They could all burn to ashes and he wouldn't care as long as he could have her back in his arms.

She'd never believe him now. And yet the woman had been compassionate enough to bestow the Breath of Life on that wretch Le Vis. If she was capable of forgiving a witch-hunter, then why not him?

Because Renard had hurt her in the worst way imaginable. Ariane's greatest fear was being deceived, having her trust betrayed just as her father had done with her mother.

"My lord—"

The timid voice roused him from his dark musings. Renard lifted his head to find one of his pages hovering timidly at his elbow.

"I—I was sent to inquire if you were done, milord— That is, if you wanted the covers cleared . . ." The lad swallowed, his adam's apple bobbing in his scrawny neck.

His fear was so palpable, Renard felt himself flush with shame. He had resolved that none of his servants would ever cringe in terror of him as they had done with his grandfather. But his humor had been so black of late, he'd been behaving worse than the old devil, roaring at anyone who came near him.

The boy gulped and tried again, "Un—unless there is something else I can fetch you. M-more wine?"

"No, lad," Renard replied gently. With some difficulty, he even managed a smile. By lingering this late at the table, he was keeping the entire kitchen staff from finishing their tasks and getting to their beds.

Scraping back his chair, he rose to his feet. He was drunk, but not drunk enough to quite drown his misery, he realized ruefully. Only enough to make his gait a trifle unsteady as he moved away from the table.

As he wended his way from the great hall, he had no desire to retire to his own bedchamber, to face another night tormenting himself with thoughts of Ariane, of that all too brief afternoon when she had been truly his, when they had lost themselves in each other's loving again and again.

But where was he to go? He could scarcely spend another night pacing the parapets. Shielding his candle from the draft, he hesitated, then turned abruptly, heading for the one part of the château he had steadfastly avoided ever since his return.

The private chapel had been remodeled sometime late in the fourteenth century. But Renard spared not even a glance at the costly, extravagant stained-glass window or the gilt trim on the altar. He headed toward the circular stair that led to the crypt below, where generations of Deauvilles had been laid to rest.

The dark was so impenetrable, his candle made little impression. Renard paused to light one of the torches embedded in the walls. He glanced about until he found the newest addition. It would have been hard to miss the sarcophagus that had become his grandfather's final resting place. The elaborate tomb had been fashioned to suit Robert Deauville's sense of his own consequence.

But the knight carved into the marble bore little resemblance to the grandfather Renard remembered. The effigy's countenance was too serene to reflect the old man's choleric temper, cruelty, and arrogance.

Renard's gaze drifted from his grandfather's magnificent sarcophagus to the recess in the wall behind it. A plain clay urn rested on the stone ledge, the urn that held all that remained of the legendary Melusine, the woman that Renard had known for so long simply as grand-mère.

It was a strange irony that these two who had been such fierce enemies should now lie here, entombed side by side for all eternity. Why the old comte had had Lucy's remains fetched here, Renard had no idea. Out of superstitious fear perhaps, or some final warped revenge. As a daughter of the earth, Lucy would have wanted her bones returned to the soil where they belonged.

When Renard had become the comte, Toussaint had pleaded with him to take Lucy's bones into the forest, see that she was properly laid to rest, but Renard had adamantly refused, saying it made no difference after all this time.

Perhaps he still harbored some resentment toward the woman who had so twisted his life to suit her own ends. Ariane's shock had been great to discover that Lucy was Melusine, but no less than Renard's own. He'd never learned the truth about his grandmother until that night he'd escaped from his Grandfather Deauville's château and made his way back to the only home he'd ever known, the cottage high in the mountains. His back was torn and bleeding from his grandfather's whip, his heart lacerated even worse from his discovery that Martine had married someone else in his absence.

He'd overheard Toussaint and Lucy talking and that had been how he'd discovered who his grandmother really was. Although he'd been stunned, his reaction had not been entirely one of horror like Ariane's.

Perhaps because when all was said and done, Lucy was still his grandmother, the woman who'd raised him. Or perhaps because he'd lacked Ariane's wisdom. He'd only been a boy of sixteen, raw with hurt and exhaustion.

He had collapsed on his knees before Lucy, clutching her skirts and pleading.

"If you truly are this dread Melusine, grand-mère, then use your power to save me. Hide me. Keep me safe from that old devil. And—and find a way to bring Martine back to me. Make her love me again."

Lucy had smiled, gently laying her withered hand upon his

cheek. "Forget about that girl, Justice. You see how easily she has forgotten you. She was never worthy to be your bride. You have a great destiny awaiting you. You are going to be the Comte de—"

"Damn my destiny. I don't want it. If you won't help me, I'll find a way to escape from here. I'll go far from Brittany, someplace where he'll never find me. And I'll get Martine to go with me."

Lucy's green eyes had flashed, those strange bright eyes of hers that never seemed to dim with age. "You think that I have planned and schemed and dreamed such dreams for you all these years to let you throw it all away? Heed me Justice and heed me well. You are going to be a great man, a man of extraordinary power."

It was at that moment that the truth had finally penetrated his thick skull, that it was not his Grandfather Deauville who had torn him away from his life in the hills, the simple future he wanted, the girl he loved. It had all been Lucy's, or should he say Melusine's, doing.

He'd recoiled from his grandmother, his voice breaking. "Mon Dieu. You—you have never really cared about me, have you? I've never been anything but a means to an end for you, a way to finish the rebellion you started years ago."

Lucy sorrowfully shook her head. "You can't defeat powerful men through rebellion. There was only one way I could make sure any grandchild of mine would never be helpless, trampled into the dirt. And that was to make you one of them, an aristocrat."

Outside the cottage, he heard the thunder of horse's hooves, saw the flare of torchlight. Peering out, he saw that his grandfather's retainers had arrived to fetch him back to the château. He glanced desperately at his grandmother. Rarely had he ever been able to read Lucy's eyes, but he saw the flicker of guilt, her final betrayal. The men had come because she had sent for them.

"Justice, I do love you, more than life itself. I only want what is best for you." She reached up to cup his face between her hands, but he'd thrust her away.

"You want me to be a powerful man? Then here is my first command, that I never set eyes on you again. It will be a damned embarrassment for a comte to have an old witch as his grandmother."

Lucy was so strong. She rarely ever showed her pain, but her face crumpled as though he'd struck her. He hadn't cared. He wanted to hurt her as much as she was hurting him. He'd flung himself out of the cottage and never looked back . . .

Renard's fingers trembled a little as he reached out to touch the clay urn. Even as he'd resigned himself to his life, he'd continued to nurse his resentment against her. Years later and he was still struggling to come to terms with his feelings about her, love and anger, guilt, regret, and shame all jumbled up inside of him.

"Justice? Lad? Are you there?"

Toussaint's voice echoing down the stairs caused Renard to jerk hastily away from the urn. Before the old man could descend into the crypt, Renard was already there barring his path.

Toussaint shuffled cautiously down the worn stone steps, balancing a candlestick in his hand as he grumbled, "This is a gloomy place to spend a fair summer night."

"What are you doing back here?" Renard asked tersely. "I asked you to remain on Faire Isle, to look after my lady."

"Your lady is well enough. I am more concerned about you."

"Well, don't be," Renard said, brusquely turning away, but Toussaint clamped his hand upon his shoulder.

"How long is this foolishness between you and Mistress Cheney to go on? You should return to her, lad."

Renard shook his head. "If Ariane decides to forgive me, she will send for me. I won't force my presence upon her again." After a moment, he added gruffly. "I am in love with her, Toussaint."

"Well, praise be. It certainly took you long enough to figure that out. So why not go and tell her so?"

"Because it is too late for that."

"Only if you allow it to be."

Renard moved away from the old man, his boots echoing off the stone floor. "You tried to warn me. I should have been honest with her from the beginning. But no, I had to be so clever, trying to bully her into marrying me as my grandfather would have done. When that didn't work, I resorted to Lucy's kind of tricks, forcing Ariane into that pact with the rings." He halted in front of the sarcophagus, staring from the old man's tomb to the urn resting behind it. "Sometimes I think I am the worst of both of them."

Toussaint stepped quietly beside him. "No, lad. You tend to forget you are also your mother's and your father's son. Only natural I expect, because you never had a chance to know them. They were kind, loving people who adored each other, who managed to steal a bit of happiness from a world that is sometimes full of dark magic. You and your lady will too."

Renard wished he could believe that. He turned to Toussaint and pressed the old man's hand, commanding more gently this time. "Go back to Faire Isle. Keep her safe for me."

Toussaint studied him for a long moment, but apparently saw the futility of trying to reason with him further. He started back toward the stairs but not before casting a sorrowful look in the direction of the urn set in the wall.

Renard wrestled with himself for a moment before saying hesitantly, "Er—Toussaint, if you want to—to take Lucy's bones, lay her to rest in the earth, you may do so."

"No, lad, you are the only one who can grant her that peace.

Lucy made some terrible mistakes during her life, but she did love you, boy. Far better than she ever loved anyone else."

Renard said nothing. He supposed the old man was right, but the thought brought him little comfort. It was his heritage from Melusine that was costing him Ariane. And yet how could he ever expect forgiveness from Ariane when he couldn't bring himself to forgive his own grandmother?

Renard lingered down in the crypt long after Toussaint had gone. He didn't rouse himself from his bleak reflections until the torch suddenly flickered and went out. Cursing softly, Renard groped his way through the darkness, trying to make his way toward the stairs when a voice carried to him, calling his name, as though from a great distance.

"Renard . . ."

Renard's heartbeat quickened. He felt the ring on his finger turn warm, the familiar tingle coursing through him.

"Ariane?" His voice was raw and desperate with hope. He pressed his hand bearing the ring over the region of his heart and concentrated as he'd never done before, sending all his thoughts, his longing for her winging through the night.

Time seemed to crawl by before he heard her voice again. Not clear like the other times she'd used the ring, but disturbingly faint and far away.

"Renard. Please come . . . to me. In danger."

His gut knotting with fear, he closed his eyes and called out to her.

"What is it, Ariane? What is wrong? Answer me."

Her voice echoed inside him again, her accent low and urgent. *"I have been captured by Le Vis. He is taking me for trial. We are already on the road to Paris. Please . . . help me."*

Her terror reached him across the distance, icing through his veins. His jaw clenching with grim purpose, he tried to send back to her his love, all his reassurance.

"Don't be afraid, ma chère. I am on my way."

٭ ٭ ٭

THE RING GLINTED AGAINST THE PALE SKIN OF THE WOMAN'S HAND,
but it fit far too snugly. For a moment Catherine feared she was
going to be unable to remove it. But with a hard tug, the metal
band scraped from her finger.

She cupped the ring in the palm of her hand, smiling slightly
as she translated the inscription.

This ring to me doth bind you both heart and mind.

Catherine had been uncertain if she would be able to command the power of the ring, use it to confuse Renard, but the
whisper of the comte's last words assured her of her success.

"Don't be afraid, ma chère. I am on my way."

Catherine closed her hand over the ring. It was all she could
do not to burst into laughter. Men were so appallingly easy to
manipulate. Just like the one that waited so anxiously behind her.

She had turned away to the window so that Le Vis had been
unable to see what she was doing. It would hardly do at this
point to have the fool realize she was just as versed in the ways
of magic as the women she had sent him to destroy.

Composing herself, she turned back to face the witch-
hunter. She had always had a distaste for Le Vis and never more
so than now. He had dared to appear before her, his robes
stained with the dust of his hard journey, his face gaunt, his mis-
shapen eye wild, and he was practically slavering like a dog.

"Well, Your Grace?" he demanded. "Will it serve?"

"Oh, yes indeed," Catherine purred. "You did not bring me
Remy and the gloves, but this ring will serve the purpose just as
well. It will lure our enemies to Paris. You have done well, Monsignor Le Vis. And you too, Master Aristide."

She nodded toward the haggard boy standing in Le Vis's
shadow. The boy said nothing, merely bowed his head.

But Le Vis rubbed his hands together, an almost insane light
glinting in his eyes. "We will have them this time. But get that

demon and his whore to Paris where your soldiers may lay hands upon them. I will build a bonfire hotter than the fires of hell. Then you will remember all that you promised me. My appointment as grand inquisitor."

"But certainly, Monsieur Le Vis. I will make certain that you receive all that is coming to you," Catherine murmured.

Le Vis detected nothing amiss in her promise, his eyes glowing with visions of future glory. She noted, however, that the boy had snapped alert, his expression troubled and suspicious.

Catherine dismissed them both, holding out her hand to be kissed with a regal smile.

She had greater matters at hand. Her heart quickened with a rare sense of excitement and triumph. Everything was falling into place. She had the king of Navarre and his Huguenot followers settled here in Paris. The miasma she had brewed had reached its full potency. She had even determined the occasion upon which to finally set her plan into motion. St. Bartholomew's Eve.

And now she had it in her power to make certain there would be no threat of exposure from Ariane Cheney.

Retreating to her private chambers, she dismissed all her servants, then whipped the cover off the cage next to her bedside. The pigeon cooed softly, regarding Catherine with puzzled eyes. Catherine had never credited birds with much intelligence, but perhaps the creature was wondering where its mistress was.

Tapping on the outside of the cage, Catherine said softly, "You must forget all about Hermoine. She has no more use for you."

Neither Madame Pechard nor Louise Lavalle would be sending any more messages. Both were lodged in the deepest dungeons of the Bastille and Catherine did not intend that either should ever see the light of day again.

Catherine bent closer to the cage and whispered. "You have one more message to send, my little friend."

Catherine only wished she could be there to see Marie

Claire's face when she received it . . . and Ariane's. Her mouth curled wryly. It was rather amusing really. That the girl's foolish challenge to Catherine's power was about to be defeated by the same weakness that had conquered her mother.

Love.

Chapter Twenty-two

RAIN POURED DOWN FOR THE NEXT SEVERAL DAYS, A SERIES OF intermittent storms casting a pall over Belle Haven and effectively cutting the entire island off from the mainland. It was a considerable relief to Ariane when the sun poked through at last.

She was anxious for any tidings from the outside world, some word of Remy's fate or a report from Louise regarding what was happening in Paris. And although Ariane was reluctant to admit it, she was even more anxious for some word of Renard.

She had not seen or heard anything of the man since he had departed from Belle Haven the night of their quarrel. But Toussaint and some of the comte's retainers continued to maintain guard over her home no matter how Ariane remonstrated. Considering how matters stood between her and Renard, she was mortified to keep accepting his protection.

As soon as the rain ceased, Ariane went in search of Toussaint, determined to demand that the obstinate old man return home. She had insisted that Renard's men begin keeping their horses in her stables when the inclement weather had struck. And it was there that she found Toussaint in the last stall, grooming his roan gelding, a horse as stolid as the redoubtable old man.

The stalls were all full now, but one. Ariane noted that Miri's pony was missing. She frowned over that fact, hardly knowing whether to be pleased or concerned. Miri had been behaving strangely, one moment moping about Belle Haven, the next almost frantic to escape the house. Miri insisted that nothing was the matter, but she also carefully avoided Ariane's eyes.

Ariane feared she could guess what troubled her little sister, that boy Simon Aristide. Miri must be beginning to suspect the same thing Renard did, that young Aristide had perished in his efforts to escape the island.

Even if Simon had lived, Miri was better off away from that dangerously confused young man. But telling Miri that would not ease the child's heartache, as Ariane knew from her own experience. Perhaps she would be better off if she did not see Renard again, but the thought gave her little comfort.

As she strode toward the last stall, Toussaint glanced round at her approach.

"Good morrow, milady." Renard's cousin was as ever deeply respectful, but his craggy face also carried an element of silent reproach.

But she called back in a determinedly cheerful voice, "Yes, it finally is a good morning. The rains have stopped, and it will likely be safe to travel by the causeway."

"Indeed, milady?" Toussaint returned to his grooming.

"You and the comte's retainers will be able to return to Tremazan today."

"Oh? Have you received word then confirming that Le Vis is dead?"

"Well, no, but—"

"Or some report from Paris that the Dark Queen has been astonishingly toppled from her throne?"

"Of course not, but—"

"Then I believe I'll be staying right here."

Ariane drew herself up stiffly. "Monsieur Toussaint, I insist—"

"Begging your pardon. No disrespect to your ladyship, but I take orders from none but the Comte de Renard and he says I am to remain here until *he* is certain there is no more danger."

Ariane regarded the old man in sheer exasperation, and she was about to charge him with a sharp message for Monsieur le Comte, but she realized it would do no good.

She leaned wearily against the front of the stall watching Toussaint's loving ministrations to his horse. Much as she despised herself for it, she could not refrain from asking, "How—how is he, Toussaint?"

"Well, I wouldn't rightly know." The old man cast a shrewd look at Ariane. "But judging from the look of him when I last saw him, I would venture to say the lad is as miserable as you are."

Ariane started to haughtily deny it, but found she couldn't. She had been much shaken by Renard's deception, so angry and distressed she had told herself she was glad he was gone. But the truth was she missed him with something akin to a physical ache.

Toussaint suggested in a gentler tone. "If you are so pining for word of Justice, you have the power to obtain it far more quickly than I, milady. All you have to do is slip his ring back on your finger and—"

"No!" Ariane shook her head, although she had been fighting the temptation to do just that. Now that she knew what evil hand had actually forged those rings, she was not about to ever touch that metal band again.

Toussaint heaved a frustrated sigh. "By God, I begin to believe there is something to that prediction of Lucy's that you and the lad are destined for each other. Because I have never known a man and woman better matched for stubbornness."

His voice dropped to a coaxing note. "Couldn't this misunderstanding between you and Justice be cleared away if you would just talk to him? Better yet, skip the talking and get straight down to the kissing."

Ariane could not help smiling a little at the old man's efforts to play matchmaker, but she replied sadly, "It is more than a mere misunderstanding that lies between me and the comte. He—he—"

"Deceived you about his grandmother, yes, I know. Lucy did some terrible things in her day. Can you blame the lad for wanting to conceal his connection to all that?"

"But I am the woman—" Ariane broke off. She'd almost said the woman Renard loved, but she was no longer so sure. "I am the woman he wanted to marry. He should have been honest with me."

"Perhaps, but that is not always so easy for Justice. The lad was very different once, so completely open and trusting."

Toussaint's face softened at the memory, but the set of his mouth turned grim as he continued. "That changed fast enough when Lucy allowed his grandfather to take him. Between the cruelty of that old villain and the mockery of his supposed highborn friends, Justice learned fast enough to guard his emotions and his secrets. Whatever trust the boy had left in him, Lucy finished when he turned to her for protection and she refused to help him."

"I knew he felt betrayed by his grandmother," Ariane said, "but I did not understand what he thought she could have done to help him. Of course, I did not know then that she was Melusine."

"I never seem able to think of her that way. She'll always be Lucy to me." His face softened and what she read in his eyes astonished Ariane.

"You—you were in love with *Melusine?*"

"No, with a bright-eyed girl named Lucy. After her rebellion had failed, it was no sorceress who fled into the hills, seeking out my help and protection. Only a vulnerable young woman. She was already far gone with child, her lover one of her raiders who had been killed by the king's soldiers. Lucy refused to speak of him. But at night, she would sit up staring into the firelight and I could see she was haunted by memories of him and others who had died fighting in her cause. And yes, she was also tormented with guilt and regret for some of the dreadful things she'd done."

Toussaint cast Ariane a defiant look, then went on gruffly. "She was not an evil woman, no matter what the world might say of her. If—if only she could have been persuaded to abandon the conjuring and all her mad ambitions. But she paid a terrible price for all her scheming in the end, didn't she?"

"Yes, I suppose she did," Ariane said softly, remembering Renard's description of his grandmother's terrible death.

The old man's eyes filled with tears. No matter how she felt about Melusine, Ariane could not resist reaching out to give Toussaint's hand a gentle squeeze.

Blinking hard, he returned to grooming his horse with a renewed briskness. "After what happened with Lucy, I was none too keen on Justice ever having anything more to do with any sort of magic. Despite Lucy's prediction, I especially didn't like the idea of him seeking to marry you . . . another wise woman. You may not care to hear this, milady, but you have much in common with my Lucy."

Ariane bridled, but Toussaint hastened to add, "Oh, I don't mean with regards to the dark magic. Unlike Lucy, you wisely eschewed all of that. But in another respect you are both much the same, fiercely proud and independent women and none too eager to ever submit your will or heart to any man."

"It is not an easy thing for a woman to surrender her entire life and happiness into another's keeping," Ariane said.

"It is none too easy for a man either," Toussaint retorted. "But you were good for Justice. You brought him back to himself and I don't think he was entirely bad for you either."

"No, he wasn't. He saved my life and that of my sisters, many times." But Ariane discovered it was not Renard's riding to the rescue that most filled her thoughts, but memories of the afternoon she had spent in his arms, that soul-deep connection she had felt between them. How was it possible for a man at once to make you feel so safe and secure and as though another part of you had been set soaring free?

She was aware that Toussaint was watching her. He said hesitantly, "I wish you would do me one favor, milady."

"What is that?"

"If you cannot ever bring yourself to forgive him for his deceit and trust him again, don't torture him by letting him wait and hope. Send back his ring. Will you promise me that?"

To return the ring would be the fair and just thing to do, but as she nodded her agreement, Ariane felt as though it was the most difficult promise she had ever made.

※ ※ ※

ARIANE KNELT DOWN BY THE TRUNK AT THE FOOT OF HER BED, HER mind full of her recent conversation with Toussaint, her heart in turmoil. She did not know what she was going to do, but she felt a need to at least see the ring that had bound her to Renard.

She popped open the lid of the trunk and tensed. Her linens, her shifts, all those garments she had left so carefully folded were in disarray as though someone had been pawing through them. Perhaps Gabrielle had been seeking to borrow something, although that explanation made little sense. Everything Gabrielle owned was far finer than Ariane's.

Uneasily, Ariane began to refold and straighten things as she searched for the pouch in which she had put the ring. She felt considerable relief when she spotted the leather pocket until she snatched it up.

The pouch felt flat and empty. Undoing the drawstring, she turned it over and shook it, but nothing dropped out into her trembling hand. Her heart gave an anxious thud and she immediately began rooting through the other things in the trunk. Perhaps somehow the ring had dropped out of the pouch.

Even as she mounted her frantic search, Ariane had a sickened sense of loss. Soon everything was scattered on the floor, the trunk entirely empty. She sank back on her heels, no longer able to deny it. The ring was gone and unfortunately there was only one person she could imagine who might have taken it.

Scrambling to her feet, Ariane marched grimly down the hall in search of her sister. Gabrielle was in her own bedchamber, perched upon the window seat.

She was staring moodily out the window when Ariane entered. But whatever unhappy thoughts had been consuming her, Gabrielle was quick to straighten, holding out her hand and saying over brightly, "Oh, Ariane, only look at how smooth my skin is. Strange as it may be, I think the Dark Queen's poison may actually have improved—"

"What have you done with it, Gabrielle?" Ariane demanded.

"What I have done with what?" Gabrielle asked in surprise.

"With the ring Renard gave me. I cannot find it anywhere."

"And what makes you suppose I would have it?"

"Because you have been urging me to get rid of the ring forever," Ariane went on, desperately trying to probe her sister's eyes. "Please tell me you haven't thrown it down the well or—or melted it."

"I haven't touched the blasted thing." Gabrielle flounced to her feet with all the dignity of an affronted duchess. But her haughty manner was diminished when she added, "Oh, I admit that there were times that I did *think* of stealing the ring and dis-posing of it, but I wouldn't do that anymore."

"Because Renard saved you from the poison?"

"No. Because you have been so cross and wretched without your ogre, I declare I am ready to send for the man myself. I don't even care if he is Melusine's grandson. It could be very use-ful to have someone who knows a bit about dark magic in the family."

At any other time, Ariane would have been tempted to re-prove her sister for that last remark. But Gabrielle's sincere de-nial only increased her anxiety.

"I am sorry for accusing you," she said. "But if you didn't take it, then who did?"

"How the devil should I—" Gabrielle began, but she must have taken in the full measure of Ariane's distress, because she stopped and wrapped her arm comfortingly around Ariane in-stead.

"Don't fret, Airy. I am sure the ring is still there in your trunk. You just haven't looked properly."

"No, I did. It is obvious that someone has been going through my things and whoever it was took the ring."

Gabrielle frowned. "Who would do such a thing? All of our servants are completely to be trusted and we have not had any strangers prowling through the house."

"Yes, we have," a small voice piped up from behind them.

They turned to find Miri silhouetted in the doorway, her gown damp and muddied as though she had just tramped the en-tire way across the island. Gabrielle immediately began scolding.

"Great heavens! What have you been doing, Miribelle?"

"I—I was out, trying to—to—"

"To do what? Catch a chill in the rain or track half the island back to our house? You never—"

Ariane cut Gabrielle off, her gaze focused on Miri's pale face. The girl looked overcome with misery, a mingling of fear, guilt, and shame chasing through her eyes. "Miri, what is it? What is wrong?" Ariane reached out to her little sister, gently taking Miri's hand in hers. The child's fingers felt so cold. She allowed Ariane to draw her farther into the room, but she completely refused to meet Ariane's eyes.

Ariane placed her fingers beneath her little sister's chin, forcing the child to look up. "Miri, do you know something about my ring?"

Miri cast her a look of such utter wretchedness that Ariane's heart ached for her.

"Yes," she whispered. "I think it is possible Simon took it."

"That witch-hunter boy?" Gabrielle exclaimed. "But he has been nowhere near the house."

"Yes, he was. I—I brought him here the day you got sick."

Gently pushing her trembling little sister down onto a low stool, Ariane hunkered down in front of her.

"Now, Miri, please tell me what has been going on."

Miri's lip wobbled. "You are going to be so angry with me. Y-you will hate me."

"No, I won't," Ariane promised, tenderly patting her little sister's cheek. "There is nothing you could ever do that would cause me to stop loving you. Now tell me."

Miri drew in a tremulous breath, then the entire story came tumbling out. How she had been helping Simon to hide ever since the night of the raid, how she thought she had persuaded him to abandon his terrible trade of witch-hunting.

"S-so I brought him to the house to talk to you. He was so afraid of you using your ring to fetch Renard, but I told him you weren't wearing it, that it was in your trunk."

"Oh, Miri," Gabrielle groaned. "You little fool."

"Hush, Gabrielle," Ariane said sharply, but Miri spoke up.

"No, she is right. I was a fool to trust him. I should never have left him alone in your room, but then Gabby fell so ill and I went to her and e-everything was such confusion. By the time I went back to your room, Simon was gone and I haven't been able to find him anywhere since."

Tears trickled down Miri's cheeks. "It never occurred to me that he had taken your ring until I heard you and Gabby talking just now. I—I am so sorry, Ariane. It is just that I—I liked him so much and I thought he liked me. Necromancer tried to warn me, but I wouldn't listen."

"Let that be a lesson to you, Miribelle Cheney. Never trust a man over your cat." But Gabrielle accompanied these sharp words by swooping in to envelop Miri in a hug.

"Never mind, little sister," she said fiercely. "Don't you cry over that wretched boy. He isn't worth a single tear."

Miri buried her woebegone face against Gabrielle's shoulder, the child suffering from her first heartbreak and sense of betrayal, bitter emotions Gabrielle understood all too well.

Ariane longed to wrap her arms protectively around her sisters, but she was forced to turn her attention to the more alarming question of the missing ring.

"So if Simon did take the ring," she mused aloud. "What would he do with it?"

"Do you have any doubt on that score?" Gabrielle demanded. "He'd scurry back with it at once to his precious master."

When Miri gave a muffled sob at her words, she held the girl tighter.

Ariane frowned. "Yes, assuming Le Vis is still alive. But what good would the ring do either one of them? They would have no idea what to do with it unless—"

Ariane froze. Unless they took the ring to Catherine. There was no telling what she might be able to do with such a dangerous weapon.

But there was no sense terrifying herself by conjuring up some alarming scenario. The important thing was to get word to Renard, warn him at once. Leaving Gabrielle to comfort Miri, Ariane hastened downstairs, preparing to send for Toussaint.

As she descended to the great hall, she was startled to discover she had a visitor. Marie Claire paced anxiously, looking far from her usual placid self.

The older woman looked exceedingly grave as she embraced Ariane. Ariane did not even bother with the pretense of greeting. She blurted out, "My God, Marie, what is it?"

"Word at last. From Paris." Marie Claire handed Ariane a folded note, her mouth so grim that Ariane did not even need to read her eyes to know that the tidings must be dire.

She hesitated to take the note, uncertain how much more bad news she could handle. But she steeled her spine, accepting the paper and unfolding it while Marie Claire explained, "That message arrived by carrier pigeon this morning written in our own code, which I fancied so secret. That is my translation of it."

Ariane anxiously scanned the ink lines, written in Marie Claire's elegant hand, but as Ariane read further, it was obvious that the words, icy, arrogant, menacing, emanated from another quarter entirely.

Greetings to my dear Marie Claire and the Lady of Faire Isle,

Much as I have enjoyed our recent intrigues, there comes a time when all games must end. I have come into possession of a certain ring, which has enabled me to lure the Comte de Renard to Paris. He will soon be in my grasp, far sooner than you will ever be able to prevent him from walking into my trap. Never fear. At this juncture, all I intend to do is lodge him comfortably in the Bastille.

I believe you can guess what my price will be for releasing him. I want those gloves, my dear Ariane. You will bring them to me or else your Renard will suffer a far worse fate than the one I meted out to Louise

Lavalle and Hermoine Pechard. My good friend Le Vis
would be quite astonished. It seems that witches don't
float after all.

Trusting that we will bring this distressing enmity
between us to a satisfactory conclusion.

The note was signed simply . . . *Catherine.*

Ariane let the parchment fall from her hands. She raised her
eyes to Marie Claire and saw her own stricken expression mir-
rored there.

"Louise and Madame Pechard—"

"Dead, by this account," she said hoarsely. "You were right.
I should never have sent Louise to spy." Marie Claire rallied with
a wan smile. "But I have many days ahead to don my hair shirt
and do penance with my rosary beads. Right now we must decide what is to be done about Renard."

"What is there to decide? I must go to Paris."

"We should not be hasty. Perhaps this is all a hoax."

"I have other reasons to believe it is true." Ariane swiftly
told Marie Claire about the missing ring.

Marie Claire continued to look dubious. "But could Catherine use the ring to summon him, by pretending she was you?
Could Renard be that easily fooled?"

"I don't know," Ariane murmured. "But even if he wasn't, if
someone else used my ring, he would assume that I was in danger."

"And go charging to your rescue even if he risked walking
into a trap?"

"Yes, that is exactly what he would do. Trust me, Marie, I
know the man so well—" Ariane stumbled to a halt, realizing
what she was saying. She did know Renard. His strength, his
courage, his willingness to die for her, and yes, how much he
loved her.

What a fool she had been to have ever sent him away. Pray God she would have time enough to mend things with him. But she needed to leave for Paris and at once.

Marie Claire trailed after her. "And so you will walk into a trap as well."

"If I must to save him. Facing Catherine is the only way to end all this, Marie. Perhaps it always has been."

"Then I am going with you."

"No, Marie. If something does go wrong, you will be needed here on Faire Isle."

"But you cannot propose going alone."

"She won't. I am going with her." Gabrielle's voice rang out. "And me!"

Ariane raised her eyes to the musician's gallery, dismayed to discover that her sisters had been standing there, listening. Gabrielle marched down the stairs with Miri trailing determinedly behind.

Ariane hastened to the bottom of the steps to head them off. "No, Gabrielle. I know what you would say, but it is utterly out of the question. There is no way I will allow—"

"This time you have no say in the matter." Gabrielle cut her off ruthlessly. "Didn't you promise after what happened with the gloves that you would stop treating both Miri and me like children? We are your sisters, Ariane, and I am sure Maman meant for us all to look out for one another."

"And if you don't let us come, we will just follow you," Miri chimed in.

Ariane glanced from one sister to the other, Gabrielle's lovely patrician features so different from Miri's ethereal countenance. But never had the resemblance between them been so marked as they stared at Ariane, chins cocked at a stubborn angle, their eyes filled with steely resolve.

Ariane made another effort to protest, but Gabrielle seized

her by the shoulders. "You listen to me, Ariane Cheney. Out of the three of us, you appear to be the only one who has any chance of finding happiness with the man who you love. I am even willing to concede that the comte deserves you."

She added with a glimmering smile, "Well, *almost.* Now are you going to waste time arguing with us or are we going to Paris to rescue your ogre?"

Ariane's throat constricted. Moved beyond words, all Ariane could do was nod and envelop first Miri and then Gabrielle in a fierce hug, choking out her gratitude.

The girl endured it for a few seconds, but as ever was quick to wriggle free.

"You don't have to thank *me.* My motives for wanting to go to Paris are not entirely unselfish."

Ariane regarded her sister with a mingling of disappointment and dismay. Surely Gabrielle could not be thinking about her own ambitions at a time like this.

After some obvious struggle with herself, Gabrielle blurted out, "It's Remy. We have had not one word about him since he left Faire Isle and I—I—Damn it! I will never be able to rest easy until I know what has happened to the noble fool."

Gabrielle cast Ariane a defiant look. It was obvious that she cared for Nicolas Remy far more deeply than she would ever be willing to admit.

"Of course, I know it is perfectly stupid of me," she went on gruffly. "Paris is a large city and the man is a fugitive." Her lower lip trembled. "I daresay we will never be able to find him."

Ariane tenderly brushed back a stray lock of Gabrielle's golden hair.

"We will find him, dearest," she promised. "And we will make certain he is safe."

※ ※ ※

MOONLIGHT SHIMMERED OVER THE LOUVRE, THE PALACE ETCHED against the night sky like a fairy-tale castle, light and music pouring from the windows of the main salon, where the reception for the newly married royal couple was still taking place.

Outside the gates of the palace, the street was thronged with Parisians celebrating the wedding of the lovely Princess Margot to Henry of Navarre. Most of the common folk were glad of any excuse for revelry, but there was a marked tension about the celebrations. Despite its magnificence the wedding had not been popular, the alliance between Catholics and Huguenots an uneasy one.

Or perhaps the unease was all inside of him, Remy thought as he stared desperately up at the walls of the palace. He had pushed himself to the brink of collapse to return to Paris, anticipating all manner of disaster. What he had never expected was to arrive in time to find himself in the midst of a wedding festival.

He had been so convinced that the Dark Queen had never meant for this marriage to take place, that she had meant to murder his king. Finding Henry alive and well and a bridegroom had left Remy shaken and confused, but more suspicious and fearful than ever.

He had marched boldly into the palace, determined to warn Henry, even if it cost him his life. Remy had fully expected to be arrested or slain on the spot, but the Dark Queen had proved too clever for that.

She had greeted Remy with a warmth that had sickened him, scolding him for being absent for so long. Where had the bold Scourge been? Everyone, including herself, had been so worried about him.

Where had he been? Fleeing for his life from her soldiers, Remy had bluntly declared before the entire court. But Catherine's performance had been entirely too much for him.

She had gasped, paled, insisted that it was all a dreadful mistake, that the men who had attacked him would be severely punished. And what could he do? He could hardly call the Dowager Queen of France a liar, especially when he had no proof.

Only he had seen the sly look in Catherine's eyes that had warned him she was far from done with him, that despite how she smiled upon Navarre and called him her dear son, this marriage was nothing but a farce.

Remy had had no chance to speak to Henry alone. He had drawn aside Admiral Coligny and several other of the king's highest-ranking ministers, trying to convince them the king was in grave danger. But it was as Remy had always feared. No one would believe him.

As he gazed back at the palace, feeling helpless and frustrated, Remy felt one of his brother officers clap him on the shoulders, urging him away from the Louvre and back to their lodgings in the town.

"But we can't just leave our king surrounded by his enemies," Remy said, making one last desperate effort to convince his companions. "We have to get him out of there."

"Get him out?" young Tavers exclaimed, his sandy brows lifting in astonishment. "His Majesty has only been wed a day ago. He's scarcely had time to enjoy the pleasures of his marriage bed."

"Marriage bed! It is more likely to be his deathbed and likely the rest of ours as well," Remy said heatedly.

"Ah, please lad," old Admiral Coligny groaned. "No more of that nonsense about Queen Catherine being a witch, plotting to murder us all."

"It is not nonsense, sir. If you had seen and learned what I did this summer on Faire Isle—"

"You should have never set one foot there." This time it was Remy's friend, Captain Devereaux who interrupted, the burly man shaking his shaggy brown head. "It is said to be a passing strange place, the Faire Isle."

"No doubt our good Remy has been sleeping with the fairies," Tavers chimed in.

"Or was bewitched by some blue-eyed Circe," the old Admiral said, his eyes twinkling.

Remy was annoyed to feel the red sting his cheeks, the Admiral's words perilously close to the truth.

"I tell you what the trouble is," Tavers said, wagging one finger at Remy. "He cannot bear the thought of a truce with the Catholics. Some men simply aren't fashioned for peace."

"Don't worry, Remy." Devereaux clapped one huge hand on Remy's shoulder. "We'll find you another war, m'boy."

"Damn it, Dev. I am as sick of fighting as you, but—"

"I think we need to domesticate our Scourge. Find him a wife," the Admiral declared.

The two others agreed and soon they were all jocularly putting forth suggestions for a possible bride. Only Devereaux seemed to realize the depth of Remy's fear and frustration. He said soothingly, "Come along now. You simply need a flagon of wine and a good meal. You hardly ate anything back there at the palace. Anyone would have thought you were afraid of being poisoned."

"I wonder why," Remy muttered.

"Come back with me to my lodgings. Claire has not clapped eyes on you for an age and you have yet to see our newest offspring, your namesake. Mind you, the lad has such a set of lungs on him, he keeps the entire house awake. We've taken to calling him the wee Scourge."

Remy attempted to smile. Perhaps they were right and he had let his imagination run wild, conjuring up dangers that had never existed. Perhaps he had been bewitched and everything that had happened on Faire Isle had been nothing more than a strange dream.

Except that those fleeting hours he had spent with Gabrielle seemed more real to him than the entire rest of his life. His return to Paris, the marriage of his king, his friends' sanguine belief that this heralded a new age of peace and tolerance for the Huguenots—that was the dream.

And one from which Remy feared they were destined to be violently awakened.

Chapter Twenty-three

ARIANE GAZED WEARILY OUT THE WINDOW OF HER CHAMBER at the inn, staring at the pale ribbon of road as though she could somehow dissolve the miles remaining to Paris. She would have pressed on farther if Toussaint had not dissuaded her. Night was falling, the old man had argued, and they were all fair dropping from the saddle. The horses had been ridden hard enough for one day and they would never reach Paris if one of the poor brutes pulled up lame.

All sensible arguments, but Ariane chafed at the further delay. She had prayed that they might overtake Renard before he reached Paris, but there had never been any hope of that. Ariane had always marveled at Renard's stamina and by what reports they gleaned of him, he was traveling like a man possessed. Barely pausing to eat or sleep, hiring fresh mounts so that he could keep pressing on.

There was no way Ariane or her sisters could match that

killing pace. Of the three of them, only Miri was a skilled rider. But even she was showing signs of extreme exhaustion. This evening, she and Gabrielle had scarcely remained awake long enough to take some supper before collapsing upon the bed.

Sleep eluded Ariane, bone tired as she was, and Toussaint was equally restless. She could see the old man moving about in the stableyard below, long after there was any need for him to do so.

Toussaint had insisted that he and several of the comte's retainers accompany the Cheneys on the journey to Paris and Ariane had put up little argument. The road could be a dangerous place. She was glad of Toussaint's escort, although for much of the journey she had been obliged to listen to his grumbling about Renard's pigheadedness, the lad's reckless folly in always charging off on his own this way.

All this fierce bluster barely concealed the old man's very real fear for the fate of his cousin. If the Dark Queen had succeeded in luring him into her trap, Toussaint drew comfort from the fact that Justice was no longer a humble peasant, but a comte, a powerful nobleman. The queen would not dare to simply dispose of him as though he was someone of no importance.

Ariane had said nothing when Toussaint advanced this opinion. She wished she could have derived consolation from such a belief. But if Catherine had had no compunction about murdering a queen, she was unlikely to have any qualms about destroying Renard. In some of her darker moments of this endless journey, Ariane despaired that Catherine might already have done so.

"Uhhh."

Ariane turned away from the window at the sound and crossed anxiously over to the large four-poster bed. Gabrielle was fast asleep, but Miri was stirring restively.

Ariane drew the coverlet more snugly over her. Miri appeared so worn out and her nightmares had been getting worse ever since they'd left home. She smoothed back her sister's fall of white-blond hair. Her sister still seemed so much the child. It was hard to remember that Miri would be thirteen in five days' time, Ariane reckoned up on her fingers. Because this was August 23, St. Bartholomew's Eve.

※ ※ ※

THE ROYAL APARTMENT WAS HEAVY WITH MIST ROLLING IN FROM THE Seine, the stars and moon blotted out by a blanket of cloud. St. Bartholomew's Eve . . . a good night for creating a few more martyrs, Catherine thought with a cynical twist of her lips.

She had always found it strange to honor a man simply because he'd been fool enough to get himself skinned alive for the sake of his God. Not very clever of old Bartholomew, but Catherine had little patience for saints and martyrs.

The fools never seemed to have the wit to realize that religion was more a matter of politics than anything else. Personally she didn't give a damn that the Huguenots refused to hear mass and preferred the Book of Common Prayer. She only cared that they had become a threat to her power.

Catherine placed the small iron burner on the window ledge. Using a candle, she lit the incense, the sweet, acrid scent mingling with the dank smell coming in off the river.

"What are you doing, Maman?" her son Charles called out anxiously.

"There are noxious odors drifting in from the Seine tonight. I am merely perfuming the air."

Smiling, she turned to face the cluster of men gathered in the king's private apartment for this secret council meeting. His Majesty's most high-ranking advisors, at least those of the Catholic persuasion.

Many of them were Catherine's political enemies and deeply mistrusted her, especially the handsome duc de Guise. But tonight she and the arrogant young nobleman were temporarily united in a common cause. De Guise's father had been killed by the Huguenots and he had long thirsted for revenge.

Then there was her younger son, the duc d'Anjou. Despite his effeminate appearance, a pearl earring dangling from one ear, he fancied himself a soldier. He was eager for any action that might bring him fame, capable of any cruelty.

The only hitch to her plans was the king himself, as Catherine had known he would be. As Charles listened to his advisors' arguments, he plucked nervously at the thin beard that did little to conceal the weakness of his chin. His receding hairline made him appear older than his years. His bloodshot eyes spoke of a man with a tenuous grip on his sanity.

The courtiers fell back as Catherine rustled forward to grasp Charles by the hand, making it seem like an affectionate motherly gesture. It stopped him from biting his knuckles, an irritating habit of his when he grew agitated.

"My liege, you must heed your subjects. There has never been a better time to strike. The wedding celebrations are at an end. The guests will soon start leaving to return home, but right now we have every important Huguenot leader here in Paris, within our grasp."

There were murmurs of assent from de Guise and the others, but Charles shook his head vehemently.

"The Huguenots are my subjects, too, Maman. We have just given our sister in marriage to my cousin, Henry of Navarre. A marriage of your arranging to bring about a truce with the Protestants. Have you forgotten that?"

Of course, I arranged it, you fool. The better to lure our enemies to Paris. But Catherine suppressed the impatient thought.

Charles's fingers twitched as he removed them from her grasp. "To attack the Huguenots now would be the worst sort of betrayal."

"It is they who will betray us," Catherine said. "They plot against Your Grace even at this moment. Do you realize what large numbers of these heretics are within our city gates? If they chose to storm the palace, they could easily overthrow you, murder every Catholic in Paris."

The king raised his knuckles to his mouth, backing away from her. "That would never happen. They would never attack me. Admiral Coligny would not allow it. He is an honorable man and I have been learning much from him."

"But the admiral has been gravely wounded, laid low by an assassin," de Guise reminded the king.

Catherine glared at the young man. An assassin she was certain the duc had hired, and he had not even had the wit to engage a man with aim good enough to finish the job. The damned arrogant fool had nearly ruined everything. The attempt on the admiral's life had spread such fear and unease through the Huguenot ranks, it was a wonder they were not fleeing Paris in droves.

Catherine cupped Charles's face between her hands. "My dear one, don't you understand? The Huguenots blame us for the attack on the admiral. They want their revenge. They must be stopped.

"What better night to rid ourselves of these heretics than on the Feast of St. Bartholomew?" she intoned piously. "The holy martyr will surely look with favor on our righteous cause."

Charles's eyes darted frantically about the room, seeking to avoid her compelling gaze. He grasped hold of her wrists to thrust her away from him. "N-no, the admiral would never allow his followers to hurt me. He has treated me with such respect and kindness. L-like—like a father."

And what of your mother? Catherine wanted to demand coldly. The woman who has worked so tirelessly to keep the crown safely upon your mad head?

But there was no reasoning with Charles. Catherine had known there wouldn't be. That was why she had prepared so carefully for this moment. Leaving the duc d' Anjou to try to reason with his brother, she returned to the window, removing the vial of murky liquid from the bosom of her gown.

Her heart beat with excitement. Brewing a miasma was the most difficult of black magic to perform. The fumes were calculated to weaken the strongest of wills, loosen the bonds of reason, heighten the darkest of emotions, hatred, fear, anger, and lust.

Catherine had never attempted such a difficult potion before. She uncorked the vial carefully. The odor was rank but the incense would help to disguise the smell. She surreptitiously added a few drops to the incense burner.

Only a few. The miasma was excessively powerful. The incense hissed, the smoke issuing from it taking on a slightly darker cast. Catherine backed away, applying a dab of ointment beneath her nose to protect herself from the fumes.

Charles and his advisors were too absorbed by their debate to notice the subtle change in the air. But she could tell the moment the fumes began to have their effect. Faces grew more flushed, voices more angry and belligerent. The impact was strongest on the man with the weakest hold on sanity. Charles began to sweat profusely, his pupils reduced to mere pinpricks.

He gasped in a deep breath, his face contorting in a terrible grimace. He clutched at his head as though his skull were about to split, and let loose a shriek that startled everyone to silence.

Shoving de Guise and his brother out of the way, he rushed at Catherine, spittle flying from his lips. "Go on then if that is what you wish," he screamed at her. "Kill them. Kill them all. Every Huguenot in the city. Every man, woman, and child so there is no one left to reproach me when the bloody deed is done."

He raised his fist and Catherine flinched, flinging up one hand to protect herself, forgetting she still clutched the vial in her hand. Charles swung out wildly, knocking the bottle from her grasp, sending it flying out the open window. The glass shattered on the cobbles below.

Sobbing hysterically, the king fled from the chamber. Heart thudding with apprehension, Catherine leaned out the window. She had no idea what the impact of the miasma might be, released full force. She watched in horrified fascination as a large green cloud mushroomed in the courtyard. Fortunately, the breeze seemed to be dispersing it, blowing the fumes away from the palace.

Catherine drew back in, pulling the window closed. Composing herself, she turned to face the men gathered behind her, still a little stunned by the king's erratic behavior.

"You heard the king's command," she said. "You must obey him. Summon your retainers and coordinate your assault. None of the Huguenots must escape, especially not Admiral Coligny or the Scourge. Let the ringing of the bells in the tower of St. Germaine L'Auxerois signal the attack."

De Guise's lips pulled back in a savage smile and Anjou gave a wild laugh. None of the men needed much urging from her. They rushed for the door, their eyes glazed with the lust for the kill . . .

※ ※ ※

MIRI MOANED, WRITHING AND THRASHING SO WILDLY SHE WAS IN danger of tumbling from the bed. Ariane bent over her, gripping her shoulders, trying to draw her little sister back from the throes of her nightmare.

"Miri! Miri, wake up." Ariane gave her a gentle shake, but to her alarm, it had no effect on the girl. She was drenched in sweat, half-sobbing in her sleep.

Gabrielle struggled up onto one elbow, rubbing her eyes and muttering sleepily. "What . . . devil is going on?"

But as she caught sight of Ariane struggling with Miri, Gabrielle snapped fully awake.

"She's having one of her nightmares," Ariane said, "but I can't get her to wake."

Gabrielle seized hold of Miri and shook her roughly. "Miri!"

Miri's eyes flew open. She gave a shuddering gasp. Clawing away from both Gabrielle and Ariane, she sat bolt upright, her eyes wild and unfocused. Before Ariane could restrain her, she scrambled off the bottom of the bed.

Her face white and pinched with terror, she stumbled over to the window. "Dear God," she panted. "They—they are coming. Men with torches, knives, swords."

Ariane rushed over to Miri with Gabrielle hard at her heels. Ariane attempted to gather Miri into her arms. "Shhh, dearest. There is no one out there. You are safe here with me and Gabrielle."

Miri struggled frantically away from her, cowering back against the wall. "N-no. They're coming . . . the m-murderers."

Gabrielle captured Miri's face between her hands, forcing her to look at her. "Miri, listen to me. You were having another of your bad dreams."

"N-not another. The same one." Miri clutched at the front of Gabrielle's nightgown. "And it was all clear this time. The witch . . . the Dark Queen, she brewed up some terrible potion. Only she dropped it and it broke, spreading this terrible green mist. And the bells—the bells started to ring and people were going mad.

"Killing Huguenots like R-remy. All of them, the women, the children, even the—the little b-babies."

With a wrenching sob, Miri flung her arms around Gabrielle's neck, clinging to her. Gabrielle stroked her little sister's hair while casting an uneasy look at Ariane.

"What is she talking about, Ariane. What does it all mean?"

Ariane believed she finally understood the significance of Miri's dream. Louise Lavalle had been convinced Catherine was plotting something truly vile. But surely not even the Dark Queen would dare release the dark power of . . . of a *miasma*?

Ariane gazed in the direction of Paris, wondering what terror might soon unfold, endangering not only Remy and his countrymen, but also Renard.

"We had better rouse Toussaint," she said grimly. "And set out for Paris at once. We have to try to stop Catherine."

"It's too late," Miri wept against Ariane's shoulder. "I know it is. They are already ringing the bells . . ."

* * *

RENARD DRAGGED HIMSELF OUT OF BED, GROPING FOR FLINT AND tinder to light a candle. The soft glow spilled over the bare trappings of his room at the Half Moon Inn. It was a warm night, a heavy mist curling over the city, but he regretted leaving the window open. The incessant pealing of those church bells was damned irritating.

He slammed the window closed and rubbed his eyes, raw from lack of sleep. But he'd already rested longer than he had intended since his exhausted arrival in Paris early this evening.

He needed to stay awake, decide what the devil he was going to do. Renard had been so convinced it was Ariane calling him, that she was in desperate trouble, but the closer he'd come to Paris, the more he'd begun to suspect he'd been cleverly tricked.

It seemed impossible, for that would mean that someone else had got hold of the ring, someone who knew how to use it. And there was only one person it could possibly be, the Dark Queen.

But how and when could the de Medici witch have seized possession of the ring? And did that mean she had Ariane as well? Renard cursed himself now for not taking the time to go to Faire Isle first before tearing off for Paris. But his mind had been in such a feverish haze, it was as though he'd been bewitched.

The last message, purportedly from Ariane, had reached him shortly after he'd arrived in Paris. The voice, silken soft in his ear, had sounded so much like Ariane except for one thing.

"Where are you, my love? I am being held prisoner in the Louvre. Oh, Justin, please come for me at once."

Justin? Renard's suspicions had hardened into certainty. He'd been tempted to reply, play along with the mysterious voice, follow its instructions. But in the end, he'd thought better of it. "Justin" wasn't going anywhere near that palace until he had a better idea what the blazes was going on.

Sinking down on the edge of his bed, Renard dragged on his boots. There was one person who might have some answers for him. The taproom had been full of gossip this evening, terse voices discussing recent events in Paris. The marriage of the Princess Margot to the heretic Navarre, the recent assassination attempt on Admiral Coligny, the return of the Scourge to Paris.

So the gallant Captain Remy had made it back to Paris and by all reports he had not managed to get himself killed yet. He was even installed in lodgings not far from this inn. There had been a point when Renard wouldn't have minded throttling Remy himself. Although he had a grudging admiration for the captain's courage and sense of honor, Renard had resented the danger that Remy had brought to Ariane's doorstep.

And yes, he was obliged to admit, he had been a trifle jealous of Ariane's regard for the young man. But if anyone could help him discover what the Dark Queen might be plotting now or where Ariane might be, it was Nicolas Remy.

Pausing only long enough to splash some water on his face, Renard gathered up his sword and cloak. As he descended the stairs to the taproom, he caught a flash of light through the windows.

The streets seemed to be full of an inordinate amount of activity tonight, mounted men clattering by on horseback. Just as strangely, the taproom was nearly deserted except for a waiter wiping down the tables and an old man nursing a bottle of wine. A cold feeling of unease stole through Renard.

There was a palpable tension in the air. Renard tried to dismiss it as the product of exhaustion or imagination. But that was one of the better things he'd learned from his grandmother.

"We are not so different from the beasts of the earth, Justice. We have the same uncanny instincts that warn us that something is amiss, that danger is approaching. But most men are fools and simply dismiss these feelings. Learn to trust yours."

The back of his neck was definitely prickling. Renard hoped that he had indeed come to Paris on a fool's errand. That wherever Ariane was tonight, she was miles from here.

As he stalked toward the door, the landlord of the inn suddenly came bursting out of the kitchens. To Renard's surprise, the portly innkeeper rushed forward to intercept him.

"M-monsieur le Comte." The little man sketched him a bow. "Surely you—you are not thinking of going out tonight."

Renard frowned at him. The man was so nervous, his palms were sweating. "Yes, why the devil not?"

"Well—well, be-because. This is Paris. The streets can be very dangerous at night."

"I am a goodly sized fellow," Renard replied. "I can look out for myself and surely this is one of the better quarters of the city. We are not that far from the royal palace."

With a friendly nod, he attempted to step past the innkeeper, but to his annoyance, the man continued to bar his path.

"Are—are you a good Catholic?"

Renard studied the man through narrowed eyes. What the

devil did that have to do with anything? His grandmother had
been a witch. He had been raised more as a pagan than anything else. But as the Comte de Renard, he knew his duties to his
people.

"I hear the mass. I observe holy days," he replied curtly.

"G-good. Then if you insist upon going out, you'd better
wear this." The landlord produced a white armband, which he
attempted to tie around Renard's arm.

When Renard balked, the landlord beseeched him. "Please,
monsieur. It may save your life."

The man was so desperately earnest, Renard submitted, allowing him to knot the white scarf about his forearm. As he did
so, Renard sought to probe the landlord's eyes and what he read
there chilled his blood.

Renard needed to find Nicolas Remy and find him quickly . . .

⚜ ⚜ ⚜

REMY DASHED FROM THE HOUSE INTO THE DARKENED STREET, HIS
sword clutched in his hand. The Huguenot family who'd given
him lodging huddled in the doorway, Monsieur Berne, his wife,
and three young daughters. Their faces were tense and apprehensive as, like Remy, they listened to the distant, relentless tolling of
the bells.

Remy thought it was coming from the direction of the tower
of St. Germaine L'Auxerois, a church near the Louvre. But what
the deuce did it mean? There was something about the peal of
the bells at this late hour that resonated more of warning . . . or
a call to arms. Remy's hand tightened on the hilt of his sword.
He'd been on edge, even more alert than usual since he'd received word of the assassination attempt on Admiral Coligny.

As he stepped another pace into the street, other sounds carried to his ears from the next square, shouts, the clatter of horses'
hooves, and a loud crack like . . . like gunfire.

Remy's gut knotted. "Get back inside and bar the door," he snapped at the Berne family.

The women hastened to obey, but Monsieur Berne remained frozen on the threshold.

"C-captain Remy," the merchant gestured with a shaking finger, alerting Remy to the shadowy figure of the man who rushed through the gap between the houses across the street.

Remy raised his sword, positioning himself protectively in front of the doorway as the stranger approached. But the man gasped, half-staggering the last few steps. As light from the house spilled over his features, Remy drew in a sharp breath.

It was Tavers, although Remy scarcely recognized him. His sandy hair was matted with the blood that streaked down one side of his face. He stumbled forward. Only the strength of Remy's arm kept him from crashing to his knees.

"Remy. G-god help us," the young soldier choked, clutching at the front of Remy's doublet.

"What the devil is going on, Jacques?" Remy demanded. "What's happening?"

"The d-duc de Guise's men. They've finished what the assassin started. They—they've dragged the admiral from his bed. K-killed him. Put his head on a pike."

Remy compressed his lips, more grieved than surprised. He'd been to call upon the old man only that afternoon, made one last desperate attempt to warn him. Although weak from his wound, the admiral had pressed Remy's hand and continued to insist, *"No, no, the attack on me was the work of one religious fanatic. The king will get to the bottom of the affair and see that the proper punishment is meted out. Charles is—is an earnest young man, eager to learn. I—I have acquired great influence with him."*

The old warrior was so anxious for peace, he'd deluded himself, Remy thought sadly. No one controlled mad Charles of France. No one but the Dark Queen.

"Come on," Remy said. "Let's get you inside." But as he looped Tavers's arm around his neck and tried to urge him toward the house, the wounded man balked.

"N-no, Remy. You don't understand," he panted. "Catholic lords . . . going on rampage. Killing every important Huguenot they can find."

"Sweet Jesu," Monsieur Berne exclaimed.

"Especially w-want you, Remy. The Scourge. Are—are looking for you."

"Then let them find me," Remy snarled.

"No!" Tavers pawed at him desperately. "You must go—find Devereaux. Get to the palace. Protect the king."

Henry . . . Remy thought with a wave of black despair. The young king he'd been obliged to abandon at the Louvre, quartered in the very midst of their enemies. If the Dark Queen was bent upon destroying all the Huguenot leaders, Henry was likely already dead.

No. Tavers was right. If there was any chance at all that Henry still lived, Remy had to get to him, save his king or die trying.

Dragging Tavers into the house, Remy consigned him to the care of the merchant and his wife. Although the fear was naked in his eyes, Monsieur Berne maintained a dignified calm as he issued Remy terse instructions how to keep to the alleys, taking a shortcut to reach the stables where Remy had left his horse, not far from where Captain Devereaux had found quarters.

Remy paused only long enough to press Tavers's hand one last time before vanishing into the darkness. He tore along back streets, scrambling over fences, slipping between houses and shops, trying to move as swiftly and stealthily as he could, all the time aware of the infernal peal of the bells and other sounds as well, growing steadily louder. Shrieks, the clatter of hoofbeats on the cobbles, the pounding of running feet. In the distance Remy could make out the movement of shadowy figures, the flicker of torches. It was as though all Paris was awakening and pouring into the streets.

But as Remy emerged onto one of the main thoroughfares, he realized he was no longer in Paris. He'd detoured into hell. He drew up short at the terrible scene unfolding before his eyes, the red flare of torches illuminating the savage faces of men set beneath caps adorned with white crosses. Assassins armed with knives, clubs, swords, pistols, every conceivable weapon.

Doors were being battered in, shrieking women and wailing children being dragged from houses. These ruthless lords and their men were not merely seeking to destroy the leaders, but to murder every last Huguenot in Paris, every man, woman, and child.

The cobbles were already slick with blood, the very walls of the close-packed houses splashed red. The fallen and dying lay everywhere. Remy had seen death on the battlefield before but nothing to equal this mayhem. Bodies being hacked to pieces, limbs and heads being gleefully brandished.

It was as though some foul wind had spread a contagion of madness over the city. Sword clenched in his hand, Remy's every muscle tensed with the instinct to dive into the fray, to rush to the aid of his people. It was with difficulty that he checked himself, sought to remember that his first duty was to the king he'd sworn to protect.

There had been no rooms available at the Half Moon Inn when Remy had arrived in Paris, but Remy had been able to leave his mount stabled there. But as Remy braced himself to make a dash for it, he caught sight of a familiar burly figure. Captain Devereaux stood braced in the battered ruins of the door that led to his quarters. Snarling, he brandished his sword, laying about him, fending off some half-dozen attackers who sought to rush the house. Devereaux was a formidable fighter, but the fear he could inspire on the battlefield was as nothing to the ferocity he displayed defending his young family.

He cut down two of the assassins and turned on a third, never seeing the coward who crept up on his left, leveling the arquebus.

"Dev!" Remy roared, but he was too far away for his warning to be heard amidst the chaos.

The arquebus spit its deadly burst of fire. Devereaux's face blossomed red. He sagged to his knees, pitching face forward into the street.

All thoughts of his king forgotten, Remy lips curled back in a savage snarl. He plunged out of the shadows and raced forward.

Clutching her infant son to her breast, Devereaux's young bride screamed as she was dragged out of the house by two loutish attackers. Remy had to leap over Devereaux's body to reach her in time. With one stroke of his sword, he cut down the brute who was attempting to wrench the babe from Clare's arms. Whirling, he drove his steel through the stomach of her other attacker.

Dev's murderer sought frantically to reload his arquebus. Yanking his sword free, Remy slit the villain's throat.

Clare Devereaux had sunk to her knees, weeping over her husband's body. Young Nicolas's tiny fists curled in his mother's hair as the babe set up a lusty wail. Remy realized that if he was going to save his friend's wife and child, the Scourge was going to have to do something he'd never done in his life. Run from a fight.

Bending down, he caught hold of Clare's elbow. He had no time to be gentle. When she resisted him, he hauled her roughly to her feet.

"Come on. Move!" he growled, propelling her away from Dev's body. He hustled Clare back across the street, frightening off one attacker merely by brandishing his bloody sword. Knocking another man out of his way, an elderly priest.

He stumbled away from Remy, tears coursing down his withered face as he pleaded, "In heaven's name, stop this killing. This is not the way of our gentle Savior." But no one was listening, not even his fellow clerics, one of whom was using a wooden crucifix as his weapon.

As Remy shoved Clare toward the nearest alley, he became aware that he had acquired others seeking his protection. An old man, a frightened woman leading her two children by the hand, a tear-streaked young boy sobbing for his father.

"Captain Remy," the woman cried, and Remy realized he'd been recognized. They pressed close to him, looking as though they'd found salvation from their great hero, the Scourge.

Some hero when all he could do was herd them into the darkness of the alley. He felt like some bloody warrior shepherd trying to save his flock from an ever-increasing pack of wolves. His fellow Huguenots were not the only ones who had recognized him. He heard the shouts from the square behind him.

"It was the Scourge. I saw him. He went that way. Get him."

"Run!" Remy gave the boy a slight push, urging Clare and the rest of them forward. He forced his helpless band down a twisting maze of alleys and back streets, nudging them onward. But he knew they could not possibly maintain this pace. The old man was wheezing for breath, the others beginning to lag. And where the devil was he taking them anyway? Remy was hopelessly lost.

He led them down yet another alley, as the heavy pounding of feet behind them grew louder. Someone loosed off a shot that whizzed overhead, shattering the glass of an upper-story window. The old man sank to his knees. The woman collapsed, sobbing quietly, her daughters cowering near her, the young boy as well. Clare's footsteps flagged, her eyes glinting up at Remy with desperation. She cradled her infant son, the child's cry now little more than a thin wail.

"R-remy," she panted. "You could still get away and—and take my boy. Save him."

"No, Clare. Keep going. You can make it. Get the others

up. Try to find some empty building, some place where you can hide. I'll hold these villains off." He laid his hand against her cheek, trying to infuse some hope into her when he had so little left himself.

Remy spun about as the first of their pursuers hove into view, the torches casting hellish shadows up the side of the buildings. At the sight of the cruel, gloating faces, Remy hitched in a sharp breath and something snapped inside him. He was seized by a black rage, an intolerance and hatred for his enemies unlike anything he'd ever known. Raising his sword, he charged, emitting a bloodcurdling cry he scarcely recognized as his own.

He cut down the first attacker with one savage stroke, but there were others now, surging forward, blocking off the end of the alley. Remy tore into them blindly, no longer seeing faces, only the red haze of his own fury. He lashed out with his sword again and again, the sickly sweet scent of blood filling his nostrils, spattering his hand, his clothing, his beard.

Someone attempted to stab him with a pathetic excuse for a knife. Remy's sword arced down, ripped through the assassin's chest. Remy caught a glimpse of an agonized countenance and froze. Smooth cheeks, a thin face, eyes wide with the shock and pain of Remy's mortal blow . . . his would-be murderer was little more than a child.

Remy blinked, staring down in shock at the boy he'd just slain, and that brief moment of sanity cost him dearly. He felt the first blade break through his guard and tear open his shoulder. Searing pain shot through him and he staggered back. He managed to recover and parried several more thrusts. But the next one pierced his side. He felt the warmth of blood soaking through his doublet, but this time it was his own.

He fought on, but there were far too many of them. He grew weaker, his sword heavier. Someone swung a club at his head and missed, the blow landing heavily on his shoulder instead.

Remy cried out in agony, losing his grip on his sword. His

knees buckled and as he slowly went down, he felt the stab of yet another blade. He fell hard, toppling onto his back. He lay there, bracing himself for the thrust that would end his life.

When it didn't come, he forced his eyes open, viewing the world through a dizzying fog of pain. He had a dim impression of a terrifying giant towering over him, but strangely this man seemed to be trying to drive back his attackers. From somewhere in the alley behind him, he heard a terrified scream.

Clare . . . Remy made an effort to rise. But it was futile. The pain . . . it no longer seemed so bad. He had a curious sensation of floating, drifting out of his body, away from this cold dark alley, away from all this madness.

Back to Faire Isle. He was on the sunlit bank by the stream and Gabrielle was waiting for him. Only this time she didn't turn away. She was smiling tenderly and holding wide her arms.

※ ※ ※

RENARD HAD FOLLOWED THE HUE AND CRY AFTER THE SCOURGE. HE arrived at the alley just in time to see Remy going down, like a mighty lion falling prey to a pack of jackals. Swearing, Renard rushed forward, sending one attacker flying to the ground, felling another with his fist.

He caught the wrist of the third just before the man drove his poniard into the captain's chest.

"No," Renard roared. "The Scourge is mine. You are needed elsewhere. The heretics are trying to escape down the Seine, loading their treasure onto ships."

The man glowered at Renard, but wrenched his hand free and backed off, as did the other assassins. From the look of their crude weapons, these men weren't soldiers, only common laborers and ruffians from the streets of Paris.

Renard didn't know whether it was because of the sight of his armband or the ring of authority in his voice. Or his rough-hewn face and formidable size. Perhaps it was simply greed or the lust for fresh blood.

Eyes glistening like rats, the men slunk away from him, vanishing back down the alley. When the last of their footsteps receded, Renard hunkered down over Remy. The captain's chest still rose and fell with labored breaths, but Renard could see he was in a bad way.

He stripped off his cloak and used it, in a desperate effort to staunch the flow of blood soaking Remy's doublet.

The captain stirred, his eyes fluttering open. He was already far gone, those brown depths so clouded that Renard doubted that Remy even recognized him.

But the captain surprised him by rasping, *"Monsieur le Comte.* What—what the devil . . . you doing here?"

"Never mind about that now," Renard said brusquely. "I have to get you out of here. Find you help."

"No!" Remy struggled to raise his hand. He clutched at Renard's sleeve. "Clare. Th-the baby. Th-the others. H-help them. Get them away."

Renard's gaze flickered unwillingly toward the shadowy forms at the back of the alley. A shaft of moonlight pierced the clouds and haloed the white outstretched arm of a young woman, the unmoving bundle that had been her child . . . a mother sprawled over the two little girls she had tried in vain to protect . . . the sightless eyes of an old man . . . the bloodied tunic of a young boy.

Renard averted his gaze. Perhaps there was one mercy in all this. Nicolas Remy need never know the fate of those he'd fought so hard to protect. The man was dying and what was more, he knew it. His hand fell away from Renard, his eyes lowered to half-slits, but Renard caught the glint of quiet resignation.

"My sword . . . all I have left," he whispered. "Take it. Give to . . . Gabrielle. Promise . . ."

"I promise," Renard said hoarsely.

"Tell . . . tell her . . ." Nicolas Remy's voice faded to silence.

Renard's throat constricted and he was surprised by the depth of emotion he felt for a man he barely knew. But Captain Remy's courage, his selflessness, his devotion to honor and duty were such to command any man's respect.

Renard didn't know if it was a proper tribute to pay to a fallen Huguenot, but he made the sign of the cross over him. He drew his cloak up over the captain's face. Retrieving Remy's sword, Renard rose heavily to his feet.

There was nothing more to be done for Nicolas Remy, but there were others who needed his aid. Despite the death-like silence that had fallen over the alley, the streets beyond still echoed with screams as this night of madness rolled on.

Grimly clutching the captain's sword, Renard raced out of the alley. As he turned the corner, he flattened himself against the wall of a shop with broken windows. A troop of mounted horsemen galloped in view, their uniforms marking them as members of the elite Swiss guard.

And in their midst . . . garbed in his flowing red robes, Vachel Le Vis's twisted features appeared even more hellish by the flare of torchlight. Renard sucked in a sharp breath, all his rage, all his hatred of the witch-hunter flared to a fever pitch, like a red-hot fire consuming his brain.

Heedless of the fact that he was impossibly outnumbered, Renard leaped out of the shadows, roaring. He charged directly at the troop of mounted guardsmen. Twice Le Vis had escaped the fires of hell and Renard meant to send him there, even if he perished in the attempt.

Chapter Twenty-four

AFTER THE HEAT OF THE DAY, THE TAPROOM OF THE HALF Moon Inn felt blessedly cool, a haven from the grim sights in the street beyond. Ariane stripped off her riding gloves and released a deep breath. She had only ever visited Paris once before, one of the rare times she had traveled with her parents as a very young child. Her memories were vague. She retained an impression of a great deal of bustle and noise.

But two days after the event that was already being called Bloody Sunday, a pall of silence seemed to have fallen over the city. The few people who ventured abroad appeared subdued, their eyes downcast.

Ariane and her sisters had ridden through the streets surrounded by the comte's retainers, Toussaint leading the way. The protective cordon had been unnecessary. They were in no danger of assault. But Ariane feared the terrible images would remain branded upon her mind for a long time . . . cobblestones stained rusty with dried blood, doors broken off their hinges, windows smashed, half-burned shops, buildings that were no more than blackened shells. The Seine itself was murky with blood, the riverbank heaped with naked corpses awaiting burial.

Miri sank down at one of the tables, her curtain of hair falling forward over her face. Only days ago, she had seemed so young for her age. Now she appeared old beyond her years, deep shadows pooling beneath her eyes.

Ariane stroked the girl's hair back, murmuring, "Oh, little one, I wish you hadn't had to see—"

"It's all right, Ariane," Miri said in a wearied voice. "Don't worry about me. I'd seen it all before. In my dreams."

Her sad attempt at a reassuring smile was enough to break Ariane's heart. Never before had she appreciated her little sister's courage in enduring her nightmares. But in some respects, Miri was bearing up far better than Gabrielle.

Gabrielle slumped in a chair opposite Miri, her face bleached white. Much to her mortification, she had been distressingly ill in the stableyard. Ariane had ordered up a basin of water.

She dampened her handkerchief and tried to bathe Gabrielle's face, but her sister reared back, fending her off.

"You don't need to fuss over me either, Ariane. I'm fine." She made an effort to straighten in her chair. "The first thing we need to do is find out where the wounded are being kept. There have to be some who were only wounded. They cannot have killed all the Huguenots."

When Miri made a small choked sound, Gabrielle glared at her. "I don't care what you saw in your dream, Miri. Some of the Huguenots must have escaped or gone into hiding."

Although she would not speak his name, Ariane knew what particular Huguenot Gabrielle was thinking of. For all her fierceness, Gabrielle was seeking reassurance, a reassurance Ariane was unable to give.

Perhaps some of the Huguenots had managed to escape, but

Gabrielle had to know as well as Ariane did that Nicolas Remy was unlikely to be one of them. He would have spilled the last drop of his blood before he stood by and allowed any innocent to come to harm.

They had come to this particular inn because Toussaint had said this was where Renard always stayed when he ventured to Paris. Although Ariane knew it was foolish, she kept hoping at any moment to see him walk through that door, smile his slow smile, and address her with that familiar teasing drawl.

"Ah, chérie, how foolish of you to have worried about me. Do you not know I am far too clever to have been trapped by the Dark Queen?"

But the only man who entered the taproom was Toussaint. Ariane could tell from the old man's expression that the tidings were not good. He wasted no time getting to the point.

"I spoke to the landlord. It appears Justice was here, but he did go out that night . . . St. Bartholomew's Eve, and the inn-keeper's not set eyes on him since. But by what reports he'd heard, the comte was arrested by a party of the Swiss Guard."

Toussaint paused to swallow thickly. "Apparently the lad didn't go too willingly. He was clubbed unconscious and dragged off to the old fortress of the Bastille."

"Oh, dear God." Ariane's heart wrenched at the thought of Renard badly hurt, tossed into some dungeon.

"We—we've got to get him out of there, milady," Toussaint said.

Ariane nodded, but she knew there was only one way of securing Renard's release. She would have to barter with the Dark Queen. Her first impulse was to rush immediately to the Louvre.

But she could not be received at the palace this way, dusty from her travels. She would have to take the time to bathe, to put on the extra gown she had brought tucked in her saddlebags, one of her mother's. Prepare herself like a knight donning his armor to face his enemy.

The most difficult part would be convincing Toussaint to remain at the inn, and her sisters as well. Grateful as she had been for their company, crossing swords with the Dark Queen was one battle the Lady of Faire Isle must wage alone.

๙ ๙ ๙

CATHERINE PACED THE SILENT HALLS OF HER ROYAL APARTMENTS. She had dismissed all of her ladies-in-waiting and attendants. Brushing back the heavy drapery, she peered out the window of her antechamber. The violence of St. Bartholomew's Eve had even reached the Louvre itself, blood splashed on the palace walls and in the courtyard. The corpses had long been removed, but the workmen were still on their knees, scrubbing to remove the last evidence of the slaughter from the cobbles.

Catherine feared that the stains of this night would never be completely removed, from the palace walls or her soul. She had not intended for the whole thing to get so terrifyingly far out of control. All she had wanted was to overcome her son's foolish scruples and set a fire under the Catholic nobles to rid her of the Protestant threat.

Her visions of a well-ordered campaign of attack had swiftly degenerated into an unruly mob. Burning, looting, killing—the rampage had continued all through Sunday until Catherine had feared she might have to send in troops to restore order.

She was relieved that the violence here in Paris had finally reached its end. There was still a little unrest in a few sections, but by and large, the city was quiet again. Her spies had informed her that the whispers were already starting, entirely blaming her for the massacre. *That Italian woman, that vile de Medici sorceress.*

Catherine herself did not know how much of the savagery was owing to her miasma and how much simply to the bestiality of human nature. But it would be a long time before she ever risked tampering with such powerful black magic again.

At least the execution of so many Huguenots should certainly pacify both the Pope and Phillip of Spain. His Most Catholic Majesty could no longer accuse France of being lax with heretics and use that as an excuse to invade. The massacre would also send a message of warning to Huguenot rebels throughout France that they would not soon forget.

But unexpected regret clouded Catherine's heart. This hideous bloodshed was so far removed from the dreams she'd had as a young girl when she had first come to France to be married. She had been so in love with her young prince and she had imagined them ruling side by side with such magnificence that they would be set down in history with all the glory of a Ferdinand and Isabella. That had been before her bitter realization that Henry of France would never love her, that the only power he would share was with his mistress.

Now Henry was long dead and as for herself, Catherine had the power she'd craved. But no matter what she might ever accomplish for France, she was seized by a bleak premonition that all she would ever be remembered for was this . . . the massacre of St. Bartholomew's Day.

She forced herself to rally when the antechamber door opened and Gillian Harcourt crept into the room. The petite blond lady-in-waiting sank into a deep curtsy. "Your Majesty, there is someone here—"

"I told you I do not wish to receive anyone," Catherine interrupted coldly.

"But Your Grace, you told me that when the Lady of Faire Isle arrived seeking an audience, she was to be escorted into your presence immediately. No matter the time of night or day."

Catherine caught the note of suppressed excitement in the girl's voice. Even the foolish courtesans of her Flying Squadron were awed by the reputation of the Lady of Faire Isle. Catherine frowned in fleeting annoyance. Never had she achieved anything close to the reverence the uncrowned lady of that one small island commanded.

Catherine grudgingly conceded that her dear Evangeline and the late Eugenie Pellentier had fully deserved such respect. Whether Ariane Cheney did remained to be seen.

Catherine's mouth curled in a thin smile.

"Show the *lady* in."

※ ※ ※

ARIANE WAS USHERED INTO THE ANTECHAMBER, THE TRAIN OF HER mother's gown of antique gold rustling behind her. She caught a glimpse of her reflection in a large gilt-edged mirror. She was by far too pale, her thick fall of brown hair dressed loosely about her shoulders. But the plain gold circlet that banded her forehead lent her a touch of regal calm and dignity.

Despite her appearance of outward serenity, her heart tripped irregularly as she braced herself to confront Catherine de Medici.

Ariane was only dimly aware of the lady-in-waiting announcing her, then slipping quietly from the room. She found herself left alone with the Dark Queen. Catherine awaited her, framed against the apartment's tall, sunlit windows.

"Ah, Ariane. So you have arrived at last," she said. "Come closer, child."

Ariane forced her feet forward with measured steps as she stared at Catherine. Was this the creature she had so long feared? Mistress of the dark arts, betrayer of her mother's friendship, employer of witch-hunters, dire authoress of the tragedy whose terrible aftermath Ariane had just witnessed.

Catherine was not very tall, her figure on the plump side. The cut of her black gown was austere, the starkness relieved only by the narrow white ruff at her throat. Her face was smooth, almost masklike.

The two women regarded each other silently, each taking the other's measure. Catherine's throat clogged with an unexpected rush of emotion. She felt as though she was looking at a ghost, Evangeline's soft brown hair tumbled around the young woman's shoulders. The girl was much taller than Evangeline had ever been. She had obviously inherited her height from her father, along with Louis Cheney's aristocratic cheekbones. But those were Evangeline's eyes that stared gravely back at Catherine from Ariane's countenance.

Catherine experienced a surge of grief and longing for her old friend such as she had not allowed herself to feel for years. But she could not let any lingering sentimentality for the girl's mother affect how she dealt with Ariane. Catherine flushed at her own folly, seeking to shrug off the maudlin emotion.

But her voice was unusually soft as she held out her hand to Ariane. "I have been looking forward to this meeting, my dear. I have not seen you since you were in your infancy."

Ariane made a stiff curtsy and took Catherine's hand, but she could not bring herself to kiss it. The queen did not appear troubled by Ariane's lack of obeisance. Her fingers curled around Ariane's.

"I attended your christening, you know. Did Evangeline ever tell you that? I journeyed all the way out to that wretched island for the first and only time in my life. I so wanted to arrange for my dear friend's confinement in one of my own royal palaces, but Evangeline insisted upon giving birth to you on Faire Isle."

Catherine gave a light chuckle. "I remember when I peeked into your cradle, thinking what a funny, solemn little thing you were. Hardly ever crying, gazing up at me with those great unblinking eyes. I *should* have been your godmother, but of course Evangeline felt obliged to accord that honor to your Great-aunt Eugenie as the Lady of Faire Isle."

Ariane repressed a shiver at the thought of the Dark Queen bending over her cradle like some malevolent fairy. She attempted to ease her hand away, but Catherine's grip tightened.

It was then that Ariane discovered the true power of the Dark Queen. It was in her eyes, cold and dark as unending night. Never had Ariane encountered a gaze so piercing.

Ariane wanted to avert her eyes, but she forced herself to meet Catherine's gaze dead-on. The queen stared at her for a long moment before releasing her.

"Yes," she murmured. "You very much have the look of my dear Evangeline about you."

These intimate references to the woman whose friendship Catherine had so callously betrayed stirred Ariane's resentment.

"My mother was never *your* dear Evangeline," she said. "May we have an end to these pleasantries and come straight to the point? You know why I am here. I have come to negotiate the release of the Comte de Renard."

Catherine's brows rose haughtily. "How do you know I haven't simply killed him?"

Ariane's heart constricted with alarm, then she realized the woman was toying with her.

Ariane glared at her. "I know he is still alive. I—I can feel it."

"How remarkably tender and romantic," Catherine drawled. "Yes, it so happens your comte is still among the living. You have me to thank for that."

"You! It was you who lured him to Paris."

"Regrettably, his arrival was a bit more untimely than yours. He entered the city in the midst of our, er, St. Bartholomew's Eve celebration. Knowing that he was of little use to me dead, I did try to employ the power of the ring to persuade him to come straight to the palace." Catherine shrugged. "Either he had finally grown wise to my tricks or he decided it would be more amusing to try to save Huguenots."

"The comte is not the sort of man to stand idly by while innocents are being slaughtered," Ariane said proudly.

"The more fool he for risking his life by meddling in what does not concern him. His late grandfather would certainly never have done so. All in all, your Renard made a great nuisance of himself. Luckily, I had sent out a contingent of the Swiss Guard to arrest him. The comte strenuously objected to taking up residence in the Bastille. I am afraid you will find him in rather poor condition."

Ariane was hard-pressed to contain herself as Catherine continued, "Monsieur Le Vis is most eager to minister to him and I'm told the Bastille has a remarkable range of torture instruments."

Ariane blanched. "You—you have turned Renard over to the clutches of that madman?"

"Not yet I haven't. At the moment he is comfortably lodged in one of the towers as befitting a man of his rank. But there are less pleasant quarters in the Bastille, dank underground dungeons that have never seen the light of day. Oubliettes where you can toss a man and completely forget about him until he runs mad or starves to death. Your lover's fate rests entirely in your hands, Ariane. Have you brought the articles I asked for?"

Ariane fumbled with the pouch tied at her belt, her fingers feeling clumsy and wooden. "What you seek is right here."

She held up the purse, not quite able to control the tremor in her hand. But when Catherine reached for it, Ariane drew it back.

"No. Not until you give me the warrant for Renard's release."

Catherine clucked her tongue. "My dear Ariane. I am sensing a marked lack of trust here."

Still smirking, Catherine drifted across the chamber and settled herself behind a large ornate desk. She reached for parchment, ink, and quill and began to write. Ariane had to check her urge to pace nervously back and forth. She found it hard to believe she could obtain Renard's release this easily.

As she watched the queen writing out the warrant, Ariane experienced a rush of anger that this woman could look so calm and unruffled after all she had done. Not one sign of regret for her use of the witch-hunters, for her attacks upon the daughters of a woman she persisted in calling her friend. No remorse at all for all those slain men, women, and children heaped like refuse upon the banks of the Seine.

"How could you do it?" Ariane demanded.

The queen looked up from her writing. "Do what?"

"Slaughter all those innocent people."

"They were not all that innocent. I was merely trying to bring a definite end to the civil war that has been plaguing this country."

"By murdering women and children?" Ariane cried.

"The unfortunate consequence of war, my dear. It was nothing I could help."

"Nothing you could help? You induced this madness, you released a miasma."

Catherine suspended the quill over the page in mid-stroke, a crack appearing in her icy composure. "You—you know about that? Then Louise Lavalle reached you when she escaped?"

"Louise escaped?" Ariane regarded Catherine accusingly. "You wrote to us that she was dead."

Catherine scowled, clearly nettled that she had parted with a piece of information she would just as soon have Ariane not know. "Both Louise and Madame Pechard should have been strangled and sunk quietly to the bottom of the Seine. But at the last moment Louise was able to exercise her charms upon the guard and procure escape for Hermoine and herself."

Catherine added dryly. "Never underestimate another witch merely because she has freckles."

Ariane clasped her hands together, unable to contain her joy at the news. She had blamed herself for using Louise and Madame Pechard, allowing them to risk their lives. It was a great relief and comfort to her to learn that they had escaped.

Catherine paused once more in her writing. "But if Louise did not tell you about my miasma, then who did?"

Ariane lowered her lashes to conceal her thoughts. She had no wish to reveal to Catherine Miri's capacity for prophetic dreams. Somehow it would feel as though she were rendering her little sister more vulnerable to the Dark Queen. Also it might give Ariane a decided advantage if she were able to mystify Catherine.

She had never been a particularly good liar or actress, but Ariane took a sweeping turn about the room, assuming a haughty stance. "I know more about you than you think, Your Grace. After all, I am the Lady of Faire Isle. I have more power than you could imagine."

Catherine made a sound perilously close to a snort. Ignoring the derisive sound, Ariane continued, "For instance, I know all about what went on at your secret council meeting. How you drove your poor son to madness. How you dropped the vial out the window. You should not presume to practice the dark arts if you're going to be that careless."

Catherine's jaw dropped, her expression hovering between disbelief and unease. "How could you possibly . . ." She checked herself, seeking to recover her composure.

"My brew may have helped things along a little, but if you think men require much prompting to behave like beasts, then you know little of their nature. I wonder if my little concoction was even necessary. Bring a tribe of Huguenots into the heart of Catholic Paris, throw together those who have been bitter enemies, and the situation was already ripe for bloodshed."

"Which you could have prevented. You could have used your gifts and abilities to heal this terrible breach, not urge men on to death and destruction."

A hint of color flamed in Catherine's cheeks. "Don't presume to lecture me, impertinent girl. You know nothing of what it takes to govern a country, to survive amidst so much treachery and intrigue. You with your quiet, sheltered life on your island.

"I have danced on the blade of a knife for most of my life, from the time I was a child and revolutionaries swept through my own country. I was taken prisoner and would have perished then if I had not swiftly learned how to manipulate and control others. Employ any means necessary to survive, even the dark arts you so despise. Why by the time I was fifteen—"

Catherine checked her passionate outburst, settling her icy mask back into place. Compressing her lips, she affixed the royal seal. Rising to her feet, she extended the parchment toward Ariane.

"Here," she said curtly. "Now give me those tiresome gloves."

When Ariane surrendered the pouch, Catherine all but snatched it from her. Ariane perused the document to make sure it was in order, all the while keeping a wary eye on Catherine as she inspected the contents of the pouch, waiting for the explosion of wrath she feared was coming.

Catherine did not lose her temper. But her jaw tightened. "There is only one glove here."

"Yes," Ariane replied with as much calm as she could muster. "I left the other one in the care of some friends here in Paris. I shall send the second glove to you once Renard and I are safely out the city gates."

"Do not trifle with me, Ariane." Catherine reached across the table and yanked the warrant away from her. "Because of my affection for your late mother, I have borne far too much of your insolent interference in my affairs. What makes you think I will permit either you or your noble lover to leave the city?"

"Because if you try to stop me, I will make sure the other glove disappears and you will never know when or where it will turn back up to haunt you."

"Bah," Catherine sneered. "Those gloves are not of that much consequence. If you had found a way to prove they were poisoned and bring an accusation against me, you would have already done so."

"But I can prove they are poisoned. All I have to do is slip one on."

"You would also end up dead."

"Not if I have the antidote," Ariane countered.

"And since when did you become such an expert in the dark arts?" Catherine demanded scornfully. "I am sure my dear virtuous Evangeline never taught you."

"No, but there was once another witch as well versed in the dark arts as you. Melusine."

Even Catherine flinched at the name. "But how would you have acquired anything from her? Melusine is long since—"

Catherine broke off and stalked around the desk, coming closer. She probed Ariane's eyes before she could look away.

"God's blood," she muttered. "Renard . . . he is Melusine's grandson?" Catherine gave a mirthless bark of laughter. "The Lady of Faire Isle has given her heart to the offspring of a notorious witch? Evangeline must be tossing in her grave."

"I am sure Maman would be far too wise to hold Renard accountable for the sins of his grandmother," Ariane retorted. "Any more than your unfortunate children should be blamed for yours."

Catherine's smile faded. "This is all bluster and nonsense. I don't know why I have even been so afraid of what these gloves could prove. No one would believe—"

"Oh, yes, I am afraid the people of France would be all too eager to believe anything of you, especially after St. Bartholomew's Day. Many Catholics are going to be horrified by what you have done and as for all those noblemen who supported you in this bloody deed, they would be only too eager to turn on you and bring you down."

Catherine pursed her lips in a stubborn line. "I am the Dowager Queen of France."

"Other queens have met with destruction. Have you forgotten that Anne Boleyn was charged with witchcraft as well as adultery before she was beheaded?"

A ripple of unease crossed Catherine's features. "That was England and she was a commoner, not of a royal house."

"Neither are you. You are little more than an Italian merchant's daughter."

Catherine's brows snapped ominously together and Ariane feared she had gone too far. The Dark Queen advanced upon her.

"Give me my other glove, Ariane or I am warning you . . ."

Ariane's heart hammered in her breast, but she refused to back down. "No, I am warning you, Catherine. I mean to revive the council of the daughters of the earth, the guardians against such misuse of the old ways as you have done."

"The council," Catherine scoffed. "I'll set witch-hunters after the lot of you."

"Go ahead, but there will be far too many of us. Even you cannot fight us all. Think of it, Catherine. A silent army of wise women. Do you really want to be constantly looking over your shoulder, anticipating the arrival of another Louise Lavalle to expose your secrets to the world? One more clever, one whose eyes you can't read next time."

"The witch hasn't been born whose eyes I can't read," Catherine snarled. "Do you know how easily I could strip you of all your secrets?"

Catherine roughly seized hold of Ariane's chin, compelling her to gaze straight into those cold, dark eyes. Ariane wanted to jerk away, but she forced herself to meet the Dark Queen's challenge, mentally erecting a wall to guard her thoughts.

Never had she been subjected to such a piercing stare, such

a clash of will. Sweat beaded on Ariane's brow as she fought to beat back Catherine's relentless probing. She stared fiercely back, unblinking, feeling as though they were locked in mortal combat, steel pressed to steel, neither willing to yield.

The veins in Ariane's head throbbed and she did not know how much more of this intense pressure she could bear. Miraculously she felt Catherine begin to waver.

Her defenses crumbled and Ariane suddenly saw the pathetic woman who lurked in the heart of the Dark Queen. The one who'd craved love and been denied, who'd filled up her emptiness with the lust for power. Who trusted no one, who believed in nothing. Whose greatest fear was being brought down by her enemies. Dying reviled and alone. Who was slowly being consumed by her own darkness.

Ariane understood now why her mother had pitied Catherine, although she was unable to do so herself. The destruction that Catherine had wrought was too great. But Ariane knew she would never fear the Dark Queen in quite the same way again. Catherine shuddered. She abruptly released Ariane. Her hand trembled as she used it to shield her eyes as she stalked back to the desk and retrieved the warrant.

"Very well," she muttered. "I agree to your terms. Just make certain I have that second glove back before sunset or I'll send my soldiers hard after you. You'll never set foot on the shore of your beloved Faire Isle again."

Catherine thrust the order for Renard's release in her direction. Ariane's fingers quivered as she took hold of it. Her urge to flee the palace was strong, to effect Renard's release and get him and her sisters out of Paris before Catherine changed her mind.

But she had just won a significant victory over the Dark Queen. It would be cowardly to retreat now.

"There is one more thing. I need to know the fate of—of Nicolas Remy."

"The Scourge? Dead no doubt. I certainly hope so."

But Catherine did not sound entirely sure. Ariane felt a flicker of hope. She continued boldly, "And what about Remy's young king, Henry of Navarre? I understand you have him imprisoned here in his apartments. I would like him to be released as well."

Catherine's lips thinned. "You overreach yourself, my girl. You can have your wretched Renard, but not the king."

"You intend to execute your own son-in-law?"

"No, that will no longer be necessary. Without his advisors, Henry is nothing, not nearly as clever and formidable as his late mother was. He is a very malleable young man and will easily renounce his heretic beliefs. Nonetheless, I prefer to keep him under my watchful eye."

Ariane frowned, but saw that Catherine would never yield on this point. She had achieved as much with the woman as she dared. She dipped into a stiff curtsy, backing toward the door when a thought occurred to Ariane. She could not believe she had almost forgotten.

"There is something else . . ."

"What now?" Catherine asked impatiently.

"My ring. I want it back."

Catherine pursed her lips, then vented a weary sigh. "Why not? I no longer have a use for it and the blasted thing never fit me all that well."

Rustling over to her desk, she unlocked one of the drawers and produced the ring. She slapped it down on the corner of the desk, but when Ariane went to retrieve it, Catherine's hand shot out, covering hers.

She forced her lips into the semblance of a smile. "Come now, my dear. There is no reason that you and I should part in this cold fashion. The Queen Mother of France and the Lady of Faire Isle should not be such bitter enemies. Your mother and I were once the best of friends."

Closing her fingers over the ring, Ariane wrenched away

from Catherine. "I am fully aware of how much your friendship cost my mother, so I leave you with one final thought, Your Grace. If you ever seek to harm anyone under my protection or those whom I love, you will discover exactly how much of a witch I can be."

Head held high, Ariane exited with quiet dignity, never looking back.

※ ※ ※

LONG AFTER THE DOOR HAD CLOSED BEHIND ARIANE, CATHERINE stood with her hands braced upon the desk, deeply unnerved by her encounter with the young woman. No one had ever been able to shatter Catherine's defenses that way, to read all the fears and vulnerabilities Catherine sought to hide. No one except perhaps Evangeline.

But even more painful to Catherine was what she had glimpsed in Ariane's face. Ariane's eyes were like some mystical mirror, reflecting to Catherine a haunting image of the wise woman she might have been if her life had taken a different path, if she had made different choices.

Trembling, Catherine forced herself to straighten. Ariane had a vein of steel in her that not even her mother had possessed. Catherine wondered if she was being a fool to let the girl leave here alive. But loath as she was to admit it, she had been shaken by some of Ariane's threats. Catherine certainly had enough other enemies to fight without having a union of daughters of the earth to deal with as well.

The girl was more powerful and clever than Catherine had supposed. How *had* Ariane known about her secret council meeting? About the miasma? Could she have already planted another spy of whom Catherine was ignorant?

She decided she had best proceed with caution. Catherine

had time enough later to decide what might need to be done about Ariane. Very likely she was getting into a fret over nothing.

Ariane would return her glove as promised, then retreat to her island. Likely that would be an end of all commerce between them. Catherine was tired of the whole affair and she still had one more loose end that wanted trimming.

That wretch Le Vis had been demanding to see Catherine since daybreak, no doubt expecting her to redeem her promises.

Moments later Le Vis was ushered into her presence. The bloodbath in Paris seemed to have put him over the edge of excitement. His eyes glinted with an insane joy. Attired in his bloodred robes, he reminded Catherine of a cardinal from hell, but she concealed her loathing and contempt, inviting the man to be seated, offering him a cup of wine.

Le Vis accepted eagerly, raising his cup in a toast to what he acclaimed as the victory of the one true faith.

"The streets of Paris are paved with the blood of the heretics," he gloated. "Such a pleasing sight for the eyes of God."

"Yes," Catherine said dryly. "I am sure the angels of heaven must be weeping tears of joy."

Le Vis did not appear to notice the irony in her voice. Catherine watched with narrowed eyes as he greedily quaffed his wine.

He continued to enthuse. "This great victory paves the way for our greater work, Your Majesty. The destruction of all the witches in France. When shall we commence the trial of the demon Renard and his sorceress, the Cheney woman?"

"Never," Catherine replied softly.

"What?" Le Vis set down his cup to frown at her.

"I have released the comte," Catherine informed him coolly. "He and Ariane Cheney will shortly be leaving Paris."

The blood rushed to Le Vis's face. "But—what of our glorious plan? Our campaign to rid France of every last witch."

"I am afraid that was never of much interest to me."

Le Vis uttered a choked sound, but it was less of protest than distress. He clutched his throat and gasped for air. He tried to stagger to his feet, only to collapse, tipping over his wine cup in the process.

Catherine came round the desk to stand over him, dispassionately watching as Le Vis writhed in his throes of agony. His eyes bulged, staring up at her in terror and confusion.

Catherine leaned over him, murmuring, "You see, Monsieur Le Vis, I may have forgotten to mention it, but I am a bit of a witch myself."

She was amused to see the horrified realization flicker across his face only moments before he gave his last pain-filled gasp and was still. His sightless eyes stared up at her, spittle trickling from his gaping mouth.

With a shudder of distaste, Catherine moved away from him. Fetching the cup that had fallen, she placed it back on the desk. One of her simpler poisons, really, crude but most effective, acting quickly. It would have been quite a waste to have employed anything subtler on a witch-hunter.

Stepping to the door of her apartment, Catherine dispatched one of the pages to fetch Bartolomy Verducci. The thin gray-haired man responded quickly, all too eager to ingratiate himself with Catherine after his recent failures with Captain Remy and the missing gloves.

He bowed and scraped, asking breathlessly, "What service can I perform for Your Grace?"

"There is a dead witch-hunter in my antechamber. Remove him," Catherine replied tonelessly.

Bartolomy's eyes nearly popped from his head, but he sought to recover from his shock. "Y-yes, Your Grace."

"And be discreet about it," Catherine commanded. "Slip Monsieur Le Vis in with the other bodies being removed for burial. One more will hardly be noticed and in any case I doubt Le Vis will be mourned or even missed. His entire order of fellow witch-hunters has been destroyed, all except for that boy."

The boy . . .

As Bartolomy moved to obey, a mischievous thought suddenly struck Catherine. Until she knew the full extent of Ariane's power, she was wary of attacking her outright. But there were indirect methods she could use.

"On second thought, Bartolomy," she said. "Run Le Vis through a couple of times with your sword and return the body to Master Simon Aristide. Tell him that his master was destroyed by the Comte de Renard and Ariane Cheney. Follow Ariane after she obtains the comte's release from the Bastille and make sure young Aristide knows where to find them.

"Tell him . . ." Catherine smiled. "That Renard is the grandson of Melusine and that she is the witch who likely destroyed his village."

Although Bartolomy blinked in confusion at these instructions, he hastened away to carry out her commands.

Would the boy believe such a tale? Catherine wondered. Maybe he would, maybe he wouldn't. If he did, and decided to seek revenge on Ariane and her comte, at least Catherine might end up rid of one of her enemies, however the affair played out.

In any event, she had accomplished all that she could. The past few days had been quite eventful and Catherine was quite fatigued. The Dark Queen gave a wearied yawn and went to seek out her bed.

※ ※ ※

RENARD SHIFTED PAINFULLY ON THE CAMP BED, ONE EYE PARTLY swollen, the other bleary from a sleepless night. Sunlight filtered through the high window of his tower room. The sound of the sentry ringing the bell to announce the quarter hour carried even through the thick walls. Renard stuffed the feather pillow over his head until it stopped, the peal calling up too many grim memories of a few nights ago.

His head still throbbed from the whack of the cudgel that had rendered him unconscious. Luckily, his skull was too thick to have been split open. His ribs had not fared as well. He was certain that quite a few of them were cracked from the blows and kicks he'd taken. His entire body was one mass of bruises and he feared he might have broken his nose. Again.

But he was better off than Nicolas Remy. At least *he* was still alive. He couldn't even complain about the conditions of his imprisonment. His tower room was spacious enough, well-aired and reasonably clean. He'd been provided with hot water for bathing, decent food, and wine. The governor had called for a doctor to see to Renard's injuries, but Renard had taken one look at the jar of leeches clutched in the man's hand and sent him packing.

He was even allowed to receive visitors, although he'd had only one. That miscreant Le Vis had shown up early this morning to gloat. It had been from him that Renard had learned how the Dark Queen had acquired his ring and also why Renard was being kept alive.

He was the bait to entice Ariane to come to Paris. Renard only hoped she'd be wiser than he had been. They had parted on such bitter terms. Perhaps she wouldn't come rushing to try to save him.

But even as he considered that possibility, Renard realized it was a slim hope. He knew Ariane's sense of responsibility too well. She'd be blaming herself for the loss of the ring. Even if she now regarded him as her worst enemy, she'd try to come to his rescue and charge straight into the clutches of the Dark Queen.

The thought was enough to drive him mad. He had no way of getting word to anyone on the outside. Nor had he come up with a plan for escape. When offered the chance of exercise yesterday, he'd dragged himself out of bed to walk along the Bastille parapets. But he'd been closely watched and in the fading daylight, he had been unable to gain any real sense of the fortress's layout.

Nor was he in any condition yet to try to overpower his guards. All he could do was lie here like a damned useless lump, try to rest, try to heal. He forced his eyes closed and finally managed to drift off for a while, only to be roused by the chink of the key in the lock.

The massive door creaked open. Baroit, his chief warder, entered, a fellow with a long face and thick gray mustache. He was a respectful enough man for a jailer, extremely mindful of Renard's rank.

"Monsieur le Comte," he said with a bow. "You have a visitor—"

Renard swore and flung one arm across his eyes. "If it is Le Vis again, tell him to go to hell. I don't care how many of you try to protect him. If he sets one damned foot in here, I swear I'll stuff his bloody arse through that window—"

"Monsieur!" Baroit exclaimed in shocked accents. "Please watch what you say, my lord. Your visitor is a lady."

Renard lowered his arm. A lady? No, the woman he glimpsed hovering behind Baroit was a golden vision, too lovely to be real, like those serene figures of ladies woven into tapestries, taming unicorns or offering knights tokens of their favor.

Except that this particular lady did not look all that serene. Her eyes were filled with consternation, her soft mouth a-tremble. Any joy Renard might have felt at seeing her was lost beneath a crushing wave of defeat and despair.

"God's teeth, Ariane," he grated. "What are you doing here?"

"This is hardly the welcome I'd hoped for," Ariane tried to tease, but she couldn't quite manage it. Her breath caught in her throat at the sight of Renard's ravaged face and she could tell by the stiff way he moved that that was not the full extent of his injuries.

Gritting his teeth, he sat up, swinging his legs over the side of the cot. As the guard slipped quietly from the room, Ariane rushed over to Renard and sank down beside him.

As a healer, she'd always prided herself on her ability to remain calm and detached. But she could not refrain from crying out, "Oh, Justice. What have they done to you?"

Renard made a grim effort to smile. "Nothing compared to what I did to them. Trying to disarm a man with a sword and take him alive puts you at a certain disadvantage. I was doing well enough until some sneaking bastard crept up on me from behind with a very large club."

Ariane ran her fingers through his hair, anxiously probing. Renard hissed when she found a large lump, but at least she felt no break in the skin. The injuries to his face appeared by far the worst, his lip split, one eye swollen, dark ugly bruises blossoming across his cheekbones. Ariane touched his cheek lightly. When he winced, her eyes filled with tears.

"Ah, don't cry, ma chère," Renard protested. "My face never was all that pretty, you know."

"I—I thought it was," she sniffed.

"Mon Dieu." He started to laugh, then stopped with a sharp indrawn breath. "The Dark Queen must have put one devil of a spell on you."

"No, it was you who did that."

Despite his hellish bruises, something in his gaze softened. Renard stole his arm about her waist only to stop with a low groan.

"Damnation, you should not have come here, Ariane. Why did you ever allow that evil woman to lure you to Paris?"

"Why did you?" she retorted.

"Because I am a great fool who would go anywhere, take any risk if I thought you were in danger."

"Then the same answer must suffice for me." She swallowed hard and then faltered, "Oh, Justice . . . about that last night on Faire Isle. The way we parted. Some of the terrible things I said to you. I am so sorry—"

"Hush, ma chère." He drifted his fingers lightly across her lips to silence her. "I said a good many things I regret myself. But none of that is important right now."

Ariane mopped her eyes. "You are right. The main thing is to get you out of here."

"I fear you will have a hard time doing that unless you have smuggled a rope ladder and pistol under that lovely golden gown."

Ariane managed to smile. "I have done something even better. I have given the governor the order for your release. I daresay he is even now instructing the guards to retrieve your sword and any other possessions they confiscated from you."

Renard realized his cell door had been left open. He regarded Ariane with confusion. "What—what is this, chérie?"

"Catherine and I have arrived at an understanding. She has agreed to let you go."

"She did what?" Renard frowned, then sighed as understanding broke over him. "You surrendered the gloves to her, didn't you? You should never have done that, Ariane. Not to save my thick hide. Those gloves were your only evidence, the only chance you had to bring down the Dark Queen, to avenge the wrongs she has done to so many innocent people, including your poor Maman."

"You have always read my eyes too well, Renard," Ariane said ruefully. "But obviously not well enough or you would know that my desire to undo Catherine could never mean as much to me as your life."

She stroked the hair back from his brow, studying an angry red cut on his forehead, her mind already racing ahead to what sort of ointment she must apply.

Renard's hand closed over hers. Holding it up to the light, he stared at the metal band encircling her finger.

"You got the ring back from her." He added in a tone of even greater wonder, "And you are wearing it."

"Yes," Ariane said. "And I promise you I will never be so careless with it again."

His eyes searched hers. "Ariane—" he began.

"I know." She whispered the gentlest of kisses across his lips. "I am sure we both have much to say to each other. We must get back to the inn where Toussaint is waiting for us."

"Toussaint is here, too?" Renard flinched as he rose unsteadily to his feet. "Of course, he *would* be. The king's entire army couldn't have kept that stubborn old fool from coming to hunt for me."

"My sisters are here as well and I am afraid even your redoubtable Toussaint may be having a hard time restraining Gabrielle. She is determined to search for Remy."

A shadow fell across Renard's face. "Ma chère," he began. He was unable to continue, but he didn't need to. A painful lump lodged in Ariane's throat as she read the dreadful truth in Renard's eyes.

ఝ ఝ ఝ

THE PRIVATE ROOM AT THE HALF-MOON INN PROVIDED A WELCOME haven in which Ariane could finally give way to her grief. Perched on the settle before the hearth, she cradled Miri in her arms, mingling their tears for the quiet captain from Navarre who had so briefly touched their lives.

Ariane feared that Gabrielle had come to care for Remy far

more than she would have admitted. And Gabrielle was just realizing that fact. Now, when it was far too late.

But she refused to cry. Gabrielle leaned up against the wall, maintaining a stony silence as Renard quietly finished the account of Remy's last minutes.

"He died as bravely and honorably as he lived. And he wanted you to have this." Renard approached Gabrielle, Remy's sword balanced across his palms. Gabrielle stared down at the weapon, making no move to take it.

"There was something else he wanted me to tell you, but he died before he could finish," Renard continued. "And yet perhaps you can guess what it was he wanted to say."

"Yes," Gabrielle said hoarsely. She took the sword from Renard at last, her eyes burning fiercely with unshed tears. "We—we have to go and find him."

Renard looked a little taken aback. "Gabrielle," he said gently. "Perhaps you have not completely understood me. Remy is—is—"

"I know he is dead," she snapped. "But we can't just leave him to rot on the banks of the Seine. We have to find him, see he is buried properly."

Renard cast her a compassionate glance. "I am sorry, Gabrielle. That is not possible. There are too many dead. We will likely never find him. And there is still much unease and tension out there in the streets, bad feeling against the Huguenots. It would be far too dangerous to go looking for Remy."

Gabrielle clenched her teeth. "I don't care. I won't leave him to be dumped naked in some unmarked grave. He deserves to be laid to rest with honor as . . . as a knight would be."

She started for the door. When Renard blocked her path, she glared up at him, furious tears streaming down her face, Remy's sword clutched dangerously in her hand. Ariane eased Miri away from her and leaped up hastily to intervene.

She rested her hand gently but firmly on her sister's shoulder. "Gabrielle, I am so sorry. But we must be content to honor Remy's memory. We have no other choice and you know he would never have wanted you to place yourself in danger by looking for him."

"Of course *he* wouldn't, the noble idiot. So busy protecting everyone else, he never had a care for himself." Gabrielle glowered at both Ariane and Renard. She stormed away from them. "We should have kept him locked in the cellar. It's all my fault. I—I could have made him stay—"

"Oh, Gabrielle," Ariane said. "You must not blame yourself. Remy's sense of honor was so strong, nothing would have stayed him from his duty. Not even you."

But she realized that Gabrielle was not even listening to her. She gestured wildly with his sword. "So now what? We are just going to go back home to Faire Isle with our tails tucked between our legs? And let that evil woman go unpunished for murdering Remy and every other terrible thing she has done?"

"Gabrielle," Ariane began. "We really—"

"I know, I know!" Gabrielle interrupted bitterly. "We have no choice, but one day . . . one day . . . I swear I'll bring her down. The Dark Queen will no longer be the most powerful witch in France."

Gabrielle faltered, the anger that had shored her up draining out of her. She slumped down at the table and buried her face on her arm. Miri crept over to sit beside her, looking sad and helpless. She rested her fingers timidly near Gabrielle's arm.

Ariane ached to go to Gabrielle and wrap her arms about her sister, but she knew from bitter experience the futility of trying to comfort Gabrielle.

She felt Renard rest his hand upon her shoulder. "Best to leave her be, ma chère. Give her time."

Ariane nodded sadly and turned her attention to the wounds that she *could* heal. Despite Renard's insistence that he was doing fine, she led him over to the settle and insisted that he sit down while she inspected the cut on his forehead. Ariane pursed her lips. The gash should have been stitched, but at the very least she would make sure that it was properly cleaned to avoid any risk of infection.

Toussaint was busy seeing to the horses, readying the provisions for their journey from Paris, which could not take place too soon as far as Ariane was concerned. She placed no faith in Catherine's ability to honor any agreement that she had made for long. As soon as the horses were readied, and Renard a little more rested, they must go.

When she heard the tramp of approaching footsteps, Ariane straightened eagerly, expecting it to be Toussaint returning to tell them that all was ready for their departure. But the door burst open to admit the last person Ariane had ever expected to see again.

Simon Aristide stormed into the room. The boy's black hair tumbling about his face was as wild as the expression in his eyes.

"S-simon." Miri leapt up. She took a faltering step toward him, but Ariane held her back.

Simon did not appear to notice her. His gaze locked on Renard with a hate-filled glare. "There you are! You—you black-hearted spawn from hell."

Renard shoved to his feet as swiftly as his battered body would allow. He positioned his broad-shouldered frame squarely in front of Simon, blocking his farther entrance into the room.

"You've one devil of a nerve, showing your face again, boy," Renard growled. "What do you want?"

"Retribution for the death of my master. You—you murderer."

Despite his bruises, Renard managed to arch one eyebrow in haughty fashion. "What the devil are you talking about?"

"As if you didn't know. Monsieur Le Vis is dead, cruelly hacked apart by your bloody sword." Simon choked. "And—and he didn't even have a chance to defend himself. He was not even armed."

Ariane moved forward to stand by Renard. "Simon, I don't know who has been telling you such lies, but the comte has been imprisoned in the Bastille. He was just released a few hours ago."

"If you want to find Le Vis's murderer," Gabrielle spoke up scornfully, "You would do well to consult the mistress that you both served. Very likely this is some more mischief of Catherine's."

"Oh, I have no doubt she was involved," Simon said, his voice trembling with fury. "My poor master was too bewitched to realize how evil she is. And I was too stupid to see that you have all been in league together."

"No, Simon, you are wrong," Miri quavered. "The Dark Queen is our enemy too."

Simon ignored her, leveling an accusing finger at Renard. "I know who you are. You are the grandson of an evil witch named Melusine and she—she was the one who destroyed my village, murdered my family."

"That is completely ridiculous," Renard said gruffly. "My grandmother has been dead for years."

"I won't listen to any more lies. At least I will give you more of a chance than you gave my master. Draw your sword."

"Don't be stupid, boy," Renard said, but Simon advanced on him, unsheathing his own weapon. "Draw! Or I will cut you down right now."

Renard muttered a vexed oath. Thrusting Ariane out of the way, he drew his own sword in time to parry Simon's first blow.

The swords met in a loud clash of steel. Miri cried out in protest, but the boy had been driven to the brink of despair by the death of the one man he had trusted.

Ariane watched the furious battle anxiously. Ordinarily she would have had no fear for Renard, but he had been weakened by his recent ordeal. And she saw clearly that he refused to go for the swift clean blow his superior skill would have allowed. He would never cut that boy down before Miri's very eyes. Renard was trying desperately to disarm Simon, giving the boy a decided advantage.

He struck and lunged with a strength born of his fury, nearly breaking through Renard's guard time and again. Ariane glanced about her, frantically seeking something she could use as a weapon to render Simon unconscious.

Before she could act, Miri rushed forward, crying. "Simon! Please! No!"

She managed to seize hold of his sword arm. But as she deflected his blade, Renard's weapon broke through. There was no way he could check the blow. His sword flashed in a downward arc, slicing through Simon's right eye and cheek.

The boy staggered back, dropping his sword with an agonized cry. He clasped his hand to his face, blood gushing between his fingers.

"Oh, S—simon." Crying, Miri hovered over him. "Let me help you."

But he wrenched free of her. "Get away from me," he ground out. "I thought to save you, but you—you are just like the rest of them. A—a witch."

He glared at Miri through his remaining good eye and her heart froze, reading that same expression she had seen too many times in creatures injured beyond repair. That dark empty look of a soul that had fled.

"N-no," she whispered brokenly, reaching out to him.

Simon shrank away from all of them. Still clutching his bloodied face, he fled, disappearing through the open door.

Miri sank to her knees, sobbing as though her heart would

break. Ariane bent down to wrap her little sister in her arms, holding Miri's shuddering frame against her.

Renard peered gravely at them both. "Do you want me to go after the boy, chérie? Try to bring him back?"

"No," Ariane said sadly. "I fear it would do little good. Please Justice, just find Toussaint and then take us home."

Chapter Twenty-five

SUNLIGHT SPILLED SOFTLY THROUGH THE WINDOWS OF BELLE Haven as the summer's day faded to twilight. But Ariane did not find the peace she had expected with her arrival home. She was, if anything, even more aware of all the responsibilities she had left behind, especially regarding her two sisters.

Gabrielle was so withdrawn, the hard look in her eyes more pronounced. It was as though the death of Nicolas Remy had obliterated what final trace remained of the innocent girl she once had been. Miri, devastated by what had happened with Simon, seemed more dependent than ever on Ariane.

Ariane had hoped that being tucked in her own bed with Necromancer curled at her side would afford Miri some comfort. But Miri had begged Ariane to stay with her until she fell asleep.

She would barely let Ariane leave her side long enough to bid farewell to Renard. Ariane found him waiting for her in the great hall. The journey home had been such a long and arduous one, she had scarcely found a moment for a private word with Renard.

When she had rushed to Paris to rescue him, she had felt that she would know exactly what to say to him if she ever had him in her arms again. Now back at Belle Haven, matters no longer seemed so simple.

The bruises that had marred his face had largely faded. His face was shadowed by weariness more than anything else as he smiled at her. "I am glad you have come down, milady. I wanted a word with you before I return to Tremazan."

Ariane nodded. "But I cannot stay long. Miri is so distressed. She needs me."

"I know that, ma chère," Renard said, and once again Ariane realized he was reading her all too well, the doubts that had arisen to trouble her.

"About my proposal of marriage," he began.

"Oh, Renard, please," Ariane interrupted him. "I know what you would say."

"No, you don't," he said with a rueful smile. "Ariane, I have had much time to think, while I was in prison and—and even before that when I was alone at my castle. I just wanted to tell you that I realize how wrong I have been, about the ruthless way I have pursued you from the very beginning, concealing the truth about my grandmother."

"Renard, I—"

"No, please hear me out. You were right to be angry with me. It was your greatest fear, not being able to trust a man, and all I did was prove you right."

"I understand why you did it," Ariane said. "It was *your* greatest fear, being rejected because you were the grandson of Melusine, and that is exactly what I did."

Renard sighed. "I cannot pretend that Lucy was an innocent woman. She did do many of the evil things she was accused of, but she paid a high price for it, and I don't mean the terrible manner of her death. She'd already been punished by the loss of her daughter. She studied all that black magic, but never learned enough of healing to save her own child.

"She raised me, loved me, and then I rejected her. She could have used her powers to save herself, but she didn't. It was not the witch-hunters who condemned her to such a terrible death, Ariane. She did that herself."

He reached for her hand. "And as for these rings. Lucy did fashion them for a ruthless purpose, hoping that with such a charm her daughter would ensnare herself a wealthy comte. Just as I tried to trap you.

"But my mother never misused these powerful tokens the way I did. She gave the ring to my father freely, out of love, demanding nothing in return. Only that he might send for her whenever he needed her."

"And that is what I should have done. This ring is yours, ma chère, even if you decide you can never marry me. I give it to you freely, unconditionally. But if you ever do want me . . . you know what to do."

Raising her hand to his lips, he kissed it tenderly, then turned and walked away.

❦ ❦ ❦

LATE THAT NIGHT, INCENSE WAFTED THROUGH THE HIDDEN WORK-room, Ariane slipping into the now-familiar trance. Her mother's image shimmered in the water of the copper bowl set before her.

"Maman, I—I love him and I don't know what to do," Ariane faltered.

"Oh, I believe you do, my dear."

"I want to be with Renard so desperately, but never have Gabrielle and Miri needed me more than since our return from Paris. I am convinced Gabrielle is planning something wild and desperate, but am not sure what, and that frightens me.

"And Miri was so crushed by what happened with Simon, her spirit seems quite broken."

"The child will recover, Ariane," Evangeline said firmly. *"As for Gabrielle, she will pursue her own path no matter how you mount guard over her. You cannot chart your sisters' destinies forever."*

"I know that. But—but what of Faire Isle? I am sworn to be its protector."

"And so you will continue to do. I never agreed with your Great-aunt Eugenie that to be the Lady of Faire Isle meant to forsake both the joy and grief of being a wife and mother. This place was supposed to be a refuge, a haven, not somewhere to hide from love and the risks of being hurt.

"There comes a time when every woman must leave her island, my daughter. And a time to leave her mother as well. You must let me go, Ariane."

"I know that," Ariane whispered. Even as she had lit the black candles tonight, she had realized that this was going to be the last time she would ever conjure her mother's spirit. "But it is very hard, Maman. I think I will always miss you and need your love and wisdom. Your image is already fading in my mind. Papa took your portrait away with him, and I am so afraid that I am going to forget you."

"You won't, my dear. You will find something hidden away in the bottom of my cupboard that may help you remember. Just look at it whenever you feel the need of me and you will find me there."

The water rippled, her mother's image vanishing in the cloudy depths, and Ariane felt her eyes grow heavy. She fell into the deep sleep the potion always induced. But when she awakened, she immediately remembered her mother's final words to her.

Heart racing, she rushed upstairs, certain that she knew what she would find. Papa had not taken Maman's portrait away after all. It had been buried all along in the bottom of the wardrobe.

Eagerly rummaging through the pile of her mother's clothes, Ariane's fingers closed around the gilt frame, trembling as she brought it out into the light. But as she turned the frame over, she sank back on her heels, stunned.

Her eyes misted with wonder as she beheld the strength and wisdom of Evangeline Cheney peering back at her. Captured forever in her own reflection in the mirror.

❦ ❦ ❦

DAYS LATER, ARIANE PICKED HER WAY CAREFULLY THROUGH THE underbrush, twigs tugging at her skirts. The open fields, the distant stone walls of the Château Tremazan were lost from view as she plunged deeper into the woods.

After the long journey to Paris, the tragic aftermath of St. Bartholomew's Eve, Ariane had thought she would never want to leave Faire Isle again. The ivy-covered walls of the manor tucked in the hollow of the island, her herb garden, her orchard, the mystical forest that whispered of fairies and unicorns . . . these places were just as sweet and dear to her as they had ever been.

Yet something had changed in her. It was as though she had become more attuned to the call of the world beyond Faire Isle. She had long neglected her father's lands on the mainland, shoving all the responsibilities onto the steward, perhaps out of anger at her father or a sense of hopelessness over dealing with his debts. But even if the property did end up passing to her father's cousin, Ariane meant to do her best by the estate. She had purged any remaining bitterness toward her father, allowing only the good memories to dwell in her heart.

Ariane was also determined that what she had said to the Dark Queen should prove no idle threat. She meant to reach out to other daughters of the earth across France and even farther afield, to reestablish the council that had once watched over the affairs of wise women and prevented the misuse of the ancient ways.

But as important as these tasks were, there was another, far more compelling reason luring Ariane off her island. And that was the towering figure of the man she glimpsed in the glade ahead of her.

Ariane carefully parted the branches to peer into the clearing, taking great care to make as little noise as possible. But she realized that Renard was far too intent upon his labor to be aware of much else.

Stripped down to his shirt and breeches, his sleeves pushed up to his elbows, Renard drove the shovel deep into the forest floor. The muscles in his forearms were taut with strain as he shifted mounds of soil, digging the grave deep.

A fine sheen of sweat glistened on his rugged countenance, damp tendrils of golden-brown hair falling across his eyes. His mouth was compressed in a hard purposeful line as he sought to make his final peace with the memory of his grandmother.

Ariane knew how difficult this was for him. She'd come to better understand the turmoil of Renard's emotions regarding the woman who raised him, love, anger, guilt, and grief.

Ariane longed to go to him, offer the comfort of her presence, but this was something Renard needed to do alone, a rite so private and solemn, even old Toussaint had not accompanied him. As she saw Renard pause in his labors to dash his arm across his eyes, it was all that Ariane could do not to rush to him.

But if recent events had taught her nothing else, it was that she could not shoulder the grief or absorb the wounds of those she loved, no matter how much she might wish to do so. Her heart aching with love for him, Ariane stole one last glance at Renard before letting the branch fall back in place and stealing silently away.

༓ ༓ ༓

RENARD USED THE BACK OF THE SHOVEL TO TAMP THE LAST OF THE soil back into place. The disturbed earth looked like a wound in the forest floor, but he knew that it would not be long before the moss, the wildflowers, the vines crept back to conceal all traces of Lucy's grave.

No one would ever know that the bones of the dreaded Melusine were buried deep beneath this spot and his grandmother would have wanted it that way. Renard drove the tip of the shovel into the ground and rested his tired arms upon the handle. How much of his grandmother's legend was true? How much evil had she truly wrought in her youth?

Those were things he'd never know and Renard had reconciled himself to that. He would never be able to think of Lucy as Melusine. He'd only remember her as the tiny old lady who'd scolded and fussed over her huge hulk of a grandson. Whose gnarled hands had brushed back his hair when he'd come in wearied from a day's work. The wise woman who'd taught him to read eyes so well and just enough of the old dark ways to protect himself from his enemies. Who had spun her visions by the fireside, dreaming dreams for him she'd long ago surrendered for herself. Who despite all her mistakes, had loved him, not always rightly or wisely, but with all the fierce passion of her heart.

Renard was uncertain what awaited in the afterlife for a woman who been burned as a witch, but he liked to believe that God was more merciful than man, and that wherever Lucy was, she forgave Renard for the pain he had caused her. Just as he had forgiven her.

"Rest in peace, Grand-mère," he murmured.

Shouldering his shovel, he headed back through the forest toward his castle, the leaves rustling a pleasant music to his ears. But beyond the sound of the woods, he caught the whisper of something else.

A voice calling his name, sweet, low, and urgent.

"Justice, I need you. Come to me."

Renard stopped dead in his tracks, the shovel falling from his hand. He hitched in his breath, fighting to contain his alarm. He pressed his ring over the region of his heart, his reply sharpened by his fear.

"What is it, Ariane? Are you in danger? What is wrong?"

A brief pause and then the answer. *"No danger . . . but I require your presence at once."*

Renard's brow furrowed in puzzlement, but he replied, *"I will saddle up and ride for Faire Isle immediately."*

"But I am not on Faire Isle."

"Then where are you?"

"You must come and find me. Look for me at the place where destiny began."

Renard scowled. The place where destiny began? What the devil—Then his brow cleared as comprehension dawned upon him. Not pausing to send further reply, he whirled about and plunged back through the trees.

His heartbeat quickened as he thrust branches out of his path, scarcely able to believe that Ariane could be so near at hand. He'd remembered what he'd told her the night of their return from Paris.

"This ring is yours, ma chère, even if you decide you can never marry me. I give it to you freely, unconditionally. But if you ever do want me . . . you know what to do."

Those simple words had taken more of Renard's courage than any battle he'd ever fought, any enemy he had ever faced. He had been so afraid that Ariane would be lost to him, swallowed up by the cares of Faire Isle.

Her sisters needed her, her servants needed her, every blasted soul on that island needed her. He'd never been a patient man, but he had tried once before to force marriage upon her. He would not make that mistake again. Ariane must come to him freely this time and when she was ready. But his resolve had been strained to the snapping point.

Lengthening his stride, Renard broke into a run, heedless of the briars and twigs that scratched him, caught at his clothing. By the time he reached the embankment above the brook, he was winded. He had to lean his hand against the smooth bark of a birch tree while he caught his breath.

As he glanced eagerly down at the stream, he half-expected to find Ariane just as he had that memorable day, skirt hitched up, exposing her shapely white legs as she waded, gathering her jars of moss. But she was seated demurely on the bank, her knees curled up to her chest, her toes poking out from beneath the plain hem of her homespun skirt.

A barefoot sorceress with glossy waves of chestnut hair cascading down her back. Her face was tipped dreamily skyward, the sunlight casting a glow over her fair profile in a way that made Renard's heart still with a strange mingling of awe and despair.

He'd always admired Ariane's gentle strength and courage, the calm that was so much a part of her. But she had changed somehow since Paris, as though she'd grown in stature, radiating some inner light of her own. Acquired an even greater strength and wisdom, a steel forged by the fires of tragedy and sorrow.

She seemed like . . . like so many Ladies of Faire Isle who had gone before her must have been. Serene, self-contained, dependent upon no man. How had he ever imagined for a moment that this remarkable woman might belong to him?

Subdued, Renard trudged the rest of the way down the embankment. When his shadow fell over her, Ariane roused from her dreamings. She glanced around and then scrambled to her feet and smoothed out her skirts.

Suddenly, she looked as shy and uncertain as he felt. Renard shuffled his boots. It was damned ridiculous, he thought, after all they had been through together. They were behaving as awkwardly as a peasant lad and a village maid meeting for the first time at a dance upon the green.

"Ah, there you are, my lord. You came rather quickly this time. You must not have gotten lost."

"No, I didn't. You see, I was once rescued by this wise woman with quiet eyes," he tried to match her teasing tone, but found his heart was much too full for that. He added softly, "Now I don't believe I will ever be lost again."

Her smile grew more tender, but she said nothing. Just gazed up at him so steadily Renard had to suppress the urge to smooth down his shirt sleeves, fingercomb his hair.

"Er—I believe you sent for me, milady."

"I did indeed."

"Well . . . was there something you required?"

"Yes." She pointed to an object half hidden by the tall grass, no more than a yard away. "I dropped my handkerchief. Would you be so kind as to fetch it for me?"

Renard's gaze flicked from her to the handkerchief and back again. Looking considerably bemused, he bent down to retrieve the square of linen. As he did so, it was all that Ariane could do to retain her composure. Her heart was beating so hard, she found it difficult to breathe. It was even more difficult when Renard lowered himself to one knee beside her and gravely presented the handkerchief.

"Th-thank you." Her fingers trembled slightly as she accepted the linen from him and tucked it into her belt. "That is the third time."

"I beg your pardon?"

"I have used your ring three times. Now I must marry you."

"Ah, no, ma chère. I told you that I released you from that foolish agreement."

"But I never released you. You said that when I used the ring three times, we would be wed. Do you now mean to go back on your word?"

Renard stared at her, clearly torn between hope and disbelief. Such a powerful giant of a man and there was still a poignant trace of that raw peasant lad about him, kneeling before her, his heart in his hands.

"Do you not still want to marry me?" she asked.

"How can you ask—you know I—" He faltered. "But you seem so different since Paris. Somehow stronger, braver, more sure of yourself. Very much the Lady of Faire Isle. I was not sure you were ever going to need me again."

"I believe I am stronger." She caressed the hair back from his brow. "Brave enough to no longer be afraid to need you, to want you, to trust you with all my heart."

"Ariane, you cannot imagine what it means to me to hear you say that."

"Yes, I can, Justice," she whispered. "I can read it in your eyes."

Renard rose slowly to his feet, taking hold of her hands, drawing her up after him. He stole his arm about her waist and bent to brush his lips against hers. His kiss tender, reverent. As he gathered her closer, his mouth became more insistent, demanding, filling her with his heat.

Ariane devoured his lips just as eagerly, returning passionate kiss for passionate kiss. Renard finally drew back to peer down at her, his harsh features softened by a look of wonder, desire, adoration. He startled her by flinging back his head and roaring out a joyous laugh that rang to the top of the trees.

Lifting her up, he spun her around and around until she was dizzy and laughing. When he set her down, she staggered and clung to him to keep from falling.

Renard's strong arms shored her up as he apologized ruefully, "Forgive me. I could not contain myself. I fear I am as

much of a great, rough ogre as your sister thinks I am. Have I offended your dignity, my Lady of Faire Isle?"

"Yes, you have." Ariane tried to look stern, but she sighed,
snuggling closer. "I only wish you will carry me off to your castle
and offend me a great deal more."

Renard was only too ready to comply, but Ariane pulled
back, saying hesitantly, "Justice, there is one thing you must understand. I will be happy and so proud to be your wife, your
countess, but I will also still be the Lady of Faire Isle. I was bred
for it, trained to be a healer, to look after the people of the island
and—and—"

Renard silenced her with another swift kiss. "Do you think I
don't know that, ma chère? If you trust me with your heart, you
must trust me in this as well. I would never ask you to be less
than you are."

Ariane's eyes misted with love and gratitude. "Thank you,
my lord. It takes a rare man to be unafraid to offer his wife such
independence. A man as strong and wise as you. I believe your
grandmother was right when she said you were destined to be
my husband."

Renard's heavy-lidded green eyes glinted down at her.
"Humph! You didn't think so when you first met me."

"That is because you were so mysterious and maddeningly
evasive. You wouldn't even tell me why you wanted to marry me.
Always insisting you would tell me on our wedding night. If I
had given in and married you when you first demanded, I wonder what you would have said to me."

Renard's lips twisted ruefully. "Oh, I have always been far
too glib for my own good. I would have probably handed you a
lot of nonsense about it being fate and what a suitable match it
was. Me with my wealth and title, you with your legacy of powerful books."

Ariane smiled. "And now, my lord? What reason would you
give?"

"Only one very simple one. I love you, ma chère. Will that do?"

"Oh, yes, Justice." Ariane tenderly laid her hand alongside his cheek. "That is quite the best reason I have ever heard."

Renard pressed a kiss into the palm of her hand, his eyes warm and open, inviting her into his heart. To remain there forever.

*Read on for a sneak peek at
Gabrielle's story, the next exciting novel
in the Cheney sisters trilogy*

The
Courtesan

GABRIELLE CHENEY PEERED THROUGH THE SLITS OF HER MASK, picking her way carefully along the path, overgrown with weeds. The courtyard of the Maison d' Esprit was as silent as a cemetery and twice as eerie. The moon cast a pale light over moss-blackened fountains and broken statuary. Some headless saint presided over the withered remains of a rose garden. The flowers were long gone, but the thorns were not, one branch catching at the hem of Gabrielle's cloak.

As she bent to free herself, she was beset by the troubling sensation that had afflicted her all evening. The feeling that she was being followed. Straightening, she curled her fingers over the hilt of the sword hidden beneath her cloak and whirled around. The iron gate and stone wall were nothing more than vague outlines in the fog-bound night. But as she stared, another figure took shape, that of a tall proud warrior.

Her hand fell away from the sword and she uttered a soft choked cry. Not of fear, but more of despair because she had seen the silhouette of this man far too many times in her dreams. She took a step forward only to check the motion, knowing it would do her no good. There would be no smile to greet her, no strong arms to welcome her because he didn't exist, this phantom man. All she would find was empty space and silence.

Ghosts left no footfalls, and memories cast no shadows, except perhaps on the human heart. She watched the figure of the man evaporate into the mist as he always did. Gabrielle had never once seen his face, but she knew beyond certainty who he was.

Nicolas Remy, the captain from Navarre. Whether it was his ghost she kept seeing or only a figment of her own tormented imagination, the effect was always the same. Gabrielle's heart constricted with sorrow and guilt.

"Oh, Remy," she murmured. "I've asked your forgiveness a thousand times. What more do you want from me? Why can't you leave me in peace?"

She knew she would never gain an answer to that question, at least not in this damp, misty courtyard. With one last glance behind her, Gabrielle turned and hastened toward the house.

The stone manor loomed ahead of her, splintered wood and a great hole where the front door should be, gaping like the jagged mouth of some fierce beast ready to devour her. But Gabrielle feared the ghosts of her own memories far more than she did the sinister aspect of the house. Besides, she knew the truth behind the legends of the Maison d' Esprit far better than the superstitious Parisians who blessed themselves every time they had to pass those rusting gates.

Easing past the shattered remains of the door, she entered the house, the darkness swallowing her. The boarded-up windows blocked out what pale moonlight there was to be had.

Gabrielle stripped off her mask and reached beneath her cloak for the large pouch fastened to her belt. She groped until she found the candle set in its small brass holder, along with the tinderbox she had brought. After much fumbling between flint and wick, she managed to coax the taper to light.

The tiny flame spluttered to life, casting a small circle of illumination. Gabrielle moved deeper into the room that yawned before her, the grit crunching beneath her feet. Holding up the candle, she surveyed the wreckage of the once-magnificent great hall. The bishop had done very handsomely by his mistress until the witch-hunters had come.

Gabrielle shivered with a mingling of horror and pity. Poor Giselle Lascelles and her daughters. How terrified those women must have been, dragged from their home, crying and shrieking to meet the worst sort of torture and death that could befall any daughter of the earth. All of them lost, save one . . .

The appearance of the great hall was calculated to make any chance intruder believe that the Maison d' Esprit was uninhabited by anyone but ghosts. Gabrielle was one of the few who knew better. Lifting her skirts, she moved to the stairs stretching upward. The small glow of her candle could not reach far enough to penetrate the upper regions of the landing, to detect whoever or whatever might be lurking there.

"Hello?" she called tentatively.

Her voice echoed, swallowed up by the vast silence of the house. "Cassandra Lascelles?" Gabrielle called more loudly.

She was met with more unnerving silence, then she thought she heard a floorboard creak. Gabrielle moistened her lips and tried again. "Cass? Are you there? It is me . . . Gabrielle Cheney. I need to talk to—"

She checked abruptly at a low rumbling sound. Staring up at the landing, she caught the shadow of movement. Her heart leaped into her throat as two baleful yellow eyes glared back at her, the rumbling escalating into a fearsome growl. The creature sprang forward, a large brownish-black mastiff with a heavy muscular body.

"*Merde!*" Gabrielle cried.

As it bounded down the stairs, Gabrielle scrambled back, nearly dropping her candle. Hot wax splashed over the brass holder, searing her hand. She winced with pain, but managed to keep a grip on the taper.

"C-Cerberus. Good d-dog," Gabrielle quavered. "Don't you remember me?"

Apparently he did not. The mastiff issued a series of savage barks.

Fortunately, Gabrielle had long ago learned the weakness of this particular beast. One wary eye on the dog, she inched aside enough to set her candle down on the aumbry shelf. She groped for the pouch hidden beneath her cloak. The cursed drawstrings refused to budge or perhaps her fingers were too clumsy with nervousness. Somehow she got the purse open, and drew forth a cluster of slightly squashed red grapes.

Swallowing her fear, she croaked, "Nice Cerberus. S-sweet beastie. Look what I have for you."

She carefully extended her arm, the handful of red grapes glistening against her palm. The dog gave a sharp bark. Gabrielle jumped and tossed the grapes wildly. The cluster hit the floor with a dull thud, causing the dog to shy back.

Cerberus crept forward again, snuffling her offering. The dog emitted a delighted whine and began greedily gulping down the fruit. Gabrielle ventured a few steps away from the wall. Cerberus would make no objection to her movement, at least not until the grapes ran out.

"*What have you done to my dog?*" An imperious voice rang out.

Gabrielle twisted toward the sound and breathed a sigh of

relief. Cassandra Lascelles stood poised at the top of the stairs, a tall, thin silhouette.

"I haven't done anything to your precious Cerberus," Gabrielle retorted. "Merely bribed him with a few grapes to keep him from devouring me instead."

"Gabrielle? Is that you?" Cass asked sharply.

"Yes."

Clutching the bannister, Cass began to descend the stairs with elaborate care. She had been blind almost from the moment of her birth. A tattered red gown half-hung off her thin frame, baring one shoulder. The weight of her mass of gypsy-dark hair appeared too heavy for her slender neck. She had an exotic face with high slanting cheekbones and an ice-white complexion that seldom saw the light of the sun. Her sightless dark eyes were fixed and without expression, all emotion centered in her mouth, which at the moment was slashed thin with displeasure.

"Cerberus! Come," she commanded.

The formidable beast whined and lowered his head, slinking guiltily over to his mistress. Cassandra groped until she seized hold of the dog's leather collar.

One hand resting protectively on her dog's head, Cass straightened and scowled.

"Damnation, Gabrielle Cheney. I have warned you before not to come here without first sending word through my servant. I do not like to be taken unawares. Bribe or no bribe, you are lucky Cerberus did not tear out your throat."

"I am sorry," Gabrielle said, taking a cautious step closer. "But I was desperate to see you and I didn't have time to contact you through Finette. I have been here enough times before that I thought Cerberus might recognize me."

"He is trained not to *recognize* anyone. Otherwise he would not be much of a protector."

Cass's rigid features melted into a reluctant smile. She bent and muttered some low command to her dog. With her hand still poised on Cerberus's collar, she walked forward with a sure step that Gabrielle always found astonishing.

Gabrielle had seen her sister Miri accomplish some astounding feats with animals, but the degree of rapport between Cassandra and her dog, the way she had taught Cerberus to be her eyes was nothing short of magic.

Cerberus led Cass straight over to Gabrielle. Another low command and the dog took up position, sitting beside her, eyes trained on Cass as though awaiting her next order. Cass reached out boldly until she made contact with Gabrielle. Drawing her forward, she enveloped Gabrielle in a brisk hug.

"I did not mean to make you feel unwelcome, my friend," she murmured. "But *next* time, let me know when you are coming."

"I will," Gabrielle promised. Cass released her and stepped back, her lips quirking upward in a faintly teasing smile. "Well, to what do I owe the honor of this unexpected visit? Surely you could not have already used up that last bottle of perfume I brewed for you. I gave you enough to bring every man at court to his knees."

Cassandra Lascelles could concoct some of the most powerfully seductive perfumes and skin ointments Gabrielle had ever discovered.

"No, I need no more perfume."

"Cream for your complexion then. Or another lotion perhaps?"

"N-no . . ." Gabrielle said, glad that the other woman could not see her face. She liked to feel cool and in control, but it had been sheer desperation that had blazed her path to Cass's door.

Now that she was here, she discovered it was more difficult to blurt out what she wanted than she had imagined it would be.

As though she sensed Gabrielle's reluctance, Cass said in a softer tone, "Out with it, my friend. What do you want from me?"

Clearing her throat, Gabrielle confessed haltingly, "I need your help, Cass. To—to find someone who is lost to me."

Remy, her heart whispered with the familiar dull ache.

Cass's fine brows arched upward in surprise. "I would be delighted to assist you in anyway I can, my dear," she said dryly. "But as you may have observed, my eyesight is not all that keen. Hadn't you better hire yourself a tracker or some mercenary who is good at that sort of thing?"

"I—I can't. The person I seek is . . . no longer in this world. I have heard—that is—Finette told me that you possess remarkable skills in the art of necromancy."

Cassandra's face darkened with annoyance. "Rot Finette! That scrawny little witch talks far too much."

"So is it true then?"

Cass didn't answer her, something in her face shutting down.

"Necromancy," she repeated slowly. "The raising of the dead. Perhaps I do possess some ability in that arena. But you are a witch the same as me. Why don't you conjure for yourself or go to your sister Ariane for help? She is the present Lady of Faire Isle, reputed to be as wise and clever as your late mother."

"You know full well I cannot do that. Ariane and I have not had any contact for the past two years." Gabrielle experienced the familiar rush of pain and regret at the thought of her older sister. "She didn't approve of my decision to come to Paris."

"Because you became a courtesan? Very few respectable women would approve of that."

"Yes, well, it is all very fine for Ariane to pass judgment on me," Gabrielle said. "She is quite happily married to her Comte de Renard. For her, everything is simple and perfect and that makes it impossible for her to understand that other women might find life a bit more . . . complicated."

Gabrielle tried to sound indifferent, as though Ariane's disapproval was of no consequence. But the loss of her sister's love and respect weighed heavily on her.

"It doesn't matter," she went on briskly. "Ariane wouldn't have helped me in any case. She confines all her skills to healing the sick. She would never dabble in the darker arts."

"How wise of her and how unfortunate for you," Cass said. "Because I don't dabble in them lightly either. I don't share my peculiar talent for necromancy with anyone. Not even you, my friend. Now why don't you just forget all this nonsense and come have a cup of wine with me?"

She gave Cerberus a light tap and the dog sprang to its feet. Both woman and dog turned as one and headed back toward the stairs.

Gabrielle stood a moment, dismayed by Cassandra's refusal. But Gabrielle never easily surrendered anything she had set her heart upon, and few things had ever meant more to her than this. The hope of seeing Nicolas Remy, speaking to him one last time.

She hurried after Cassandra, seizing her by the elbow.

"Cass, wait, please—"

Cerberus bristled and issued a warning growl. Gabrielle hastily drew her hand away.

"Cass, you must help me or—or I don't know what I shall do. There is someone who has passed to the other side whom I am desperate to contact. It is more important to me than you can possibly imagine. I—I will pay you any amount you require."

"Money doesn't interest me. If it did, I have ways of getting it myself."

"What about jewels then? Gowns from the finest dressmaker in Paris."

Cass flushed and shoved the drooping sleeve of her tattered frock farther up her shoulder, the gesture a trifle self-conscious. Her jaw jutted to a stubborn angle. "I don't care about such fripperies either."

"Then name your price," Gabrielle pleaded. "I'll give you anything, do anything you ask."

Cass gave a bark of laughter. "*Anything?* You are very rash,

Gabrielle Cheney. Didn't your Maman ever tell you of the old fairy tales about what dire things happen to ladies who make such promises?"

"Well, what could you possibly demand? My firstborn child?"

"No, I abhor children," Cass drawled. "I doubt they'd even taste good in a stew." She fell silent for a moment, then said slyly. "I will do what you ask, but I warn you. There is a reason the conjuring of the dead is considered black magic and forbidden. A séance is a dangerous proceeding, one that can easily go awry. Sometimes the soul one wishes to contact does not care to be disturbed, whereas there are others, more evil, who might welcome a portal back into our world."

Gabrielle frowned, wondering if Cassandra was merely seeking to frighten her. "Are you telling me that if you conjured wrong, you could—could what? Let loose some sort of ghost or demon?"

"Anything is possible when you tempt fate by playing with the darker arts."

"If it is so dangerous, then why do *you* do it?" Gabrielle demanded.

"Because my days are spent in darkness," Cass replied softly. "But when I conjure the dead, I can actually *see*. This is the only way I have of looking upon another face and so to me that makes it worth any risk. The question is, is it worth it to you?"

Was it? Gabrielle had to admit that Cassandra's words had daunted her. But then she thought of Remy, the way she had parted from him the day he had ridden out to meet his death, so much between them left unsaid.

"Yes," Gabrielle said, steeling her spine. "The risk is worth it."

"Then I will help you."

Gabrielle warily returned to Cass's side, her elation tempered with suspicion of this sudden capitulation. "You will? What made you change your mind?"

Cass shrugged. "Perhaps I might one day find it useful to have you in my debt. I will give you one séance, one conjuring of the dead in return for some future favor."

"And what would that be?"

"How I can possibly decide right now?" Cassandra protested. "But you will agree to perform some service for me, no questions asked, no refusal. Is it a bargain?"

"Do you require an oath in blood?" Gabrielle asked dryly.

"No, a simple handshake and your pledge will do." Cassandra extended her hand toward Gabrielle.

Gabrielle hesitated. She had not survived this long in Paris without learning some caution, and surely there could be nothing more rash than undertaking a commitment without knowing what it was.

"Come now, Gabrielle," Cass said. "I am not one of those backstabbing intriguers you associate with at court. I admit our acquaintance has been of short duration, but you may trust me in this. I would never ask more of you than you can give."

Somewhat reassured, Gabrielle shook Cass's hand. "All right. I—I agree. Do this for me and I am in your debt. You have the word of Gabrielle Cheney."

An odd smile tugged at the corner of Cassandra's mouth as they sealed their bargain, sending a chill through Gabrielle. But the disturbing expression was gone so swiftly, Gabrielle thought she must only have imagined it.

Cass turned toward the cupboard, groping along the lower shelf. Her hand collided with the candle Gabrielle had left burning there. Cass swore as she nearly knocked it over, hot wax splashing her hand.

"Move this candle out of my way," she said. "And then stand back."

Although mystified by the abrupt command, Gabrielle did as she was told. She stepped away from the cupboard, holding her candle aloft. With an intent look of concentration upon her face, Cass continued to feel her way along the shelf.

Gabrielle could not see what Cass did, but suddenly the entire aumbry shuddered and creaked. Cass scrambled back and Gabrielle gasped in astonishment as the cupboard swung outward, revealing a yawning hole in the floor. She crept closer, the light from her candle flickering over carved stone steps that spiraled downward, leading to a darkness that was cold and uninviting.

A hidden cellar. So that explained how Cass must have escaped the witch-hunters all those years ago. Gabrielle wondered why the other Lascelles women could not have been saved as well, but Cass was loathe to discuss the tragic loss of her family. As one who fiercely guarded her own wounds, Gabrielle understood and respected Cass's reticence.

"You allowed me to read your palm, now I am trusting you with the secret of my innermost sanctum. Welcome to my real home," Cassandra said with a mocking flourish of her hand. When Cerberus attempted to brush past her and lead the way down, Cassandra collared him.

"No!" She bent down and muttered some command that sounded to Gabrielle like, "Go. Guard."

Head erect, the dog trotted away, looking like a soldier ordered to do sentry duty. Cassandra inched forward carefully and started to descend the stairs, pausing to call back to Gabrielle. "Clutch your candle tight and follow me closely.

"The way down is always a very dark and treacherous one," she added with one of her strange ironic smiles, leaving Gabrielle with the uneasy feeling that Cass was talking about much more than the stairs.

Gabrielle swallowed hard, but she had already come too far to turn back now. Gripping her candle, she plunged after Cass into the darkness.